THE SUNNYVALE GIRLS

Three generations of Stewart women share a deep connection to their family farm in western Australia, but a secret from the past threatens to tear them apart. Widowed matriarch Maggie remembers a time when Italian prisoners of war came to work on their land, changing her heart and home forever. Single mum Toni has been tied to the place for as long as she can recall, although farming was never her dream. And Flick is as passionate about the farm as a young girl could be, despite limited opportunities for love. When a letter from 1946 is unearthed in an old cottage on the property, the Sunnyvale girls find themselves on a journey across the world to Italy. Their quest to solve a mystery leads to incredible discoveries about each other, and about themselves.

FIONA PALMER

THE SUNNYVALE GIRLS

Complete and Unabridged

AURORA
Leicester

First published in Australia in 2014
by Penguin Group (Australia)

First Aurora Edition
published 2019
by arrangement with
Penguin Random House Australia

A catalogue record for this book is available
from the British Library.

ISBN 978–1–78782–198–9

Published by
F. A. Thorpe (Publishing)
Anstey, Leicestershire

Set by Words & Graphics Ltd.
Anstey, Leicestershire
Printed and bound in Great Britain by
T. J. International Ltd., Padstow, Cornwall

This book is printed on acid-free paper

To the Murray and Mosca families

Oceans apart but connected together

2 December 1946

Bella Maggie,
I am finally home, back to my Italy a free
man. My thoughts continually return to
you. I miss the wide open space of your
country and I miss you, greatly.
   I promise you I will be back to Australia
so we can be together. Please wait for me.

Ti amo,

Rocco

1

2000

The screeching of galahs in the early morning sounded like church hymns. Nothing made Maggie feel closer to God than this moment in the dawn. The air was fresh, scented with rosemary, basil and wild lavender. The light was soft and glowing as if filtered through stained glass, and the sounds of the birds assured her that she was alive.

Maggie was happiest in her garden. It was her little wonderland, although there was really nothing small about it — the pumpkins and watermelons sprawled beyond the rabbit fence. She bent over to squeeze some of the basil, releasing a burst of scent. Her back groaned slightly as she stood up and stretched. At seventy-two, she had no complaints except a tired body.

A smile tugged at her lips as she admired the tomato plants. They were only small now but soon she'd have to get Toni to truss them up. Come January/February they'd be making their own sun-dried tomatoes. Eating fresh from the land was one of life's pleasures for Maggie. If the world fell apart tomorrow, they'd survive, just as they always had. They were three generations of women who lived off their own land. It was just the three of them, too — Maggie, Toni and Flick.

The Sunnyvale girls. They would thrive on what they grew, and on how they supported each other. Wasn't that what family was all about?

Tending the garden daily, watching it all flourish, also made Maggie feel closer to Rocco. His memory came to her more frequently than ever when she was in the garden. After all, through his gentle nurturing, he was the one who had opened her eyes to the magic of growing your own produce. How different life would have been if the war hadn't made it all the way out here, to their remote farm.

Maggie always greeted her day with time in the garden. It was her special ritual. Toni, her daughter, would be at the sheds, already elbow-deep in farm work, while her granddaughter, Flick, was off to see the sunrise with her beloved horse in her own favourite place. All three of them belonged on this farm, entwined in Sunnyvale's earth like the deep roots of the gum trees, and their spirits hovered over it protectively like wedge-tailed eagles. Maggie had been born on this farm and it was here she hoped to see out the rest of her life.

★   ★   ★

Felicity Stewart held her breath for a moment as the sun rose from the horizon. Golden light brushed the tops of the pale grass in the pasture paddock before her. The crisp morning air stung her cheeks but she refused to move. Even Contractor stood firm beneath her, snorting his breath into the cold air and shaking his mane as

4

if also impressed with the dawn. Flick leant forward and rubbed his neck. The combined scent of Contractor and his leather saddle was her favourite smell in the world, and it made this moment perfect.

'It's always worth it, hey, boy?'

His body trembled beneath her. He knew that with the sun now up, their time here was coming to an end. But Flick wasn't quite ready for work. Last night's events haunted her, and her mind was in turmoil. She wasn't sure if she should approach Chad about what she'd seen last night or not. He was coming out to the farm today anyway, so maybe she'd just wait and see.

'Time to do some work,' she said to herself, but the dog beside them barked. 'Oh, I know, Fella. You're always ready for work.'

Fella looked up at her, tail wagging and eyes sparkling with mischief. He was a Red Cloud kelpie and had short brown fur — it was a colour he shared with Contractor, although Contractor had a big white blaze down his nose and white socks on his back legs. Her boys were a perfect pair, her best mates, and could read her moods better than her own mum. The farm's worker, Jimmy, had a dog too. Gypsy was Fella's sister, and both were only two years old, still just pups.

Flick clicked her tongue and nudged Contractor on his way. With one hand on her hip and the other on the reins, she glanced back at the sun. The magic of the sunrise and all its amazing colours was nearly gone, leaving just the sun brightening a new, long day. She'd seen many sunrises in her twenty years, but to her eyes they

5

still got bigger and better every day.

Contractor broke into a gallop, knowing they were headed back home and towards breakfast. Fella's lean body stretched out alongside them, his tongue flapping in rhythm with his strides. Flick leant forward in the saddle.

'Come on, boy.'

The wind against her face was glorious and she felt safe on Contractor's powerful body. Her mum preferred the Honda motorbike, but Flick loved the strength of her horse and the fact that he would protect her. A bike would never go back to the house for help, no matter what her mum had to say about the benefits of her Honda. But then again, Toni had always been a hard arse.

As the farmhouse came into view, Flick dropped Contractor back to a walk. Fella was racing to catch up, breathing heavily but tail still wagging madly.

Flick spotted Maggie's plump bum as she bent over her herbs in the veggie patch next to the house. The Stewarts were known throughout the district for having a thriving vegetable garden. Nan was always giving away armloads of produce to anyone who visited. You name it, they grew it. Olive trees, smaller than the huge ones over by the old house, edged the garden. Every year they bottled up jars and jars of olives. People put in orders for them, and for good reason. They were delicious.

'Morning, Nan,' Flick said as she approached.

Maggie stood up. She was wearing her favourite apron. It was faded blue gingham with

6

a white pocket at the front, where she tucked her pair of scissors. She picked up the basil and parsley she'd just snipped.

'Hello, my darling. How was the sunrise this morning?'

'Absolutely glorious. I saw the wedge-tailed eagle back by its nest. I'll have to keep a closer eye on the lambs in that paddock.'

Maggie nodded. Her face was wrinkled and dotted with age spots, her soft grey hair pulled back into a neat, practical bun. She was fine-boned and petite, with the exception of her rear end. Maggie said her backside was her storage tank in case the Depression ever hit again.

Flick could see the traces of her nan's beauty, and the proof was in the old photos. She'd been a stunner in her day. Grandad had always said he was the luckiest man alive on the day she married him. He had lost the use of his legs in a farming accident long before Flick was born, so he'd got around either in his wheelchair, on the motorbike or in the converted ute. Never had he walked the farm with them or strolled through the crops of an evening, but he'd always been around, overseeing the farm, until he passed away four years ago.

'Hurry up and put Contractor away,' Maggie said. 'I'll have brekkie ready in a few minutes. And if you see Jimmy in your travels, can you let him know, please?'

'Sure, Nan.'

Flick headed towards the horse shed and locked Contractor away. 'There you go,' she said, handing him his wide plastic bucket of mixed feed. Flick kissed his long nose, put the saddle away, and ran back to the house. Fella ran beside her, glancing up excitedly as if to ask, 'What are we chasing?' Fella was clearly disappointed when they got to the verandah and Flick pulled off her boots. No boots meant no play. His head dropped as he flopped down beside them. Knowing that she never worked without her boots, Fella practically sat on them now. That way he wouldn't be left behind. Flick scratched his ears. She couldn't resist his gorgeous face.

'You're a sook, Fella,' came a voice over her shoulder. Jimmy strode onto the verandah followed by an energetic Gypsy. Instantly, Fella leapt up and nipped at Gypsy's ear. Then they sprang around, jumping at each other, playing.

'Mad as cut snakes, those two,' said Jimmy, his hands on his hips. At forty-four, Jimmy was still fit and handsome. His blond hair was trimmed short and his jade-green eyes changed intensity in the light, but James Painter had always been Jimmy to Flick. He'd worked on the farm for nearly four years, ever since Grandad passed away. Jimmy wasn't just their worker any more. He was more like family now, and the only father figure, besides her grandad, that she was ever likely to have.

'Bit like us two,' said Flick, and launched herself at Jimmy as he bent over to take off his boots. Flick tried to put him in a head-lock but he stood up, lifting her off the ground. She squirmed as he threw her over his shoulder. Fella and Gypsy paused to watch them.

8

The screen door snapped open. 'Knock it off, you two. Mum's inside waiting.' Toni was always so stern, her skin tanned from all the outside work, her body lean and strong. Her hair was short, almost pixie-like, and was streaked with grey. If it weren't for the beautiful hourglass figure that filled out her jeans and stretched her shirts across the chest, she'd fit right in with the men in the yards.

Toni's dark-brown eyes flashed with impatience, and Jimmy set Flick down. He straightened his shirt, gave Flick a wink and squeezed past Toni. At least Toni cracked a smile.

'Come on. Nan's made us omelettes.' Toni turned and they both headed inside the homestead. It had a verandah on three sides and a big patio out the back, but if you asked Flick, the house lacked character. She had always preferred the old house in the gimlet trees further down towards the back paddock, with its jarrah floorboards and high ceilings. But she'd grown up in this house, so it was home. It had its own quirks: the toilet door that didn't shut, the cracks in the lounge room walls that opened and closed with the seasons, and the buckshot holes in the pantry from the time that Nan tried to shoot a snake that had snuck inside. And there were wider doorways and ramps instead of steps, which had been put in for Grandad.

In the dining room, the table was set with plates and Nan's homemade tablecloth. Nan was serving the freshly cooked omelette to Jimmy, who sat at one end. Grandad's seat at the other end always stayed empty. Flick sat on one side of

9

Jimmy, Toni the other, and Nan usually sat beside Flick. It had been this way since Jimmy had arrived.

Nan always fed them and kept house while they ran the farm; she was not ready to retire. She'd said that the moment she stopped working would be the moment she'd start to die.

'Oh, Maggie May, this looks great. Thank you,' said Jimmy, who wasted no time digging in.

Nan squeezed his shoulder, delighted at pleasing him. While Flick waited for her breakfast, she tried to ignore the pile of university brochures at the edge of the table. Was her mum really going to start on about this again today? Flick flipped her long chestnut plait over her shoulder but it wasn't enough to deflect her mum's disappointed glare. Luckily, Nan was back within minutes, flopping an omelette onto Flick's plate.

'Thanks, Nan. The herbs smell divine.'

'So, did you catch up with Chad last night?' Jimmy asked.

Flick drew in a breath. 'Yeah.'

His brow creased. 'You were home early. Heard your car,' he explained.

Toni shot her a worried glance. No doubt she'd been thinking the same thing.

'He had an early start so I only stayed for a beer.'

Nan sat down with her muesli, and Flick hoped they'd forget about Chad. That was one subject she wasn't in the mood for. She gave her full attention to eating her breakfast instead.

'We weren't expecting you home last night,'

Toni persisted. 'Is everything okay?'

Flick attempted to keep her feelings of confusion and hurt from her face, trying for a casual smile. 'He had to get up really early so it was just easier to come home and get a good night's sleep.' She wasn't sure if she'd pulled it off. Jimmy, chewing as slowly as a jersey cow, studied her expression.

'Oh, all right.' Toni seemed convinced. She cleared her throat and reached for the travel brochures she had strategically placed on the table beside the bunch of university brochures.

Flick's stomach dropped. *Here it comes again*, she thought. She didn't know what was worse — a lecture about travel or the Spanish Inquisition on Chad.

'I, um, picked these up when I was in Narrogin yesterday getting the hose fittings,' Toni said.

Flick glanced at her mum. She was trying to act casual as she slid the pamphlets across the table. The four travel brochures were for Italy, France, America and Vietnam.

'These look great and the girl said they're very popular destinations,' Toni continued. 'There's the money Grandad left you just waiting for you to pick a trip.'

'I told you, I'm happy here, Mum,' Flick said. 'I don't want to travel. Fella and Contractor need me and I'd prefer to use the money to do up the old place.'

Toni clicked her tongue. 'You don't want to be stuck here your whole life, Felicity. Go, explore the world before it's too late and you end up like me!'

11

Flick finished her omelette and turned to her mum, a woman she'd grown up idolising, a woman of strength and determination. Nothing was impossible for her and she'd done everything on her own. Always. 'What's so wrong with being like you, Mum? Your life seems pretty perfect to me.'

'There's so much more out there on offer,' Toni replied. 'I know you love it here, but this place isn't going anywhere.'

'This place is all I've ever wanted. When are you actually going to listen to me?' Flick stood abruptly, collecting her plate while Jimmy tried his best to look invisible.

Toni got up too but Maggie raised her voice. 'Antonia, leave her be.'

Before anything else could be said, Flick darted for the kitchen, dropped her plate in the sink and charged out the screen door.

She needed time to cool down. Her mum just seemed to like pushing her buttons. Why was she so persistent? And why couldn't she hear what Flick was saying? Flick found it hard enough dealing with her mum, but now it seemed she had boyfriend issues to contend with, too. This was definitely not her week.

★   ★   ★

Toni flinched as the screen door slammed. She wanted to go back to half an hour ago, when the light had spread through the shed and warmed her skin as she'd sat cleaning motor parts in petrol. It had been so peaceful, just the galahs screeching and the odd sound of a small branch they'd nibbled off as it hit the ground with a thump. Back before she'd made Flick angry.

Pushing her empty plate away, she pulled back the travel brochures. Each photo of exotic lands and different cultures drew her in. Why wasn't Felicity interested? She'd give anything to have the opportunities her daughter now had laid out before her.

Jimmy reached around her and collected her plate, his rolled shirtsleeves exposing his muscled forearm.

'Thanks, Jimmy.' She smiled up at him. It was hard not to notice James Painter. He was far too handsome for his own good. After losing her dad, it had been so nice to have a male figure around again, and Jimmy was tall and strong, but upbeat and optimistic, too. That was something she'd missed her whole life. Her dad had depended on Toni for nearly everything, but being wheelchair-bound, he'd also suffered from bouts of depression.

She resisted the urge to watch Jimmy's denim-clad backside and instead focused on her mum. Toni wondered how she'd managed to stay on the farm for so long without complaining even once.

'Thanks for brekkie, Mum. We'll be off moving a mob to the south paddock. See you at lunchtime.'

'Okay, dear. And don't forget to check the dam pump. I'm not getting the water to my veggies.'

'We'll check it out on our way back. See ya.'

Jimmy was waiting outside for her. His boots

were on and he was leaning against the verandah pole, the morning sun casting bright light across his unshaven jaw. The stubble only came off when it got too long and itchy for him. Toni didn't mind it, and had often wondered what it would be like to have his strong arms around her and to kiss his lips. But that was a ridiculous notion. He was eight years younger than her, still in his forties, still young enough to have a family of his own. Toni had been thirty-three when she'd had Felicity, and by the time she'd realised she was pregnant, the father, Simon, had already moved on, leaving Toni behind with the most amazing gift.

Toni slipped on her Rossi boots and glanced towards Contractor's stall.

'She's not there,' Jimmy pre-empted, putting on his tan akubra hat and passing Toni her dark-brown one. 'She'll be down at the old place.'

Toni realised Jimmy was right. The old brick farmhouse had always been Felicity's thinking place.

'Shall we go move this mob, then?' he asked.

'Righto,' Toni replied as they headed for the ute, boots crunching on gravel. Gypsy, at Jimmy's heel, launched herself up onto the back tray of the old Hilux they used for paddock work. The noise from the Hilux's holey muffler was great for moving on the sheep.

Toni drove them down the track past the gimlet trees and the old house. She spotted Fella lying outside the front door, the telltale sign that Flick was inside.

'Do you think I'm pushing her too much?' Toni asked, clenching her hands on the steering wheel. Her nails were short, her hands marked with cuts and ingrained dirt. Jimmy remained silent. Toni stopped at the paddock gate and glanced at him.

'You really want to know what I think?' he said, looking at her.

'Of course.'

'Even if you never take my advice?' he replied with a smirk, then jumped out of the ute to open the gate. When he got back in he fiddled with his hat in his hands.

'Come on, Jimmy. Please.'

'Well, honestly, I don't think you can force Flick to do anything. She's stubborn, like you.'

'*Me?* Don't you mean my mother?'

'All you Stewart women are stubborn, but that's not a criticism. Being stubborn is also one of your strengths. It's what makes you all survivors.'

Toni shrugged, unable to look into his intriguing green eyes.

'All I'm trying to say is, it has to be Flick's idea. She'll go to uni if she can see a benefit in it for her, maybe to do agribusiness or an equine course. And maybe the travel will come a few years later when something grabs her interest. She's still only twenty. But if you keep pushing her, she may close herself off just to spite you.'

Toni mulled over his words as she drove closer to the sheep. Gypsy had already jumped off and was bringing them into a close group. She risked a glance at Jimmy's face. 'How did you get to be so insightful?'

Suddenly the ute lurched and they both hit their heads on the roof. Toni braked and rubbed her head.

'What the hell was that? Did I just run over a sheep?' she said, glancing at the mob ahead.

'I don't think so. It sounded solid.' Jimmy leapt out and gasped. 'Oh my God,'

Toni rushed to his side where he knelt down. 'What? What is it?'

Jimmy was trying to talk but he was laughing too hard. He reached for Toni and pulled her down to see under the ute. They hadn't hit a sheep or a rock, but the old rusty bullbar from the front of the Hilux. It had somehow come off and they'd run right over it. Toni burst out laughing too.

As their laughter eventually died, Toni became aware that Jimmy was still holding her arm. She also realised she was leaning into him.

Jimmy didn't move away and there was a new expression in his eyes she hadn't noticed before, one she couldn't handle.

'Toni . . . ' he whispered, staring deep into her eyes, but just at that moment Gypsy barked at them, as if to say, 'What the hell are you doing? Are we moving this mob or what?'

Toni jumped up off the ground and brushed the dirt from her pants. 'Well, we need to shift this bloody thing,' she said.

Moments later Jimmy was pulling on a section of rusty steel. Together they dragged it out from under the ute. It squealed as metal ground against metal and they lifted it onto the back tray.

'Seems like the rust ate out the brackets,' she said as she walked to the front of the ute. 'The old girl looks a bit different now.'

Jimmy chuckled. 'She sure does.' His gentle laugh was enough to put them both at ease. But Toni couldn't forget their moment. What had Jimmy been about to say to her?

Gypsy barked and they started moving the sheep again.

'The lambs are looking good,' said Jimmy.

'They are, aren't they? We've had such a good drop rate.'

'Yeah, you were right to change the lambing dates. They're going great on all the green feed,' he said, shutting the gate on the mob in the next paddock.

Toni clenched her teeth to stop her smile spreading. 'Thank you. I appreciate that.' Her father had scarcely given her any praise over the years. When she'd used her initiative or suggested an easier way, her father had never acknowledged it. Although she felt a pang of guilt admitting it, even to herself, deep down Toni loved running the farm without her dad's overbearing self-righteousness.

She leant back against the frame of the gate and watched the merinos, their heads down eating as they settled into the different paddock. The growing lambs beside their mums did look really healthy, and Toni felt a sense of accomplishment. She worked damn hard on this farm, and it took everything she had to offer.

Toni had no idea what 'personal' time was. She'd never taken a real holiday. A weekend down the coast fishing was as good as it got. And to think she'd spent her childhood dreaming of getting on an aeroplane and flying far away from Sunnyvale.

'You look like you're a million miles away,' Jimmy said.

Toni sighed. 'I guess I was.' She swatted a fly and turned to face him. 'Do you ever wonder how different our lives could have been?'

His face was unreadable and Toni instantly regretted her wayward question.

'Yes, I've thought about it. Like if the bank had given me the loan to buy my father's farm instead of him having to sell it? But then I wouldn't have gone looking for work and I wouldn't have ended up here.' He shrugged. 'I wouldn't have you three in my life and it'd be pretty empty. So I'm glad it worked out this way. Maybe fate had this planned out all along.'

'Wow.' Toni knew Jimmy enjoyed working at Sunnyvale but to put the three of them before having his own farm?

'Sometimes life has a way of working out, even if you don't realise it at the time. Sometimes — '

'Sometimes you talk too much.' She smiled. 'But I know what you're trying to say. So, thanks. I know I'm lucky.'

'Is this about your dad?' Jimmy asked softly.

Toni couldn't bring herself to respond. How did he know? Was she that easy to read?

'Who do you talk to, Toni? You never leave the farm. You don't seem to have any fun — '

'I have fun,' she said vehemently.

'Really? I've asked you to come to the club with me for a feed and a game of pool and you never do. Or head to the lake for a swim and just relax. You work too hard, you know that.'

'I . . . ' Toni closed her mouth again. What could she say? *I don't go anywhere with you because it would be too much fun?* She didn't want to like him any more than she already did. It was easier not to be around him — especially in his swimming shorts! It was bad enough in summer when he'd strip off his shirt and stand under the outside shower.

'What is it that you wanted to do before your dad had his accident?' Jimmy pressed.

Oh God. The million-dollar question. Toni winced as her dreams flooded her mind. 'Dad couldn't help it. They had no other choice but to bring me home to help.'

'That's not what I asked, Toni.'

Toni hated the way his jade eyes ate right through to the most fragile part of her. She glanced back to her sheep, the paddock opening up before them along the horizon. 'I wanted to travel,' she said at last. She'd never spoken about her desires to anyone before.

'So what's wrong with starting that now? You can always take me along,' he added with a wink.

Toni laughed, but that shimmer in his eyes was back. She'd always been able to read him, but now he seemed to be sending new messages.

'I'll remember that next time I head to the sale yards,' said Toni, slapping him playfully on his arm.

'Toni, you never know what life might be about to throw at you.' He shrugged. 'Look at me — fate threw me in with three extraordinary Sunnyvale girls. Sometimes things just work out.'

For some reason Jimmy's words rattled inside her mind and caused a tingle down her spine. Maybe this would be the year that brought about change for them all. The more she thought about it, the more she felt it was true. She breathed in deeply, the air tinged with dust and eucalyptus, but also something else.

What did fate have in store for them all?

2

Flick turned off the old vacuum cleaner and arched her back as she surveyed her efforts. It had taken her two hours to finish scraping off the old carpet underlay that had stuck fast to the jarrah floorboards. Grandad had always said that floorboards were a sign of being poor, so the moment they could get rugs or carpet, they did. Now jarrah floorboards like these were hot property. This whole house was filled with them, and Flick wanted the boards in glossed glory.

Maggie's old room was the last one she'd cleaned. Now Flick could start up the sander she'd hired. She'd already bogged up the cracks in the walls, repainted them and replaced all the ceilings in the rooms where rain had got in and damaged them. The house was transforming before her eyes. Flick didn't need much effort to imagine it all fixed up. It would be full of character and charm: high ceilings, wide passageways, a huge built-in pantry in the kitchen, lots of rooms. Flick picked up the vacuum cleaner, took it out the front and dumped it on the verandah by the door. The outside of the house was still the original bricks. Flick touched the perfect rectangles with their swirl pattern. She couldn't imagine making each one of these by hand.

Heavy boot steps creaked along the verandah. 'You need a moment alone with your house?'

21

Jimmy teased as he stopped beside her. Gypsy found Fella and they ran off into the bush as if they were rally cars, skidding around the trees.

'How did they do it, Jimmy?'

'How did who do what?'

'Rocco and Giulio. You know, the Italian prisoners they had working on the farm. Nan said that they made each one of these bricks by hand and built this whole house with just a tape measure, plumb and level. It must have taken ages.'

Jimmy touched a brick too, his dirty finger tracing the pattern. 'I guess it would have. But they worked hard in those days. Would have done a whole day's work on just a bit of bread and cheese too, probably. They were bloody clever, I'll give 'em that.'

'Nan said they used a shovel to slap the mud into a mould. Imagine trying to make all the bricks and then still having to build the house. She said when it came time to put the roof on, the house was only a smidgen off perfectly square.'

Jimmy shrugged. 'It's like asking how they made the Colosseum, or Petra in Jordan.'

Flick studied Jimmy. 'Have you ever been?'

'Me? No. My sister has. She loves travelling. I wouldn't mind going one day, but what's better than what we've got?' he said with a wink.

'I agree.' She smiled. 'So, what are you doing here? Escaped Mum for a bit, have you?'

Jimmy cleared his throat. 'Something like that. Thought I'd see how you're going. Tried sanding yet?'

22

'Just about to. Can you run me through it again? I really don't want to stuff up.'

He nodded and followed her inside and down the wide passageway. There was a lounge room to the left and a bedroom to the right, and further down it opened up into a dining area with another room on the left. There were fireplaces in the lounge and dining rooms, with a big old stove in the kitchen that was a thing of beauty. Flick was so glad it hadn't been ransacked over the years. She planned to put in a new one, but alongside the old one. Sometimes Nan still came over to light a fire in the old stove to cook her pavlovas. They were the best ever.

The kitchen wasn't large but it extended out off the dining area and had a walk-in pantry. A door off to the side took you to the enclosed back verandah, to the bathroom and the sleep-out bedroom.

The large sander was in the corner of the main bedroom, plugged in and ready for work.

'Have you hit down all the nails?' Jimmy asked.

'Yep. The lounge room was last and it was in really good shape.'

He bent down to look at a few spots. 'Good job. I could take you out doing tradie work if your mum ever sacks me.'

'It's easy when someone shows you. And as if Mum would sack you. She'd never admit it but I don't think she could do without you.'

Jimmy smiled, even though Flick could tell he was trying not to. She was glad that news made him happy. Her mum should tell him stuff like that herself but she was too much like Grandad, never any good at showing her emotions.

Jimmy stood up and handed her a dust respirator and goggles. 'Okay, just like I showed you before. Never bounce the sanding drum or stand in one place, or you'll get hollows in the floor.' Jimmy started the drum floor sander and walked forward. 'See? Just like that. Go in the direction of the planks and wood grain.' He did a patch and then it was Flick's turn.

She was a little nervous, but Jimmy was a good teacher. She learnt more from him than she would at any agriculture school.

'That's it, keep going.'

As she moved forward again there was a loud vibration noise. Confused, she stopped the machine and pulled off her dust mask.

'What did I do wrong?'

'It was a loose board. You must have missed one.'

Flick hadn't noticed a loose board before. She stepped to the wall and pressed on the boards along it. None of them moved but as she knelt down, the edge of one of the shorter boards rose up.

'This one doesn't have any nails in it at all.'

That was strange. Flick pushed it down again and slid her finger under the other end. The short board lifted out completely from under the edge of the wall. She shot Jimmy a look.

'Huh. I hope this isn't how the mice get in,' she said, bending down to look into the hole. 'Hey, I think there's something down there. Hang on.'

Flick jumped up and ran to the kitchen to get the torch. When she returned Jimmy was trying to fit his arm down the hole. She laughed. 'That's what having too many muscles does. Here, mine are skinnier.'

'I could feel the top of a tin,' he said, excitement in his voice.

Flick shined the torch on his face. 'Who's supposed to be the kid here?' She crouched down to peer into the black slit. 'It's a box. God, I hope there are no snakes hiding down here.' Handing Jimmy the torch she squeezed her hand into the gap.

'It's probably a snake pit filled with spiders of every shape and size.' Jimmy reached over and tickled her arm.

Flick tried hard not to scream and drop the box but she did pull it back so fast she knocked skin off her knuckles. 'Damn you, Jimmy. You know I hate snakes and spiders.'

'You're just like Maggie. You gonna fill this house up with buckshot too?' he said with a chuckle.

'If I have to.' Flick turned the narrow tin box, which was almost as wide as the floorboard, so she could ease it out. 'Whoever put this here would have had arms like me. It's a tight fit. Do you think it was Nan?'

'I don't know. Hurry up and open it. Maybe it's old coins worth a fortune.'

Flick brushed off the dirt from the top and rested the box on her lap. It was a little rusty and looked old. She prised open the lid. Inside was a stack of envelopes gathered by string. The top envelope had some moisture damage, and the address was hard to read. Two fading stamps were lifting off the corner.

'Letters. To who?' Jimmy asked.

'I'm not sure. I can't quite read it.' Flick counted ten letters in all and looked at one towards the middle. The ink on the envelope was much easier to read, although the handwriting was unfamiliar. 'It's addressed to Nan. Look, see? *Maggie Fuller, care of Sunnyvale Farm, Pingaring.*' Flick held it up for Jimmy and as she did, she realised something. 'It's never been opened.' She checked the others. 'All for Nan and none have been opened. I wonder who they're from.'

Jimmy took one and studied it. 'The stamps are Italian.'

'No way, really?' Flick studied the rectangles and sure enough, Jimmy was right. 'Amazing.'

'Do you think Maggie hid them? Or maybe someone didn't want her to see these.' He looked around. 'Who's room was this?'

'It was my great-gran's. A scandal, do you think?' On the back of the second letter was an address. 'Oh, I have to go show Nan right now. I wonder what they say.'

'What about the sanding?' said Jimmy as Flick stood up.

'It can wait — this is like finding buried treasure! I won't be long, but if you get bored . . . ' she said with the sweetest smile she could muster.

Jimmy just waved her off and put his dust mask back on.

'Thanks, Jimmy. Love ya!' Then she was off, running towards the main house, past the gimlets and the veggie garden. 'Nan!' she yelled as she got closer. '*Nan!*'

Maggie opened the back door. 'Goodness, girl, what's going on? Is someone hurt?'

'No, but look what I found in the old house.' Flick was trying to catch her breath as she handed over the pile of letters. 'They were hidden under a floorboard and they're addressed to you. All ten of them. And they have Italian stamps. Who are they from, Nan?'

Maggie stepped out from the doorway and took a letter. Her finger went to the stamps and then both hands began to shake. Clutching the letter to her chest, she closed her eyes.

Flick watched her sway and reached for her. 'Sit down, Nan.' She helped Maggie to the bench seat against the back of the house. 'Are you feeling okay?'

Maggie nodded and smiled, but there were tears in her eyes. She gently opened the letter, some of the fragile paper tearing. Flick held her breath with anticipation.

'Can you read it, please, darling? I haven't got my glasses,' said Maggie in a strained voice.

Flick sat beside her and took the letter from her nan's grasp.

'It says *Bella Maggie*, I think?'

Maggie gasped and nodded. 'Oh yes, *beautiful Maggie*. What else does it say?'

'Um . . . *I am looking for work but there is none. I help my family. I am trying to get back to you. I haven't heard from you but I will not* give up hope that you wait for me. I made a promise. I will come back to Australia so we can be together. Ti amo, Rocco.'

Flick dropped the letter on her lap and looked up at her nan. Tears were falling silently down her lined face.

'Oh, Nan.' Flick embraced her, clutching her hand in hers as her strong nan cried. 'I'm sorry it upset you. I thought you'd be happy.'

Maggie sniffed back some of her tears as she snuggled into Flick's hug. 'Oh, I am happy, dear. I waited so long for these letters. I thought they never came.'

Flick handed her the tin. 'There are more. Are these from the Italian prisoner you talk about sometimes?'

Maggie nodded, fingering the letters. 'He was the love of my life once, Felicity. It seems so very long ago.'

If the emotion on her grandmother's face was anything to go by, time didn't seem to be a factor. 'But you never forget your first love, right?'

Maggie dried her tears with her apron. 'Where did you find them?'

'Hidden under a loose floorboard in your mother's room. Do you think she hid them from you?'

'Perhaps she did. Maybe she knew how I felt about Rocco, even though we tried hard to hide it. Or maybe she just didn't want the connection to him. She never would have approved. He was a prisoner, an Italian and he had no money.' Maggie sighed angrily. 'I asked her if she'd seen

28

any letters from Rocco. She lied to me. I should have known.'

'Did he have to go back to Italy?' asked Flick, not liking the flash of regret and pain on her Nan's face.

'Yes, all of them were sent back after the war. It broke my heart.' Maggie glanced at the letters again.

'Would you like me to read another one, Nan?'

'That's okay, dear. I'll go find my reading glasses. You probably want to get back to what you were doing.'

Actually, Flick wanted to stay right there and ask Nan heaps of questions about her and Rocco. But she realised Maggie probably wanted some time alone, and she couldn't blame her. What a thing to find. All those years Nan was waiting to hear from Rocco . . . she'd thought he never cared, when all along he did. It was so sad, Flick could have cried. All that lost love.

'All right, Nan,' she said, kissing her soft cheek. 'I'll get back to work. If you need anything you know where I am. We'll talk after dinner, okay?'

Maggie nodded but she was staring at her letters, her eyes brimming with memories and tears. Flick had never seen her blue eyes so vibrant and youthful. She got up and walked to the edge of the verandah but Maggie didn't notice. She was already back in 1944.

3

1944

Maggie was up early again. She had six cows to milk and only one had waited outside the cottage. But she'd had Nessy a long time; Nessy knew the routine. Maggie set down the bucket of Nessy's milk inside the cottage for her mum. Phyllis would put it through the separator until Maggie had finished milking, and then it would be Maggie's turn to finish the separating. She liked the old way better: they used to leave the milk on the large setting pans overnight and then scrape the layers of cream off in the morning. But her mum had insisted on getting a separator so they could sell the cream to Watsonia in Perth. When they first got it, Maggie had turned it so fast the cream had been thick enough to stand a fork in. But she'd been scolded. They needed the cream for money, except for the bit they kept to make their own butter.

Phyllis picked up the bucket and put it next to the separator. The cottage kitchen was small, with the dining table in the middle and a smaller table against a wall with a large tin dish on top that they used to wash up the dishes. The wood stove was already burning with the sticks Maggie had collected earlier.

'Hurry up with those cows now, Margaret,' said Phyllis as she pushed back her neat curls. She had blush on her pinched cheeks, and the same blue eyes as Maggie. Her clothes were always impeccable; even her apron was spotless.

Maggie nodded and headed outside past the old bough shed, which her father had built from trees and covered with broom bush. They used the bough shed more in summer or when they had the neighbours over for a party.

As she walked by, the chooks ran to the edge of their pen, hoping for scraps. Mother sold some of the eggs too, and Maggie would have to collect them later and scratch them clean with steel wool.

Maggie walked along the dirt, through the gimlet trees and around the large salmon gums. Near the stables were Splinter and Flossy, their large bodies resting in their wooden stalls. The other Clydesdales were with her brother Charlie and her father, who were clearing the land her father had bought back in 1927. Her father had applied to get a 2000-acre block three hundred and sixty times, but the land was highly sought after. It didn't help that the government was giving land to the Poms before the Aussies, and by the time Father was offered land it was way out near Pingaring — and eighty others had also applied. Father believed he was selected because he'd been to agriculture school and had the skills to make it work.

It was a very long way from the city, over five hours in their old ute. Mother spoke about the isolation — nothing but untouched natural bush around them and the odd farm — and how she'd hated the place to begin with. Father had wanted better land closer to a bigger town but it was all taken. Eventually he took this parcel of land because he'd heard the railway would be coming close by. As it turned out the railway went past further west, which became the siding of Pingaring, twenty minutes by car. But father said he

31

had his chance at land so he took it, naming it 'Sunnyvale'.

A year later Maggie had been born. Now at sixteen, Sunnyvale was all she knew. And she loved it much more than her mother did. It was home for her and her three older brothers, George, Thomas and Charlie. Well, it had been. Thomas and George had gone to war. George had been killed and Thomas was still missing, presumed dead. Now it was just her and nineteen-year-old Charlie left to help their mother and father on Sunnyvale. It was lonely at times without her other brothers.

A magpie flew overhead and Maggie moved cautiously, knowing it might try to swoop her to protect its nest. She was safer with the screeching galahs, although her ears took a battering. It wasn't a long walk to the cows. They usually liked the edge of the fence by the road and Maggie enjoyed the quiet of the walk. Both of their dogs, Roy and Roo, were with Charlie. Roo would always be off looking for a kangaroo while Roy, the sheepdog, was happiest by Charlie's side.

Sucking in the morning air, Maggie rubbed her arms against the cold. Pain shot up her foot as she trod on a sharp rock and she cursed her thin shoes but kept going. She could hear the girls now; they saw her too and started to moo.

'Hey, Miss Maggie!'

Maggie turned to the gravel road to see Arthur riding towards her on his bike.

'Morning, Mr Stewart.' He was wearing brown pants and a jacket that were too big, probably hand-me-downs from his older brother. His greasy hair was plastered off to the side, like it had been recently combed. Arthur was riding the treasured Malvern Star bicycle that he'd bought with over a month's wages. He was two years older than Maggie — they'd been to school together — and she knew he was sweet on her. His family's farm was ten kilometres away, at the end of the road. Their mothers spoke of marriage while the fathers discussed a farm merger. Maggie wasn't so keen on either idea.

Arthur rode his bike close to the fence and then stopped the big spoke wheels. 'I wondered if you'd be here bringing in the cows,' he said with a smile.

Maggie had to bite her tongue. He met her here nearly every week and she half wondered whether he sat behind the big tree further up waiting for her. 'Yes, Mother is waiting. Off to town again for work?'

He nodded shyly.

'You might pass the war officer. The Italians are arriving today.'

'A few are none too pleased about having them around these parts.'

'It'll be good. Give the gossips something to really talk about,' she said. *Might offer some respite from all the talk of marriage*, she added in her head. Maggie could hardly wait for the Italians to arrive. They came from a world so different from hers. What would they look like? Would they be skinny and fair like Arthur?

'Are Mr Fuller and Charlie still clearing?'

'Yes, not much left in that paddock. We can get a crop in soon.'

'Um, have you any news on your brother?' Arthur asked, blushing.

Her good mood vanished. 'No. He's still missing in action.' Maggie shivered at the words. They sounded strange coming from her mouth, like she was just reciting the telegram they'd received a year ago. It had said there was a possibility he could have been taken prisoner but they had no more information. Maggie had listened to her father read out the news as her mother collapsed on the chair while clinging to Charlie. Sometimes it seemed like yesterday. Even though time had passed they still held onto hope that Thomas might return after the war, or that they'd find him in one of the prison camps.

'Mother won't give up hope but I fear he's gone like George. I'm so glad they couldn't take Charlie. The war has taken enough of my family.'

George had joined the 2/11th Battalion in 1939 and saw action in Libya and Greece. But it was in Crete in early 1941 that George was shot and killed. Thomas had joined another Battalion in 1940 and had gone missing a few years later. Maggie knew it all so well now; over the years it had been repeated by her family as if helping them to understand what their boys' fight had been for, and maybe also to feel closer to them in some way.

If the doctors hadn't refused Charlie due to his severely broken arm, they might have lost him too. Maggie tried hard to imagine what her brothers had gone through, tried to imagine the strange lands they'd walked along and the battles they must have fought. Had they killed anyone? Had George died painfully? She'd heard bits on the radio at night and it always made her heart race. She missed her big brothers dearly. It seemed not that long ago that they'd all been out shooting foxes together or playing in the bush. It was hard to think of them as dead. It was as if they were just away on a trip, and one day they would reappear to pull her hair and undo her

34

ribbons. She still hoped this was true for Thomas.

'I'm sorry, Maggie. I didn't mean to upset you. I'd best be on my way or I'll be late. It's a long ride into town. I might see you tomorrow,' Arthur said hopefully. His skinny legs pushed hard to move the bike along the gravel.

'Goodbye, Arthur.' Maggie turned and followed the group of cows home, pulling apart some wild oats she'd plucked from the paddock.

By the time she'd milked all the cows, her father and Charlie had come home for morning tea. Normally Maggie would take it out to them — maybe a slice of cake and some tea made up in a big beer bottle — but today they returned to the cottage, as the Italians were arriving before lunch.

'Maggie May, how's my girl?' her father said after he'd washed up. Charlie was behind him, trying to fold up his cotton sleeves so he could wash.

John was the best father a girl could have. He was gentle, funny and always had time for his only daughter. Maggie knew her mother thought he spoiled her too much. But Phyllis spoilt Charlie plenty too.

'How was the clearing?' Maggie asked.

'Going well,' her father replied. 'Won't be long and then we'll have a real crop.'

'Roo caught a mid-sized kangaroo, so we brought it home for dinner,' said Charlie, scratching his head. At nearly nineteen he was already shaving. He had one of those sweet faces that made you want to hug him and trust him wholeheartedly. Maybe it was his gentle smile, or the way he moved calmly like their father as if they had all the time in the world. In fact, Charlie was a lot like his father: they were both medium build, a little on the thin side, with short sandy hair and narrow jaws. Charlie was a strapping young man but he wasn't afraid of showing his affections. He wrapped his arm around Maggie and gave her a squeeze. 'Think Mother would mind making roo tail soup?'

Maggie laughed. It was Charlie's favourite, so of course it would be made. Phyllis clung to her remaining son with every ounce of love she had left — so much so that it felt sometimes as if there was not much left for Maggie.

Phyllis came in from outside, saw Charlie was home and smiled.

'Sit down, Charlie, I'll get you something to eat,' she said, holding out a chair and then patting his shoulders as he sat. 'Maggie, is the tea ready?'

'Yes, Mother.' Maggie filled the cups with hot tea. Phyllis took the first one from Maggie and passed it to Charlie's good hand before sitting beside him, leaving Maggie to deliver the rest. When Charlie was younger he'd fallen off Contractor, their big racing horse, and had been thrown hard to the ground. His arm had been broken in many places and had never healed right. It still ached a lot and had no strength.

John sat down beside Maggie and brushed her arm affectionately. Maggie had liked it when her father used to carry her on his shoulder so she could see the world from up high. Now she was too big for that, and besides, she was nearly as tall as he was.

'Do you think the Italians would like roo tail soup?' Maggie asked.

'I don't know. I can't imagine they've been eating all that well in the camps,' said John.

'Will they understand us?'

'I hope so! It'll make things pretty hard otherwise. I

36

imagine they've picked up some basic words. Maybe you could teach them, Maggie?' he said with a wink.

Maggie thought that was a wonderful idea. She would have loved to have been a teacher.

'Certainly not, John Fuller,' said Phyllis sternly as she clunked her cup down on the small wooden table. 'She'll be going nowhere near those wog prisoners. I don't trust them. I still don't see why we need them.'

'Now, we've talked about this, Phyllis. We need the help on the farm. Charlie and I can't keep up with all the work.'

'If the war hadn't taken my boys, we wouldn't be needing these dagoes. What a waste,' she muttered. 'They kill my son and then take refuge on our farm.'

Maggie cringed. She hated the names people were calling the Italian prisoners but it was even worse when it came from her own mother.

'I can hear a truck,' said Charlie, wiping his hands on his trousers, which were held with braces over his white cotton shirt. He headed outside with the rest of the family hot on his heels. Morning tea was forgotten.

Outside a Chevy truck pulled up. An officer in uniform got out the front and two men in maroon-coloured clothes stood up on the back tray of the truck.

'Mr Fuller, Captain Jack Tweedie,' said the man in uniform, holding out his hand to her father. As they talked and shook hands, Maggie studied the men on the back. Besides their dyed purple clothes, she found them no different from other men: they still had two legs, arms and eyes. Both men looked lean, clean-shaven and tall, and one of them seemed no older than Charlie.

They climbed down and Maggie stared at the

37

ground, unsure of how to behave in front of prisoners. She felt her mother's hands on her arms, pulling her back, and Maggie wondered whether her mother was trying to protect her or shield herself.

'These are your men,' said the officer. He pointed to the older of the two, the one with thick dark eyebrows. 'This is Giulio Mosca, he's twenty-seven and is quite skilled in building things.' Then the officer pointed to the younger man. He had black hair and deep brown eyes, and — Maggie had to admit — he was very handsome. Instantly she straightened her dress and wished she'd checked her hair.

'And this is Rocco Valducci. He's twenty, a quiet bloke but a good worker.' The officer stood straight in his dark-green uniform with big front pockets. It reminded Maggie of seeing her brothers before they left. That would be the last mental picture of them she'd ever have, eternally in uniform.

'Giulio, Rocco, this is your new boss, Mr Fuller, and his wife, Mrs Fuller,' said Captain Tweedie.

Maggie's father held out his hand and both men shook it firmly.

'Mistair,' said the oldest one with a nod.

'This is my son, Charlie,' said John. Charlie also shook hands with the Italians. 'And my daughter, Margaret.'

Maggie gave them a smile and felt a blush rising under her skin. Having the eyes of the Italian men on her was both scary and exciting. They were so nice to look at, with their strong bodies and dark eyes.

'You lads speak much English?' John asked.

'A little, Mr Boss,' said Rocco pointing to himself.

'Good. Charlie, show them where they'll stay while I talk to the captain.'

'Yes, Father.' Charlie gestured for the men to follow him, and Maggie tagged along, pulling out of her mother's grasp, knowing Phyllis wouldn't want to cause a scene in front of the captain.

Charlie led them past the bough shed to the tin hut they had recently built for their new workers. It was a little A-frame shed with a wooden door and floor. Maggie and Charlie both wished it could be their room, a way to get out of the cottage and have some privacy.

'You'll both be in here,' Charlie said slowly and opened the door. Inside there were two steel-frame beds and a small table with a bowl for washing up and shaving. 'I hope it will do?'

They both nodded. 'It fin,' said Rocco.

Maggie stifled a giggle but repeated it for him. 'It is fine?' she said slowly.

'It is fine,' Rocco said more clearly.

She nodded her approval and they walked back to the truck. The officer was on the back of the truck and handed over some more lurid burgundy clothes to Giulio and Rocco.

'I'll be back with the canteen truck to resupply them with clothes and boots,' he said, jumping down. 'Until then, good luck.' Mr Tweedie shook John's hand again and got into the truck. 'Don't let them near the firearms,' he added as he started the vehicle.

'Why is that, Father?' asked Charlie who'd spoken Maggie's own thoughts.

Mr Tweedie leant out the window. 'They're still prisoners and not to be trusted with weapons.'

As the truck disappeared in a trail of dust, the family turned back to Rocco and Giulio, standing there in their odd-looking uniforms, with only the spare clothes in their hands and whatever was in their pockets.

Maggie wondered what they must be thinking about this place, how different it must seem from their own homes. Did they have families they yearned for? Loved ones who were missing them in return?

'Well, boys, if you work hard, then we're all going to get on great,' said John. By the blank looks on their faces, not even Rocco could keep up with what her father had said. 'Put your clothes in your room,' John said slowly, and pointed as he spoke. 'Then we will show you around.' He gestured to the farm.

Phyllis was standing beside John with a pained expression, like the time Roo had dragged in a smelly dead fox. Maggie wondered how many other people around this area would greet the Italian prisoners so warily.

John had to wave the prisoners off and eventually they headed to their little hut. They seemed unsure about leaving on their own. Was this the most freedom they'd had since being captured?

'How much do they get paid, Father?' Maggie asked curiously.

'Fifteen pence per day. One day's work will test them and then I'll know what we're dealing with.'

Phyllis tutted and went back inside the cottage.

'What do you think, Charlie?' Maggie whispered to her brother. 'Do you think they're dangerous? I've heard all the talk at church every Sunday.'

Charlie shrugged his good shoulder. 'They seem harmless. They're just men caught up in a war like our brothers. As Father said, time will tell. Here they come,' he said.

'I'll show you the stables,' said John, waving them

towards the horses. Charlie walked beside him, the Italians a few steps behind.

Maggie was just about to follow when her mother yelled out. 'Inside, Margaret. I need help with the bread.'

Maggie rolled her eyes. She always missed out on everything. As she watched the men walking away, something flitted in her stomach, something exciting and unusual. She was sure that the two new workers were about to make farm life on Sunnyvale just that little bit more exciting.

4

Flick turned off the sander, pulled down her dust mask and surveyed her work. The jarrah boards didn't look like much yet, but she knew when the finish went on they would be stunning. Then hopefully she was going to move in.

'Hello? Flick?'

Her belly lurched. Chad was here. She'd been so preoccupied with the floors and Nan's letters that she'd momentarily forgotten about what she'd seen last night.

'I'm in here,' she shouted back.

Chad walked into the room, his sandy blond hair kicking up at the ends and his blue eyes full of fun. 'Hey, good-looking.' He pulled her into his arms, oblivious to her rigid movements and missing smile. But that was Chad for you.

Being tucked up in his arms, Flick relaxed instinctively. He smelt good, even with his blue cotton workshirt tainted with sheep.

She hadn't taken to him straight off. Sure, he had good looks, but he was loud and vivacious. He'd asked her out a few times but she'd always said no. Her track record with guys wasn't so great, so she tried to pick wisely. But then one night at a party in Kulin she found herself sitting outside on an old couch with him under the stars. It was the most quiet and mellow she'd seen him. That night she'd uncovered a sweet guy, patient and interesting. They had talked farming and world issues. They had laughed and joked. Flick had seen the man behind the bubbly personality and she'd liked it. Chad had asked her out on a date again, only to the pub, but she'd accepted this time. It had been a great night, more talking and laughing. He'd shown more substance than she'd expected and when he'd asked her out again she accepted. They'd been dating now for nearly a year.

Chad kissed her on the lips, and when Flick only half-heartedly responded, he pulled back, an eyebrow raised. 'You okay?'

'Sort of. You?'

'Slightly hung over.' He pulled a face. 'Missed you last night though.'

'Really?' It was Flick's turn to raise her eyebrow. 'I actually ended up going in to see you.' She watched him carefully for a reaction, a sign of anything that might give him away.

'Did you? I didn't see you,' he said, his voice even. 'Mind you, I was blind drunk early on. I should have had more water after a big day in the yards but beer tasted better.' He laughed.

'Well, I saw you. You were wrapped around a pretty blonde with big — ' Flick rolled her hands out over her chest.

'Mandy? She's the Pommy barmaid at the pub. She cut my drinks off and took my keys.'

'She was all over you outside the pub.'

Chad cupped her face. 'Aw, baby, are you jealous?' He kissed her forehead. 'She helped me home, that's all. Not that I can really remember. She was just being nice.' He shrugged, a smile tugging at his lips. 'You look so cute when you're jealous.' He kissed her nose and she felt the tension easing from her neck and shoulders. 'Can I help you here? I have a few hours up my sleeve.' Chad ran his fingers through her hair. He'd always been besotted by it.

'You could help me clean this up, that would be great.' She wasn't sure why she'd jumped to the worst conclusion, and her gut unclenched as her fears washed away. She remembered the tender moments they'd had, lying snuggled up together in bed, chatting softly as he stroked her skin. He wasn't a guy in an unhappy relationship. Assuming the worst was something of a habit for Flick. She put it down to the fact she'd never had a father, and the only male figure in her life had been her grandad, who had always seemed so angry with the world. Chad was more like Fella, such a ball of excitement — the exact opposite of her grandad. Maybe that's why she was attracted to him. But sometimes that energy was hard to keep up with.

'I'm all yours.' Chad flashed her a smile and picked up the used sand pads. 'Do you think I can hang around till lunch?'

Flick laughed. Just like Jimmy, Chad was a sucker for a good feed. 'You know Nan would love it.' She reached for his face, brushing her thumb along the dark rings under his eyes. 'So you hit it pretty hard last night, hey?'

'Hmm, what can I say? Winning a premiership and being fairest and best is taking a toll. No one ever said it would be this hard,' he teased.

The local footy team was still celebrating after their hard-fought grand-final win. And Chad

44

winning fairest and best had made him Mr Popular, with everyone wanting to shout him a beer and chew his ear off about the game. She was proud of him, but she couldn't keep up with the constant parties.

'Well, you'll have to not try so hard next year,' she said with a smirk.

Their clean-up lasted as long as it took Flick to tell Chad about the letters she'd found before he pulled her into his strong arms. Chad was solid, almost her height, and he could weave through a crowded football field like no other. Flick rested her head on his shoulder. It was nice to be loved.

'Do you know what I'm thinking?' he whispered as his hands roamed over her backside, drawing her closer to him.

'I'm sure I could guess.' Flick wasn't really in the mood. She was covered in dust and worn out from the sander, but it could be days before she saw Chad again. 'Let me show you the pantry,' she said with a grin.

★ ★ ★

Outside, Flick brushed the dust off her clothes and shook her head. She could see the particles falling from her hair in the bright sunlight. While she was bent over, Fella jumped up and his big tongue licked her face.

'Ah, gross, Fella. Get down.' She pushed him away and reached for Chad's hand. Together they headed towards the main house.

Twisted stumps of old roses indicated where

an old garden bed had once been; the small fence had fallen down years ago. Flick had dug wells around the roses and started watering them again, and slowly they were showing signs of life. With a bit of TLC they would be big and bright and make this house welcoming.

'I can't wait to hear more about the letters and Rocco. I wonder why Nan never told us about their relationship.' Flick used to pull out the old black and white photo albums and quiz her grandmother about the prisoners. Nan could have mentioned it then, surely?

'Who knows? I think we even had a prisoner on our farm but from memory he only stayed a few months. I can't remember why. I'll have to ask Dad,' said Chad.

'Oh, great,' Flick mumbled when she realised the farm ute was parked by the house. Mum was back for lunch. She gave Gypsy a pat before stepping up to the verandah and pulling off her boots.

Familiar with the routine, Chad washed his hands in the laundry before Flick. They found the others in the dining room, eating cold meat and salad.

'Sorry I'm late, Nan. I just wanted to finish off the room I was in. I also have an extra.'

Chad stepped forward with a beaming smile.

'No worries, love, and hello, young man,' said Maggie. 'Funny how you always stop by around meal times.' Maggie stood up to fetch another plate.

'How could I resist, Maggie? You know I come for you too,' he said with a wink.

Maggie rolled her eyes and shook her head. 'Go on, sit.'

'So, did you read the rest of the letters, Nan?' Flick asked softly.

Maggie nodded on her way back to the kitchen.

'What letters?' asked Toni, who'd been eating quietly next to Jimmy. If she'd been angry with the way Flick had run out this morning, she didn't show it.

'Didn't Jimmy tell you?'

Jimmy, the typical male, shrugged while stuffing a chunk of lamb into his mouth

Toni was still waiting, her fork hanging in mid air.

'I found a loose floorboard in the old house and underneath it was a tin full of letters for Nan from Rocco, the Italian prisoner who was here years ago.'

Maggie waddled back in and put the plate and cutlery in front of Chad.

'Is that true, Mum? What's all that about?'

'What else did he say, Nan?' Flick persisted. There was nothing more romantic than love letters.

Maggie took her time to sit back at the table. Only Jimmy was still eating, at least pretending to mind his own business.

'I guess you won't let up,' Maggie said with a sigh. 'Well, you know Rocco was on our farm for two years . . . ' A deep breath. 'In that time we fell in love. But then the war ended and he was sent home.'

'What? Why didn't you ever tell me this? You

and Rocco. Wow.' Toni was stunned.

'Nan, that's not the end if he wrote to you,' said Flick.

Holding her hands together on the table, Maggie smiled. 'He promised to write and to come back for me. But I didn't get any letters and figured he'd moved on once he got home.'

'Which isn't true, because his letters are here!' said Flick. 'He did want to come back for you!'

'I'm not keeping up,' said Toni. Her eyes were like dinner plates.

'Nan thinks her mum hid the letters so that Nan wouldn't run off with a prisoner,' said Flick. 'She must have been so awful.'

'It was a different time back then, Felicity.' Maggie glanced at a black and white photo on the wall opposite of her father John on top of a huge horse called Contractor. The very horse Flick had named hers after.

'It would have been frowned upon,' said Toni.

'Yes, very much. My mother would have died from the shame and embarrassment if it ever got out. We hid our love because I knew how my mother felt about the Italians. All she could see was her son's killer. So if she found out they would have been sent back to camp. I was young and in love. I wanted to be with Rocco forever.' She sighed. 'I really thought he'd forgotten me.'

'But he didn't! The proof is there in the letters. He loved you too, Nan!'

Maggie smiled briefly. 'He never returned, though. Even if my mother hid the letters from me, she could never have kept him away, surely. I imagined him coming back and not letting

48

anyone stand in his way.' She was gazing at the opposite wall, not really focused on anything. 'He never did come back for us.' Maggie blinked a few times and then stood up. 'Which was for the best, because life wouldn't have turned out the way it did and I wouldn't have married your grandfather. He was a good man. Now, I made a sponge cake. Would you all like some for sweets?' She headed for the kitchen, not waiting for a reply.

Flick was taking a while for her Nan's words to sink in. Something had come out wrong. 'Nan,' she called out. 'What do you mean he never came back for 'us'?'

The whole room fell silent. Even the wall clock seemed to miss a few ticks.

'Mum?' said Toni. Her face was ashen, her cutlery abandoned.

Maggie didn't come back out, nor did she reply.

Flick and Toni leapt up at the same time, their chairs scraping against the floor. Jimmy and Chad were left sitting at the table eating slowly and shooting awkward glances across the room at each other.

Flick and Toni found Maggie, a hand either side of the sink, her back slumped and head hanging. It took a moment for Flick to realise her shoulders were shaking. 'Nan?' She went over and caressed her shoulder. 'Are you okay?'

Maggie shook her head.

'Mum?' Toni probed again. 'What did you mean by 'us'?'

Slowly Maggie straightened her shoulders and

wiped away some tears but she didn't turn around. 'You and me, Toni. He never came back for us.' A shaky breath. 'Rocco is your father,' she whispered.

Flick heard it and she was sure her mother had too, but the words were so faint and so hard to comprehend that she thought she must have imagined them.

'What?' they both said at once.

Toni reached out and turned Maggie towards her. 'Say that again?'

Flick felt her heart lurch for her Nan. Never had Flick seen her this upset. Her face dripped with tears.

'Rocco is your real father.' This time her eyes rose up to meet her daughter's, her head nodding.

Toni stepped back as if she'd been slapped. 'No.' She bumped against the kitchen table and gripped on for dear life. 'I don't believe it.' She pressed her fingers into her eyes as if it might take the pain away.

'It's true. I swear it.'

'How could you keep this from me? My whole life — a lie!'

Flick was unravelling fast. She hated seeing her Nan so upset but she'd also never seen her mum this tattered. Who should she turn to first?

Before Flick could make a decision Toni stormed out of the kitchen, slamming the back door hard enough to fracture the hinges. Maggie turned back to the sink as huge sobs wracked her body. And as Flick rubbed her Nan's back gently, she finally realised what this meant — her

50

grandfather wasn't her biological grandfather, or her mum's father.

Yet again the men in her life had been taken away from her.

★ ★ ★

Toni almost tripped over Fella in her haste to flee the house. She swore as she clung to the verandah post that stopped her skittling along the ground. Tears blurred her vision as she stomped her way to the shed and she roughly wiped them away. She needed to get to the bike, to ride it fast and to feel the wind against her face. She needed to blow away the turmoil in her mind.

Toni wasn't aware of starting the bike and didn't think about where she was going as the fence posts flashed past. She just rode it hard, the wind squeezing the tears from her eyes.

When she came to the end of the road she finally stopped. Turning off the bike she just sat there, thinking while the quiet of the land stretched out around her.

She was fifty-three years old. Fifty-three years of thinking that Arthur was her father and that she was a Stewart. But if she wasn't a Stewart, who the hell was she? She didn't even know this man Rocco's last name.

As the tears dried up they were steadily replaced with anger. Maggie had helped her raise Flick, had always been there by her side, the one person she could rely on. Yet all the while she'd been keeping this massive secret from her, the biggest secret of all. How could she do that? For fifty-three years! There was a niggling sensation at the back of her mind, something about her being hypocritical, but Toni pushed it away. She couldn't think of that now.

As the reality of it all finally seeped into her bones, other questions began to surface. Had Arthur known she wasn't his? Could that be why they'd always locked horns? Was this what had made life hard, the difference between Arthur and herself? And who was this Rocco anyway? A man in a black and white photo. A name that popped up now and then alongside memories of the war or the old house. This shadowy figure — he was her father?

All the years of assuming she'd turn out like Arthur, wondering if his depression was hereditary. She'd been so much more strong-willed than him and she'd always assumed that came from Maggie. But perhaps it actually came from Rocco? In what other ways might she be like him? Would they look the same, or even laugh the same? Had Maggie been thinking along these lines all this time?

Rocco. Her father. Was he even alive?

Toni wanted all these emotions to stop. Her head felt heavy and achy. Her eyes and temples stung from crying. It struck her that the last time she'd cried was at Arthur's funeral four years ago. She suddenly felt tired and old. And just so angry.

After a very long time Toni ventured back to the sheds to do what she always did when things felt tough: bury herself in farm work.

5

It was very quiet in the house. When Flick felt it was okay to leave Nan for five minutes she ducked back to Chad, who was now standing awkwardly by the collection of photos on the wall. Jimmy must have snuck out.

'Hey, you're still here?' Flick said, walking towards Chad.

He turned and reached for her. 'Are you all right?

Flick fell into him. 'I'm not sure. What a bomb.'

'Yeah.' He pulled a face. 'I think I should probably make myself scarce. I feel like you guys need some time alone.'

'Are you going to come out to the club with me and Jimmy tonight? I thought of cancelling but I think I need the drink. Besides, I know Mum won't want to talk and Nan has shut down too.' A strained laugh left her lips. 'They are so similar.' Flick sighed and rested her head on his shoulder. 'I would really like you there. Everything is just so weird.'

Chad nodded and kissed her. 'Okay, babe. I'll try. Call me if you need.'

After he left, Flick went back into the kitchen to help clean up the dishes with Maggie. 'Nan, can I do anything to help?'

'There's nothing more to say or do, love. I've let the cat out of the bag and there's no way we can ever stuff it back in.' Maggie gave her a weak smile.

'Would you like me to stay? I'm sure Mum can shift the sheep on her own.'

'I'm okay, I'm just worried about Toni. It's not how I thought things would go. I didn't really think this through. No, you go and get the sheep in, love.'

'Only if you're sure?'

Her nan stood up straight. 'I may be old, Felicity, but I'm not frail and I don't need watching over. Go do what you have to. I'm fine.' She gave Flick a tight hug as if to show her resilience.

Flick was reluctant to leave but knew once Nan had said her piece that was the end of it. Besides, she also wanted to go and see how her mum was doing. As she turned to leave Maggie grabbed her hand.

'There is one thing. Tell Toni I'm sorry. I didn't see the point of telling her, since Rocco never came back. I was trying to protect her, you understand? It was bad enough he hurt one person — I didn't want him to hurt her too. Do you think she will ever forgive me?'

The desperation in her eyes was gut-wrenching. Flick patted her on the hand.

'I'm sure she'll come around. Just give her time. You know how pigheaded Mum can be. I'll talk to her — well, I'll try. I'll be back later. You rest up.'

Flick went to saddle up Contractor. Knowing her mum, she'd be at the shed.

* * *

54

Sure enough, when Flick arrived, Toni was sitting on the Honda motorbike next to the Hilux, just staring into space with glassy eyes.

'Wow, the ute looks weird without the bullbar,' said Flick. Contractor neighed and stamped his foot impatiently. He loved sheep work and was oblivious to all the drama.

Toni glanced up vaguely. 'I know. I'll see if I can get it back on but it might be pointless. It's not like the ute goes fast enough to need it. Here, Fella, get up. Let's get these sheep moved.'

Flick opened her mouth, ready to talk to her mum about all that had gone on, but Toni started the bike and revved it while Fella leapt onto the back. He stood, balancing as she took off towards the east paddock.

Flick leant down, resting her face against Contractor, and rubbed his neck. 'Well, that went well . . . not. Let's go, mate. Follow that bike.'

It was a warm spring day and Flick was glad she'd put on her wide-brim hat. There was a hint of a breeze, which pressed against her blue-checked shirt as Contractor galloped along the track. What a perfect Friday afternoon. Almost good enough to forget the last few hours.

They rounded up the mob and moved them towards the gate. Toni shut off the bike to close the gate but when she tried to start it again, it wouldn't kick over.

'Are you out of fuel?' Flick asked, turning Contractor back towards her.

'No, it's over half full.' Toni got off and looked over the motor. Then she unscrewed the spark plug. 'Ah, shit.' She stood up and put the spark plug in her pocket. 'Can I catch a lift?'

Flick bit her lip so she didn't give her mum the smug look that was just dying to spread across her face. 'Sure.' Flick took her foot out of her stirrup and hooked her arm so her mum could lift herself up onto the Contractor's back. Toni wrapped her arms around Flick's waist and, after a slight pause, hugged her tight before resting her head against her shoulder. Flick drew her lip in between her teeth to hold back her tears. Fighting to control her voice, she asked, 'Dirty spark plug?'

'Yep.'

'Do you want me to take you back to the shed or shall we pen these sheep up first?' asked Flick.

'Think you can handle it?'

'With Contractor and Fella, not a problem.' Flick nudged Contractor and they headed off.

'How are the floors coming along?' asked Toni as she relaxed her grip and sat upright.

Flick paused for a moment then chose her words carefully. 'You really want to talk about that? How about we talk about what happened in the kitchen?'

Toni huffed, her mood drastically changing.

'You can't avoid it, Mum. I know it must be a shock — '

'Of course it's a bloody shock. What am I supposed to think? I've just found out my whole life was a lie. I just can't believe my mother would do this. I'm so angry,' she said through her teeth.

Flick felt her body trembling and tried to

understand what her mum was going through. 'You know Nan was just trying to do what she thought best. Without Rocco coming back, maybe it was?'

'No, I don't care. There are no excuses for not telling me. I've lived my whole life thinking Arthur was my father. I busted my arse to get him to appreciate my efforts and to get his approval, and for what? He wasn't even my dad.'

Tears prickled as Flick took offence to her words. 'Mum, Grandad was a part of our lives. He was here, he loved us. Where was Rocco?' Sure, her grandad could be hard to take sometimes but there were moments when he showered them with love, moments that Flick missed now he was gone.

Toni sighed and Flick knew she'd given her something to think about.

'I don't want to talk about it any more, Felicity. I just can't handle it right now. We're shearing soon so we have a lot to do.'

Her stern tone was one Flick never messed with. Much the same with Nan. A change of conversation was needed. After a few minutes of silence Flick perked up.

'You should come and see the floors at the old house, Mum. They look great now that Jimmy showed me how to use the sander properly. That bloke has no end of talent.'

'I know. He should be putting them to use on the farm, not helping you play house.'

Flick sighed. 'You could just be happy for me. At least I'm here on the farm and not off doing drugs and having kids to lots of men.'

57

'Sorry, you're right. And I am interested, really.' Toni squeezed Flick's arm. 'I'm just worried it's a waste of money. We already have a home.'

'Why don't you come and see how it looks? Once the floors are polished up I want to move in. Maybe Jimmy should too, so he's not stuck out in the old shearing quarters. He deserves better.'

'Yeah, you're probably right there,' said Toni quietly.

Flick changed the subject again. 'So are you coming out to the club with us tonight for some pool? It'll take your mind off things.'

'No, Flick. I'm just not up to facing people at the moment.'

Flick moved Contractor to the left behind the mob, which was wandering too far out. Fella was in a bit deep so she called him back.

'You know, you really should get out more, Mum. How are you supposed to meet a man and have some fun?'

'Oh, you are a funny girl. Why would I need a man? I have everything I need here,' said Toni.

'Come on. I haven't seen you with anyone in ages. If I wasn't here I'd actually think you'd made up my dad too,' she teased.

Toni cleared her throat like something was stuck hard. 'He may as well be made up. Sometimes I even struggle to remember what he looked like. But you have his eyes and if I really think hard, I can picture him from that starting point.'

'I wish you knew more about him. Fancy not

even knowing his last name! And you thought *I* was reckless at school.'

Toni sighed heavily. 'What can I say? One night of recklessness brought me you. I don't regret any of it. I had a good time and I'm sure he did too.'

Flick groaned. 'I don't need any more details, thanks, Mum.'

'What? I was thirty-three and single.'

Flick thought for a moment. 'Did you plan on having me?'

'I've told you before, I don't really know. I didn't plan it, but I didn't really worry about contraception either. I wasn't upset when I found out I was pregnant; maybe I was hoping. But I was disappointed I wasn't in a relationship. Getting married would have been ideal, having a husband to share life with.'

'Then why didn't you try to find him again?'

Fella barked at the sheep as they ran through the next gate, cutting off her last word.

'Because we didn't know each other from a bar of soap. He was with the Co-operative Bulk Handling mob constructing the new bin. I only saw him in passing a few times at the shop and then at a big party we had. Before I had a chance to run into him again, they'd left.'

'You didn't think it would be important for him to know he was going to be a dad?'

'He was long gone by the time I found out I was pregnant. It didn't seem important to find him. I didn't need him, just you.' Toni sighed. 'For all I know, he was already a dad. Maybe he had a girlfriend. It was better just being happy with what he'd given me.' Toni played with Flick's long plait. 'You were a gift from a stranger.'

'Just like Nan? She thinks you're a gift from Rocco,' said Flick carefully.

'It's different,' Toni spat, her mood hardening again.

'How's it different? You didn't know Rocco was your dad, and I don't even know who mine is. The only man I had was Grandad, and now I find out I don't even really have him.'

'Oh, Felicity, you always had Grandad. You grew up with him, you were the apple of his eye.'

'But so did you, Mum. Just because Rocco is your real dad, didn't mean you didn't have one either. You didn't miss out. I'm the one who never had a dad. I'm the one who should be angry. Unless you help me find Simon, I'll never have one.'

'Finding him won't make him an instant father.'

Flick huffed. 'Maybe not, but he might have a chance to learn. Maybe I have half brothers or sisters out there. How will I ever know? You think you have a right to be angry at Nan — well, I think I should be angry at you.' But she put her own issues behind her, shelving them for another day. She'd had twenty years to come to terms with her fatherless life, whereas her mum had the lot on one day.

Flick had tried to find Simon herself one time by calling people at Co-operative Bulk Handling, but no one had wanted to help her. Locating a passing worker from a hired crew all those years

60

ago seemed impossible. Even so, Flick still dreamt of finding him. It had been hard growing up without a dad. Grandad Arthur and the odd workman were as close as she could get. It made her wish Jimmy had been on their farm since the day she was born. He would have made an awesome dad.

'Why didn't you find someone to marry? I don't really remember you ever having boy-friends, not anything long-term. At least Nan found you a dad,' she said with difficulty.

She felt her mum's hand on her arm. 'Oh, Flick, believe me, I would have if I could. It's just so hard to find a good man out here, let alone one willing to take on a child.'

'What about Jimmy?'

Toni stiffened. 'Jimmy would have been twenty-four when I had you. Little more than a kid himself. And of course there's the minor detail that we hadn't even met him then.' She sighed. 'But I tried. I dated a shearer for a while but that was too hard with his job and me with the farm and you. I just didn't have time for relationships that needed extra work, if you know what I mean. And you remember Drew? The Pommy fella? We had a month together before his visa ran out and he went home.' Toni shrugged. 'I wished all that for you, but I couldn't make it come true. Dating is not easy when you have a child and a farm to manage. Besides, you seemed happy just having Grandad.'

Flick rolled her eyes. Sure, she'd seemed happy on the outside. She'd always been an easygoing kid. But it was hard to forget the

61

nights she'd longed for a father to do things with, or those days she'd see her friends at school spoilt by their dads. She'd turned green with envy watching them riding on their dads' shoulders, or later, getting driving lessons. Not even Grandad could help her with that. It was Nan who'd showed her how to drive the old ute. At least Toni had had a father figure around, regardless of whether or not he was her biological one.

6

Toni adjusted her numb bum on Contractor's back but the discomfort didn't disappear. Flick's words about Jimmy had shocked Toni more than she realised. Did Flick really not see a problem with Toni dating Jimmy? Why had it seemed such a natural assumption for her? That was so typical of Flick's attitude — if you want something, just go for it. Easy for her to say, when she'd got everything she ever wanted. A dog, her horse, coming back to the farm. Toni had never got anything she'd wanted, besides Felicity.

Toni had joined clubs, played hockey and tennis — she'd even tried golf just to get out there in the hope of meeting a future husband. Living in a small country town with fewer than a hundred people made finding someone you wanted to spend your life with all but impossible. After all, married men and women and children made up most of that population.

Once she'd had Felicity she'd struggled to keep looking. There had been the odd night here and there but nothing that was going to be everlasting. Farming and a child had kept her exhausted and then she'd just felt too old. Who would want a weathered, manly woman like her? She'd been happy enough on her own, hadn't she? Until Jimmy had slotted into their life. If only she could have found him years ago.

'Mum, looks like Jimmy's had trouble.'

Toni followed Flick's gaze to the shed, across from the sheep yards where the ute was still parked, the boom spray connected behind it. Jimmy was leaning over the green-painted frame near the blob dobber tank, his snug blue singlet not leaving much to the imagination. Toni couldn't look away — the arm that was holding the weight of his body was so tightly shaped with muscles. She could see them continue across his back.

'Pretty hot, hey?' said Flick, causing Toni to blink finally.

'What?'

'Jimmy. He's got a hot bod for an old dude. I saw you checking him out.'

Toni felt the burning flush crawl across her face and quickly tilted her hat so Flick couldn't see. 'I was just trying to see what was wrong,' she said.

'Sure,' said Flick with a chuckle before she moved Contractor towards the sheep.

Toni reminded herself that this was exactly why she couldn't go out in public with Jimmy. She had to stay here on the farm where she was reminded that it was about the job. Who knew what she'd do after a few drinks and a bit of fun? The poor guy was a great worker; she couldn't put him through that. She doubted he'd appreciate his older boss trying to crack onto him. After four years of working so well together, she couldn't do anything to jeopardise his happiness here. She'd rather work alongside Jimmy as friends than not have him in their lives at all.

'You'd better go see if he needs a hand, Mum. I got this.'

Toni slid off Contractor and headed towards the shed. 'What's up?' she asked.

He didn't turn around, as if he'd already sensed she was there. 'The bloody blob dobber isn't spitting out right. I adjusted it — let's see if this helps.' He started the motor and turned to watch the end of the folded-up boom where the white foam was dripping. The foam thickened and big bubbles dropped out like massive marshmallows.

'Now you've got it,' said Toni.

Jimmy turned off the motor and then wiped his big hands across his work jeans. His eyes ran the length of Toni's body and for a moment she felt exposed in her black singlet, her shirt tied around her waist.

'Aren't you missing something?' he said.

Toni stared at him blankly.

'The motorbike?' Jimmy smiled. 'It's a Honda, about this high, two wheels and usually has Fella on the back?'

God, of course. 'Oh, yeah. It died.' She pulled the spark plug out of her jeans. 'I'd better go clean it up.' Quickly she headed into the workshop in search of the wire brush.

She was leaning over the bench, scrubbing the plug when the hair on her neck prickled. Jimmy stood right behind her and she could almost feel his presence on her skin.

'If that wire brush won't fix it, I think there's a new plug over by the ute parts in the cupboard,' he said.

Toni shivered but she focused on her job, despite the wire brush digging into her fingers every now and then.

Jimmy leant over, covering her hand in his. He was reaching for the spark plug but the contact was electric.

'Let me see.' He tugged it from her grasp and inspected it.

Toni tried to slow her breathing so the manly scent of sweat and soap didn't make her hyperventilate.

'It's still got some life left in it yet.' He handed it back. 'I'll drop you back at the bike if you like.' He paused and shifted some tools on the bench. 'Um, so how are you going?'

'Okay,' she said, her jaw tightening until her teeth ached.

'It was quite a bombshell Maggie dropped. If you want someone to talk to, I'm here,' he offered.

'Thanks, but I'm fine,' she said too quickly. She turned to leave but he grabbed her arm.

'Maggie's very upset,' he said.

Toni shook his hand away. 'So am I,' she said, before walking out of the shed. 'And don't worry about the lift. I'll walk.'

⋆　⋆　⋆

When all the sheep were in, the shearing shed set up and the rest of the day's work was done, Toni and Flick headed home. While Flick sorted out Contractor, Toni went and grabbed the first shower while avoiding her mum. Maggie had a roast cooking and the smell permeated the house, causing blowflies to hover by the back door. Roast was her favourite dinner but she wasn't falling for that old trick.

After showering, Toni opened her bedroom window. The Doctor had blown in, fluttering her thin blue curtains. The cold shower had been just what she'd needed. Her skin felt alive as she slathered it with moisturiser. Toni couldn't take back the damage the sun had done to her skin over the years from the outside work but she tried to keep it soft at least. Being lean kept the skin taut, so long as she didn't lose all that muscle.

Reaching into her cupboard for her usual trackpants and singlet, Toni paused. Should she wear something a little more summery? She considered a little cotton dress. If she wore that, would everyone wonder why? Would they think she was trying to impress Jimmy? Maybe she just wanted to feel a little bit feminine for a change. And besides, she had only worn it once. The moths would probably get to it if she didn't actually use it.

The soft white cotton and thin straps were casual enough, especially with the little drop of material to the top of her knees. With this bodice she wouldn't have to wear a bra either, making it extra comfortable to lounge around in after work. Okay, she was sold. She tugged the straps off the hanger and slipped the dress on over her head, then stepped towards the mirror. She didn't even notice the dress; what she saw was her brown eyes. So different from Maggie's blue ones, and now that she thought about it, they weren't like Arthur's either. His had been hazel with an almost green tinge. But hers were deep chocolate-brown. She moved closer to the mirror, her face inches from her reflection as she studied the intricacies of her eyes. The truth had been looking back at her, her whole life.

Stepping back with determination, Toni pulled out her bag and threw in a few sets of clothes. She needed more time away from Maggie. Tonight she'd sleep in the shearing quarters in her swag.

'Toni, can we talk?' Maggie peered around the door.

'Not now.' She walked past Maggie, stopping at the office to pick up the swag before walking out of the house with her bag.

'Toni, wait. Where are you going? I have dinner ready.'

'I'm not hungry.' She let the door bang shut and marched to the shearing quarters. She set herself up in the end room, leaving a room between her and Jimmy. With a bit of luck, he wouldn't even notice she'd moved in.

But she needed a drink. Heading back to the house, she grabbed a beer from the outside fridge. The afternoon was starting to cool and from the verandah Toni could see towards the west paddock where the sun was setting. Flick was walking back towards the house and Contractor was in his yard watching her leave, his body silhouetted by the golden sun.

'You look nice, Mum. I like that dress. Have you changed your mind about coming with us?'

Flick stepped onto the verandah and helped herself to a beer.

'No.' Toni hoped Flick just left it. She couldn't handle any more talk today.

Flick chewed on her lip. 'Fair enough. Well, I'd better go and have a shower.' Flick kicked off her boots and took her beer inside.

Toni breathed a sigh of relief and thought about walking back towards the quarters. She didn't really want to go back there but didn't want to stay by the house either. She was starving but there was no way was she going to sit across the table from her mother. Maybe after Maggie had gone to bed she'd sneak in for some food, or raid Jimmy's two-minute noodle stash.

The sun was setting in vivid orange, swirling into reds and yellows. The rush of wind brought with it an amazing scent. Toni closed her eyes, trying to breathe it in, and it only took a moment to realise why it touched her so.

His footfall should have alerted her earlier but she'd been distracted by the sunset.

'Beautiful afternoon.' Jimmy was in clean stonewash jeans and a white T-shirt. His hair was still damp from the shower. He looked good. 'You got a hot date?' he asked as his eyes trailed the length of her body.

'No. Any more hassles with the spraying?'

'Nope, all done.' His eyes wandered back down to her dress while his tongue darted across his bottom lip. 'Are you coming with us?'

'No.'

'Hmm, what a shame. I'm almost tempted to stay, with all that's happened, but Flick wants to stick to routine, said she needs a drink. I think this news has messed with her too, more than anyone realises.'

'Yeah, I forgot that she hides her emotions well.' Toni felt awful. In her own chaos, she hadn't really thought of the effect on Flick. Her daughter was such a tough person, who put others first. 'Thanks for being there for her, Jimmy. She really looks up to you.' Toni took a big drink of her beer, hoping it would relax the tightness swelling in her throat.

'It's no problem. She's a great girl, keeps me on my toes,' he said with a smile. 'Is she ready?'

'Just having a shower. Go grab a beer and head inside, dinner's ready. I think I spotted a pavlova too.' It was her favourite.

'What?' He slammed the fridge shut and spun around, beer in hand. Jimmy linked his arm in hers and practically dragged her back to the house. 'You trying to get me to stay home?' he asked with a teasing glint in his eyes.

Toni nearly tripped over her feet. 'No.' *God, what made him say that?*

Jimmy strode inside. Toni didn't want to follow, but he wasn't letting her go. They found Flick doing up the buttons on her shirt while her damp hair dripped down her back. She was looking at a photo album open on the table in the dining room.

'Did Maggie make a pav?' Jimmy demanded.

Flick glanced up and frowned. 'I don't know, I just got out the shower. Nan's in the kitchen plating up.'

Toni let out her breath. Mum was busy. Good.

Toni glanced over Flick's shoulder. 'What are you looking at?'

'This was open at the old photos. God, it was so different back in those days,' said Flick.

'Oh.' Toni had seen these black and white photos before. Only now they had a completely different meaning.

Flick pointed to a black and white photo. 'That's Phyllis and John Fuller out the front of the old cottage. Amazing what they had to live in back then. Are they hessian bags, Mum?' She indicated a room that was built on the side of the cottage. It looked so rustic against the wooden slats of the main cottage.

'Yes. Mum said that room had a tin roof but they had sewn the hessian and made a wall with it. Apparently a great spot when summer was at its hottest. They could wet the hessian and the breeze would make it cool.'

'And these are the Italian prisoners, right? Which one was Rocco?' asked Flick.

Toni's fingers caressed the edge of the photo. Two men stood by two big gum trees, guns in their hands and a massive kangaroo propped up between them. Her focus was on the photo of the man in boots, pants, and a dark V-neck jumper over his collared shirt, the long barrel of the gun pointing to the ground. She studied Rocco, but it was so hard to get a clear picture of him in the blurry image.

Without colour she couldn't really see his eyes. But looking at him now brought out a whole new feeling. This was her real dad. And she was half Italian.

'He's handsome. No wonder Nan fell for him,' said Flick.

It was then that Toni noticed how worn the edge of this particular photo was. As if someone had been back to look at it many, many times over.

7

'Have you got the cake?' Phyllis was by the stove putting the tea into the beer bottles.

'Yes, Mother. A big slice each.' Maggie had wrapped them in butter paper and then again in newspaper.

'Just don't let the paper fly away — '

'I know, it will scare the horses. I'll be careful. It's not that windy outside.' Sometimes her mother talked to her as if she were still eight instead of sixteen. Maggie put the cake into the small wooden crate. Phyllis finished corking the bottles and put them in too, along with four cups.

'Don't be down there too long. They need to get back to work and I'll need you here to clean up and get ready for dinner. Charlie got an emu so that will be a nice change from rabbit and roo.'

Maggie tried not to screw up her face. Emu wasn't her favourite. Picking up the crate she headed outside and started walking to where the men were working in the new paddock. It had only been a week since the Italians had arrived, but already they had done so much. Last night she had overheard her father telling her mother that hiring the Italians was the best thing he'd done. Not that Phyllis would ever agree. She was far too worried about what the locals thought, but John had reminded her that they weren't the only ones who needed the help of the prisoners.

Since their arrival John and Charlie had gone to some funny extremes to explain things to them — seeing her father impersonate a kangaroo and emu had been a highlight. Phyllis, of course, would never stoop to that, and just spoke normally as if they could understand every word she said.

Maggie felt sorry for them. They'd been thrust upon a completely different land, with no family or friends, and treated like they were dangerous. Maggie often wondered if Thomas had been captured and was feeling the same way. It was this thought that often had her wanting to give Rocco and Giulio a hug, just to make them feel less alone. Giulio and Rocco often sat alone together after work, speaking in hushed Italian. Sometimes she heard them singing a song. She didn't understand the lyrics but it sounded sad and haunting, as if they were singing about their loved ones back home.

It was easy to like them both. They worked hard, were quiet and polite, kept to themselves and cared for their horses. She couldn't imagine them wanting to hurt anyone. She'd overhead Rocco having a huge conversation with Contractor in Italian; someone with a cruel heart would not offer so much affection and graciousness. Rocco and Giulio seemed so thankful just to be here and not in the prison camp. She could tell by the way they gazed out across the land, were ready and waiting for work each morning and followed her father as if he were their idol.

It took Maggie nearly twenty minutes to walk to where they were working. The rocks and roots were stacked in neat piles, and she was amazed at how quickly the four of them worked. Rocco and Giulio were wearing their short-sleeved shirts tucked into their pants, which were held up with belts. Sweat stained their shirts and glistened on their skin. She'd much rather look at them than at the stern face of her mother.

'Afternoon smoko. Ease up, lads,' said John when he saw Maggie. He put the rock he was holding onto the cart, waited for the others to load up their rocks and then he led Splinter and Winks over to the tree line at the edge of the paddock.

Maggie headed to the spot where they liked to stop. Cut logs were already set up in the shade. She put down the crate, opened the cake up and got the tea out.

'Hello, thank you,' said Rocco as he took a cup she handed him. 'Tea good.'

'Yes, the tea is good,' said Maggie. She often repeated words to show how they should be pronounced. 'Cake?' she asked, nodding to it.

Charlie had already helped himself to a piece. 'Chocolate cake.'

Giulio waited until John had taken a piece before helping himself. 'Shocolat cak,' he said, trying the new words.

'Chocolate cake,' said Maggie, sounding it out carefully. Both Giulio and Rocco repeated it until she nodded that they had it.

Then she laughed as they ate some and groaned in pleasure.

'Groans mean the same thing in any language,' said Charlie with a chuckle.

Then her father and Giulio put down their cups and rolled cigarettes. Maggie was used to the smell of tobacco, but walked over to Winks and Splinter, the two Clydesdales harnessed to the cart, and let the men smoke in peace. She rubbed the horses' noses and talked to them softly. One had to admire the thick legs and solid powerful bodies of this breed. They were worlds apart from Contractor.

John got up first, emptying the dregs from his cup and putting it back in the crate, and the others followed suit. Maggie collected the crate and the empty tea bottles.

'Thanks, little sister,' said Charlie, before following their father to the horses.

'Thank you, Miss Margaret,' said Giulio. His words were spoken clearly and confidently.

Rocco stepped up to her and Maggie felt a tingle of joy at his closeness.

'*Grazie*, Margaret,' he said with a smile.

'*Grazie*? Is 'thank you'?' she asked. Rocco nodded and so she took the cup he held out and tried the new word again. '*Grazie*, Rocco.'

His whole face lit up and at that moment, Maggie decided that she would try to learn a bit of their language too. Why should they be the ones to make all the effort to fit in? Besides, his Italian sounded so wonderful. In the early mornings when she went out to collect sticks for the fire she could hear them talking in Italian. She would often pause by their shed, wondering what they were saying. She'd never heard anything like it before.

'Goodbye.' Maggie turned and began to walk back to the cottage, her mother's instructions at the forefront of her mind. But it didn't stop her from glancing back to watch the men at work, especially Rocco with his strong arms and back.

She turned, before she was caught watching, and saw a Chevy ute driving towards her.

'Margaret!'

Arthur was leaning out the side, waving madly. The ute stopped.

'Hello, Margaret,' said Arthur's father.

'Afternoon, Mr Stewart. Are you here to see Father?'

'Yes, just need to talk about some farm business.' Mr Stewart nodded to the men working in the paddock. 'How are the Italians working out?'

'Really good, Mr Stewart. As you can see, this paddock is nearly done. They're hard workers,' she said, a little proudly. She could only imagine what the rest of the town was thinking about them. Hopefully Mr Stewart would report good things.

'Good to hear.'

Arthur got out of the ute. 'I'll walk up in a minute,' he said to his father.

Mr Stewart smiled and nodded his goodbye before driving off.

Arthur stood beside her, braces holding up his pants. He just didn't fill them like Rocco. They flapped about his legs like ship sails on skinny masts.

'I can't talk long. Mother needs me,' she said.

'I understand. I just wanted to make sure everything was all right with the prisoners?'

Maggie tried not to wince. On their farm they were not prisoners, just hired workers. At least, that's how she liked to think of them.

'Everything is going fine,' she said brightly.

They watched Mr Stewart get out to talk to John. Rocco glanced their way as he put another rock on the cart. Maggie felt funny under his gaze. Would he think she was with Arthur? Why did that bother her?

'Are they kind to you?' asked Arthur.

Maggie continued to watch the men, holding the crate against her chest. 'Yes, they are. I'm trying to help them with their English,' she said with a smile.

'Do you think that's wise?' he said, causing her smile to vanish.

Maggie realised Arthur didn't mean anything harsh by his words; he was just being cautious and overprotective — unlike her mother, who would have only been worried what the community thought.

'It's fine, Arthur. I need to go so I don't upset mother. Goodbye.'

Arthur looked crestfallen. 'Goodbye, Margaret.'

She could feel him watching her as she began walking home. This time she didn't look back.

At the cottage, her mother had her doing the washing, helping to cook dinner and darning Charlie's socks. Maggie had been happy for the chores, which passed the day quickly. Soon enough the men arrived from work, washed and came in for dinner.

The table arrangements on their first night here had caused mother no end of grief. Where to sit the Italians so they weren't near her, or at the head of the table, or anywhere near Maggie? Phyllis had eventually decided that father and Charlie would sit at either end of the table, with the women on one side and the prisoners on the other. Maggie actually liked the new seating arrangements, as Rocco was right in her line of sight. She tried not to smile as she laid out the bone-handled cutlery on the table along with the Rosella tomato sauce and salt. When they all ate together, it was like it used to be with her whole family, as if Tommy and George were still home. Except that Rocco was more handsome than her brothers.

Phyllis handed Maggie a plate with sliced bread on it, which she placed on the table as the men came in. With all six of them in the one room, it was really cosy. Rocco and Giulio waited until John and Charlie sat down before pulling out their own wooden chairs.

Maggie helped pass out the bowls of emu stew. Everyone waited until she and Phyllis sat down before lifting their forks to eat. Maggie waited to see what the men thought about dinner before she started. Rocco squinted an eye as he swallowed. It was much the same as her own reaction to her mother's emu stew. Giulio had eaten a few mouthfuls when her father spoke up.

'You like? It's emu,' he said slowly.

Both Italians froze. By now they were well aware of the word emu.

Giulio's face contorted. He sprang from the table and rushed outside while holding a hand over his mouth.

'I know how he feels,' mumbled Maggie while John and Charlie were laughing. Phyllis gave them cold stares.

'It's not that bad, is it, Rocco?' asked Charlie.

Rocco's dark eyebrows moved as he frowned. 'Is good. Food India, not much.' He shook his head.

Maggie forgot the food on her fork as she watched Rocco. 'India? You were in India?'

'Si. Long time. No food.' His lovely tanned skin paled by the candlelight.

Maggie could see the pain dancing across his deep brown eyes. What had they endured there?

Everyone was silent. Rocco's admission had changed the mood and filled the atmosphere with discomfort. Luckily Giulio came back in.

'Mi dispiace, mi dispiace,' he kept repeating.

'He say sorry,' said Rocco.

John waved it away. 'Don't worry, Giulio. Sit, sit. Eat the bread.' He picked up the plate and Giulio gratefully took a slice, his shoulders relaxing after

79

seeing the smile on John's face.

Maggie turned back to Rocco, 'So 'sorry' is *mi dispiace?*'

Giulio and Rocco both looked at her with surprised expressions. Giulio said something to Rocco in Italian.

'*Si, si.*' Rocco agreed, and smiled at Maggie. 'Giulio say good. You good.'

'What is the point, Margaret?' huffed her mother. 'I don't think you should humour them. They need to adapt to us.'

'Maybe Maggie might visit Italy one day,' said Charlie.

'I might,' she said. Giulio and Rocco went back to eating. She could tell the family was talking too fast for them. 'I like the challenge. It's something new, and like Father always says, new things keep the mind ticking over.'

John grinned at Maggie, then turned to Phyllis. 'It's not hurting anyone. Let her at least help them learn.'

Maggie didn't dare glance at her mother but when Phyllis didn't contradict her father, she did let the breath she was holding escape slowly.

'Oh, guess what we found out today?' John said to Phyllis. 'Rocco tells me that Giulio is a mason. His father was a good one and he learnt from him.'

Phyllis stared at John blankly.

'He can build us a new house. A real one, with bricks.'

'Are you joking with me, Mr Fuller?' said Phyllis. She dabbed her lips with the worn napkin on her lap.

Maggie knew her mother dreamt of a nice home. This bit of news would be a delight. Hopefully it would ease her disdain for the Italians.

'I assure you I am not joking. Maybe tomorrow we

80

can find the spot you'd like your new house to be.' John was grinning, waiting for Phyllis to understand what he was actually telling her.

Phyllis dropped her napkin and clasped her hands together. 'Oh, John.'

'So you'd better draw up some plans soon so we can give them to Giulio,' said Charlie.

Phyllis was looking at John like he'd built it already, when in fact it was Giulio who'd be doing all the work.

'Charlie can have a real room instead of the sleep-out,' said Phyllis. 'Oh, this is wonderful news.'

Maggie shifted her feet under the table and accidentally touched someone's foot. She looked straight up at Rocco, who was smiling at her. She was embarrassed and excited at the same time, and couldn't help the heat crawling towards her face. Maggie hung her head towards her bowl. Luckily her mother was too busy talking about plans for the new house. Hopefully this would keep her in a good mood for a long time.

Maggie refused to look up again in case she saw Rocco watching her. Instead she quickly got up, started collecting the empty dishes, and took them to the tin dish on the side table to wash up. That way no one could see her face, as she was sure it would be bright red.

8

'I love these old photos. Look how beautiful Nan is,' said Flick.

'She's a looker, all right,' said Jimmy with a chuckle as he leant against a dining chair.

'Are you trying to get yourself a big slab of pavlova?' said Maggie as she walked back into the room in a grey tracksuit.

Toni stepped back abruptly. The air grew thick with tension.

'And there's the original Contractor. See, Jimmy? Tell him the story, Nan,' Flick begged, hoping to distract everyone.

Toni cleared her throat and mumbled something about needing another beer before leaving the room, her eyes downcast.

Flick grasped her grandmother's hand and pointed to the photo.

'Well,' started Maggie slowly, 'I think I was about fourteen when we went to Kalgoorlie as a family.' She sat down on the closest chair. 'One of my father's mates had told him about the Boulder Cup. It was the first time I'd seen anything like it and it was a splendid day. Contractor was in that race and he came third. Dad heard that Contractor had pulled up lame and they were going to put him down. But Dad believed he could heal Contractor, that he didn't deserve to die, so they gave him to Dad instead. We borrowed a float and brought him home and

Dad nursed him until his leg healed. He couldn't be a racehorse any more but he suited us just fine. He had guts, that horse, and he was so grand. Made the poor Clydesdales look short and fat, but Winks was his best mate.' Maggie pointed to the photo of all the Clydesdales and recalled each of their names.

'Uncle Charlie fell off Contractor, didn't he?'

'Yes, yes he did. Wrecked his arm too. But it was a blessing; if his arm had been good then the army would have taken him and he would have died in the war like my other brothers.'

The room fell silent.

'I didn't know that, Maggie. I'm sorry,' said Jimmy.

Maggie shut the photo album and sighed. 'It was a long time ago. Sometimes it does no good to get stuck in the past.' She rose from her chair to put the album back. 'Come on, let's eat so you kids can get to the club.'

Dinner was a quiet affair, with Toni's vacant chair causing some conflict. Jimmy wanted to find her but Maggie stopped him.

'She knows it's here. Leave her be, Jimmy.' And she gave a pinched smile that was borderline grimace.

'I'm so full,' said Jimmy once he'd finished. 'Too full to fit any pavlova in.'

Maggie chuckled. 'Best you be heading off to the club. Say hi to Cookie if you see him, if he's not too busy in the kitchen.'

'I will, Nan,' said Flick, and they all got up to clear the table.

In the kitchen Flick noticed that Nan had

made up a meal for Toni, and it sat waiting on the bench.

'I'll just put it in the fridge,' said Maggie. 'She can come eat it later.'

Jimmy watched her carefully. 'Will you be okay?'

'Yes, of course. Shoo,' she said waving them towards the door.

'We can stay,' Jimmy added.

'No. Shoo, shoo. Off you go.'

Jimmy baaed like a sheep and linked his arm through Flick's on the way past. 'See you later,' he called back to Maggie.

Flick went with him but glanced back to watch Maggie reach for the knitting she'd left on the edge of the kitchen bench. Nan would be all right if she was knitting.

Outside they headed to Flick's new VX Commodore, a red six-cylinder executive sedan. She'd bought it a few months earlier, using some of the farm wage she'd saved since leaving school, and it had hardly made it out of the shed. Most of the time she drove the farm ute. It still had that new-car smell.

'Do you think we'll be able to sneak some pav when we get back?' asked Jimmy.

Flick laughed. 'Jimmy, I swear you can read my mind.' She glanced around, wondering where her mum could have got to. Maybe she just needed a walk to clear her head. Fella wasn't around so he must've been with her.

Jimmy stopped by the back of the car. 'And is your mind saying it's Jimmy's turn to drive us to the club?' he asked hopefully.

She opened the driver-side door and shook her head. 'Pigs might fly. Good try, though.'

'I wonder who'll be there tonight,' Jimmy said as they reversed out of the shed.

The last of the light was fading fast. But it was September and the days were getting longer. Flick wasn't sure if she liked that, as it usually meant they worked longer hours too. Before too long harvest would be here and she'd be on a header.

'It's a shame your mum isn't coming. For a minute I thought she was going to.'

Flick drove down the driveway and turned onto the gravel road heading towards Karlgarin. 'I know. But she's not really taking this news well. I don't think she's talked to Nan all day, and when I tried to talk about it with her she shut me down.'

'Hmm, yeah, she did the same with me. She's a hard woman to get through to,' he said softly. 'I just wish she'd stop trying to be so strong. She's allowed to fall to pieces and she's allowed to ask for help, or even just talk to me. I wouldn't think any less of her.' Jimmy pressed his fingers against his temples. 'I can't help her through this if she won't let me in.'

'Yep, well, that's Mum. She keeps her cards close to her chest.' Flick wondered where Jimmy was going with this. Just how much did he care? 'Are you and Mum . . . ' she blurted out, and then didn't know how to finish her question.

'Are we what?'

Flick cleared her throat. 'You seriously want me to say it? Can't you read between the lines?'

'Not when those lines are blurry,' he teased. 'If you're asking if we have something going on, then no.'

'Oh.' She glanced at him but it was hard to tell what he was thinking in the dark so she focused back on the road. They were coming up to a reserve and it was always thick with kangaroos.

'Why? Do you want us to have something going on?'

Flick shrugged. 'It doesn't worry me. I just want both of you to be happy. She's getting older and I don't want her to be lonely.'

'I'm sure she'd appreciate the 'getting older' comment,' he said with a chuckle. 'You know, maybe she's happy that way.'

'Maybe, but now with this Rocco stuff. You know how she is, she'll bottle this up for God knows how long. I'm not sure I know how to fix it.'

'Maybe you can't. Maybe only she can.'

She slowed down to turn onto the bitumen road. 'Yeah. I don't know. I just worry about them both.'

'You're a good girl, Flick. I think your mum would be stoked to know you care so much.'

'God, don't tell her,' Flick groaned. 'She'll use it as an excuse to ram some more holidays down my throat.'

'Would a trip away be that bad? Maybe go for a week, see something new and be back to the farm before you know it. Is it really that big a deal? At least she'll be off your back.'

'I guess.' Deep down Flick knew her mum was hoping that if she went on one trip, Flick would have a ball and wouldn't want to come back to the farm. What scared Flick was thinking her mum could be right.

The clubhouse came into view, and Flick pulled up on an angle out the front.

'Looks like an all right crowd,' said Jimmy as they got out the car and headed to the door, drawn in by the clang of balls on the pool table and the sound of cheerful voices.

★ ★ ★

'Hey, it's Flick and Jimmy. Up for a game next?' said Dolly, who was at the pool table with a few mates. One of the local truckies, Dolly had got his name when he lost the dolly he'd been carting on his flat-top trailer. The name had nothing to do with his hairstyle, which was a long curly mullet.

'Sure, I'll just get us a brew,' said Jimmy, heading to the bar.

'So who're we playing? You two?' Flick pointed at Dolly and Fred, Dolly's mate who worked in Hyden. Both men were closer to Jimmy's age than Flick's, and had families.

'Yep, that all right?' said Fred.

'Fine by us, as long as you don't mind losing,' she teased.

A big roar went up as the guys laughed at her bravado.

'Everything okay?' asked Jimmy as he handed her a beer.

'Of course. Just giving them fair warning.' She spotted her friend Jane at the bar with her baby on her knee and went over to say hi while the boys racked up the balls.

'Hey, Flick, how's things?' Janey was one of Flick's few close friends nearby. Most girls her age were still away travelling or at university. On occasion, her friends from school would come out to the farm for a visit, but that's all it ever was.

'Hi, Janey. How's little Emmett?' Flick tickled the little guy's toes, which he was trying to grab with plump fingers while Jane held his waist.

'Hungry and tired as always,' she said with a laugh. 'I'm hoping he starts sleeping through the night before harvest gets here.' Jane glanced at her husband, who was working a shift behind the bar. Most of the local farmers pitched in to help keep the local watering hole, which was part of the bowling club, operating all year round. 'Once Turk's on the header I'll become a harvest widow and it will be all up to me.'

'If you get stuck or need a break, you know I'll have him. Just sing out, okay?' said Flick.

'Turk or Emmett?' Jane said with a laugh. 'Thanks Flick, you're a gem.'

Flick really wanted to tell Jane about Rocco and the incredible day they'd all had, but something held her back. It was all too new, too fresh. Only Jimmy and Chad knew. Thinking of Chad, she looked around but couldn't see him.

'You playing or what, Stewart?' said Dolly.

She rolled her eyes at Jane before taking another long sip of her beer then leaving it on the bar. 'Duty calls.'

Jane laughed as Flick stepped to the pool table.

Jimmy passed her the cue. 'I broke for us. We're bigs.'

They won the first game easily, and just when they were about to win the second game a few new workers came in and called dibs on the pool table.

'Lucky,' said Dolly. 'We were just about to win one back.'

Flick and Jimmy wandered to the bar and sat down. There were a few families with kids eating at the far end, causing the room to hum with voices.

'Didn't you say Chad was coming?' Jimmy said, catching her looking at the door.

She shrugged. 'He was going to try.' She hoped he was still going to make it. She needed a shoulder and his were big and strong. 'Must have got stuck at the farm.'

She turned her attention to Jimmy. His elbows were on the bar, his hands clasped together as if he was praying, jade eyes dazzling under the lights.

'What?' he asked, wiping a hand self-consciously across his face.

Flick hesitated, wondering if she should go down this path but decided to take a chance. It seemed like the day for it. 'Do you think my mum's hot?'

Jimmy choked, his hand covering his mouth as beer dribbled out between his fingers.

'Jesus, Flick, don't spring stuff like that on a drinking man.'

Flick passed him a napkin and he patted his mouth and hand dry. She wondered if he was going to answer her or not.

Jimmy leant forward, the chair creaking under his weight. 'Why do you want to know?'

'It was a fair question and it's a simple answer. Yes or no? I happen to think she's pretty good for her age but I wanted a man's opinion. I sometimes forget that she's a woman, and wondered if men actually saw her as a genuine option. Or do you just see her as another bloke?' Flick swished the beer in her glass before taking a sip.

Jimmy gazed back. 'You're right, it's a fair question so I'll give you a truthful answer.' He looked around the bar before leaning closer and dropping his voice. 'I think your mum is gorgeous. She may cover up her curves but that doesn't mean men haven't noticed.'

'Nice way of saying you've noticed her big — '

'Flick,' growled Jimmy, cutting her off. 'As I was saying, she's perfect.'

'So why haven't you tried anything? She just not your type?'

The blush spreading across his skin made her even more curious. He shifted in his seat and started to pick at his nails.

'Wow, Flick. This conversation is a bit much.'

'Don't go all shy on me, Jimmy. You're my best mate. You can talk to me,' she said with a smile. 'And today has been a day of major revelations.'

He gave a nervous laugh. 'God, I know this will come back to bite me on my arse. Fine.' He took a deep breath. 'There is nothing wrong with

Toni. She's gorgeous, funny, gentle and clever. And she is my type. Happy?'

Flick spluttered. 'Gentle?'

'Yeah. You've never noticed how gentle she is with the birthing ewes or the new lambs? And she's always talking to the dogs and spoils them when no one is looking.'

'Huh.' He really did notice things. 'So then why?'

He let out a massive sigh. 'I haven't tried anything because I don't think I'm *her* type. She probably thinks I'm too young for a start, and I think there is that whole 'we work together' issue, our friendship being more important.'

Flick waved her hand. 'Rubbish. What if it did work? Is that something you'd want?'

'Isn't that what everyone wants? A person to spend their life with? Don't you?' Jimmy picked up a beer coaster and played with it.

'Yeah, I guess that's the end game. For me, though — I think I could be happy living without a companion if I had the farm and my animals.'

'Easy for you to say that when you have Chad.'

She shrugged. Maybe he was right. But Flick hadn't thought about anything long-lasting with Chad.

'Hey, um . . . ' Jimmy bit his lower lip. 'You're not going to mention this conversation to anyone, right?'

Flick thought on it for a minute, letting Jimmy stew. She could try to play cupid and set them up, but if it backfired then she'd be the one to wear it. Flick smiled at the thought of the ever-cool, relaxed Jimmy bumbling his way through asking Toni out.

She grinned. 'You have my word. It stays between us.'

9

Toni could hear the dogs barking and for a moment she thought she was dreaming. When she realised it was their dogs she jumped out of bed and collided with something, forgetting she was in the shearing quarters. Staggering outside she headed blindly through the night towards the headlights that shone by the house.

The dogs stopped barking the moment they saw her. She walked into the beams and yelled out, 'Hello?'

Who would be calling so late at night? For a moment her heart raced as she thought of Flick and Jimmy in an accident. But her brain kicked in as she remembered them getting home at about ten. It was hard not to hear Jimmy settling in for the night. A herd of bloody elephants would be quieter.

'Toni? Sorry to call in so late.'

A man started walking towards her, and she instantly recognised his lopsided walk and rattly voice. It was Morris, a farmer in his sixties from Warragil, a farm ten kilometres away. His wife, Jude, had often looked after Flick when she was little.

'Hi, Morris. What's up?'

'I've just come back from the pub and there's a mob of your sheep on the road.'

'Oh, great.' She groaned. 'You all right?'

'Yeah, nah, I'm fine. But I did hit a few with

the bullbar. Not a scratch on the ute but I think you'd better take the gun with you. Sorry. Sorry to wake you too. I thought it best to drop straight in.'

'Don't worry, I'm just glad you're okay. I'll go check it out,' she said, hugging her body. She was just wearing her T-shirt and pyjama bottoms, and her feet were starting to go numb.

'Righto. They're near Hendo's place along Kean Road.'

Toni thanked Morris again before he hobbled back to his ute. She was lucky it hadn't been worse and lucky that Morris was still half sober. Toni headed to the house, the outside sensor light blinking on.

It was eleven o'clock. She headed down the passageway to Flick's room and crouched by her bed. 'Flick, get up, darling.' Toni gently shook her.

Flick groaned. 'Is it morning already?'

'No. A mob of sheep's out on the main road. We have to go move them before a truck comes through. Get up, sweetie,' she said, turning on the light.

Flick threw her arm over her eyes. 'I don't want to,' she said, reverting back to her childhood voice. 'Can't you take Jimmy?'

'Aren't you the one who wants to be a farmer?'

Flick sighed and threw back her covers. 'All right. Give me five.'

'I'll go and get Jimmy too. If it's the mob I'm thinking of, we might need all the help we can get. Oh, and grab the torches on your way out too, please — and the gun.'

Toni heard Flick mumble, 'Yes, sir', but let her be. At least she was getting up.

Toni didn't bother with a torch; there was moonlight, and besides, she knew how to get to the shearing quarters blindfolded. She'd had many a fun night there over the years, when she would get on the turps with the shearers at cut-out. Back before Flick came along.

Gypsy barked, realised it was Toni and greeted her with a wag of her tail. Toni got to Jimmy's door and was tempted to go inside to wake him like she'd woken Flick, but figured that was crossing some sort of line. Instead, she opted to bang on his door. 'Jimmy,' she called. He was a lot more responsive than Flick. After a few seconds she heard his feet touch the floor and pad to the door.

'Is everything okay?' he said, opening the door.

He stood there in just a pair of thin trackpants. The worn elastic hardly held them on his waist. The moon shone across his bare chest and Toni bit her lip so she wouldn't gasp out loud as her eyes drank him in. If his pants fell any lower, she'd know a lot more about Jimmy than she'd ever intended.

'Sorry to wake you,' she croaked. 'We have a mob out on Kean Road. Might need your help.'

He flicked on the light and they both stood there, blinking. Toni didn't like the way the light emphasised his toned physique, nor how it highlighted just how little the material of his pants hid. When she lifted her eyes she realised Jimmy had been staring at her. She crossed her arms automatically over the thin singlet stretched across her breasts. The cold night had probably made them more noticeable.

'No probs, I'll just get dressed.' Jimmy reached for his shirt and tugged it on. It was about then that Toni realised she should probably have left, but it was too late. He dropped his dacks there and then. His lean legs went right up to where tight trunk boxers hugged his backside.

'If you're just gonna stand there, at least help me find my socks,' he said with an edge of humour. He turned towards her but she focused on his face, those electric eyes that were teasing her in this odd moment. How could he find this funny after she'd so rudely awoken him from his sleep?

Toni was torn between actually helping him and running screaming in the opposite direction. 'I'd better go get the torches sorted,' she said awkwardly, and he chuckled as she strode away. Quickly she ducked into the end room, which she'd occupied. She pulled on her work clothes then walked back to the ute by the house. Flick already had it started, trying to warm up the cab, and Fella was waiting on the back.

'What's that look for?' Flick asked.

Toni hated how Flick saw everything. Even from a young age she'd had the ability to pick up on body language.

Toni shrugged as the sound of footsteps grew louder behind her. Her skin prickled in awareness. 'Move over, I'll drive,' she said, gesturing Flick into the middle. There was no way was she going to be sitting next to Jimmy with her mind swimming with images of his body.

'It's okay. You can drive back,' said Flick.

'If you two are going to fight then maybe I should drive,' said Jimmy with a laugh. Gypsy was beside him until she saw Fella. With a big flying leap she joined Fella on the back of the ute.

Toni gave up fighting Flick and moved to the passenger side. Jimmy held the door for her while she scooted across to the middle. Then he got in beside her, his body pressed up against hers. And just as she knew it would, her body reacted. Tingles from head to toes.

'Ma, how do you think they got out?' asked Flick as they began to drive towards the Houdini sheep.

But Toni was having trouble concentrating. Her mind was scattered like the pellets from a shotgun. Things were changing around Jimmy. She was sure he was doing things differently, but why now? His eyes were always swimming with a playfulness that bordered on flirting. Was all this starting to turn her into a lovesick loony? Had her body unconsciously been making this stuff into more than it was? Even now she was sure there was more room on Jimmy's other side, yet he felt plastered against her like double-sided sticky tape. It was all too much for her right now.

Jimmy gently touched her leg. 'Toni?' She just about leapt through the roof.

'You all right, Mum?'

'Yeah, I was miles away and Jimmy scared the crap out of me.'

'Sorry, I thought you might've nodded off,' said Jimmy.

He took ages to drag his hand back. Each finger left a scorch mark against her leg. *Drive faster, Flick*, she begged silently, and forced herself to answer her daughter's question. 'I'd say that Brian has been out for a wander around his land and forgot to shut a gate.'

'I feel sorry for him,' said Flick. 'It must be hard living in town when he spent most of his life out here.'

'I'd say so. Hopefully he'll sell it to us one day rather than just leasing it,' said Toni.

'Not until he's dead,' said Jimmy. 'He'll never see it sold while he's alive.'

Flick slowed down the ute to turn onto Kean Road. 'I guess we should have a word with him about checking the gates. You know it's only going to get worse as he gets older and more forgetful.'

'Well, that will be our problem. Brian will always be welcome around here, regardless of his memory. He's been in this district for years and he used to bounce me on his knee. Oh, there's some of the sheep,' said Toni leaning forward.

'So, um . . . ' Jimmy began tentatively. 'How come you're sleeping in the quarters?'

Flick stopped the ute and glanced at her, opened-mouthed. 'Mum? Are you?'

'Just for a few nights.'

Jimmy opened the door. The interior light came on and Toni shot him her best pissed-off expression. After four years he knew it well.

He got out with a weary grimace, torch in

hand. 'I'll take the dogs and work this lot up.'

Toni felt the cold seep in and pulled the door shut, almost taking him out in the process.

'Okay, we'll see how far up the road they've gone and push them back to the gate,' she said to Flick, expecting her to drive off. When she didn't, Toni glanced at her. Flick still looked stunned. 'It's nothing. I just need time out.'

Flick shook her head but didn't say a word. Toni was relieved. Now was not the time for a lecture from her daughter.

A hundred metres up, Toni spotted something in the light. 'Flick, let me out here. I can see the injured ones.' The road was marked with black rubber and some blood. Toni reached for the unloaded gun behind the seat and put some bullets in her pocket. 'Once I'm done here I'll start pushing these back while you go search up further for any strays.'

'Righto.'

'Oh, and can you put the dead ones on the back of the ute on your way back? I don't want to leave them here.'

'Yep,' said Flick before driving off, the sound of the ute getting quieter.

The road glistened in the moonlight. Toni checked the sheep: one was already dead and two were badly injured, so she put them to sleep with a precision bullet. She dragged them to the edge of the road for Flick's return.

The sheep in front of her were *baaing* after the gunshots, which had sounded like thunder in the quiet, still night. The sky was filled with twinkling stars, and as Toni walked along the road, searching the bushes with a torch, she couldn't help but feel thankful. It was always sad losing sheep, but simple things like the massive night sky and the crisp, clear air made Toni appreciate this life.

Before long they had the mob rounded up and tucked away back in their paddock.

'Gate's shut tight,' said Jimmy, giving it a rattle for good measure. He jumped in and Flick drove them home.

'I'm so wide awake,' said Flick. 'Anyone want a cuppa before bed?'

'We don't want to wake Nan,' warned Toni. She didn't want to go back in the house.

'We can have it at my place, under the stars. How does that sound? They're beautiful tonight,' Jimmy said.

'Cool. May as well seeing as Mum is now living there too,' Flick said with a dig. She parked at the shearing quarters and they all headed towards the room with the kitchen, Jimmy leading the way.

'I've got two cups in my bedroom,' Jimmy said to Toni, who was just walking past his door. 'Can you grab them? I only have three in the quarters.'

'Must get you some more,' she said before flicking the light on in his room. It was just a small one, big enough for a single bed and some drawers. There was a TV on a crate in the corner and some books by Jimmy's bed. It was more than Toni had in her room at the end; she'd just laid her swag on an old bed.

Toni picked up one of the books. Bill Bryson, *In a Sunburned Country*. And he had another one by Lee Child called *Running Blind*. She tried to picture Jimmy, lying on his bed reading after work. He probably didn't need glasses like she did.

Toni put the book back and spotted his trackpants, still on the floor where he'd dropped them. Her fingers itched to pick them up. *Cups.* She was here for cups. Two sat on the wooden bedside drawers and she grabbed them. He had a photo of his parents and his younger sister, Tracy. Tracy had two kids who were eight and ten and Toni knew Jimmy missed seeing them all. Any time he had off he travelled to the city to see them, but they didn't visit him often. Jimmy had said it was too hard on his dad to come back. Leaving his farm was the hardest thing he'd done but he'd had no choice. Looking at his room she realised Jimmy couldn't really bring the kids back to the farm either. It was just a normal bloke's room, probably tidier than most, but it was poky and small.

She reached out and felt the soft blue sheets he'd been sleeping in not that long ago. Did he ever bring women here? The thought shocked her and she left his room quickly. In the kitchen the other two were busy talking while the kettle boiled. They hadn't even realised she'd been gone a bit too long. She washed the cups but she was still shaken. Jimmy could do what he wanted; this was his space and he often had little parties with his mates out here, but Toni had never thought that maybe there were women here too.

An idea came to her as they headed outside to

drink their coffees under the twinkling sky. 'Hey, Jimmy, once Flick has the floors done in the old house she plans on moving in. One of those rooms is yours if you want it.'

'For real?'

'Yep. I think you need that place more than Flick does, but I know she won't part with it. And besides, you've done just as much work on it as she has. You can't keep living in this shithole,' she said, gesturing to the shearing quarters. 'This is not good enough for you.'

'Awesome,' Flick said. 'Does that mean Jimmy can help me finish the floors and sort out the kitchen?'

'He can do as much as he wants to do. It'll be handy having the place liveable again. Your sister might even bring her kids out for a visit, with somewhere nice to stay.'

'Yeah, actually she might. Brilliant.' Jimmy grinned as if she'd just told him he'd won lotto, and pleasing him blasted shivers down her spine. 'Thanks, Toni. I really appreciate that.'

'Are you going to move in too?' asked Flick almost sarcastically.

'No, I'm not.' But right now avoiding Maggie sounded like a great idea.

'I wish you would just talk to Nan,' said Flick with a huff. 'You have stuff to talk about. Have you even stopped to wonder if Rocco is still alive? Don't you want to know more about him?'

Toni didn't know how to handle the questions. Maybe if she'd found out about Rocco when she was younger she'd be more understanding, but right now she felt lost. Was her place even on this farm? Where did she belong? And most of the time she kept thinking about what her life would have been like if she'd known the truth. Would she have got on better with Arthur? Instead of fighting against their differences, would they have respected them? And she hadn't even started thinking about Rocco. Was he alive? Did she even care?

She hadn't had enough time to figure all this out. Flick was asking for miracles.

What was she to do? Maybe she would find the answers in the stars if she watched them long enough.

10

Maggie wiped her hands on the tea towel after clearing away the breakfast dishes. Only Flick and Jimmy had turned up; no sign of Toni. She should have expected that after she didn't show for dinner but it still cut deep. To top it off, early this morning Maggie had woken for the toilet, padded past Toni's room and noticed her bed hadn't been slept in. Her daughter never forgave easily.

Maggie clearly remembered the time she and Arthur had said Toni couldn't go away to a party with her friends. Toni had stopped talking to them for a whole week and camped out on the lawn in a tent. Even as a fourteen-year-old she'd been full of fire and passion. Just like Rocco.

Maggie pulled out a stool and sat down, looking out the kitchen window. She felt sick, her gut twisted and acid bubbling deep in her belly. Her child was hurting and it was all her fault. Maybe if she'd kept her mouth shut none of this would be happening. Maggie hadn't intended to let the secret she'd kept for so long slip out but since getting Rocco's letters she hadn't really been herself. The memories had engulfed her and it was like being plunged deep into water. The vivid memories washed over her like waves, replaying her life over and over.

But knowing Rocco had planned on coming back for her changed everything, and with

Arthur long gone she couldn't feel guilty about telling Toni the truth. Arthur died with a daughter, but Toni lived on and deserved to know her real father. If only she would calm down, just enough for Maggie to tell her about Rocco. About the kind of man he was. Maggie wanted Toni to love him like she did.

Her hand automatically went to her pocket. Maggie pulled out her favourite letter, the one she'd been carrying with her. It was the shortest letter of the lot. It simply said, *Dear Maggie, I'm coming for you. Ti amo, Rocco.*

The years she'd dreamt about him coming back for her and Toni, how happy they'd all be. A family. What would have happened if she'd got the letters back then, when they were intended? Would she still have waited out the years with Arthur until Rocco returned? Would she have told Arthur that Rocco was coming for her? Would Arthur have walked away without a fight?

Arthur Stewart wasn't a fighter, and he hadn't been much of a farmer either, but he'd tried his best. His brothers had called him the runt of the litter when he was younger and he never did seem to grow into his lanky body. But he'd had a heart as big as Sunnyvale and a gentleness not seen in many men. It wasn't his fault that he lost the use of his legs and she understood that it had changed him. That's why she'd never given up on him, even though he'd grown bitter, lost and depressed. She couldn't imagine what it was like to be waited on by your loved ones, losing so much independence and not feeling whole.

But she clung to the man he'd been. She'd

seen his eyes after Toni was born; he'd loved her instantly and claimed her as his own. While she was young he doted on her but as she grew older, she began to look more and more like Rocco, and her strong will twisted Arthur up, more so when he was confined to his wheelchair.

Maggie carefully refolded the letter and tucked it away. She pulled out a small bag of home-grown potatoes from the bottom cupboard for her shepherd's pie. She found a small one, about the size of an egg. A smile crossed her face. Another vivid memory. She closed her eyes, willing it to take her back.

But an approaching ute caused the memory to slip away like fog in the morning light. Maggie pulled out a peeler from the drawer and peered out the window. It was young Chad.

'Flick, darling,' she called through the house. 'You have a visitor.'

Her granddaughter was supposed to be off working on the old house but had snuck back to check her emails.

'Coming!' she yelled back. Flick thumped through the house as she ran to the door. Chad had stepped up onto the verandah and Flick slowed when she saw him.

'Hey, baby, how are you?' His voice floated through to the kitchen, and Maggie shuffled towards the open door, ears straining while the half-peeled potato sat forgotten in her hand. She could still see them out the window.

'I didn't think you cared,' Flick said softly.

'Of course I do,' he said, pulling her close.

Flick let him but she was still frowning. 'I

thought you were going to come out to the club last night. I needed you.'

Maggie sighed heavily. She hadn't realised the toll all this was taking on Felicity too. Would they ever forgive her? Could they all get past this? No matter how much it hurt, deep down Maggie was still relieved her secret was out. Fifty-three years of holding the truth inside had taken its toll. It was not something she could ever discuss with Arthur either. Maggie told stories about Rocco and Giulio while Arthur wasn't around but there were times when Toni would ask about them and Arthur would pale. Had he worried that Rocco would return? Had he feared he'd lose Toni? Or even Maggie? It was too late to ask Arthur those questions now.

'I'm sorry I wasn't there.' Chad didn't offer an explanation.

Flick tilted her head, giving him a stare Maggie knew well. 'Were you stuck at the farm?' she asked.

'Ah, yeah. We had a fence down and lost some sheep to the neighbours. Had to draft them off.'

'Right. I see. Funny that, 'cos I heard from Shannon that Justin said you were the life of the party at his place.'

Chad's eyes rolled to the side. 'Sorry, Flick. We had such a shit run with the sheep I stopped for a few at the pub. I was going to come but Justin was there and wouldn't take no for an answer.'

'So he forced you to his house for an impromptu party?' she said frankly.

'Pretty much. You know what they're like,' he said, caressing her face. 'After a few at the pub I couldn't drive anyway. I'll make it up to you, I promise. You shearing tomorrow?' he asked.

Maggie noticed the subject diversion and she could see Flick hadn't missed it either. She felt guilty about listening to their conversation but she worried for her granddaughter.

'Yes, we are. Can you stay and help me work on the house? Jimmy and I have got all day to work on it.'

'Um, no.' Chad frowned and kissed her lips. 'Sorry, babe. I actually have to get back and help Dad. I had to come out this way to pick up some parts for the old truck. Turned out Noel had some at his workshop in Karlgarin. He's saved us a packet.'

Maggie felt Flick's disappointment. Chad hadn't actually come here for her. He just happened to be passing by.

'But I'll call you tonight and we can have a long chat if you like. You can tell me what's been going on. Okay, babe?'

Maggie looked down at her potato, clenched against her apron. Lately something about Chad had started a niggling sensation deep in her chest. He was a lovely boy and they all enjoyed his company, but recently his life seemed to have become more important than Flick's. Maggie didn't like seeing her granddaughter put aside, and she was worried Chad had lost his way.

If only she could talk to Toni about this. Maybe she'd come in for dinner tonight. Maggie didn't want to push her; Toni deserved time to process everything. Maggie could wait. After all, she'd waited this long. With a sigh, she stepped back to her pile of potato skins, worrying about them all.

11

Shearing was the last thing Flick felt like doing. She sat at the table eating her eggs on toast but her mind was still obsessing over her conversation with Chad the day before. Not even the crispy bacon could take her mind off it. What to do about Chad? Didn't he realise how much this family chaos was eating at her? Why hadn't he cared enough to ask? Even to take some time out of his day so they could talk.

He didn't even stay for long yesterday, and as for that 'I'll call you tonight' comment — well, she'd waited and his call never came. Automatically her mind threw in some excuses: he'd got stuck at the farm, he'd had an accident, he'd fallen asleep after a hard day's work. But she couldn't help thinking he'd just found the pub again. Maybe that's why she never called him — she was too afraid of what she'd find out.

'How are you going, love?' asked Maggie, placing the bottle of tomato sauce on the table for Jimmy. Hopefully he would arrive soon because Flick felt rather lonely at the table by herself. Nan had already eaten and apparently her mum had already grabbed something too.

'I'm fine,' she said rather shortly, then regretted it. Maggie's eyes softened and Flick knew there was something on her mind.

'I didn't get a chance to ask yesterday, but is everything all right with Chad?' Maggie asked, giving Flick's shoulder a squeeze. 'He didn't stay for long.'

Why did everyone in her family, including Jimmy, have to notice all the small things and keep tabs?

'Yep, all good. He's going to come out one day while we're shearing and give us a hand.'

Maggie sighed. 'I'm sorry.'

The words came out of the blue, and Flick looked up at her nan, who stood there with a pained expression.

'I never meant for this to hurt anyone and I know you're all caught up in it,' said Maggie softly.

Flick patted her hand and smiled. It had obviously upset Nan that Toni was still sleeping over at the quarters. She was probably living on two-minute noodles and tins of spaghetti, all so she didn't have to cross paths with her mum.

'Don't worry yourself, Nan. We're a tough bunch. It will all blow over soon, trust me.' Flick hoped she spoke the truth.

Jimmy walked in with the gun in his hand. 'Morning all. Save me some of that coffee, please, Flick. Someone forgot to put the gun away from the other night.' His gaze was directed at Flick but his tone was teasing.

'Morning, Jimmy,' Maggie said. 'You remind me so much of Rocco in that photo, standing there with the gun, all handsome.'

Jimmy gave her a grin. 'Am I handsome enough for a bit of bacon too?' he asked with a wink.

Maggie chuckled. 'Oh, you're a scoundrel. Go

get that gun locked up and come get your eggs.'

'Give him nothing, Nan,' said Flick with gusto.

Jimmy poked out his tongue at her, then went to lock up the gun in the cabinet.

'You know, it's been ages since we did a roo cull. Have you seen how many there are near the top paddock?' said Flick when he came back

'I had noticed. The dogs could go some roo meat too,' said Jimmy.

Maggie put Jimmy's eggs on the table. 'Back in my day we were the ones eating the roo meat. Mother's roo tail soup was my favourite.'

Flick screwed up her face. 'Gross. I'll pass, thanks.'

'I should make you a rabbit stew. You'd love it if I didn't tell you what it was.'

Flick shivered at the thought. 'I don't know how you lived like that back then.'

Maggie wiped her hands on her apron. 'We didn't have much of a choice. We were on rations, had to use coupons just to get tea and sugar.'

Jimmy chewed his mouthful quickly so he could speak. 'I remember my dad talking about the Italian prisoners a few times. The ones he knew came back and settled on farms nearby. We called that area Little Italy.'

'I think you'll find there a quite a few around. Look at Mr Di Franco, he came back after the war,' said Maggie.

Flick started thinking about Rocco and the letters. He had said he was coming back for Maggie. Flick could tell from the letters how much he loved her, so what could have happened to stop him from getting back?

'Hey, Nan, where was Rocco from? What part of Italy?'

Maggie's face crinkled as she thought hard. 'He did tell me but it was a long time ago, I can't remember the name of the place. It was somewhere in the middle area of Italy but not far from the coast. Giulio was born nearby too.'

'You know, Rocco could still be alive, Nan.'

Maggie's eyes darkened. 'I'd like to think so, sweetheart,' she said and headed back to the kitchen. 'You'd better get a move on,' she called. 'The shearing crew just drove past.'

Chairs scraped against the floors as they stood up. Jimmy took his plate with him, still shovelling the last of his eggs as he went. He detoured to the kitchen to drop off his plate and Maggie pressed a bacon and egg toastie into his hands.

'Make sure she eats it, please. She won't have time to sneak back in to pick at the fridge today.'

Jimmy nodded and followed Flick to get their boots.

'See you at smoko, Nan!' yelled Flick.

Smoko was her favourite time, especially during shearing. Maggie always made the special stuff for them all: jam and cream scones, hedgehog and caramel slice, Anzac biscuits.

Down at the shed the shearers were already picking a stand and setting up their gear. Each year they had the same crew: Mouse, Bottle Top Bill, Donnie and Squeak, and this year they had a new kid they called Pup. He was still trying to pick up his numbers but Mouse said he worked hard and was a clean shearer. Jimmy did the pressing, Toni classed and Flick helped roustabout when she wasn't pushing up sheep into the pens with Jimmy. Her mum was already at the shed. No doubt she'd been here since five, setting up.

'Hey, Mouse, how've you been?' asked Toni as she shook the big guy's hand. He was the opposite of his nickname — tall and solid, and he stomped around like an elephant.

'Great, Toni. Looks like we have a clear run, no rain forecast, touch wood.' Mouse rested his hands on his hips. 'Thanks for letting Pup tag along, he really needs the shed time. He's a good kid.' He nodded to the scrawny pimple-faced kid on the end stand. 'Just turned eighteen.'

'Hey, Squeak,' said Flick to the girl who walked towards them. She'd just set up the CD player in the usual spot by the side wall.

'Flicky Flick, how are ya, mate?'

The two girls hugged. Squeak, whose real name was Sara, was Mouse's daughter, five years older than Flick. She's been rousing for her dad since she could throw a fleece. She was nearly as big as her dad, and had the lean muscled arms of a basketball player. Squeak could drink Flick under the table with both hands tied behind her back.

'Great. Ready to go? Brought some good tunes?' she asked.

Squeak nodded as she tied up her blonde hair into a topknot. 'You bet. Hey, have you met Pup yet?' Flick shook her head before Squeak dragged her over to his stand.

'Hey, Pup, this is Flick. Pup's one of my

second cousins.' Pup gave her a half wave and a smile then went back to putting on his moccasins. 'Yeah, he don't talk much.' Squeak glanced at her watch, looked up at her dad, then turned on the music. 'Let's get this show on the road! Yeah, baby.' She smacked her hands together and rolled her shoulders.

U2's 'Beautiful Day' was cranked up to full volume. Flick followed Squeak to the shearers, who had turned on their handpieces, the whirring motors echoing off the tin walls. Sheep shuffled in their pens, hoofs against the boards. Soon the *clunk clack* of the press would join them.

'Mouse and Bottle Top still the quickest?' she yelled in Squeak's ear.

Squeak nodded. They both took up positions by the two fastest shearers, waiting for the bellies.

Flick's mood picked up and she felt like she was on a high. The music pulsed through her and the camaraderie with the crew was fun and infectious. She found herself skipping with the scraper and flinging the shorn bellies with pizzazz. Wheatus was the next tune with 'Teenage Dirtbag'. Squeak always made sure they had the latest tunes, but the good old favourites like AC/DC, Bon Jovi and Def Leppard still made the rounds.

Half an hour in and Flick had discarded her checked shirt, rousing in just a black singlet (now covered with wool) and her jeans. She'd be head to toe in sweat and lanolin by the end of the day, her hands encrusted with sheep poo and

115

blood and nails all black and dirty. But it made her feel like she'd done an honest hard day's work. Plus it was always fun with this crew.

Squeak paused the CD player on Pink's 'There You Go' when it was smoko time. The sight of Maggie walking in with three massive Tupperware containers was enough to stop a herd of stampeding cattle — or in this case, very hungry shearers who knew just how well Maggie fed them.

'Missed you, Maggie,' said Bottle Top. His smile was dotted with black holes where his teeth had once been; his party trick was opening his beer bottles with his teeth.

'They all go soft around Maggie,' said Squeak, who was scraping up the wool under the table.

'I know.' They weren't the only ones. Flick approached her nan and gave her a kiss. She was a sight in her boots, dress and apron. 'Thanks, Nan.'

Toni turned her back and made a cuppa before taking it out of the shed in silence. Flick started grinding her teeth.

Maggie dropped a plate of food into Flick's hands, pleading with her eyes. 'Can you take this out to your mum? I don't want her starving herself for my benefit.'

Flick hated how this tension had visibly aged Maggie. Overnight she seemed tired and slower moving. 'Okay, Nan.'

With a sigh she headed outside to where Toni was sitting on the steps with her coffee. A predictable smile spread across her face when she saw the handful of food.

'Is that for me?'

Flick nodded and handed it over. Toni bit straight into the marshmallow slice and groaned with pleasure.

'Nan doesn't want you to starve,' she said and regretted it when her mum froze mid bite.

Toni immediately handed the food back to Flick. 'I don't need it, thanks.'

She knew full well how Nan would feel if she returned with the food. It would be another rejection. 'Mum, don't you think you're being — ' *childish* was the first word that sprang to mind, but Flick wondered how she could put this nicely,' — difficult?'

'I'm trying to deal with this, Felicity. I don't want her help, she's done enough already.' Toni resumed sipping her coffee, but Flick noticed she'd kept one piece of slice in her hand.

'You can't hate Nan forever. She loves you and thought she was doing what was best for you. We all make mistakes, Mum!'

Toni didn't respond. Now Flick had lost her appetite, and that was a rarity. She snuck back into the shed, hoping to sit down with the food before Nan noticed. But Maggie had been waiting. Even though Bottle Top was telling her a story, her eyes found Flick and immediately dropped to her hands. Flick could hear her heart tearing a little more.

Feeling caught in the middle again, Flick dropped heavily onto the wool bale beside Donnie. 'Hey, Donnie, going all right?'

'Yeah, love. Getting a bit of arthritis these days. Need the extra Export medication to keep it in check,' he said with a wink.

Flick almost smiled. 'Donnie, I don't think the doctors would classify beer as medication but I'm sure it's really working for you.' She took a bite of caramel slice. For the first time ever it seemed bland.

'Oh, it does — by the eighth one I don't feel anything.' He gave a deep belly laugh, one which was never missed in a crowd. Donnie's blond mess of hair hung around his face like scraggly wire. Half of it was almost turning to dreadies. He sobered up when he realised Flick wasn't joining in. 'What's going on, love?' He nodded towards Maggie and leant closer. 'What's the deal with Toni and Maggie? As soon as she arrived it was like Antarctica in 'ere.'

'Something's goin' down, Donnie.' Flick rolled her lip between her teeth. 'And I'm stuck in the middle, you know?'

He patted her knee. 'Hang in there. I'm sure it will blow over. They're both tough old birds, they'll come around.'

And he was right. They just needed more time. But Flick didn't want to feel like this for the rest of the day. She rolled her shoulders back and stretched her neck, letting her mind clear. Then she gave Donnie a real smile.

'Ready to keep up with me now?' he teased.

'Bring me everything you got. You're gonna love the next run, Donnie, I have four pet sheep coming through.'

Donnie's laughter died. 'Don't you dare put them in my pen,' he said. Then his eyes lit up. 'Actually, can you put them all in Bottle Top's pen?' he whispered. 'I'll shout you a few beers.'

Flick raised an eyebrow. Typical Donnie, up to no good yet again. No one liked shearing pet sheep as they were often difficult. These four, Snowy, Penny, Baa and Bruce, had been Flick's pets for a long time. Even now they would still *baa* when called, but only Penny and Snowy came up for pats.

'I'm sure that can be managed. Deal.' They shook hands as Jimmy walked past them. His expression said he knew their handshake wasn't good news.

Jimmy continued outside, emptied his cup and began chatting with Toni.

'Those two make a nice couple, don't ya think?' said Donnie.

Flick turned to the old shearer and closed her mouth. 'You getting a bit soft in your old age, Donnie? A bit sentimental, me ol' mate?'

He shrugged his big shoulders, his beer belly jiggling with the movement. 'Got a soft spot for ya mum. She's a good woman and she deserves to be happy. Been watchin' them two over the years but this time something's different. Time they got their act together, I think.'

Flick leant towards him. 'You know, Donnie, I think you're right. And to tell you the truth I'm a little amazed that you noticed. What's going on?'

He chuckled. 'Too many years listening to Pam and watching *Home and Away*, I reckon.'

'You're a card, Donnie.' Flick pushed the rest of the slices into his hands. 'Here, eat up.' She slapped the shearer's arm and stood up. 'Better sort them sheep out.' She gave him an

119

exaggerated double wink before heading out behind the stands to the pens.

As she pushed her way through the sheep, she called out for her pets. She knew two of them were in here. Penny found her first, pushing her head against her leg.

'Hey, girl. Been good?' She rubbed the sheep's woolly back and head and put her in Bottle Top's pen.

The sound of the shearers back at their stands moved her along. She couldn't leave Squeak and her mum for too long or they'd be snowed under. They still had a long way to go yet.

* * *

It was eight o'clock that night before Flick was finally back home and showered. It felt so good to wash the dirt and grit from her body and her skin zinged from the scrubbing.

While Maggie was in the kitchen, Flick padded barefoot to the office. She had ten minutes before dinner. She turned on the computer, waited for it to start up, then connected to the internet.

Flick had decided that it was time for action. Something had to snap her mum out of her sulkiness. She needed to realise that she could still have a father who was alive, that Flick could have a granddad. Looking for Rocco was the only thing Flick could think of that could really help her family.

Flick started her search with Rocco's full name, Rocco Valducci. Nothing relevant came back. Next, she tried 'Italian prisoners of war rural WA'. The first result was a link to the National Archives, which led her to a fact sheet called 'Wartime internee, alien and POW records held in Perth'. She clicked on the Italian prisoner of war files, and it brought up more than four thousand items, all set out in alphabetical order like an extensive library system. Flick clicked again and the website brought up the first twenty names, starting with 'ANGELOZZI Alfonso'.

She rubbed her fingers together excitedly. She was on the right track, she was sure of it. She clicked to the last page, looking for the Vs. Just seeing the list of Italian names gave her goosebumps. She couldn't imagine so many of them in Western Australia alone.

Flick was so deep in concentration she was only vaguely aware her nan standing at the door. It wasn't until Maggie rested her hand on her shoulder, causing her to jump, that she realised she was talking.

'Dinner will be ready in five minutes. What are you looking for?'

Just as Flick was about to say 'Rocco', her eyes spotted that very name on the screen. 'Oh my God, I've found him!' she shouted and almost jumped up. It was her turn to scare Maggie. 'Sorry, Nan, I'm just so excited. Look, I found Rocco.' She pointed to the screen.

VALDUCCI Rocco — PWI63259

Flick clicked on the link and it brought up another page of details.

121

Date range: 1942–1946
Location: Perth
Date registered: 25 March 1996
Physical format: paper files and documents
Access status: not yet examined.

'Nan, I'm going to request a copy and see what they have. How cool is this!'

'Do you really think this is a good idea, love? Does your mum know?'

'I can't sit back and do nothing. He was your first love and he's mum's father, my grandfather. I think it's only fair that we try to look for him. Look, I can order a copy of this. How amazing! I wonder how long it will take to arrive?' Flick kept staring at the screen. Just seeing Rocco's name made all the stories from Nan all so real. 'I wonder if there will be photos too.' Flick turned in her chair to look at Maggie. She looked rather pale, her hand clutching at the desk. 'Nan, you all right?'

Maggie swallowed. 'I'm fine, dear. All this is just bringing back so many memories. I'm even dreaming about the days when I was seventeen.' She smiled weakly. 'Some days I wish I could live in my dreams forever.'

Flick reached for her hand. 'Here, sit down.' She gave her the computer chair. 'I'm so sorry, Nan. I didn't mean to upset you.'

'Don't be, love. Those moments were so magical and to be able to remember them so vividly after all these years . . . I . . . I thought I'd forgotten most of it.' Maggie smiled, and it looked like her mind was elsewhere. 'Turns out

122

in my dreams I can remember exactly how Rocco looked. He had this calming sweetness and deep, dark eyes that just melted my heart.'

'Nan?' Flick asked after a moment. 'Do you mind if I look for Rocco? Are you okay with that?'

Maggie steadied her breathing. 'Well, I guess I'm a little scared of what you'll find. At the moment I can pretend he's still alive, growing tomatoes and building things. What if he's gone?'

'But what if he's alive and well? Wouldn't you want to see him again if you could?'

She watched her Nan's face change, the corner of her mouth tilting up. 'Yes. Yes, I think I would.'

12

Maggie was grateful to be out of the cottage and away from her mother for a few hours, even if it was to collect the rabbits from the traps. She carried two dead ones back with her now, walking along the dirt track. They were a little on the small side but would still feed the family, and the fur would give them some money. Maggie loved their little tails and had one by her bed for good luck.

It was a beautiful morning, the birds were chatty and the sky was a brilliant blue. Father and Charlie were out with the horses, seeding the paddock with wheat. It was amazing to see the paddock finally done and being put to use. Meanwhile, Giulio and Rocco had started on the new house. Mum had finally found a location she was happy with, nestled in a big bush area where some salmon gums grew tall. It was a fair way from the cottage; she wanted it closer to where the new main road was going to be. The men had cleared and levelled off the area, and as Giulio begun work on the foundations and started making bricks, Father and Charlie had gone back to the paddock work. Everyone was in a great mood, Father finally getting his paddock seeded and mother with the promise of a new house. Phyllis was even attempting to be nicer to Giulio and Rocco, which meant she'd actually started to use their names.

And the best thing about collecting the rabbits was passing by the house where they worked.

Her mother had warned her she was not to dally

near them, but Maggie had always waved to them and each day she'd walked a little closer. Now she usually stopped if she could spare the time.

'Miss Margaret,' called Rocco, waving as he spotted her.

Before she'd made it out of the bush she'd quickly checked her hair and skirts. She'd grown awfully fond of Rocco and Giulio. Especially Rocco.

'Hello, Rocco.' Maggie met him by the edge of the house. Giulio sat nearby, working a pile of wet mud on a flat bit of tin with a shovel. It amazed her how he used his leg to lever the shovel to mix the mud. Then he would put it into moulds and make the bricks. They would lie outside until they were dry, and when they had enough they would brick up the next row on the house. Rocco had told her all this, as he was also learning from Giulio. He hoped to build his own house one day.

'Nice day. More rabbits,' he said, smiling.

His English had improved with her assistance, and he was also helping to teach Giulio. It made things a lot easier, and even Mother forced a smile when Giulio thanked her for dinner.

'Yes, another two. I hear Father is taking you out shooting tonight?' she said, tugging on her long skirt.

'We are excited. No shoot emu, scared Mrs Boss cook it,' he said with a grimace.

Maggie laughed and together they walked to Giulio.

'*Buongiorno Giulio, fa bel tempo, no?*' she said, hoping she'd got it right.

Giulio stood up and grinned. 'Yes, Miss Maggie. It beoofull day.'

'It is a beautiful day,' she repeated clearly for him. She walked to the front of the house, around the

125

lumps of wood and drying bricks. 'You get so much done each week.' The bricks were now three high off the ground and she could see the size of the house. It was going to be wonderful, and they were so lucky it was being built for them. She turned back to Giulio. 'It's splendid,' she said. 'I'd better get back.'

Giulio nodded and sat back down to make his bricks. Maggie walked off, holding her breath and full of hope, but needn't have bothered as Rocco joined her. He had started doing this — walking with her to the edge of the bush before they were visible from the cottage.

He walked beside her, so close that if she moved a fraction sideways their shoulders would touch.

'Let me,' he said, reaching for the rabbits.

Their hands met and they stopped moving. Maggie was trying to let go of the rabbits but her whole body had frozen — not from fear, from the sheer delight of his touch. Maggie looked up into his deep brown eyes. She could get so lost in them. Like the big sky at night, they twinkled and held her fascination.

'You very beautiful, Maggie.'

She caught her breath. She loved it when he called her by her nickname. It sounded so personal and private, a little bit naughty but so sweet coming from his lips. He wouldn't dare call her Maggie in public.

'Thank you, Rocco,' she said, finally finding her voice. She relaxed her grip on the rabbits and slowly he took them from her. Already she missed the touch of his fingers.

They continued walking. Maggie thought of the moments she lived for nowadays. Collecting the plates at dinner or passing him a cup of tea so she had a chance to touch his hand. Fetching the rabbits so they could be alone, when they did most of their talking. Then there were the rare times when Mother went into town with Father and Maggie would teach Rocco and Giulio more English. Charlie would help too. It was their little secret. Charlie was becoming great friends with Rocco and Giulio too.

Their steps were small and slow, neither in a hurry to get back to what they should be doing.

'What was the war like?' Maggie asked. She had been wanting to ask and had finally worked up the courage. 'Were you scared?'

Rocco sucked in a breath, his chest expanding. To Maggie it made him look even more grand and strong. Maggie was ready to hang off every word.

'I didn't want war. I captured in Sidi Barrani, Egypt. War not nice, Maggie.' He looked away but not before she saw pain engulf his face.

That was all he was going to tell her. She wondered if he thought it might be too hard to explain with his broken English, or maybe it was too hard to talk about. Did he talk about it with Giulio? She hoped so; everyone needed somebody to talk to.

Maggie slowed. She knew the edge of the tree line was approaching. 'I lost both of my brothers to the war. I miss them very much,' she said, her voice quavering. She looked at the earth beneath her feet but a gentle touch caused her heart to jump inside her chest.

Rocco had taken her hand in his. She looked at where his callused, strong fingers wrapped around hers. She tingled all over.

'I am sorry, Maggie. I am sorry,' he said.

She looked up to see those beautiful eyes full of pain, regret and sadness. Did he feel responsible, being on the other side? Maggie could never blame him, even if he was the one who'd shot her brother. For all she knew, her brothers could have killed any of Rocco's family, or Giulio's. Maggie was realising just how ridiculous war was. Everyone had family, loved ones they cared for, yet they had to go and fight because of a few people who wanted more.

Maggie couldn't handle what she saw in his eyes; it was so raw. She reached up and touched his face with her free hand. Then she realised what she was doing. If her mother found her now she'd be furious. Maggie dropped her hand and felt the prickle of a blush rising. She reached for the rabbits.

'Thank you. I'd better get back.' Then she turned and walked quickly towards the cottage. She couldn't bring herself to look back, but his touch kept her fingers tingling all the way home.

She didn't see Rocco until dinnertime. Mother insisted on packing the Italians their lunch in the morning so she didn't have to see them till night.

While Maggie waited for the men to arrive, she collected some water from the four-gallon water bag hanging from a beam and sipped it, trying to quench the thirsty ache in her belly. Or maybe it was a nervous flutter? She would be lying if she said she wasn't worried about seeing Rocco again. She still couldn't believe he'd held her hand and she'd touched his face. Maggie closed her eyes for the tenth time that day as she tried to remember every frame of that moment. *Did it really happen?* she asked herself again.

'Make sure you get your church clothes ready for tomorrow,' said her mother as she walked past holding the pot of rabbit stew. She'd cooked up both of the rabbits Maggie had skinned and cleaned. With six mouths to feed, they constantly needed food. Just as well the men were going shooting tonight.

'Yes, Mother.'

Maggie hated going to church. They all got dressed up and drove to the hall and the priest came out from Lake Grace. It wasn't so much the church itself Maggie hated, but her mother's friends — all dressed up and gossiping about the prisoners and Maggie. They hadn't forgotten about her, and talks of her and Arthur were only getting stronger. And that was the other reason she didn't want to go to church: it meant leaving the farm, leaving Rocco and being stuck with Arthur. He always asked to sit by her and would smell of greasy hair and moth balls. Maggie wanted to like Arthur; he was nice enough. But she couldn't get past thinking of him as a brother. Rocco, on the other hand — well, he evoked thoughts she shouldn't be having. Oh, wouldn't Mother be horrified.

She heard men's voices and squeezed her hands in delight, forcing herself to walk rather than run outside to see them.

'Afternoon, Father,' she said.

John and Charlie stood outside with guns in their hands. They were giving Rocco and Giulio the rundown on how to shoot them.

'Maggie,' he said with a smile.

'Put them away, dinner is ready,' said Phyllis, coming up behind Maggie.

Maggie could sense the disapproval in her mother's tone and headed back inside to set the table. Phyllis was still seething about John letting the prisoners fire the guns, which was against the army's instructions. Rocco and Giulio had been shooting with her father many times before but now father was letting them do the firing. Phyllis still didn't trust them, even after all this time.

Dinner was a quiet affair. Mother was stony silent so the men just talked about how seeding was going or the house. Maggie remained quiet too; she didn't want to join the conversation and end up paying for it later. If Mother wasn't happy, no one else should be, especially Maggie.

The only relief came from occasional glances at Rocco and the brief moments that their eyes met. Once, his foot brushed against hers and she looked up suddenly. He was waiting with a smile, and it made her heart soar.

Maggie didn't get to clear away the dishes, as Phyllis was angry and needed an excuse to do something. She clanked the plates loudly in the wash tin, and Charlie shot Maggie a worried glance. He knew Maggie would bear the brunt of their mother's anger after their departure.

'Well, we'll head off then,' John announced. Rocco and Giulio gave her a quick wave while Phyllis's back was turned and Charlie grimaced and mouthed the word 'sorry'.

Maggie wished she could go out shooting with them. She could shoot — she was a great shot, in fact; Thomas had trained her well. But Mother would never let that happen now, not with two possible killers in their midst. Maggie sighed heavily as she wrapped up the bread.

'I don't know what your father was thinking, letting them have the guns.'

Maggie retied the calico flour bag, trying to be inconspicuous.

'If something happens tonight, I will be telling him

I told him so. Can't be trusted. You know that, don't you, Margaret?' she said, turning to face Maggie and giving her a stern look.

'Yes, Mother.'

Honestly, had the men not earnt their trust already? They hadn't run away or hurt any of them. They knew where the guns were kept and could have taken them long before now if they had mind to.

Maggie went to bed early, not wanting to listen to her mother's ranting a moment longer. She used the excuse of getting sleep for church. She knew Phyllis was thinking of Arthur but she didn't care if it meant she could escape to the quiet of her bedroom.

*   *   *

The next morning she dressed in her best outfit, a white cotton dress with blue flowers printed across it. She took time to untie the rags from her hair that she'd set last night and tried to get the waves right. She even put on a little blush and lipstick that her mother had given her.

'Maggie, can you bring out the camera, please?' said her father from the doorway.

He was also dressed for church. Maggie grabbed the camera, as she had learnt how to use it before the others. When she went outside she followed her father and Charlie to a large tree. Giulio and Rocco were standing beside it with the guns in their hands, and between them was a massive kangaroo. Its head came up to Rocco's shoulders.

'He's huge. Did you get him last night?' she asked.

'Rocco did. Good shot. He said they shoot birds back home,' said her father.

131

Charlie stood next to her and whispered, 'He didn't want to ask Rocco how many men he shot while in the war. I bet it was a lot.'

Maggie shuddered. She didn't want to think of it either. She walked up to the kangaroo to get a closer look. There was a bullet hole right in the centre of his head. A clean kill.

'Well done, Rocco,' she said softly.

'Thank you, Miss Margaret,' he said. Then he dropped his voice to a whisper. 'You are lovely, beautiful today.'

And there was that butterfly flutter in her chest! His words moved her. But it wasn't just his words. It was the way he stared at her as if she truly were the most beautiful thing on earth. She felt his power, strong and gentle at once. No one had ever conveyed so much to her in such a small moment. She couldn't help comparing him to Arthur. Nothing Arthur could say or do would ever make her feel so alive as she did when she was near Rocco. She turned back to the kangaroo and touched its ear, trying desperately to hide her joy from her family. Her mother could never know about the feelings she had around Rocco and she worried just how obvious it might be.

Charlie told them to get ready for the photo, and Maggie raised the camera. She couldn't even think of the lives Rocco might have taken while in the war. He seemed too quietly spoken and gentle to be capable of any harm. But he did look so strong and manly standing there with the gun in his hand — and with his dark eyes, even slightly dangerous.

Somehow, that didn't seem to worry her one little bit.

13

Toni strode towards the shearing shed in the early morning light. The air was cool against her skin but she welcomed it, for soon enough she'd be craving it after working in the hot shed. Today they would be finished. The shearers hadn't turned up yet so she had time to get some bales done and put the last of the sheep in the pens. She started up the steps to the shed but paused on the first one. Something wasn't quite right.

The cockies were screeching in the large gum tree by the sheep yards, the sky was a wide pale blue and there was not a cloud in sight. Her eyes sought out what her gut had warned. There were fewer sheep in the outside yards, and at the top of the steps sat Gypsy, watching her quietly except for the thump of her tail.

Damn. Jimmy. Sure enough, she headed up the steps and spied him down near the piles of graded wool, walking a massive armload back to the wool press. Some of the wool trailed behind him like lumpy strands from a spider's web.

'You beat me to it.' Toni stepped towards the pile of fleeces and gathered up an armful of the same grade. Jimmy stood by the press as she pushed in her load.

'Sorry, a bloody mouse woke me up at four, scratching around the roof, so I got up. I chucked some baits up there. Didn't you hear it?'

'Ah, no. Pretty restless night actually. I only

got to sleep at two, but slept like a log till six. Didn't even hear you get up.'

Jimmy's eyes pierced hers. 'Still thinking about Rocco?'

Her shoulders dropped. 'Yeah, I guess. I don't know how to forgive my mum for this. It's just . . . ' Really, she had no words for the torment twisting inside her. She didn't know who she was any more, besides half Italian.

'Hard?' He reached out, holding her arm briefly.

'Very.' She rubbed some sleep from her eyes.

'Wanna put the kettle on?' he said eventually. 'I'll finish this up.' Jimmy set the press on its way and then hooked in the bale fasteners before releasing it.

With the kettle on, Toni helped him move the bale towards the end of the shed where the old flat-top truck sat. They nearly had a full load.

They chatted about the quality of the wool while the kettle boiled. Jimmy made their cups of coffee and they took them to the steps where they could watch the sunrise.

Jimmy sat down on the boards, one leg over the edge and the other one propped up so he could lean on it. Toni slipped off her boots and crossed her legs, her jeans pulling tight across her knees.

'Man, how do you do that?' said Jimmy, putting down his cup.

'Do what?'

'Sit like that? That's something Flick would do. You're very flexible,' he said.

'For my age . . . Is that what you were

134

thinking?' Toni kept a straight face, even when she could see Jimmy starting to squirm.

'No, not at all. I mean, I couldn't do that. You're practically twisted up like a pretzel.'

'I may be old but a bit of yoga is good for the body. Being flexible stops a lot of aches and general tightness across my back.'

Jimmy tilted his head and the sunlight filtered through his blond hair, making a halo glow. 'See, I didn't know that. After all these years there is still stuff I don't know about you.'

Toni laughed. 'That's probably about it. Not much you don't already know.' She felt him watching her as she sipped her coffee.

'Well, what happened with Flick's father? Did you not want to find him? Do you know where he is, and how come you didn't meet anyone after him?'

Toni turned to him with her mouth open. 'Jesus, Jim, I think you got the wrong job. We do farm work here, not PI stuff. Talk about bombarding me with the tough questions.'

'Hey, they were all the ones I could think of at the time.' He was still waiting for her answers.

What harm would talking to him do? She'd never had anyone to talk to about this stuff except for her friend Alice, who'd moved to town ten years ago. She couldn't talk to Flick or Maggie. She took a deep breath.

'Right. Well, Flick's father — his name was Simon — was a one-night stand. Which you already know. He left town with his crew before I even knew I was pregnant. Flick has tried to look for him but we don't have enough information.

Besides, I'm not sure if I want her to. He might be a disappointment, he might reject her — or even worse, Flick might want to go spend time with him.'

'You're worried you'll lose her?'

Toni shrugged. But Jimmy had hit the nail on the head. She didn't want to risk Felicity's heart or her own.

'You know that would never happen. Flick loves this place. She loves you.'

'I know, it's silly, right? But life is great how it is, why go and complicate things by digging up old graves?'

Jimmy's eyebrow raised and she knew she was about to get a lecture of sorts.

'This sounds a lot like something Maggie might have thought about with you and Rocco.'

Toni turned away, gazing towards the sheep in the yard. She heard what he was saying but chose not to let it sink in.

Jimmy pushed no further on that subject. 'What if Flick's father is delighted? And don't you think she deserves to know who made up the other half of her DNA? I know for a fact she feels like she's missing something and she'd chew off her right arm to find him.'

Toni looked into her cup. 'She's talked to you about it?' she whispered.

'Yes, of course. She's craving any little details. Anything that can make her understand who she is.'

Jimmy was right. Toni had figured not talking about him would solve the problem, but she hadn't realised how much it consumed Flick.

136

'Put yourself in her shoes. Right now it's not that hard, is it?' Jimmy leant closer. 'Don't you want to find Rocco? Don't you want to know what he's like and to see if you look like him, walk like him or have the same stubbornness?'

Toni would have contradicted him on the last part but she was too tired. Mentally she was drained like a dam in a drought. Her fight was dwindling.

'And what about my other question?' Jimmy persisted. 'How come you didn't meet anyone after Simon?'

Toni would have much rather talked about the micron of their wool. 'As if the flies aren't bad enough today,' she said with a sigh.

Jimmy shot her one of his best smiles and Toni relented.

'After I had Flick there was just no one around, especially anyone who would want an older single mother.' She clenched her hands around the cup. 'It's not like I shut myself away. I was still open to the idea of finding someone. I guess it just wasn't meant to be.'

The shearers drove around the corner of the shed in a white Mazda minibus with a blue stripe down the middle.

'Maybe fate had you waiting for me,' said Jimmy as he stood up and took their empty cups back to the table without another word.

Toni was left sitting there, aghast. She watched him go, his words echoing through her mind. *Did he really just say that?* she wondered, but just then Flick came running towards her, Fella leading the way.

137

'Sorry I'm late, took Contractor out for a quick ride,' said Flick as she darted straight inside.

Mouse was already at the base of the steps wishing Toni good morning.

'Morning, Mouse,' she said, but she was annoyed by the intrusion. Her head felt so mixed up, stretched tight like an over-full balloon. How long until she exploded?

As shearing began and Toni started sorting the fleeces, her mind was still wandering. Jimmy's questions had rattled her and they were far too profound for her to tackle while working.

'Hey, Mum,' said Flick as she started skirting the fleece she'd just thrown. 'Did you get all the beer for the cut-out?'

'Yeah, it's all in the fridge at the shearing quarters. Got some nibbles too.'

'Awesome. We can fire up the barbie afterwards.'

Toni nodded and Flick left to catch the belly Donnie had just thrown into the air.

Bon Jovi's song 'It's My Life' came on and Toni found herself singing along with it. Jimmy nudged her shoulder, smiling cheekily. For the moment she let all her thoughts fade away and focused on the sounds in the shed and the task at hand. It was a sweet release.

★   ★   ★

In the afternoon, Toni saw Chad walk into the shed. Flick dropped the scraper and went up to hug him.

'You made it!' Flick yelled over the music. But

138

Chad wasn't alone. A blonde girl wearing tiny shorts stepped in beside him. Her tank top hung straight down from her large breasts, exposing her belly button. They stood a few metres from Toni as she worked at the skirting table, just close enough for her to hear the exchange.

'Yep, I brought Kel along, hope that's okay. She's never seen shearing. Flick, meet Kel.' Chad gestured to the new girl.

Toni saw Flick's shoulders stiffen as she said hello. She didn't even offer a smile.

'Sorry, I have to get back to it,' Flick indicated with a jerk of her thumb.

Chad took Kel on a tour of the shed, explaining what everyone was doing. Then they stood over Flick and he described how she was skirting the fleece.

Flick looked uncomfortable, her face even a little red. Toni's skin prickled. *What kind of idiot brings a girl dressed like that to where his girl-friend is working?* She cursed under her breath.

'Chad, push up some more sheep for us, please?' asked Toni, hoping to give Flick some breathing space.

'Sure thing. Kel, you wanna help?'

Toni groaned. That wasn't what she had in mind. 'Who's she?' Toni asked Flick as they both watched them disappear to the pens.

'The new Pommy barmaid,' she said with a shrug as if she didn't care.

But Toni wasn't fooled. Something was definitely not right. 'You guys okay?'

'Yeah.' Flick smiled and moved back to the shearers.

'What's all that about?' said Jimmy, appearing by Toni's side.

'Beats me. But I don't like it.'

'Me either.'

Shearing finished up a little later, at five-thirty. Toni counted up the sheep for the day and let Mouse know the tally.

'Yahoo, I beat you this time, Bottle Top,' said Mouse. 'Young Pup's done great after a week.'

'Yeah, I thought so too. By next year he'll be out-shearing you.'

Mouse scoffed. 'Now, now, don't get ahead of yourself. Takes years to get as good as us,' he said, patting his small beer belly.

Pup had paused on his way past and gestured with his hand. 'It's this movement,' he said, pretending to do a long blow. 'Not this one.' He mimed drinking.

'Get out, you cheeky bastard,' said Mouse, trying to clip him over the ears.

'When you guys are sorted, just head over to the shearing quarters, the fridge is full,' Toni said. 'Chad's over there, and we'll be across once we've sorted this out.'

Mouse nodded and carted his shearing gear out to the bus.

Toni let the sheep out into the paddock while Jimmy finished off a bale. They'd decided to finish the rest tomorrow. Tonight was time to celebrate, except she wasn't exactly in the mood.

When Toni arrived at the quarters, Maggie was there putting some food out and she made an immediate beeline for her daughter.

'You can't keep avoiding me, Toni, we need to

140

talk this through,' she begged.

'Not now. I've got too much on my mind.' Toni stepped straight into the small bathroom to clean up and hoped her mum would be gone by the time she was done.

She was. But it only made Toni feel sad and lonely. She wasn't sure what she wanted. Moving on autopilot, she went straight for a beer and found a chair.

By twelve o'clock they were all relaxed and happy. Mouse was in good form, singing loudly with Flick. Donnie had pulled out his guitar and was playing some great old tunes like 'Ring of Fire' by Johnny Cash. Kel was flitting around the crowd, laughing and dancing. Toni kept her eye on her.

Jimmy was sitting by the fire he'd started on the ground; he was insistent that every great party needed a fire. As she watched the flickering red and orange flames, Flick dancing behind them and Donnie strumming away, who was she to argue? Bonfires just had this amazing ability to spread warmth and merriment.

Toni had given up the beer and switched to cans of Cougar and dry. She was feeling a warm glow and it wasn't from the fire. At least some of the noise in her head had died down.

'I s'pose I should get these buggers home before I drink too much,' said Squeak with a laugh. 'Pup's already passed out in the bus. I don't think he drank enough water before all those beers.'

'You might want to check on Bottle Top. He took off for a leak and hasn't come back,' said

141

Jimmy. 'He might have fallen asleep by a tree or just got lost in the dark.'

'That would be right,' snorted Squeak. 'We put out a search party at our last shed and eventually found him curled up in the wool in the shed. Sleeping like a baby. Took all of us to get him up.' She shook her head as she headed off into the dark.

Toni picked up the stick she'd found and started poking at the fire.

'Perfect night, hey?' said Jimmy, leaning over and nudging her with his shoulder.

'Yep, I love it when Donnie brings his guitar.'

'Hey, Ma,' said Flick, glancing around. 'Have you seen Chad?'

'Not since I saw him shuffle off towards his ute. Hope he brought his swag.'

'I hope he didn't drive home,' Flick said with a grimace. 'I'll go find him before I go to bed. Night, Mum, Jimmy.' She was still glancing around when the boys yelled out their goodbyes. 'See ya, Donnie, thanks for the tunes, man. See you next year. Catch ya, Mouse,' yelled Flick as she followed Mouse into the dark towards the bus.

Donnie came and kissed Toni's cheek. 'See ya, love.'

'Bye, guys. Thanks again.' Toni waved them off. They'd all gone to the local primary school together back in the day.

Within ten minutes the place was quiet and deserted, except for her and Jimmy by the fire.

'Wow, where did the noise go?' he said with a chuckle. 'Need another drink?'

Toni shook her can. 'Nah, I'm good, thanks.'

They stared at the fire, Jimmy now poking it with a stick. 'I just love it out here on Sunnyvale. Promise you'll never sack me,' he said, turning to her.

Toni leant forward too. 'Depends,' she said.

'On what?'

'If you're still useful,' she teased.

'Come on.' Jimmy put his hand on her knee and shook her gently. 'You know I'm useful.'

She laughed. 'Yeah, you can stay, as long as you can still open gates and push me around in my wheelchair when I'm old. Us Sunnyvale girls can't do it all on our own.' She gave him a brave wink.

'You crap on as if you're an old woman, Toni, but I know for a fact that you're none of that.'

Toni threw her empty can into the nearby bin and started picking at her nails until she felt his hand on her face, turning her towards him.

'You work harder than most blokes I know. You're fitter, stronger and nothing slows you down.' His breath caressed her face.

Toni was lost. She was trying to take in what he'd said but the fire flickering across his jade eyes had her mesmerised.

Before she could even find her words, Jimmy had found her mouth. Leaning across, he pressed his lips gently against hers. It was like nothing she'd ever experienced before. Her pulse lurched as the warmth of his lips caused fireworks within her body.

The moment he pulled back she shot up out of her chair.

143

'I . . . ' She didn't know what to say.

Jimmy stood up beside her. 'I haven't finished yet.' He grabbed her arms and pulled her closer. 'Besides all that, you are so goddamn sexy. I'd be lying if I ever tried to deny it.' His fingers remained firm, not letting her move away. 'And you don't even realise how amazing you are. I can't fight this any more, Toni.'

Jimmy leant in to kiss her again and this time his arms circled around her. Her body responded to his touch, and she was aware of his fingers caressing her skin and the way his lips melted against hers. Was this really happening?

Toni put her hands up against his chest, feeling the shape of him, and then gripped his shirt. He groaned against her mouth and she parted her lips, hoping to remember how to kiss. It had been so long.

She could taste the beer on his tongue and as he pressed closer panic flared.

Toni pulled away and covered her mouth.

'I can't do this. I think I've had a bit too much to drink.' She turned, stepped away from the chair. 'Sorry. Um, I'd better get to bed,' she said, pointing her finger towards the house. Tonight might be the perfect night to be back in her own room. Right now she could handle her mother more than she could handle Jimmy.

'Toni . . . ' Jimmy began, but she backed away, refusing to look at him. She didn't want to see the expression on his face.

What just happened? she asked herself on the walk back to the main house. She touched her lips, which still tasted like him, and her body

144

could still recall the impressions of his hands. How many times had she told herself to avoid this very situation? What the hell was he thinking?

14

Flick moved carefully in the dark as she headed towards Chad's ute. The crescent moon gave enough light to see certain shapes and as her eyes adjusted she could navigate the worn track through the scrub bush easily enough. She hadn't drunk much; she was still too annoyed. Furious, actually. Why would Chad bring Kel here to her place? Maybe some warning would have been nice, or even asking if she'd mind. Had he forgotten that it wasn't exactly an easy time for them all right now?

It really was the last thing Flick needed, especially the way Chad and Kel laughed and talked as if they'd been best friends for ages. Just how much time had they been spending together?

At the cut-out Chad had sat with Flick by the fire, reaching for her hand and giving her kisses. They'd even sung some songs together, but Flick felt awkward when Kel joined them.

'Oh, remember when Justin did this?' Kel had said, explaining some party trick.

'I don't know how he did it. And what about Tipper the other night? Crazy, hey?' Chad had replied.

Each story was like a little secret only they knew. Chad had clearly spent more time with Kel at parties than he had with Flick the last few months. He was with her when he should have been with Flick. With jealousy simmering, Flick had moved, finding it more enjoyable to sit by Donnie and Bottle Top. At least the shearers' stories were funny, and she felt included.

The last big bush brushed her arm as she made it to the clearing by the shed. She stopped as her eyes strained to make out his ute. She saw something moving, dark shadows against the tin wall of the shearing shed.

The bus started up behind her and its lights flicked on. She could hear Squeak yelling at the crew to sit down. It sounded like she was driving a busload of rowdy school kids. Flick chuckled. Poor Squeak.

In the edge of the bus lights she could see one of the shadowy figures now. It was Kel. Her first thought was that she was leaning against the shed, being sick. She had drunk a lot of their free beer. Flick hoped she felt rotten.

But Kel wasn't alone. Flick's heart lurched as the bus came closer, the lights making everything visible.

Chad and Kel were kissing.

'What the hell?' she yelled. 'Chad?' Blood pounded in her ears, drowning out the bus as it passed, launching her back into darkness again.

Flick dropped to the ground. Stunned. Shocked. Numb.

The worst part was that she'd so known something like this would happen. She'd been sensing it all day — weeks, if she were really honest. But why here, now, on her very own property?

'Flick?'

147

Chad's fearful voice snapped her back to attention. She jumped up and forced her legs to take her towards the house.

'Wait, Flick. Let me explain,' he begged. He was a few metres behind her, trying to catch up.

'Leave me alone!' she yelled without turning around. 'Don't you dare follow me, Chad. I'm not doing this tonight.' She picked up her speed, running now because she knew he probably couldn't keep up. Flick made it to the safety of the house and her room before she let the tears fall.

It was Chad who'd hurt her, yet why did she feel like she was the inadequate one? Why did this always happen to her? That now made it three guys who'd cheated on her, and she was only twenty. Why was it always this same predictable, painful story? Eventually her tears dried up but she lay on her bed, staring at the ceiling until sleep finally overcame her.

⋆ ⋆ ⋆

The following morning Flick let her body move along with Contractor as they headed down the gravel driveway to the mailbox to gather yesterday's mail.

Flick rocked in her saddle limply. She didn't even have the words to talk to Contractor about Chad. In some ways she hoped it had been a dream. She'd heard his ute start at around five this morning, and now it was gone. She didn't know whether to feel relieved or even more insulted.

Contractor shook his mane and Flick tried to forget it and live in the moment. A beautiful morning shouldn't be wasted on Chad.

On either side of the road were river gums, their light-coloured trunks a beautiful contrast to the dark-green gum leaves, their branches thick and twisted. Flick had spent so much of her childhood climbing them while she waited for the school bus, or practising how to whistle using a leaf. Being an only child she'd spent her youth following either Maggie around the kitchen or Toni and Arthur in the paddocks. The rest of the time had been spent entertaining herself, with the bush as her playground. She'd made swings in the trees, constructed cubbies and got really dirty. A brother or a sister was what she'd dreamt of most.

Fella was sitting beside the improvised mailbox, which was an old toolbox on a post. Flick dismounted and picked up the bundled mail and flicked through it while Contractor nudged her back.

'No, there's nothing here for you. The *Outback* magazine comes next week.' Flick rubbed his nose before he turned away to pull at some grass. 'Yeah, that's all you were waiting for, hey?' Fella sat by her feet, looking up expectantly. 'No, I'm afraid we all missed out,' she said with a sigh. Maybe it was still too early for Rocco's records. She'd been religiously checking the mailbox to make sure Toni didn't find the records she was expecting, but with the cut-out on she'd forgotten to get it yesterday. It had been nearly a week and she still hadn't told her mum about finding Rocco. She would tell her soon, once she figured out how she'd take it.

But Flick needed to know if Rocco was still alive. She never had liked an unfinished story. Especially her own. One day she was going to set sail and find the answers to all her questions, including the one about her own father, but this was certainly enough to go on for now.

Flick tucked the mail into her shirt and climbed back onto Contractor. Fella had already begun to run back.

Back at Contractor's stables she took off his saddle, gave him a brush and checked his water. Flick rubbed his neck and nuzzled against his long nose. His ears twitched, picking up the sound of a car before she did.

It was a bit early for visitors.

The ute came closer. *Chad*. 'Damn.' She had nowhere to hide, he was already headed towards her. 'Stay with me, Contractor,' she whispered.

'Flick,' Chad called, rushing out of his ute. 'Please, let me explain. I'm sorry.'

She turned to face him, holding up her hand to stop him. Two metres was close enough. He looked terrible: eyes dark, his skin pale, and his hair knotted. Chad dragged his hand over his face and licked his dry lips. 'I'm so sorry. She kissed me.'

Flick closed her eyes, shutting him out. She couldn't even handle hearing his apology. 'I've had enough.'

'What?'

He stepped closer and she felt her anger spike. 'I said I've had enough!' she yelled, scaring some nearby birds and causing Contractor to move away.

Chad stared back at her, his mouth open.

'I've had enough with useless boyfriends. I don't even know who you are any more,' she said, dropping her voice.

'I'm sorry. I'll try harder, I promise. It won't happen again.'

He went to step closer, but he couldn't just smile and make it all go away. Not this time. 'I can't take that risk. And besides, you weren't there when I needed you most, Chad. And you bring some strange girl to my place and disrespect me like that? It wasn't just all Kel either.' Images of his hand running through Kel's blonde hair were burned into the back of her eyes. She swallowed, slow and hard. The change in his blue eyes told her everything she needed to know. He'd enjoyed that kiss; it would have been plain to anyone who'd seen it. 'You act as though you care about me, Chad, but the truth is, you don't really. I can't believe it took me this long to figure it out.' It dawned on Flick that she didn't care enough for Chad to work through this either.

'Flick . . . ' But he didn't say anything else. Maybe he was too hung over to think.

'It's over,' she said calmly. 'I've got enough crap to deal with right now.' She went to walk away but changed her mind. Instead she stepped closer to him, shaking her hair from her face. 'I think you know we've run our course,' she said softly. 'Bye Chad.'

Flick walked away and didn't glance back, not

even when he revved his ute and drove back down the driveway.

Jimmy was heading towards her, and she gave him a smile. His face was hard but his hands came out and held her gently.

'Are you okay, Flick?' His face was torn up with concern. No doubt he'd overheard her yelling.

Tears welled in her eyes at Jimmy's kindness. She didn't want to do this now, but already drops began to fall as a sob burst free.

Jimmy pulled her into his arms tightly, rubbing her back. Everything crashed over Flick all at once. Mum and Nan, Rocco and Simon. And now Chad.

'I'm sorry,' she mumbled between sobs. Jimmy held her, letting her cry until she was spent.

'No. I'm sorry, Flick,' he said, walking her to the steps of the shearing shed, where the scent of lanolin was strong.

Flick finally stopped crying and told Jimmy the whole story. He had this way of unearthing the truth with just one look.

'When I see him next . . . ' Jimmy pushed his breath out through his teeth. 'I'm so sorry,' he said again.

She shrugged. 'Me too. But it feels good to make a stand, you know? I think we were just coming to the end of it.'

He nodded. 'You did the right thing. You can do so much better. Will you be okay?'

Flick gave a weak smile. 'Eventually.' She glanced around. 'Where's Mum?' The morning had ticked on and it was nearly ten.

Jimmy dropped his head and picked at a loose thread on his shirt. 'My guess is she took the sheep back to the paddock.'

'By herself?'

Jimmy shrugged, intent on pulling the thread. 'I guess so. The ute and sheep were gone when I got up.' Finally he looked up. 'Hey, do you want to come see the old house?'

'Why? What have you been up to?' She hadn't had a chance to get back over there, with shearing on.

'Just been putting together a little something, and I think now is the perfect time to show you.'

Together they headed to the house and kicked their boots off by the front door. Before shearing they had just finished the protective coat on the floors, so only socks or bare feet had been allowed in since.

Flick smiled as they stepped into the house. The jarrah boards were magnificent, dark and glossy.

'I can't believe how perfect they turned out,' Jimmy said as if reading her thoughts.

They entered the kitchen area.

'Wow, this place looks amazing.'

Jimmy had fitted out the kitchen with supplies. Tea towels hung from the old stove, cupboard doors had been fixed, a tablecloth covered the MDF table he'd made, and the rough wooden chairs were scattered with little homemade cushions — no doubt made by Nan. The old fridge and microwave from the shearing quarters had been brought in too, making it a liveable kitchen.

'Maggie even baked us some scones,' said Jimmy as he flicked on the kettle. 'I was just coming to get you when I overheard . . . '

Flick nodded. He didn't have to continue. 'Looks like Nan has helped out quite a bit, unless you're a closet sewer?'

He chuckled. 'Yeah, Maggie's been helping. We wanted to surprise you.'

'Aw, thanks. Does this mean we can move in?' A genuine smile tugged on her lips. 'This is good.' Something she'd been looking forward to and now something to keep her busy.

'Hey, how about you sit down and have your cuppa and scone first?' He smiled but a worry line creased his brow. 'Then you can start moving some stuff.'

'Okay. What would I ever do without you, Jimmy?'

He threw his arm around her shoulders. 'Let's just hope you never have to find out, eh?' He squeezed her again. 'I still need to finish some work in the bathroom — grout those tiles and install the new heater, then we'll be good to go.'

'Will it need long to dry?' she asked as she sat down with the coffee he handed her.

Jimmy shook his head. 'Not long. Could probably use it tomorrow night. But I think we should get the outside loo sorted. It's a jungle in there.'

Flick shuddered. 'I know!' As outside dunnies went, that one was a corker. She'd almost prefer a portaloo. One wall had broken so everything could get in: dust, snakes, mice, rabbits — a bush had even grown through the hole. Add the

154

spider webs, and that small room was one scary place.

Jimmy reached for a scone.

'Hey, should we leave Mum some?' she asked.

Jimmy shrugged. 'I doubt she'll stop by.'

Flick frowned. She'd detected an edge to his voice. 'Why do you say that?'

Jimmy was pushing the cream around on top with his finger. He didn't lift his head or reply.

'What's going on?'

'It's nothing. She's just busy.'

Flick squinted and leant forward. 'Did you two have a fight? She takes you everywhere.'

Jimmy put his scone down and leant back in his chair. 'I think it would be easier if we were fighting.' He sighed heavily. 'She's avoiding me, I think.'

'What did you do?' she asked in an accusing tone.

He stayed silent, looking sheepish.

'Come on, you can tell me. Did you tell her how to run the farm?'

Nothing.

'Did you not agree with something she wanted?'

Still nothing.

'Did you quit?'

'No.'

'Has this got something to do with what we talked about at the club?'

Jimmy's eyes shot up.

Bingo. 'Oh no, what happened?'

He squirmed in his chair. 'Felicity, I don't feel comfortable talking about this with you.'

155

'James, shall I ask my mum?' she countered.

'No!' He threw his hands up. 'It will be all right. Don't worry. She'll calm down, she always does. Just let it go.'

Flick gave up. Jimmy was looking a little pale.

'Last night really was a weird one,' she mumbled, feeling sickness swirl in her stomach as the image of Chad and Kel sprang up again.

'You going to tell your mum and nan about Chad?'

'No. And please don't say anything. I don't want them to worry.'

'If that's what you want.'

'It is. Thanks, Jimmy.' She sighed heavily as she picked up another scone. 'Seriously, how much worse could things get around here?'

15

Toni had tried her best to forget the night by the fire. She'd tried really hard to forget the taste of Jimmy's lips and the feel of his caress, but it seemed her mind had other ideas.

She chucked all the gear in the back of the ute. The trough was working again. Jimmy could have found the problem and fixed it faster than Toni had but she wasn't up to having him working alongside her alone. Not yet. She was still struggling with the endless playback reel in her mind of their kiss. Just the thought of it sent her body into a euphoric frenzy, then in the very next moment she felt almost sick and silly for behaving like that. She was nearly ten years older than him. The community would have a field day.

Toni drove back to the shed in the early afternoon, unloaded the tools and began tidying up. An electrical cord had been dumped on the floor so she picked it up and started rolling it up properly.

'Did you get the trough sorted?'

Toni spun around. 'Jimmy! I didn't hear you turn up.'

The corner of his lips twitched. Was he amused or was he as scared as she was right now?

'Sorry, just walked over from the old place.'

Toni took a deep breath to settle her nerves.

'Um, the trough is fixed. No problems.' She hung the cord back up on its hook. 'So how's the new house?'

'Yeah, fine. Heater is working so we have hot showers. Ten times better than the quarters. You should come over and check it out.'

Toni agreed. She'd moved back into the house for the comfort of her bed but truth be known it was to put some distance between herself and Jimmy. She still snuck out of the house early to avoid her mother. 'Yeah, I will,' she said, walking to the workbench. With nervous hands she started stacking and putting away tools. Meanwhile her body felt Jimmy's presence. When the hairs went up on her neck, she knew he was too close.

'Now that I have you cornered, are we going to clear the air?' he said softly.

Toni swallowed, her throat so tight it almost hurt.

'Toni?'

She was scared but the way he said her name always had a way of winning her over. Like the time he'd broken the tailgate on the ute. 'Um, Toni,' was all he'd said, and she'd found it impossible to be angry, or even just a little annoyed.

'What are your thoughts on the kiss?'

She dropped what she was holding. Part of her rejoiced in knowing it must have been real but the other part was panicking and wanting to run like a mouse in rising floodwaters. She couldn't deal with this now.

'You can't avoid me forever, Toni. I don't want

that. I want us to talk about this. Get it out in the open.'

Toni almost snorted a laugh. 'Everything is so easy for you, isn't it? I don't know how you go about life so easily and so optimistically.'

'Someone has to balance you out. I think that's me,' he said teasingly.

She didn't know where to start. Talking had never really been her thing.

'Toni, I need to know what you're thinking, how you feel. I don't want this to become a problem,' he said, touching her shoulder.

She would love to know how he was feeling inside. Was his heart racing like hers was? Did he feel as confused as she did or was he really this calm?

'Why can't things just stay the same as they were?' she whispered, afraid of her own voice and the words she might accidentally speak.

Both his hands caressed her arms as he leant against her. 'Is that really what you want?' he said softly against her ear.

She felt his heart thumping against her back.

'Mum!' yelled Flick, followed by heavy footsteps. '*Mum!*'

Jimmy sprang back just in time to look busy doing something else.

'Don't be mad,' Flick continued, coming into the shed, 'but I just couldn't stand this thing between you and Nan. It's hell being stuck in the middle,' she said, slightly out of breath. She waved some pages in the air; her face unsure. 'I went looking for Rocco.'

Toni felt as if she'd been punched in the gut.

159

'What?' She sat down on the pile of tyres next to her.

Flick flinched. 'I found his war records and paid for a copy. The files have just turned up. I hope you're not mad?'

'I . . . I don't know what to think.'

Flick grabbed her hand. 'Mum, if I had a chance to find my father, to know what he was like, I'd take it. Maybe you need to do this. Find out who he is and maybe you'll find a part of you. Then with a bit of luck you might forgive Nan and we can go back to normal.'

Her daughter's eyes portrayed just how much she hated the conflict. Toni steadied her breath. Curiosity got the better of her, and her eyes fell to the pages in Flick's hand. 'What do they say?'

'Mum, it's amazing. We're on there.'

'What do you mean?'

'Look here.' Flick shoved a sheet at her. 'This one is his personal description and it even has a photo and fingerprints. And on this side it lists his registered employer — and it's us! See? John Fuller, Sunnyvale, Pingaring, and the dates Rocco was here.'

Toni held the page, saw her grandfather's name and the name of their farm. It was amazing: history in her hand. The photo of Rocco drew her gaze next. Just a simple head shot of a handsome young man. This was her biological father. A nervous tingle raced throughout her body. She realised she did want to know this man. She did want her questions answered and she did think it would help them all to find him.

160

Flick handed her another page. 'What do you think, Mum? Is this okay?'

Toni finally smiled. 'Yeah, Flick. I guess it's okay.'

Excitement lit up Flick's face, and Toni was pleased to see something giving her daughter this much enjoyment.

Flick rushed on with her explanation. 'This one just has his name and the personal property he had, which was 20 lira.' She pulled out another sheet. 'This is his dossier, listing his dad, place of birth, date of birth. He was born in Ancona in 1924. It also has the place and date he was captured: 9 December 1940 in Sidi Barrani, and the ship he was on to Australia. Mum, it has so much stuff. It's awesome.'

'He was twenty-three when I was born,' Toni said, doing the maths. 'And he'd be seventy-six now.'

'See, he could easily be alive.'

It came so easily for Flick, the excitement. But Toni was scared of the unknown. If he was alive, would he want to meet her, or even get to know her? And what if he'd died? She'd have lost two fathers.

'And on this page it says he left Australia for Naples on 30 November 1946 on the HT *Chitral*.'

Toni turned back to the black and white photo of Rocco. 'It is pretty cool. Has Nan seen these?'

Flick shook her head. 'No. I wanted to tell you first. Nan knew I was searching for him though.' Flick's face tinted pink. 'What do you reckon, Jimmy?' she asked, changing the subject.

Jimmy picked up a sheet. 'I think it's amazing. You'll be able to use all this to find him now.' He seemed generally interested and not at all put out about Flick's timing. 'Character sketch. Worked splendidly for employer who regarded him and second POW as the best men he had ever had. Polite and reliable, conscientious, excellent workman, helped build a house and can be trusted alone. J. M. Tweedie Captain W17.' Jimmy glanced across to Flick. 'Rave reviews, no wonder Maggie fell for him. You should get the records of the other bloke too.'

'Giulio? Yeah, we should.' Flick did a little jig on the spot. 'I'm going to google these dates now, see if I can find more on Rocco.'

'Okay,' said Toni. She wasn't really sure if she was okay but there was no stopping Flick now.

Flick took off as fast as she'd come. Jimmy lingered by Toni's side. His eyes told her he was not finished with their conversation yet, and that scared the heck out of her. 'How do you really feel about all this?' he asked.

Toni was relieved his question wasn't about their kiss. But this one was just as hard to answer. 'Honestly? I have no idea. I'm glad that Flick seems happy.'

'Yeah, she's really excited. I think it's good for her to have something to focus on.' Toni wasn't sure what he meant by that but he continued without pause. 'It was kinda cool seeing all that information and history. Just think, Toni — your father fought in the war, was captured and spent years in prison camps. Coming to Sunnyvale

162

would have been a ray of sunshine by comparison.'

'It's hard to visualise it. I mean, I'm still trying to get my head around the fact that he's my father, but to go looking for him? I just can't figure out how I feel about all of this. Do I have to?'

Jimmy shrugged. 'I guess not. Just as long as you take each day as it comes. What harm can come from knowing more of the truth?'

She shrugged.

He put his hand on her shoulder and guided her out of the shed. 'Come on, let's go see if Flick can find anything else.'

* * *

They found Flick in the office, still searching on the computer.

'Any luck?' Jimmy said.

Flick's eyes didn't leave the screen. 'I can't find anything. One website says that in Italy they keep all birth and death records at the city council. Nothing is on the net.' Her shoulders slumped as she sighed.

'Well, that's it then,' said Jimmy, giving Toni a wink. 'Flick, you have your reason for a trip to Italy now. Why don't you both go, do some sightseeing and visit the place he grew up — Chiaravalle, or whatever it's called — and search the records there?'

'Wasn't he born in An . . . ' Toni gestured with her hand as she tried to remember the rest of the town's name.

163

'Ancona,' said Flick. 'I looked it up on a map. Chiaravalle is a place further inland, kind of like a distant suburb. Seeing as his father's address is listed at Chiaravalle we think this is where he actually lived.' Flick turned to Jimmy. 'I totally agree, Jimmy. Mum, let's go find Rocco.'

Toni opened her mouth but nothing came out. Sweat broke out along her forehead.

'Come on, Mum. If he's alive you actually get to meet your real dad. Or if he's not, you might be able to get a photo of his headstone, get some closure. It would be good for Nan too. Maybe she could come? Don't you want to see this out till the end? Get some answers?'

Toni's first thought was *no*. She felt as if her chance had long past, and to go away now would be impossible. Who would look after the farm?

'Come on, Toni. You've always wanted to travel,' said Jimmy. He gave her that look, the one that dared her to disagree with him.

'Really, Mum? You want to travel? I never knew that,' said Flick, turning around on her chair.

Toni shrugged. That dream had long ago faded. 'When I was your age I wanted to see things, and Italy was near the top of my list.'

Flick chewed on her bottom lip for a moment. 'Well, I do have Granddad's money sitting there. And it seems a shame to get this far and still not find out if Rocco is still alive.' She smiled up at Toni. 'Let's use some of it to go to Italy, Mum. Please?'

They were words she'd always wanted to hear from her daughter. Jimmy had been right; Flick

164

just needed the right reason to leave the farm. Flick was still waiting for her answer, hope making her eyes bright.

'Oh, I don't know.'

'I'll go and see if Nan wants to come too,' said Flick, racing off to find Maggie.

Toni started at the computer screen. 'Me in Italy?' she mumbled.

Jimmy shook her shoulders. 'Come on, of course you'll go. Now is your time too.' He smiled and gently touched her cheek, holding her in his gaze.

'But the — '

'The farm will be fine. I'm here. Nothing is happening until harvest, so now is perfect. And I know you still have your passport and you made Flick get hers too. You can't tell me you never planned on using it one day, otherwise why would you keep it up to date?' His thumb brushed just below her lips before he let her go.

'But — '

'No buts!' said Jimmy forcefully.

Toni screwed up her face.

'Hey,' said Jimmy more gently, taking her hand. 'Don't you shut down and try to get out of this trip. It's what you always wanted and right now I think it's what you, Flick and Maggie need. Finding Rocco would be a good thing.'

'Since when were you promoted to the Sunnyvale Shrink?' said Toni.

He grinned, showing his perfect teeth. 'I am a man of many talents,' he teased. In a split second his face became serious again. 'Take this opportunity for yourself, Toni. Make up for what

165

you missed out on. You can do what you want. Your dreams are still reachable. Should I keep going?'

Toni laughed and for the first time in ages, she felt a new and wonderful feeling. It was a lot like freedom. 'No, please stop. I've got the gist of it.'

'Mum, come and check this out!' shouted Flick from down the hall.

Jimmy let go of her hand and they walked to the lounge room to find Flick and Maggie looking at something.

'How did that get in here?' shouted Toni, staring at the black slithery thing on the table. It wasn't until she got closer that she realised it was a fake snake. The fact that Maggie taking pot shots at it with the gun made it obvious.

'Isn't it cool? Rocco made this and gave it to Nan for her seventeenth birthday,' said Flick. She gently picked up the wooden snake in the middle and the whole thing moved and wiggled like a slithering snake. 'It's made with wood stuck to a bit of canvas.'

'I know,' said Toni. 'I used to play with it, until I accidentally knocked off one of the bits and Nan had a pink fit and put it away.' Toni glanced at her mum, who was sitting there quietly. 'Now I know why it was so special.' For the first time in a while Toni gazed at her mum without the pain. At that moment she realised what her mum must have gone through, and she felt a little remorse and sadness.

Maggie's eyes were glued to the snake and Toni could almost see the memories flashing past. That snake had been something she'd

166

treasured for all these years. Maybe going to find Rocco *was* the right thing to do. For Maggie, for Flick and for herself.

16

It was finally Friday. As usual Father drove into town for the bread, mail and the occasional order they had rung through using the phone at the siding. Maggie normally went with her father — her mother loved going into town but had been sending Maggie because she didn't want her daughter alone on the farm with the Italians. But this week Phyllis accompanied her husband, as it was Maggie's birthday on Saturday and her mother had to get her present. For Maggie, being left on the farm alone with Rocco, Giulio and Charlie was a gift in itself.

Mother had given her a long list of chores to do, no doubt to keep her too busy to visit the men. But Maggie had worked hard and fast to get most of them done in record time. Checking her hair in the small mirror her mother kept in her room, Maggie pinched her cheeks and put on a little lipstick. On her way out from the cottage she saw Giulio carrying some sticks towards the copper by the wash house.

'What are you doing, Giulio?' Maggie looked into the copper to find water heating up, and beside it sat a pile of his maroon work clothes.

'I boil clothes.' He dropped the sticks by the copper. 'Make mine like Mistair,' he said.

'Ah, I see. Is Rocco at the house?' she asked him.

Giulio nodded and smiled. 'Yes, he smoothing bricks.'

Maggie said goodbye and raced to the house, not wanting to waste a second of her free time.

She found Rocco by the house, using a special tool he'd made for smoothing the mortar. The bricks now reached up to his head height. They'd had to construct wooden ladders so they could finish the rest.

'Hello, Rocco,' she said, trying to sneak up on him.

Rocco turned and smiled. She lived for these moments and she sensed that he did too. 'I saw Mr and Mrs Boss head in for town. They gone a while?'

Maggie nodded.

'I just finish this,' he said, gesturing along the line he was working on. 'Five minutes.'

'That's okay.'

She loved to sit and watch him work. One stinking hot day she'd arrived to see Rocco and he'd had his shirt off so he could wet it. Ever since then Maggie had that image with her always: Rocco's strong lean body, shirtless. He'd quickly got dressed when he'd seen her but it was too late, she'd seen him and now she wanted more. If her mother knew of her thoughts she'd take to Maggie with Father's belt.

'I see Giulio is trying hard to fade his new set of clothes rations,' she said.

Rocco laughed. 'Yes, Giulio gets them faded then Mr Tweedie come and see them. He gives him new ones. But Giulio want to look like Boss not prisoner so he keep trying.'

Maggie liked it when Mr Tweedie came with the canteen rations. He brought the men new uniforms and boots if required, and they could also get cigarettes, matches and lollies. Rocco always gave her lollies and she loved it. But that was their little secret. He would sneak them to her sometimes when they could find a moment without her mother watching.

'I bet your mother is nicer than mine,' she said.

Rocco nodded. He was at the end of his row. Once he was done he put the tool down and came to sit by Maggie. 'I miss my family. My mother, Antonia, is happy woman. She cook . . . ' Rocco kissed his fingers. 'She drive my father — ' He gestured with his hands. 'Ah, the word . . . With her talking, he drive her . . . silly?'

'Crazy?'

'Yes, si. She talk, talk, talk. But big heart.' He touched his chest and then dropped his head slightly. 'Like you, Maggie. She special woman.'

'Thanks, Rocco.' They sat staring at each other for a moment, the wind rustling the leaves in the trees the only sound. 'It's my birthday tomorrow,' she said shyly.

'Charlie told me. Come, I give you gift now.' He stood up and held out his hand.

Maggie slid her hand into his. It was the most amazing feeling in the world. Together they walked back to Rocco's little shed. They could hear Giulio singing an Italian song while he boiled his clothes.

'He sings about the hills of our Italy,' said Rocco as he opened the door to his room. Maggie had never been inside before, even though they'd nearly been here a year. He waited for her to enter, nodding that it was okay.

She stepped inside and was glad he kept the door open so she could run out in case mother arrived home early.

'Giulio show me how to make this for you.' Rocco turned and she realised he had something in his hands. She jumped when she realised what it was.

'It not real,' said Rocco. He held up the snake and

170

showed her how it wiggled.

'Oh, Rocco, you made this? For me?'

He nodded shyly. 'I not have much. But I make for you.'

Maggie reached out and took the delicate snake. It was over half a metre in length and each piece of wood had been carved perfectly to represent the snake's body, even down to its skinny tail. The canvas centre allowed the snake to move and the timber pieces were curved to allow it.

'It's beautiful. No one has ever made me anything like this.' It finally made sense: all those afternoons she'd seen Giulio and Rocco sitting on the steps of their room, whittling away. He'd been making this for her.

Moving with her heart, she wrapped her arms around Rocco and thanked him again. He was stiff for a moment, caught by surprise, but quickly his arms engulfed her and they hugged tightly. Rocco bent his head, tucking it towards her neck while she rested hers against his shoulder. He smelt like a man, sweat and dirt, and his arms felt strong and safe. His hand found her hair, his fingers playing with the ends. Neither of them said anything and neither one moved away.

So much had been building towards this moment, all the holding hands and touching feet under the table at dinner. He whispered her name, and it was like music from the heavens. Nothing was more perfect than this moment in Rocco's arms. Maggie tried hard to memorise everything as they stood holding each other for ages. If only time could stand still and she could stay here forever. But Mother would be home soon and Maggie was scared that if she ever found out about this she'd send Rocco back to the prison camp.

A noise outside pulled them apart quickly but it was just Giulio emptying out the copper. They both sighed with relief. But Maggie missed being in Rocco's arms.

'I'd better tell Mother I got this from the both of you. That way she won't get too upset,' she whispered. She could still feel the hum of their connection in the small room.

'I get back to house too,' he said, knowing they didn't have long left. He reached for her hand and gave it a squeeze, then let it slip away as he stepped out of his room, checking that no one had arrived while they were preoccupied.

'Go.' He started heading back to the house. 'Tell Giulio I will start next row of bricks.'

Maggie nodded, holding the snake to her chest as she watched him leave. She wanted to tell him that she loved him but the words didn't come. She was too scared to speak them out loud. Scared her mother would somehow hear them on the wind and take him away.

* * *

It was another month before Maggie was able to hold Rocco again. After their embrace, it was as if they had secretly confirmed their affection for each other. Neither of them had spoken about it but their glances meant so much more, and every night for dinner they would rest their feet together under the table. Every touch set her alight with longing. But she was ever so careful to hide it around her mother.

On this particular night in May, dinner was finished, the dishes done, and Father brought in the battery from the Chev 4 ute to run the radio so the family could listen to the news, as was their custom. They gathered around the table in their usual spots while Rocco and Giulio returned to their room.

The prime minister's voice came on. 'Fellow citizens,' he said. 'The war is over.'

'Oh my lord,' said Phyllis, her hand flying to her mouth.

Maggie was elated, but only for a moment. Would this mean Rocco would be leaving? She turned to Charlie.

'It's over,' he said, grinning. 'Can you believe it?'

'Shhh,' said John, straining to hear the report.

Maggie got up quietly and headed outside. No one seemed to notice her departure but once outside she ran to Rocco's room.

He was sitting on the steps in the dark with his small knife and some wood. He dropped both when he saw her running towards him.

'Maggie, what is it?'

Giulio was just inside the door smoking and quickly stood up. Maggie ran straight into Rocco's arms, not even caring if her mother had followed. She was breathing so hard and was so distraught that she couldn't speak. But with Rocco's warm body against hers and his gentle stroking of her hair, she calmed.

'The war is over,' she said. 'It's over.'

'Madonna!'

Maggie had heard Giulio and Rocco's Italian swear words and she felt like uttering a few of her own.

Then Rocco hugged her tightly and she knew then that he'd realised the same thing she had. How much longer did they have together?

'I have to get back,' she said, not wanting to move.

Rocco took her face in his hands and kissed her

firmly on her lips before letting her go. Maggie walked back to the cottage in a daze and sat on a chair outside the door. She couldn't go back in, not with Rocco's kiss lingering on her lips. Her first real kiss. It had been only quick but it carried so much. Arthur had kissed her once when she was only fourteen, just to see what it was like. Maggie hadn't liked it one bit and had made sure it never happened again. But she craved more of Rocco's kisses already.

'Maggie, did you tell the boys?' said Charlie as he came out the door.

She nodded.

'That should make them happy.' He sat down on the ground, leaning his back against the wooden slat wall. 'Are you thinking about Thomas and George?' he asked.

Maggie felt a bit uncomfortable, realising she was thinking only of herself. But nonetheless she nodded. 'I don't think we'll see Thomas. I fear he is lost with George, but I know Mother still holds out hope.'

'I agree, little sister. I can't help but hope she is right though.'

Their father came out. 'Here you all are.' He leant back against the wall and lit his rollie. 'They're just repeating the same newscast. Can you believe it?'

Maggie felt a knot grow in her throat over the question she most wanted to ask. Charlie ended up beating her to the punch.

'What does this mean for Giulio and Rocco, Father?'

John puffed out smoke with his sigh. 'I'm not sure, mate. No doubt Mr Tweedie will get into contact with us and let us know the situation. I guess they'll have to go back to camp for processing before they can board a ship home.'

174

A barrel of rocks made a home in her belly. She didn't want Rocco to go.

'Could they stay on, Father? The house isn't finished yet,' she said, hoping her concern for Rocco and herself was covered by worry for the house.

John chuckled. 'You sound just like your mother. I don't think they can stay. It doesn't work like that, darling. It would be nice if they could. I'm quite fond of those blokes. Hard workers. I might go have a word with them.'

As her father walked off, Maggie pondered the time she had left with the Italian prisoner who had captured her heart.

17

Flick and Toni arrived back home from their trip to Narrogin and it seemed as if Fella had never left his post. Flick got out and stretched while he danced around her feet.

'At least someone missed me,' she said, giving him a pat.

'Can you take my bags in and I'll drop the motor off down the shed?' said Toni.

'Yeah, no worries.' As always, a trip to town was usually filled with lots of jobs to do like motors to fix and parts to collect. They had to make the most of their three-hour round trip.

Flick lugged their stuff inside and dumped it on the kitchen table to sort out.

'Good grief, what's all that?' said Maggie, who was stirring a stew in the crock-pot.

Flick laughed and pulled out a new backpack from a plastic bag. 'Well, this, this is for Italy. And this — ' she pulled out a new pair of shorts ' — is for Italy, and so are these walking shoes. And also these tops and a new little bag for our passports.' Flick kept pulling things out, realising how well she'd done at the shops.

'I thought you were going to travel light,' said Maggie.

Flick grinned. 'We are! I even got Mum to buy some cute dresses and nice walking shoes. We actually had a bit of a girly day. Haven't done that for years.'

Maggie held up one of the dresses. 'I'm glad. You both need that every now and then.'

Flick dropped her shoulders. 'But I wish you would come with us.' When she'd told Maggie about the trip, she'd seemed excited for them but had refused to go, saying she wanted to stay and help Jimmy with the farm. Flick knew it was also because things were strained between her and Toni, and had let it go, realising she couldn't change her nan's mind.

'Is it all booked? How long did you decide to go for?' asked Maggie.

'Yes, it's all sorted. We leave on the twentieth and go for eight days. We can't really afford to go longer with harvest approaching but we really want to find Rocco, so Mum said we could do another trip next year if we need to, and bring you with us.'

Maggie raised an eyebrow. 'Really, Toni said that?'

Flick smiled. 'Well, that's what she was implying, I'm sure. Look, Nan, even if we don't find Rocco, we might find relatives for Mum. Wouldn't it be great to have that connection, and travel to Italy to meet them?'

'Rocco's sister might still be alive,' said Maggie quietly.

'Exactly. So we'll head over and see what we can find. We still might get a few days of sightseeing in, so it's a win-win situation. It'll do Mum good to have a break before harvest anyway.' Flick reached into her bag and pulled out all their forms. 'We've booked four days in Montone as our base. The travel agent recommended it.'

Flick ran her finger over the picture on the paper. It looked like a castle on a hilltop, much like Hogwarts from the trailer she'd seen for the new Harry Potter movie out next year. It seemed like such a fairytale.

'*Casa Valdeste is a beautiful late fourteenth-century terrace-style cottage in the medieval village of Montone,*' she read out. The words 'medieval' and 'fourteenth century' weren't exactly mentioned much in Australia.

'We have a two-bedroom villa here in Montone, which is in Umbria, and it's owned by Aussies.'

'Oh, it looks stunning,' said Maggie.

'If we find Rocco easily, we can head off and explore some more of Italy. I really hope we can track him down, Nan. For you and for Mum.'

Maggie folded up the dress she'd been looking at and put it in the bag gently. 'Now, Felicity, don't get your hopes up. Just go and have a great time with Toni. We'll all survive if you come back empty-handed.'

Flick hugged her. No one gave hugs like her nan. 'Okay, Nan. I'll try. I love you.'

Maggie cleared her throat. 'I had two calls from Chad again this morning. Anything you want to tell me?'

All her excitement over the trip disappeared in a second. Flick slumped into a chair. 'That obvious, is it?'

'I had a feeling things weren't going along so great. You had a fight?'

'Something like that, Nan,' she said with a sigh.

'He rang yesterday too. Does he need forgiving?'

'I don't know if I can. But it's just not what he did, it's everything leading up to it. I've been down this road too many times before and I think it's time I looked out for me. Is that too selfish? Should I give Chad another chance?'

'Oh, love. Matters of the heart are never easy. As much as we want to, sometimes we can't change people.' Maggie gave her a smile. 'What do you feel? What are your instincts telling you?'

'That I don't want to be in a relationship with him any more. I haven't really felt like we've been in one lately anyway.'

'Well, if you want my two cents, I think you've done the right thing. You're still young and you're beautiful and I think you deserve the very best.'

'Aw, thanks, Nan.'

Maggie went to the stove, gave the bubbling pot a stir, then switched on the kettle before coming back to sit beside Flick. 'Must be time for a cup of tea, with all this serious talk,' she said with a grin.

'I know. Please don't say anything to Mum. I don't want to worry anyone.'

'I doubt Toni would stay in my presence long enough to let me get the words out.'

Flick reached for her hand. 'She'll come around. Mum needs time. This trip will help.' Well, that was her plan. As long as it didn't backfire and cause even more of a rift. 'Hey, Nan, Rocco's papers said he left Australia in

1946. That's a whole year after the war finished, isn't it?'

'Yes, that's right.' A melancholy expression washed over Maggie. 'When we heard the war was over, we were elated, but I was devastated at the same time. My heart just ached.'

Flick jumped up and made them both a cuppa while Maggie sat with her hands clasped.

'By this stage I was already in love with him. He'd been with us a year and we were at a point where we knew something special was going on between us but neither of us had said anything about it.'

'What do you mean? You didn't talk about it?'

Maggie was staring out the window, no doubt picturing Rocco, young and handsome. 'Well, now days you kids call it going out or having a boyfriend, but back then we didn't — we just felt it in our hearts. I knew he cared for me in his gestures, the gifts he gave me or the way he held my hand. We were also too scared to talk about how we felt, knowing that it had to be kept quiet. My mother lurked, watching me, and I was afraid to tell Rocco how much I loved him in case the wind carried it to her.' She glanced up at Flick, who passed her a cup of tea. 'You probably think it was silly but back then times were so different. If it had got out that I was in love with a prisoner of war, well, the scandal would have killed my mother. She would either have sent me away or sent Rocco away and I couldn't do that to him or Giulio. I knew they loved it on the farm, where they felt free and not stuck in the camps. They'd had it really bad in the Indian camps before they reached Australia.'

'Did you eventually tell him how much you loved him?'

'Oh, yes.' Maggie took a sip of her tea as Toni came into the kitchen.

'Kettle's hot,' said Flick. Toni nodded and made a cup while Maggie continued, her voice quieter.

'We had a special spot, hidden in the bush by the new house he was building. It was away from all the tracks so I knew mother wouldn't ever see us. We would meet there sometimes when she'd gone to town, or we'd leave things for each other. Once he left me a bunch of wildflowers and a wooden heart he'd carved. I still have that little heart.' Maggie scrunched up her face as if wondering why she'd kept it for so long.

Flick knew why. Her nan couldn't forget her first love.

Toni was pottering about, pretending she wasn't listening.

'I guess in my heart I thought I'd run away with him when he came back. But when he never wrote to me . . . eventually I let him go and moved on with Arthur. I grew to love him very much,' said Maggie. 'I don't want you to think I settled for second best with your grandfather. He was sweet, gentle and caring. He was one of a kind and I don't regret one moment with Arthur and the life we made on Sunnyvale.'

Flick watched her. 'Do you ever wonder what your life would have been like if Rocco had come back for you, Nan?'

'I used to. The first few years were very hard

181

but I pushed on. I had Toni and she kept me going. I did care for Arthur, so it didn't take long before it grew into love. He was a wonderful father and a tentative husband in those early years and he'd always loved me.'

'Would you have left with Rocco if he had turned up?'

Maggie sighed. 'I don't know, love. That is something I guess we'll never know. And it doesn't really matter any more. The past is the past.' Maggie leant across the table towards Flick. 'I know you're picturing some great romantic meeting of lost loves but, Flick, so much has passed. I'm old now. Even if he's alive he could be happily married.'

'But what if he's not? What if he's alive and alone? Wouldn't you want to see him again?'

Maggie shrugged and Toni left the room with her cup.

Flick tried to imagine herself in the same situation. Would she want to meet up with a lost love, or would it be better to leave them in her mind where they'd stay young and perfect forever? For the first time she wondered if she was doing the right thing.

18

Toni stood in the veggie garden, the metal zappa in her hand. She'd made this zappa herself when Maggie's old one had worn to nothing. Maggie had always called it a zappa. Toni wasn't ever sure why, when Grandad had always called it a hoe.

Toni pulled out the punnet of tomato seedlings and planted them in the furrow she'd just made. The ones she'd planted earlier were tall enough to be staked. By the time they got back from Italy the seeds she planted would be out of the ground. Especially with her mum's green fingers.

'Mum, hurry up, we have to go!' yelled Flick from beside the house, and Toni headed back inside.

Toni washed her hands and zipped up her backpack and tow-along suitcase for tonight's flight. She threw on her blue knitted jumper over her black tank top, picked up her bags and headed out of her room. Today she was starting the next journey of herself. Today she could lift some of that chip off her shoulder.

'Come on, Mum. The bus is about to leave!' shouted Flick.

Toni still took her time, walking through the house and outside to Flick's car. Jimmy stood at the back with the boot up, waiting for her bags.

She realised she would miss him just as much

as she would miss Maggie. He was wearing his stonewash denim work jeans, threadbare short-sleeved cotton shirt and his dark sunglasses. He was looking all kinds of hot. She noticed a hint of a smile. *Damn him.* She'd been trying so hard to avoid being around him.

He was watching her carefully. She knew that look; something was weighing on his mind. He opened his mouth but it was a few moments before his words formed.

'Toni, I . . . ' He closed it again. And then the horn tooted, causing them both to jump.

'Is that everything?' asked Flick from the driver's door. She had her hair gathered on top of her head in a loose bun and was wearing black shorts with a red flowing top that just brushed her waist. Toni had to admit she looked fabulous.

'Yep, fine.' Jimmy reached for the last bag and put it in the boot, the moment gone.

'Thanks. I just have to get my glasses,' Toni said, and raced back into the house. Jimmy didn't need any more excuse than that to follow her.

Toni grabbed her sunglasses from her bedside table but suddenly felt her arm being grasped.

'Jimmy, what — ' She was silenced by the fire in his jade eyes.

He pushed her back against the wall and she was like a cornered animal, with no escape.

'Just wait. I have something to say.' He glanced down at the floor for a moment as if searching for his words before lifting those amazing eyes. 'Now, I've tried to let this go but then I realised, what if your plane crashes — '

'Gee, thanks.'

' — or something happens while you're in Italy. It made me realise that I can't let you leave without telling you how much you mean to me. I might not have this chance again.'

Toni swallowed hard. 'Are you serious?'

Jimmy pulled back, but only by a fraction. 'I've never met anyone like you, Toni. But I don't want to force you to do anything you don't want. It wouldn't be right.' His body was so close, yet so far, and his eyes were intent on hers. 'So I'm giving you what you want. It's going back to the way it was. When everything was safe and easy. I won't bother you again.'

Jimmy took her face in both hands and she thought he was going to kiss her. Toni forgot she was in the house; she forgot she was flying to a strange new land and she forgot all her reasons for not being with Jimmy. She couldn't afford to let him kiss her again but she felt like she might die if he didn't.

Then he dropped his hands, and as quickly as he had appeared, he was gone again. The corridor was empty and she was left feeling slightly rejected

When she finally found her legs and managed to get them to function, she headed back outside. Jimmy was talking with Flick and didn't even look her way.

'Promise me you'll take Contractor out for a few sunrises. He likes that,' said Flick from the car, fixing Jimmy with a steely gaze.

'I promise. He and I will be best buds by the time you're back.'

'But don't spoil him too much. I'll do that when I get back. And no taking Nan out on the town either. She's banned from the club,' joked Flick.

Jimmy glanced at Maggie, who was shaking her head. 'Don't you worry, I've got my eye on this one.'

Maggie was laughing now.

Toni wanted to ask if her mum was sure she'd be okay. But she couldn't get the words out. 'Now, remember, the phone number for our place in Montone is on the fridge. Ring if anything happens,' said Toni seriously, glancing between Jimmy and Maggie.

'Mum, they'll be fine,' said Flick as she got out of the car and came to stand with them all. 'Gee, anyone would think the farm would fall apart without her,' she muttered. 'Bye, Jimmy. We'll miss ya.' Flick wrapped her arms around him.

Toni smiled at her mum. 'Bye, Mum. You take care.' She hugged her. It was the first real contact they'd had in weeks. Maggie gripped her almost to the point of squeezing tears from Toni's eyes. She realised just how much she'd missed her mother and how comfortable she felt in her embrace. Like coming home.

Jimmy released Flick from his big bear hug, and turned to Toni. 'You enjoy this trip, okay?' he demanded, before pulling her in for a customary goodbye hug. It was short, quick and awful. Then he was opening her door for her.

Toni was thrown. Something didn't sit right, and Jimmy wouldn't meet her eyes. He was

186

giving her what she wanted, she realised, just as he'd said. Jimmy stood with Maggie, who pulled out a tissue to dab at her eyes. Toni got into the car and shut the door, and Flick started the car.

Toni had her gaze set out the window on Sunnyvale. She felt a strange sensation of loss wash over her.

'It will still be there when you get back,' said Flick.

'Funny, I'm sure I've said that to you a few times.'

Toni and Flick headed down the driveway, waving. They turned onto the main road and Toni watched Sunnyvale slip from view. It wasn't her mum's teary face that she pictured while following her daughter blindly across the world. No, it was the distant look in Jimmy's eyes, almost dejected and shut off, that caused the chill on her skin.

★ ★ ★

The airport was huge. People were coming and going, and there were massive planes outside taking people all over the world.

'I'm so excited,' said Flick, wide-eyed. She would be one of those people very soon, and Sunnyvale would be just a dot. 'Our first plane trip.'

Her mum didn't look as excited; she looked slightly anxious. *So much for wanting to be the big adventurer when she was younger,* Flick thought.

They worked out where to go to check in, and

afterwards they looked around to find some-where to wait.

'Mum, there's Uncle Charlie!' yelled Flick, dropping her stuff and running across the terminal. 'Kylie, Floss! What are you guys doing here?'

'Had to come and see you off,' Charlie said as they walked back to where Toni was standing. 'Maggie told me all about your adventure.'

In other words, Uncle Charlie knew about Rocco.

Toni wrapped her arms around her uncle. 'Hey, Charlie. It's great to see you.'

'You too, Toni. Looking good as always,' he said with a wink.

Charlie was ageing well. He had a bit of a belly on him and his hair was very thin, but other than that he was still the same as when she'd seen him at Christmas last year. Toni hugged her cousins, Kylie and Floss. 'Great to see you both too,' she said.

'Dad didn't want to miss an opportunity to see you, especially before you leave. You're going to have so much fun,' said Kylie. She was only a year younger than Toni. Her mother, Val, was the reason Uncle Charlie had left the farm. He'd gone to the city to follow his heart.

'Where's Aunty Val?' asked Flick.

'Mum's looking after all the grandkids so we could come,' said Floss. She resembled Charlie the most, with blonde hair and blue eyes. 'But she said to give you all a hug and to wish you a safe trip.'

They found a place to sit and chat while they

188

waited for their flight. Kylie was telling Toni all about Charlie's diabetes and the chronic arthritis in his bad arm.

'I'm fine, don't listen to Kylie,' Charlie said. He leant closer to Flick and whispered, 'How's your mum going?'

'Okay, I guess. I think finding Rocco will really help her, and hopefully she can forgive Nan. I've never seen them estranged like this.'

He patted her hand. 'I hope you find Rocco, he was a great bloke,' said Charlie.

Toni must have overheard, as all of a sudden she was sitting closer. 'Uncle Charlie, did you know?'

Silence. Then he cleared his throat. 'I knew Maggie loved Rocco and that he loved her.' His face reddened slightly. 'And she didn't have to tell me, but I knew that he was your father.' He put his hand up to calm Toni. 'Before you ask, it wasn't my place to tell you any of it. That's between you and Maggie.' He reached out, taking her hand. 'You can't go back and change the past. We all make mistakes and have to live with our choices. Don't let this weigh you down. Keep moving forward.'

'What if we find him?' Toni asked. 'What then?'

Charlie smiled. Even in old age you could see the family resemblance.

'Darling, the Rocco I knew was an amazing bloke. He was like a brother and I missed him when he left. Him and Giulio brought our farm back to life and made our family feel whole almost like it was before the war took Thomas and George. If Rocco is alive then I would love to meet him again, and I'm sure he'd be delighted to know you're his daughter.'

Flick blinked back emotion, hoping that his words got through to her mum. She knew Toni was worried about finding him and what that would be like, but on the other hand they also were scared it was too late. God, Flick hoped it didn't come to that. She glanced at her watch.

'Mum, it's time we went through.'

'Have a wonderful time,' said Floss, pulling Toni into a bear hug.

'Keep Charlie out of trouble,' Toni replied.

Kylie laughed. 'You know him so well. Have a great trip.'

They all hugged each other and Charlie, Kylie and Floss turned to leave. They glanced back at Flick and Toni, who waved a final goodbye.

Flick looked at her mum. 'All right. Italy, here we come.'

19

The airport doors opened on a whole new world. Florence, Italy. There were masses of people, most smoking, and chatting with their hands. It was kind of the same, but different. Florence had cars, but they were smaller and unfamiliar makes. There were streets, but they were cobblestoned. It was a city, but the buildings were older than any they'd seen in Perth.

It took them a while but eventually they found a taxi that would take them to their hotel. They passed many double-decker tourist buses, and the taxi driver pointed out the Ponte Vecchio, which, he told them in broken English, was Florence's first bridge and the only one surviving from the medieval days.

They arrived at their hotel, where they would be staying for just one night before catching the train to Arezzo the next day.

'I can't wait to go for a walk and stretch my legs,' said Flick, fishing out the euros they'd changed at the airport and paying the taxi driver.

'Let's get booked in and see what we can find,' said Toni as they pulled their suitcases up the stairs of the hotel. 'We still have half a day. May as well make the most of it, and I'm way too excited to sleep!'

After booking in — which was difficult as Valdo, the concierge with yellow teeth, spoke rough English — they dumped their stuff in their tiny room. It had a rickety bed, the smallest TV Flick had ever seen and a window that seemed to overlook the roof of a small restaurant.

Heading back down eagerly, they got a map from Valdo and rough directions to the Accademia Gallery to see Michelangelo's *David*.

'*Buonasera*,' called out Valdo as he waved his arms, causing his padded white jacket to rise up to his ears.

'*Buonasera*,' they both called back. 'I think he likes you, Mum,' teased Flick as they headed off at a brisk pace, hoping to take in as much as they could.

'Ha, ha,' said Toni. 'God, am I glad to stretch my legs. Hopefully the walk will help us sleep, probably help with the jet-lag too. I'm totally confused,' said Toni. 'I have no idea what the time would be at home.'

'Me either. Who cares?' said Flick as she studied the map.

They made it to the Accademia, which seemed from the outside like all the other three-storey buildings around Florence. The only clue to their destination was the massive queue of people. They joined the line, which seemed fifty metres long.

Flick grabbed her mum's hand and jumped up and down on the spot. 'Mum, this is so amazing. I mean, look at the road made out of small cobblestones and all the old Renaissance buildings. It's unbelievable to think we're here.'

A man was sitting nearby painting, and another was selling big colourful pictures that he had laid out on the ground. In the twenty

192

minutes they'd been in the line, four people had nearly trod on the pictures. Flick coughed as a wave of smoke floated past.

'Everyone seems to have a fag in their mouth,' she said as she leant against the wall of the Accademia.

'I should have gone to the toilet before we joined this queue,' said someone nearby.

Flick glanced at the three ladies, about her mum's age, behind them. They were all in tourist gear: shorts, walking shoes and cameras, but one was wearing a West Coast Eagles polo shirt. 'Hey, are you Aussie?' she said to them. 'We're from WA.'

'So are we!' said one of the ladies, laughing.

'What a small world,' said Toni. 'Have you been here long?'

'What? In this queue?' said another lady. They all laughed. 'No, just two nights for us. We leave this afternoon.'

They introduced themselves as Lorna, Gaye and Sue, and together they chatted for another half an hour about the best spots to visit before they finally made it in the museum. A man stood there as they went in, asking them not to take photos. As they strolled around, it was hard to grasp the age of the things they were looking at. Flick wished she could pick up some of the display pieces and feel them, just to make them seem real. There were old books and stones and sculptures, but the one thing they really wanted to see was the *David*.

'There he is, the man of the hour,' said Toni, dragging Flick towards the massive marble statue. It took their breath away. 'He's huge.' Toni looked up at the statue of David in awe. 'He looks a bit like Chad, don't you think? The face part,' she clarified with a grin.

Flick frowned and stepped forward, away from her mum's watchful eyes. She still hadn't told her mum about what happened.

'How did Michelangelo get everything to look so real? Look at his hands, the muscles in his arms.' Flick stared. It truly was the most amazing sight — solid marble that looked as soft and supple as real skin.

'Come on,' said Toni, taking her arm. There was a bench seat in a half circle around David so they went and sat down, facing his perfect marble backside.

'Now, that's a rock-hard arse,' said Flick with a smirk. But when she glanced at Toni, she wasn't smiling. 'What?'

'Has something happened with Chad?'

'Ah, yeah.' Flick squirmed on the seat. 'We, um, broke up.' She'd had time to adjust but the mention of his name still stirred up painful memories.

'Oh, honey. When?'

'Just after shearing.'

'What happened? Are you okay? Why didn't you tell me?'

'Mum, I'm fine. Chad just wasn't the right bloke for me. Just another one in my string of bad choices. I didn't want to worry you. You had enough on your plate.'

Toni pulled her into her arms. 'Never do that. I want you to always feel you can come to me and tell me anything at any time. I can't believe you kept this from me. I would have been there for you.'

They sat like that for a while, huddled together, watching the crowds of people see David for the first time. Even though it was noisy, it still felt like they were sitting in church, experiencing something powerful.

An hour later they saw the Duomo. It was like nothing Flick had ever seen, and no picture seemed to capture what her eyes saw. The cathedral stood tall over the city with its magnificent Renaissance dome, decorative arches and embellishments. Its exterior was covered in a mix of pink, white and green marble, making it stand out from the neighbouring terracotta-roofed buildings. The interior by comparison was quite plain, with the mosaic pavements the main attraction. Flick felt like lying on her belly to study the intricate mosaics that people had been walking over for hundreds of years. Then there were the elaborate stained-glass windows, each with a story to tell. Next they climbed the elegant bell tower, in matching pink, white and green marble, up the four hundred-odd narrow stairs that only fit one person at a time. They had been warned about the stairs but never expected this many. They were steep, with no handrails.

But the view was worth the climb. Flick threaded her fingers through the protective wire and gazed out the arch window. Thousands of red-tiled rooftops were scattered below like mismatched bricks. Streets seemed to disappear as buildings pressed against each other. Flick shook her head in awe. She was in bloody Florence, Italy! She was seeing things that used to belong only in books.

'Pinch me, Mum.'

'Pinch me too,' Toni said with smile.

Toni wrapped her arm around her and together they looked out over Florence. Flick took her eyes away from the incredible view to take in her mum's profile. So strong and beautiful. Flick had never been so proud, standing here beside her mum.

20

The train rocked along the tracks as Toni and Flick stared out the window at the passing land. Upon seeing the green rolling hills and small farms, Toni felt a calming peace, as if she had room to breathe. It was so different from home, which was heading into a dry, hot harvest. Here, trees were thick with colour, not like the spindly Australian mallees and gum trees with leaves only at the top. And the variety here was amazing. Cypresses, olives, Swiss pines and maples, the different colours, shapes and sizes giving the landscape such depth and interest. But it didn't make Toni love her homeland any less; if anything it made her miss it.

'What are you thinking about, Mum?' said Flick with concern.

'I don't know. I was just thinking how much I'm loving this, yet I still miss home.' Toni waved her hand over the scene before them. 'Look at this, look at where we are, and I'm here wondering if we've had a frost.' Toni laughed.

'That makes sense,' said Flick, leaning against window.

'Really?'

'Of course. The farm is you. You are the farm. It's been your whole life and I don't think you realised just how much it means to you.'

Toni smiled, in awe of her daughter. 'It's funny how life changes on you, without you even realising. I have trouble remembering you're twenty. I can still remember putting your hair up in ponytails.' Toni turned back to the window. As she watched the small farms flash past, another lurking thought made its way to her mouth. 'I wonder what Rocco does now — if he's alive, that is.' She wondered what he was passionate about. Was he still building houses? Had he been a fisherman? Or did he end up in an office? Had he been on this train before? Had he worked in any of the places they passed? And the biggest question of all — did he have any other children? If so they'd be half-siblings for Toni.

'By the end of this trip, hopefully we'll know,' Flick replied.

They lapsed into silence as they went through places like San Giovanni Valdarno and Monte-varchi in eastern Tuscany, where two-storey stone homes had small square windows and vegetable gardens crammed into available dirt, then back into the countryside, characterised by mountains, olive groves, vineyards and chestnut forests.

'Do you miss Jimmy, Mum?' said Flick, eventually breaking the silence.

It was so out of the blue that Toni had to take a moment to process her words. 'What?'

'Jimmy. Do you miss him?'

Toni raised her eyebrows. 'Is this a trick question?'

Flick laughed. 'No. I'm not blind, you know, and I just want you to know that I'm happy either way. Well, so long as either way means Jimmy still gets to hang around.'

Toni sighed. 'Well, I don't think you have to worry about that any more.' Toni couldn't help think of the way Jimmy had let her go. It was frustrating, yet wasn't it what she wanted? 'I know you love him and I don't want to do anything to jeopardise that.'

'How could it?' said Flick, leaning forward on the table between them.

Toni couldn't meet her daughter's gaze. They'd never spoken about Toni's relationships before. 'I'd hate for him to ever leave.'

'Are you worried he won't want you?'

Hell. Had Flick hit the nail on the head? Was Toni worried she wasn't good enough to keep him?

'I know Jimmy thinks you're beautiful and you guys get on so well. I just want you both to be happy. And for what it's worth, I think you're perfect for each other. He calms you down, and you inspire him.'

'Have you quite finished?' Toni asked, grinning. But she didn't forget Flick's words. 'My head just isn't in the right space for anything difficult at the moment. It's bloody complicated enough.'

'But what if you could be deliriously happy, Mum? Life's all about taking chances. If you're holding back because of me, don't. I'm old enough now to handle whatever you do.'

'Is that why you broke up with Chad? Because you weren't happy?'

'Pretty much,' said Flick. 'I think I deserve better.' She slid her hand across the table and Toni took it and gave it a squeeze.

'I did all right raising you, didn't I?' Toni's eyes glassed over with tears.

'Most of the time,' teased Flick.

When they arrived at Arezzo they went straight to the car hire place, which was across from the train station. After some quick paperwork they jumped into their little grey Mercedes five-door.

'Now we have our wheels we can search Italy for Rocco,' said Flick with a grin, which soon slipped from her face as she watched the crazy traffic around them. 'Holy crap, how are we going to get out of here?'

They didn't leave until they had their route out of Arezzo sorted. As it was, they still took a wrong turn and had to cross back over the road three times before heading in the right direction. On the way to Montone they drove on a two-lane road that was patched like a quilt. On either side of the road, mountains rose up, covered in lush, leafy maples and pines, while clouds made dark shadows over them.

'I can't find my rear-vision mirror,' groaned Flick. 'I keep looking up to the left not the right.'

Toni laughed. 'Just use your side mirrors, at least they're still the same.'

Not far out of Arezzo they came to another turn-off, but the car started to slow while the motor was revving loudly.

'Oh, crap,' said Flick. The car started moving again while she cracked up with laughter.

Toni had no idea what was so funny.

'I went to put the flicker on and I ended up putting the car out of gear,' Flick explained.

For the next few intersections Flick was all

hands as she tried to remember which side the indicator was on, and then when they turned off onto smaller roads, Toni had to remind Flick to get onto the other side of the road. At one point a car was coming straight for them and Flick had to lurch to the right to get out of its way.

They drove up a mountainside along a skinny, windy road, and a few sharp corners later they found Montone and stopped the car on the side of the road. They both had sore bellies and cheeks from all the laughing.

'Who knew driving could be so entertaining?' said Flick. A huge stone wall rose up from the edge of the road on their right, dwarfing them. 'Wow, that's, like, ten metres high.' Flick leant forward, her mouth open.

'Magnificent.' Toni pulled out the map sent to them by Steve, the Aussie guy who owned the place they were staying in. 'He said stay right and hug the massive stone wall.'

They followed the narrow one-way road around as it curved up the mountainside, the wall on their right and the other side falling away to large pine trees. Around another corner the road opened up to allow room to park cars, and nearby stood a stone arch.

'This must be the entry to the town centre,' Flick said, and parked the car.

With stiff legs they climbed out. Toni stepped towards the edge of the road, where a waist-high rock wall stood for safety. She didn't look down — her stomach wouldn't allow it; instead she gazed out across the 180-degree view before her. It was like being in a low-flying plane, able to see the patchwork paddocks and the ridges of the hills that rippled into the distance for miles. The sky was a soft blue, with not a cloud in sight. The Umbrian countryside was a slice of heaven. Here in Montone everything seemed so lush and alive. Thriving, actually. Toni wondered what Rocco's first impressions of Sunnyvale would have been. Would he have thought it flat and harsh in comparison? Had he missed the hills of his homeland?

They got their bags from the car and locked it before heading towards the immense stone archway. Only those who lived inside the walled community were allowed to bring in their small cars. Italian flags of green, white and red hung from old metal holders sunk into the wall on either side of the archway, while to the left was a collection of signs pointing directions to the *municipio*, *centro*, *informazione* and *ufficio postale*.

'Cool, we can send Nan a postcard from here,' said Flick.

At least most of the Italian words were easy to figure out, even if they couldn't pronounce them. They stepped into the archway, which became a tunnel guiding them forward. Toni could picture horses and carts on the rough-cut rectangular stones under her feet. It was like stepping back in time. The tunnel was spacious, big enough for cars to drive through, and rock arched overhead among thick wooden beams. The excitement was beyond anything Toni had ever felt; she knew they were walking towards something special. And the one thought that topped it all was knowing Rocco had grown up less than two hours from here.

21

Flick's smile was unstoppable, as was the feeling of pure awe. The tunnel opened up onto a big square made of long rectangular slabs of stone. Three — and four-storey buildings, some raw stone, others rendered in yellow, orange and peach colours, edged the area, enclosing it. The windows on each level of the buildings were dressed with dark wood or painted white shutters, and some had small flat balconies with metal railings, Italian flags draping over them. The lower floors seemed to be shops and restaurants with little awnings. Flick glanced around, spotting the post office, a newsagent and local bank. This square was obviously the heart of this quaint mountaintop village.

'Oh, it just gets better,' said Toni with a delighted sigh.

'I know. Just gorgeous. So where is our little house?' Flick asked, glancing up at the buildings. Would one of those windows be theirs for the next few days?

'Um,' said Toni, searching the piece of paper she pulled out of her bag. 'We're staying at a house called Casa Valdeste. Where are the street names?' she said, turning to look at the walls.

'*Buongiorno*,' said a young man walking past with a gentle swagger. He looked at home in his surroundings, as if he knew them well; his wide shoulders were square but relaxed. His smile reached right to his deep brown eyes. Instantly Flick felt as if she'd trust him with her life. He had rich, dark hair that flicked up at gentle angles, but it looked sexy, like he'd just ruffled his fingers through it and managed to have a style that others would pay for.

'Hi, um, *ciao*,' said Flick. 'Excuse me,' she said. She couldn't remember what that was in Italian, but it didn't matter as the man stopped.

'You need help?' he said in English.

Flick sighed with relief. He probably saw confused tourists like them every day. 'Yes, please.'

The man stepped closer and Flick got a closer look. He was the stereotypical Italian heart-throb, and she had to fight to stop her chuckle.

'Thank you.' Toni held out her map. 'We are looking for Casa Valdeste,' she said. 'Have you heard of it?'

'*Si*, this way.'

He led them off to the right of the open square and down a narrow street. There were no cars in this part of the village; the streets were too narrow. Black wrought-iron lights hung every-where, and the massive wooden doors to the homes were things of beauty. All the windows had shutters, some with pots of colourful flowers. The contrast and colour of it all was spectacular.

'I'm Toni and this is my daughter, Felicity,' Toni told their guide. 'Do you live here?'

He stopped and turned to them, holding out his hand. 'I am Stefano. I work at the restaurant for my family.'

205

'Oh, no wonder your English is good,' said Toni.

Stefano smiled, obviously pleased. '*Grazie*. I learn it at school. I practise with the tourists.' He turned and beckoned them along. He took a left, down an even smaller walkway to a dead end.

'You are here,' he said, pointing to a beautiful timber double door surrounded by original bricks and stonework. A big white tile with a blue number eighteen sat above it in the render. The black coach light above the door added to the picture-postcard effect.

'Thank you so much, Stefano,' said Toni.

'Thanks,' said Flick smiling, and sensing a blush creep up her face. He was incredibly good-looking.

'If you need me, you can find me in the Piazza Fortebraccio.' He must have noticed their blank looks. 'The main square in the village,' he added. 'Where we came from.' He pointed back the way they walked.

'Oh, right. Thank you,' said Toni. '*Grazie*,' she added.

Stefano raised his eyebrows in appreciation. '*Prego*.' Then he left.

Flick liked his dark denim jeans and deep-red polo shirt, which might have been the uniform for the restaurant.

'He's a bit cute,' said Toni while she fished out the door key from her bag. Steve had posted it to them before they left.

'Yeah, he was.'

Toni unlocked the door and they stepped inside. They were greeted with white rendered

206

walls and stunning terracotta floor tiles. They stood in a modest entry area with steps to their right. The room in front had two single beds, with a small bathroom and laundry.

'Cool. What's upstairs?' said Flick as she dumped her bags and ran up. The next level was the dining and kitchen area. It had huge exposed oak and chestnut beams on the ceiling and the timber windows were all adorned with neat little shutters. Flick opened one and was shocked to find that she could lean right out. No bars, no flywire.

'Oh God, this place is just stunning,' said Toni as she followed in behind Flick, putting her bags down. 'The kitchen is so modern.'

'And there are even more stairs!' Flick bounded up to find the last room at the top, which had a double bed and generous ensuite. 'Mum, there's even a sitting area by the window. You should see the view from up here. It's just amazing.'

Toni joined her and they both gazed out over the rooftops to the rolling hills of Italy beyond.

'It's so much better than I could even have imagined,' Toni said.

'How lucky are we? We'll even be able to see the sunset from here.'

Toni put her arm around Flick. 'I can't believe my real father grew up in this amazing country,' she said wistfully.

'If we unpack, we can go for a quick explore before dinner. What do you reckon?'

'Sounds like a plan.'

'Shall we try out Stefano's restaurant?' Flick asked.

'We must! And we have to try out the local dishes.' Toni headed for the stairs. 'You can have this room, I'll go downstairs.'

'Aw, thanks, Mum.'

Flick unpacked her toiletries, and within ten minutes they were ready to sight-see and then have dinner.

'Should we go straight to Chiaravalle tomorrow?' asked Flick.

'Yes, it's what we came for, isn't it?'

'Uh-huh. I saw a dictionary at the top of the staircase. I might look up a few words and write them down so we can show people, to save us having to play charades. The guidebook we brought doesn't seem to cover looking for lost relatives,' Flick said with a chuckle.

*　*　*

Toni shut the door behind them and they followed the stone path up and around more three-storey medieval homes. As they rounded a corner they found themselves standing beside the massive city wall. High on the hill they stood, trying to catch their breath from the climb and from the majestic view that now spread out before them. Huge pine trees grew around the wall, and Flick felt as if she could almost touch the tops of them. Rolling hills rippled into the distance, covered with all shades of green and brown patchwork paddocks. But they weren't like the big square paddocks back home. Here they were smaller and of many different shapes and sizes, interrupted by ancient oaks and olive trees.

Flick embraced her mum as they just stood there. They had run out of superlatives and another 'wow' just didn't cut it.

They continued up around the edge of the wall towards a church, the countryside following them. They decided they loved this rural part of Italy even more than the cities, which wasn't surprising. Both had been most eager to see this side of Italian life, how people farmed and lived out here.

'We have to do that 12-k walk, Mum. The guidebook said it goes right through all the farms.'

'As long as we don't get shot by gun-wielding farmers.'

'That's why Steve has that warning not to leave the road. They go bird shooting at any time, apparently,' Flick said, pulling a face. She looked up at the church as they walked towards its courtyard. Flick leant over the stone wall that surrounded the courtyard; it was a sheer drop down to the road.

'Please stand back,' said Toni.

'But look, I can see our car.' Flick leant over a bit further and watched her mum pale.

'They really need to make the walls higher,' said Toni. 'Anyone could accidentally lean too far. Imagine kids. You would have been climbing all over that as a kid.'

'Come on — looks like these steps take us back down to the main square. Let's find some food.' Walking away, Flick ducked her head under the wide branches of the shady trees planted along the wall and dodged cute little bench seats. 'It's so quiet and peaceful.'

'I don't think this would be a safe place at night. So many steps and uneven ground.'

'Not too many grappas for you, then!' Flick teased.

In the square they found the yellow rendered building that housed the restaurant.

'*L'Antica Osteria*,' Flick read from the sign, with terrible pronunciation, as they got closer. Cast-iron tables and chairs sat outside the restaurant, surrounded by green leafy plants in terracotta pots to section off the area. 'Shall we eat outside? It's such a nice evening.'

'Sounds perfect,' said Toni as she surveyed the menu. 'Oh, thank God, they have English translations.'

'*Ciao, belle!*'

Flick looked up to see Stefano strolling towards them. '*Ciao, Stefano.*'

'You eat with us tonight?' he said and she nodded while trying not to bat her eyelashes. She shouldn't try so hard to forget Chad.

'Yes, we'd love to sit outside if that's okay,' said Toni.

'*Si, si, per favore*,' he said, waving to the empty tables.

They took their seats and Stefano handed them the menus. '*Ecco!* I recommend anything with the truffle. It is what we are known for,' he said, then left them to decide.

Toni reminded them that they didn't have to

try everything tonight. 'I'm sure you won't mind coming back again!' she teased.

Stefano returned for their order, pen poised.

'I'll have the egg and white truffle to begin with, then the ricotta gnocchi in black truffle cream, and I'll try the *bees-te-ka*?' Toni attempted the word for steak while pointing to the one she wanted.

'*Bistecca Fiorentina di Angus Irlandese. Fantastico*, yes.'

Flick ordered a pasta called *pici Toscani* in *crema di carbonara*, and when Stefano brought their food they took their time, enjoying each offering and the atmosphere. It seemed like there was an even mix of tourists and locals. To finish off, they had the best tiramisu they'd ever tasted.

'Jimmy would be so jealous,' Flick said and watched her mum's expression with interest.

'Someone has to keep the home fires burning,' she said, without giving away anything.

It wasn't until Stefano came back to see if they needed more wine did it seem like he had time to chat.

'So why you ladies come to Montone?' he asked.

'We've come to look for an Italian prisoner of war who was on our farm many years ago. We want to find him, see if he's still alive,' said Flick.

'*Assolutamente* no! No way! All this way?'

'Yes. He built the house I live in.'

Stefano was so interested he asked if he could join them at their table.

'Please,' said Flick, and continued to fill him in on her quest. 'So tomorrow we are going to

Chiaravalle to see what we can find.'

'*Fantastico*! If you need anything or have problems, you find me here, okay?'

'Thanks, Stefano, how kind.' Toni got up. 'I'll just go pay,' she said quietly. Flick hadn't mentioned Rocco was her mum's father. She'd leave that to Toni's discretion.

'So, Stefano, how old are you?' Flick asked, hoping it wasn't too forward.

'I am twenty-three, and you?'

'Twenty,' she said, smiling. 'I work on our farm, Sunnyvale, with my mum and my grandmother. We have just over 8000 acres and about 2500 sheep. Keeps us busy.'

Stefano's eyes bulged. 'That is a lot. You must be very rich.'

Flick laughed, she couldn't help it. She could see how he could come to that conclusion. 'No, not rich. Lots of land but it doesn't make much money. We have lots of land in Australia, compared to here.'

'Yes, your farm would take up all of Montone and more.' He shook his head, still trying to picture it.

He kept asking her questions about the farm and Australia, so she didn't get a chance to ask him any. Toni came back and Stefano was called away.

'Sorry, I must work. *Arrivederci*.'

'Yes. *Ciao*. Thanks for a lovely night, Stefano,' said Flick with a pang of disappointment as they stood to leave.

Stefano collected the last of their dishes while watching them depart, a cute smile on his handsome face. Flick could feel his gaze follow them across the piazza until they turned down their street and giggled their way along the cobblestones, all the way back to their new home.

22

Toni was up early and snuck out of the house to watch the sunrise from the area by the church. As she neared the seats between the trees she saw a figure leaning over the rock wall, looking out over the countryside. Only one person would feel the need to lean that far over.

'And here I was tiptoeing out of the house so I didn't disturb you,' Toni said with a chuckle.

'Hey, Mum.'

Toni joined her by the edge of the hill and kept her eyes on the horizon and the many shapes of the hills around them. She was fine with that; it was the steep death-drop straight down that freaked her out.

'A sunrise anywhere is beautiful, hey? Just like looking at the stars to feel closer to home,' said Flick. 'I miss Fella always being at my side. I miss them all. But I'm glad you're here.' She pressed herself against Toni's side.

'Me too.' Toni put her arm around her daughter and they stood, watching as the sunrays hit the tips of the hills while the valleys appeared as if they were filled with fine smoke. She took in the village of Montone beside them, the sun basking the stone walls in light while everything else still lay in darkness, as if the town had been singled out by the big man himself.

'Are you worried about today? Nervous?' said Flick softly.

'I'm trying not to think about it,' Toni said truthfully. 'That way I can't be disappointed, you know? Just go in with no expectations.'

But Toni's mind was already defying her, as it kept wandering off to consider whether she'd meet Rocco today or find his resting place at the local cemetery. She bit her lip at the thought.

'You seem a million miles away. If you tell me you were thinking about our lambs going on the truck this week, I'll leave you behind!'

Toni laughed. 'No, I wasn't. I was just lost in all of this.' With one last glance they walked back to their little borrowed house and got ready for their day trip.

They headed out for the car and Toni noticed Flick eyeing the restaurant for signs of the young Mr Stefano.

'No shops open for breakfast yet,' Flick said.

'We'll find something on the road,' said Toni as they reached their rental. They were yet to get to a shop for some breakfast supplies. Maybe after they'd found Rocco. *If* they found Rocco.

Toni was impressed with Flick's driving as she navigated down the extremely narrow roads, slotting the car between the parked cars and the rock wall. 'Your car would never fit down here,' Toni laughed. They passed another one of those three-wheeled small utes. It was so small that a man was lifting it to change the tyre. Flick stopped the car.

'Quick, Mum, take a photo of it. We have to show Jimmy.'

'Yeah, he'd find that really funny.' Toni reached for the camera and quickly leant out her window and snapped a shot.

They continued down the hill towards Umbertide.

With Flick in the driver's seat, the navigating was up to Toni. Putting on her reading glasses, she unfolded the map. 'Okay, we need to get onto the E45 and then the SS219 and SS76.'

At some point things no longer made sense on the map, so they stopped at a roadhouse off the main road. 'I think we took a wrong turn,' said Toni.

Flick rolled her eyes. 'Let's grab something to eat while we're here.'

Inside the roadhouse was a massive coffee machine. They ordered two cappuccinos and two sweet croissants, all for two euro — less than two dollars fifty Australian — and ate at the bar like the locals.

'Best coffee ever,' said Flick licking her lips.

Toni couldn't disagree. She was fast learning that you didn't get a bad coffee in Italy, no matter where you went. She studied the map.

'Whoops. We seem to be heading in the wrong direction to where we want to go,' Toni said, and they burst out laughing, as they'd done something similar on their way to Montone.

Luckily there were so many little towns that it was easy to pick up on the mistake and turn around, and it had been a beautiful drive through the mountains and experiencing the tunnels. How could they be upset about taking a different route? They'd hoped to see the Mediterranean but only caught odd glimpses between the houses. They drove straight in to

216

Chiaravalle and parked on the main street.

Toni got the parking ticket sorted before they locked the car. Flick fished out the Italian words she'd looked up last night. 'I think it would have been easier to have Stefano help us with this,' she said.

'I'm sure people will work it out. Let's try in here first,' said Toni, pointing to an open door. It was hard to know what the shop was from the outside as there were no large display windows, just a sign they couldn't read over the wide door. But inside was a big display fridge with fresh meats and cheeses. Toni was a farmer — she knew her different cuts of meat and varieties — but this was Italy, where rolls of cured meat ruled: pancetta and prosciutto, plus others she'd never heard of like speck, culatello, coppa and guanciale. It was a feast for the eyes and made her mouth begin to water.

Flick bypassed the array of deli food and went to an older lady waiting in line to be served. '*Ciao, mi scusi*,' said Flick. She pointed to her sheet of paper, at the Italian words she hoped meant, 'Can you help me, please? I'm looking for . . . ' Then she pointed to '*citta municipio*', '*palazzo comunale*' and '*consiglio comunale*'. To hedge her bets she'd written down the translation for 'city hall', 'town hall' and 'town council'.

'*Si*,' said the lady, who then rattled off words they had no hope of understanding. She took them back outside the shop and gestured further down the road they were on.

'*Grazie*.' They continued down the street,

217

which had cars parked on the right while one-way traffic drove past, making it feel like a bustling city. The buildings on either side of the road were two or three storeys, with shops on the ground floor. Some of the shops had cute little awnings arched out over the pathway.

'It's so hard to see what these shops are. There are no big signs on the buildings,' said Flick. Only the pharmacies had a neon-green cross that made them easily recognisable.

'There are signs, we just aren't familiar with their branding so we don't see them. We just have to keep looking.'

When they had walked as far as they dared, Flick asked another person on the street. But this woman only waved her hand further up the street, with a left turn in there somewhere.

'*Grazie*,' said Toni, and off they continued, wondering how they'd ever imagined they could just turn up and find what they needed.

A small courtyard opened up to the left, and they saw an oval logo on a large glass-fronted building. 'That might be it. Looks quite official.'

Inside they found an empty foyer with stairs. They climbed these and reached a long corridor with many doors leading off it. All the signs were written in Italian. Just then Flick spotted a man in a police uniform.

'*Ciao*, um . . . ' She faltered, then shoved her trusty piece of paper towards him. 'We are trying to find records,' she said while pointing out words.

'Help?' he asked.

'Yes, please.' Relief for them both. 'We are

trying to find information on Rocco Valducci. He was an Italian prisoner of war.' Flick shuffled the sheets until she found the record sheet from the National Archives showing Rocco's name and date of birth.

By the look of the policeman's face, his English wasn't too good.

'Slow down, Flick,' said Toni.

Flick tried again. 'We came from Australia to find information on Rocco. Is this the right place?' she said more slowly.

The policeman took the record sheet and gestured for them to follow him to the desk at the end of the corridor. Then he started talking rapidly in Italian to the lady who sat there. He finally turned back to them. 'You need down,' he said, pointing down through the floor.

He obviously took pity on them and their blank faces, as he smiled and said, 'Come.' He was a nice-looking man, probably in his thirties.

'Thank you. We really want to find out if Rocco is still alive, or find his family. He stayed at our farm during the war,' said Flick.

Toni wondered if the policeman understood any of what Flick had just said.

They followed him back downstairs and into an adjoining building. He ushered them through a queue of locals to an office lady who tried to assist them but unfortunately she knew no English. They could only stand there like mutes as the policeman spoke to her in Italian.

The lady started waving her hands wildly across her body in what looked like an emphatic

'No!' Then she was shaking her head and saying words like *'personale'* and *'privato'*. Toni knew she had to try another option, as this lady clearly wasn't going to share any private information.

'He's my father,' she said clearly while pointing to his picture and then to herself. *'Papà?'*

'Padre?' said the policeman.

Toni smiled and nodded.

He spoke to the lady again and Toni got the feeling he'd just gone in to bat for them. It sounded like he was trying to persuade her. Australia was mentioned a few times, as if he was pointing out how far they had travelled. Then they disappeared back into the office.

'Okay,' said Flick, sitting on one of the chairs against the wall. 'I guess we just wait then.'

'I think he was trying to help us,' said Toni.

'Poor guy. I hope we aren't taking him away from his work.'

The locals in line glanced at them curiously.

'Man, what are they doing in there?' Flick sighed heavily. It had been nearly ten minutes. 'I hope he's not organising our deportation.'

Finally the policeman reappeared. He handed over a piece of paper with a name and number on it. 'His brother,' he said. 'You call him.'

'Oh, wow, thank you,' said Flick, taking it.

'Oh.' Toni felt a swell of emotions. Excitement, nerves and even panic. She had an uncle?

'Speak no English,' the policeman warned, shaking his head.

Flick smiled. 'That's okay. We have a friend who may be able to help.'

Toni knew straightaway who she was thinking of.

'Thank you so much for helping us.' Toni realised she'd forgotten her manners in all the kerfuffle. 'My name is Toni,' she said. 'My daughter, Felicity.' She smiled at the friendly man who looked so smart in his uniform.

'Mimmo,' he said.

Toni touched his arm briefly. 'Grazie, Mimmo, thank you so much. We wouldn't have this without you.'

He smiled, nodded and opened the door for them.

Outside they just stood there, trying to process what had happened.

'Wow,' said Flick looking at the name and phone number.

Toni was dying to see the name written on it but her hands stayed by her side. 'If it wasn't for Mimmo we wouldn't have that. We might not have even made it past the lady at the desk on the second floor.' He had helped her get that much closer to finding her real father. Only she couldn't express just what that meant to her. Not when she didn't fully understand it herself. All she knew was that with each passing day, finding Rocco had become more and more important to her, as if she was searching for the other half of her soul.

'We were sent an angel, I think,' said Flick with a grin. 'All in a day's work for the local policeman, right? But I think he has his words mixed up. This isn't Rocco's brother. It's a girl's name, see?'

Toni took the scrap of paper. Block print spelled out a name: Valducci Francesca.

'I guess they write the last name first,' Flick said.

But Toni wasn't listening. She was too busy staring at the name in front of her. *Francesca*. Was this her aunty? Was it really possible?

'So you think this could be his family?'

Toni shrugged. 'Let's just wait and see. We should head back and see if Stefano can help us get in touch with this person. I don't think we're going to find anyone here who can speak English and I think we've taken up enough of Mimmo's time.'

'I agree. Let's go see Stefano! Just because his English is so impeccable, of course,' she laughed.

Toni wished they could just call Francesca now.

Then all of a sudden she was hit with a terrifying thought. Why had they just been given Rocco's sister's number and not his own?

23

On the way home, they stopped into Umbertide, a bigger town near Montone, and stocked up on some lunch and fruit before heading off to their little hillside home. Flick merged with the traffic and found her way out of town. She was starting to love the little grey Mercedes. It was so compact and fun to drive around the narrow streets.

They parked and walked to the Piazza Fortebraccio, where Flick glanced at the restaurant.

'Why don't you go see and if Stefano is there and I'll put the kettle on? Maybe he can come back and use our phone?' Toni suggested.

Flick smiled at her mum, noticing that her legs looked amazing in her soft blue skirt. She appeared so different out of her work clothes and with the unfamiliar scenery behind her. Toni may have looked carefree and beautiful, but Flick saw an anxious, almost confused, look in her eyes. This would be a really hard time for her.

Flick headed straight past the outside tables and into the restaurant. The last of the lunchtime crowd was just about gone. Inside were more beautiful rock walls. It made her wonder about the person who had built them, and what life was like back then.

'Felicity,' said Stefano, waving, and she waved back and made her way to the counter. She loved the maroon polo shirt on him as it brought out his dark eyes, plus it fitted him nicely too. He turned to an older man beside him at the counter and said something in Italian before turning back to her.

'*Ciao*, Felicity. This is my father, Massimo.'

He spoke more Italian to Massimo. He was a lean man, his eyes were wrinkled with wisdom and age but his smile was youthful and just like Stefano's. She heard her name mentioned and had to admit she loved the way it rolled off his tongue. *Felicity* — so playful and romantic.

Massimo asked his son a question and Stefano replied, 'Australia', then turned back to Flick. 'My parents speak no English, I am a translator,' he said. 'How did you go today?' He leant in, his whole face captivated as he waited for her reply. Chad had never seemed that engaged with her unless she'd just taken her clothes off.

'That's actually why I'm here. We need your help, but only if you're free?' she asked, wringing her hands.

He grinned as if she'd just done him a huge favour. 'Of course I can help.'

Beautiful straight white teeth and perfect plump lips; no wonder his smile was so fascinating. 'Oh, thank you. I don't know what we'd do if we hadn't found you.' Flick waited while Stefano cleared things with his father. Massimo waved him off good-naturedly.

'So, how can I help?' He gestured to a table. 'You want to sit?'

'Actually . . . ' Flick felt awkward proposition-ing him. 'Would you mind coming back to our

224

place?' She gave him her most innocent smile. 'I promise we're not out to harm you,' she teased.

Stefano held his hand to his chest. 'I'm sure I be okay. So tell me how it went. You find him?'

Side by side, they headed out of the restaurant. 'Kind of. You wouldn't believe what happened . . . ' Flick told him the whole story, and how Mimmo had come to their rescue. 'Only thing is, she doesn't speak English.'

'You need me, yes?'

'If you don't mind, we were hoping you could call her for us and see if we could meet with her. We could either meet here or at her place, if she didn't mind . . . only, then we'd need a translator to go with us.' Flick made a sweet face.

Stefano waved his finger at her. 'You need me more.'

She chuckled. 'Yes, but only if you want to. We will pay you for your time. How much time do you have? I don't want to take you away from your work,' she said.

They paused by the big double doors. Stefano was just that bit taller so she had to look up to meet his dark eyes. He smelt good too, like the seasoned steak and white truffles from the restaurant.

'No, no. I help you. It is nice to be with an Aussie.'

Flick realised that he was probably waiting for her to let him in. Feeling a little silly, she pushed the door open. 'Come in, just head up the stairs.'

Toni was sitting at the table looking over Rocco's records. 'Oh, wonderful,' she said. 'Thank you so much for coming to our aid,

225

Stefano. Can I get you a drink?'

'No, thank you.'

'Please take a seat.' Stefano sat down beside Toni, and Flick sat opposite. 'How long can you stay?' asked Toni.

'I am free until six,' he said with a relaxed smile. His hands, fingers woven together, lay on the table. They were long, lean fingers and his hands were clean, unlike the calluses and dirt ingrained in Jimmy's hands.

'We won't keep you that long, I promise.'

Flick slid the sheet with Rocco's photo and details to Stefano. 'This is Rocco, and here's a photo of him on our farm.' She took the photo of Rocco and the kangaroo out of the folder for him.

'Wow, that is a big kangaroo. Do you have many?'

'Yes, we do.'

He was focused on the photos, and from this angle she realised just how long and dark his eyelashes were.

Stefano looked up. 'So you want me to ask the sister if Rocco is her brother and if you can visit her?'

'Yes, please. We'd still like to meet up with her, if she doesn't mind. We could give her the records we have of Rocco's. And show her the photos.' Flick was picking at her nails while she spoke. She wasn't sure why this was nerve-racking. Maybe it was Stefano and his eyelashes, or maybe it was being so close to finding out more on Rocco.

'Actually, Stefano,' Toni said, 'I've just found

out that Rocco is my father. So this lady could possibly be my aunty.'

His face lit up. 'Ah, so you half Italian,' he said warmly, as if she were his relative.

'I guess so.'

Flick felt a surge of pride for her mum. It seemed like she'd just taken another step forward. Maybe by the time they got home she'd be happy to see Nan and put her anger behind her.

'I call her now?' asked Stefano.

Toni reached for Francesca's phone number. 'That would be great. The phone is upstairs.'

'This way,' said Flick, standing up, thankful she'd at least made the bed this morning.

All three went up the stairs and gathered near the desk by the window. Stefano stuck his head out and looked around. 'Ah, you get the music,' he said, pointing to a large building with a wide front staircase. 'The children do music lessons there.'

'I wondered,' said Flick. She'd heard drums and violins. 'It's beautiful, something we certainly don't get at home.' She pulled the chair out for Stefano and Toni gave him the number. Then they stood back by the stairs to give him some breathing space.

Stefano had the phone to his ear and was soon speaking rapid Italian. He nodded his thanks when Flick handed him a pen and he began writing things down. Flick stepped back beside Toni.

'I wish I knew what they were saying,' whispered Toni.

Stefano looked up. 'Can you go back to Chiaravalle tomorrow morning?'

'Yes!' they both said.

Stefano smiled and nodded while jumping back into Italian, then finally ending the call.

'Well?' Flick couldn't contain her curiosity. Toni was wringing her hands.

'She has a brother Rocco and we will go meet her tomorrow at her house. You can talk more.'

'Brilliant.' Toni reached out and gripped Stefano's arm. 'Thank you. Is Rocco alive?'

'*Si*, she talked as if he alive and not past.'

Flick's jaw dropped. She hadn't dared let herself believe it, and glancing at her mum's similar expression, she wasn't the only one. 'Oh my God, Mum. Your real dad is alive!'

Toni staggered to her bed and sat down. Flick shot to her side, unsure whether she would faint or throw up.

'I didn't really want to get my hopes up,' Toni said softly.

Flick really wanted to ring Nan and tell her the good news but the phone was only for local calls. She would have to wait until they returned home; not even a postcard or letter would reach her before they themselves would.

'She's happy to talk with you, interested why you find Rocco. I didn't say. Thought it better we tell her in person.'

'Thanks so much. You said 'we', so you'll come with us tomorrow?' In her mind she was crossing her fingers. 'You can get off work?'

He nodded. 'Of course. I get to help two beautiful Australians.' His eyes found Flick,

228

causing the air to thin as if they were on a mountaintop rather than a hill.

Flick mumbled another 'thank you', but it just didn't seem enough for what he was offering. But then again, if he ever came to Australia, there's no doubt that she would drop everything to do the same for him. It was good to know that human kindness was still alive and kicking.

They returned to the kitchen to work out their schedule for tomorrow and check the maps. Stefano was so easy to talk to, and soon they were chatting about the differences between Italy and Australia — comparing the cost of things, what his schooling had been like and whatever farming-related information Toni could get out of him.

'So have you seen all of the village here?' he asked Flick an hour later.

'A little.'

'I will walk you around the rest if you like?'

'Oh, that would be great.' A personal tour guide, and a handsome one to boot.

Toni was staring at the world map that they'd used to show Stefano where Sunnyvale was. Flick would have bet money on it that she was feeling homesick or stressing over Rocco. Knowing he was alive would give her something to think about all night.

'You coming, Mum?'

'Sorry, what?'

Flick repeated herself. Toni shook her head. 'I might give it a miss and write in my journal instead. But please, take lots of photos for me.' She smiled with a slight twinkle in her eye, and

Flick knew exactly what she was up to.

'If you insist.' Flick grinned back, then hugged her and followed Stefano down to the door, forgetting all about her camera.

As they walked up steep brick-paved streets, down rock steps, under arches and through little tunnels, Stefano told her about the history of Montone, including the noble family of Fortebracci. He embellished with detail on the festivals, dancers on stilts, the colour, music and medieval dress.

'On Easter Monday the Montonesi dress up in medieval clothes and play some of the medieval sports such as archery. La Donazione della Santa Spina, which is the Gift of the Holy Thorn — this is a festival day for us. It is said a thorn from the crown of Jesus was presented to Carlo Fortebraccio and is now held by the church since 1473.'

Hearing him speak and say the Italian names for things was like listening to music from another country: hypnotic, beautiful and different. Flick stretched her arms out and swung them freely as if scooping up every word. She felt like jelly, all loose and relaxed. 'Wow, you have so much history. It's amazing to be able to see it and touch it.' Flick admired the balconies above them, draped with colourful flowers. It was all so enchanting.

Stefano reached for her hand and gently pulled her towards another high sloping street. 'Did you know that the Umbria Film Festival is here also? They show many of the world's latest films in the Piazza Fortebraccio.'

'Really?'

'Yes, a big event and always fun. Come this way, at the very top is Rocca di Braccio.'

She let him lead her up, enjoying the warmth of his hand and the connection. They passed a stately bell tower and came to magnificent remains.

'It was destroyed in 1478 by Pope Sixtus IV.' He let her hand slip away as they stopped.

Flick wandered around until she came to the edge of another wall with yet another stunning panoramic view. The air seemed as clear and vibrant as the landscape itself.

'I don't think I could ever get sick of this view,' she said, more to herself than to him.

'Maybe you will come back?'

She turned to Stefano. He was leaning against the short wall, watching her carefully.

'That would be cool. It's so different from home. You should come to Australia. I'd show you around, you could help out on our farm,' she said with a grin. 'We'd give you a job.'

He squinted. 'How much would you pay me?' he asked teasingly.

Flick told him the going hourly rate and laughed as his eyes exploded.

'*Incredibile!* Maybe I should come. You would take care of me, *si?*'

'Yes, Aussie bush hospitality at its best. Bonfires, sheep work, walks up the granite rock, wildflowers and kangaroos. You'd love it.'

Some of her fringe was blowing across her face in the slight breeze. Stefano was watching it intently. For a moment she thought he was going

231

to reach out and touch it. She smiled nervously.

Softly, he said a few words in Italian. '*Hai un bel sorriso.*'

'You do remember I don't know any Italian.'

'Lucky for me,' he said, turning away from her and starting to walk back along the path.

It just made her more curious. She reached for his arm, and he paused. 'What did you say?'

'*Hai un bel sorriso*,' he said slowly, and shot her a cheeky smile.

'Stefano,' she growled. 'In English.'

He chuckled. 'Not today. Come, I go back to work and see if someone can work instead of me tomorrow.'

Flick hurried after him. 'You said you'd come with us without even checking on work first?'

His polo shirt rose up above his belt as he shrugged giving Flick a glimpse of his narrow waist. Her breath caught in her throat.

'I know it will be okay. It is a family business, my parents will understand.'

Back at the restaurant, a similar-aged girl was setting up some tables but stopped to stare at them. Flick wondered if she was Stefano's sister. She had dark wavy hair and a generous mouth.

The pretty girl approached Stefano and started talking to him while looking Flick up and down. Something in her gaze was uncomfortable and Flick got the distinct impression that she probably wasn't a sister.

'This is Sofia, she works with us. She will cover my lunch shift tomorrow.'

Stefano looked pleased, which was more than she could say about Sofia. Her dark eyebrows were pressed together, eyeing Flick accusingly.

They spoke more Italian, and Flick felt like a third wheel. 'Um, look. I'll go and leave you be,' she said, cutting in.

'You coming for dinner?'

There was hope on his face and it set her heart aflutter.

'Sure, you know a good restaurant?'

Now Sofia was watching their interaction with a scowl. It wasn't fun being the odd one out.

Stefano's lips curled up at the edges. 'I do.'

His wink was so quick she nearly missed it.

Flick waved, including Sofia in her goodbye. '*Ciao.*'

She jogged back to their house with a stupid grin. She was glad they were coming back for dinner. It felt like she'd known him for weeks instead of a few days. How could that be? And then tomorrow they would be spending even more time together. She couldn't wait.

24

The next day Toni sat in the back of the car as she watched Stefano driving, with Flick in the front keeping him company. The two were hitting it off so well. He was such a lovely young man, so kind, and with beautiful manners. He had a cheeky streak, which reminded her of Jimmy, a characteristic that made life a little interesting and fun. Flick, it seemed, had inherited similar tastes.

Toni wished she hadn't thought about Jimmy again, but it was hard not to. She saw visions of him in the morning light, she caught aspects of him in Stefano and she recognised him in some of the things Flick said. He was embedded in everything around her and their time apart was proving much harder than she'd anticipated. She felt as if she'd lost half her brain; she was so used to being with him every day and he could always predict her actions. He would be taking good care of the farm and Maggie, she knew that without a doubt. Her trust in him was faultless. In her eyes, he was perfect.

'I care for you,' he'd said. Did he really mean that? Was he aware of what all that entailed? Is that why he let her go? Toni had never really loved anyone besides her family. Could she handle things if they didn't work out? Could you mend a 53-year-old heart if it broke?

Tracing her lips with her finger, she

remembered his kiss by the bonfire. Closing her eyes, she felt his breath as he whispered against her ear. With a sigh, she realised she was just tormenting herself.

The kids in front were laughing and Toni tried to focus on their conversation. They had such easygoing natures and bounced off each other as if they had been friends for years. Since dinner last night, she had noticed a change. They joked and teased, and the looks did linger. Stefano hadn't waited on them like the previous night, instead they had a girl who wasn't as friendly. Her English had been basic, to the point of being rude.

'What do you reckon, Mum?' said Flick, looking back. She wore a sweet white lace dress and had her hair out. Even without make-up she was gorgeous.

'About what?' Toni knew the extra effort was for a certain young man driving their car. Luckily for them the weather had been lovely during the day. But Stefano had mentioned it had been raining on and off lately.

'Stefano said he would take us out to Gubbio tomorrow. It's not far from us and there are medieval, Gothic and Renaissance monuments and an old Roman amphitheatre.'

'It is also known for its ceramics. You have some in your place in Montone,' said Stefano without taking his eyes off the road.

'Wow, that sounds great.' Toni leant forward. 'Are you sure you can spare the time?'

'I don't work till dinner, so if we go early we can be back in time. You will need a few good

235

hours there to explore.'

Flick was watching her, eagerly waiting for her decision. 'That would be wonderful, Stefano. Thank you.'

'*Prego*,' he said.

Toni was used to the Italian word for 'you're welcome'. Every time they thanked someone, '*prego*' followed. She could just about add the basic greetings to her Italian vocabulary now. For a moment, she wondered how nice it would be to go home and say something to Jimmy in Italian. What was Italian for 'I care for you too, but I'm scared'?

'We're here, right on time too. Thanks, Stefano. Last time we took a detour without even realising,' said Flick as a sign for Chiaravalle went past. Flick guided him to the right street and he parked out the front of a simple house just on the outskirts of town.

Toni grabbed all the records and photos as they got out.

They all fell into step as they walked through the knee-high gate. The house was rendered, with one half in an apricot colour and the other half, which jutted out towards the road, a shade of green. There was a small vacant block by the house that had a vegetable garden, and grass grew through pavers that connected it to the house. They paused at a pine front door with two gold knobs. Two sets of eyes watched Toni. They were leaving it up to her. Lifting her hand, she clenched her fist to stop the shakes and knocked quickly.

Flick rubbed her hands together. 'I'm so excited.'

Toni nodded, unable to speak. Last night they had talked into the night, running on tea and nerves, discussing where Rocco could be. Was he married? Did he have kids? Was he happy? Would he see them? They had talked until their eyelids had drooped and yawns grew many.

Stefano slid a hand into his jeans pocket. He wore a white T-shirt with a red strip across the front. Today he smelt young, fresh and manly, no lingering scent of restaurant food. The sparkle in Flick's eyes brought a warmth to Toni's heart; she loved seeing her daughter so happy and alive. She wore a similar expression when she returned from watching a sunset with Contractor and Fella. Toni was blessed to have such a charismatic, bubbly daughter. Simon had given her the gift of an angel. Shame stabbed at her — Simon didn't know how amazing his own daughter was, but over the years Toni had grown to live with the pangs of guilt. Why did they seem even more intense today?

The door rattled open to reveal a medium-built woman wearing slippers and a tracksuit, similar to something Maggie would wear.

'*Buongiorno*,' she said softly. Her faded brown hair was cut short, and lines tracked along her face.

'*Buongiorno*. Francesca?' asked Toni.

The older lady smiled and gestured for them to come in.

Stefano continued with introductions as Francesca led them to a sitting area. Toni and Flick smiled, greeting her with '*ciao*' when they heard their names mentioned.

Francesca waved to the worn yellow couch while she sat in an upright chair next to it. It was a tight fit as all three of them sat down. The room was small and had white walls decorated with photos, plates and some religious mementos. A chest sat in the corner of the room, overflowing with kids' toys.

It was difficult to know what to say, especially when poor Stefano had to repeat it for them. But seeing as though he knew a lot about their story, he took the lead and spoke to her at great length. Toni handed over the records and showed Francesca the photo.

She nodded emphatically and grinned. '*Si*, Rocco. *Fratello*.'

'Yes, he's her brother,' said Stefano.

Toni's stomach released the twisted knot it had been forming since they arrived. She knew without a doubt they had the right family.

'Where is he?' asked Flick.

Stefano repeated it and more discussion continued, then a look of shock spread across Stefano's face. '*Scherzi!*' he said.

'What? What'd she say?' pressed Toni. She scooted forward on the couch. She needed to know now. She was almost sure that Francesca had said Australia. But that couldn't be possible, could it?

'You not believe where Rocco is.' He paused, his eyes wide.

'Montone?' said Flick. 'Arezzo?'

Stefano shook his head. A smile tugged at his perfect lips. 'Western Australia.'

'What!' Flick and Toni said in unison.

238

Francesca nodded as they gazed at her.

'How? Why? When?' Toni rattled off.

'She said he returned to Australia after the war and now lives there.'

Toni was so astonished she couldn't process what this meant. She turned to Flick, her eyes as huge as party balloons.

'No way. We came all the way to Italy to find Rocco and he's in our own state?'

Stefano smiled at Flick and confirmed it. He seemed almost as excited as they were by the discovery, swept up in their saga.

Toni blinked back tears of surprise while her mind raced. 'Please ask her why he went back,' she prompted Stefano gently.

Francesca stood up after his question, went to a petite wooden cupboard and pulled out a small album. She flicked through it as she sat back down, sliding a few photos free from under the clear cover and passing them across to Toni. She instantly recognised the same picture they had, of Rocco and Giulio with the kangaroo. Tears welled in her eyes. Flick was also blinking rapidly, and her smile reflected how Toni felt. This was a major connection. Something linking Italy to Sunnyvale, their history intertwined.

'These are some that her brother gave her,' said Stefano.

'Oh, we have these same photos.' Toni got out the ones they'd also brought, of Rocco by the new house and one with the Fullers. She passed them to Francesca, who laughed and nodded while mumbling something in Italian. She looked just as amazed at what they shared.

Francesca held out the photo of Uncle Charlie, Maggie and their parents and pointed at Maggie.

Stefano translated Francesca's words: 'Rocco returned to Australia for this woman. He said he loved her. It was three years before he was allowed back.'

Toni's jaw dropped. Flick was staring with the same expression. Rocco *had* come for Maggie.

'But Nan never saw him.' Flick looked grief-stricken. She reached across Toni for Stefano's hand. 'Please ask her what happened after he got to Australia?'

Waiting for Francesca's words to be translated was excruciating.

'She said that he went to Australia, got work with a farmer who had um . . . sponsored, I think is the right word?' When they nodded he continued. 'They sponsored him and then after time he bought his own farm. She says he never talked of this girl again.'

They all looked at Maggie in the black and white photo and fell quiet.

Toni pulled some of the other photos Francesca had closer, ones of an older Rocco — maybe in his late twenties — standing by a tent between gum trees, and another of him on what must have been his wedding day, looking older again and very handsome beside his blonde bride. It was surreal to think that this was her father. Emotions rolled around her like waves, bringing a new feeling each time: sadness, joy, loss, regret.

'He got married. Wow.' It was very likely she had siblings too.

'This is him a few years ago, when he last visited Italy,' said Stefano, indicating the photo Francesca had mentioned.

'Could we have this one, please?' asked Flick. 'Tell her I'd like to take it to show my grandmother. I can make a copy of it and post it back. Tell her that this is my grandmother.'

Francesca reached for her hand and nodded, talking to Stefano some more.

'She said you can take it. She doesn't know what happened. He did mention the farm and talked a lot about the girl he was going back to marry, but once he was there it all suddenly stopped.'

Toni moved to Francesca's side, kneeling on the floor beside her chair. Her focus stayed on Francesca but she spoke to Stefano. 'Please tell her I am Maggie's daughter and that Rocco is my father. I want her to know that she is my aunty.' Toni croaked out the last words.

Francesca's eyes grew wide as Stefano talked. She started talking in Italian to Toni, her worn hands reaching out to touch her face.

'She didn't know about a child, but says she believes you. Now that she looks closely, you remind her of him. You have his eyes.'

Tears were rolling down Toni's cheeks, and she was unable to stop them. Francesca then took her in her arms and hugged her. It was hard to believe that she was her aunty, her blood, and they'd only just met and couldn't even speak to each other. Toni had so much to ask her.

When they finally pulled apart and mopped up their tears, Francesca reached for her album, flicking through it excitedly. She threw her arms up when she found it and gestured for Toni to look. It was Rocco and Francesca together, sometime after the war.

'She said you look like her.'

Toni agreed. Back before her hair had started to grey she had definitely resembled Francesca when she was younger. It was amazing to see herself in these people; a side of her that didn't seem to fit in before, not with Arthur or his family, now seemed to belong somewhere.

Next to this photo was a family portrait. Rocco looked about twelve. An older brother stood on one side and Francesca on the other, their parents standing proudly behind them. Francesca saw Toni looking at it and took it out for her to study, talking to Stefano.

'Francesca was twelve when the war stole both her brothers. Only Rocco survived,' Stefano translated.

Just like Maggie's parents, Rocco's parents had lost children to the war. Toni turned the photo over, and read the names written on the back in sloped ink: *Rocco, Francesca, Giuseppe, Carlo* and *Antonia*.

Toni sucked in her breath. *Antonia*. She pointed to herself. 'My name is Antonia too.'

Francesca put her hands to her mouth in joy and disbelief before reaching for Toni's hand again, grasping it tightly for an elderly lady.

Stefano again translated Francesca's words. 'She is so happy you came. She lives alone, her husband passed away but her two children visit and she helps look after the grandchildren.'

242

'Can I ask for Rocco's address?' Toni glanced at Flick, who had shuffled up the couch next to Stefano. 'I'd like to meet him. Does he have kids?'

'He married at thirty-eight and has two children,' answered Stefano as Francesca got up to write his address for them. She pressed it into Toni's hand.

Rocco Valducci
'Maggie Downs'
RMB 120
Quairading WA 6383

Toni sat back on the floor, reread the address a few more times and then glanced up at Flick. 'He's in Quairading. Bloody hell, it's not even two hours from home. How is this possible? I've lived this close to him my whole life.'

Flick sighed heavily and held her head. 'All this time he was right under our noses. Can you believe this, Mum?'

Toni was still speechless. *Maggie Downs*. If his letters hadn't spelt it out clearly enough, the name of his farm did. He'd loved Maggie.

Francesca asked them to stay for longer, giving them time to see more photos and learn about her family. Poor Stefano was going to need a break after this.

She took them outside to show them her veggie garden. Toni stayed glued by her side, knowing that it could be a long time before she saw her aunty again. Already her thoughts were racing with what her new heritage might mean to her — maybe she should learn Italian? Or connect with other Italians back home? Perhaps she should start planning a more extensive tour of Italy, her new homeland. She could visit Francesca again and meet her cousins. It was such a surreal feeling, as she had always felt so Australian — and of course she still was — but already she had started to feel a strong connection with the rolling green hills of Umbria. Yes, she would have to return — with Maggie, maybe? Or even with Jimmy? Her mind was just reeling with it all.

Stefano was having a break from translating and was chatting with Flick as they explored the garden.

Francesca bent to show her the tomatoes but held her arm again as they moved onto the next row, which was dug up and ready for planting. There was something so familiar about the way she tied up her tomatoes and made the channels in the ground for the water. At the end of the row lay a tool. Toni went to it and picked it up, amazed at what she was holding.

'*Si tratta di una zappa,*' said Francesca, pointing to the tool.

Toni turned it over in her hands. They had one just like this at home. *Zappa.* Even Maggie called it a zappa. Toni felt the hairs on the back of her neck stand up as she tried to swallow the lump in her throat.

Even with the language barrier, Toni felt a connection to Francesca, to her Italian roots and to Rocco. It was as if her eyes had been fully opened and parts of her soul had been found.

25

Maggie was out in the garden trying to work the dirt for a veggie patch when the men rolled some more water up for the tank. She'd been so sure Rocco and Giulio would be sent home as soon as the war ended, but it had been nearly a year and the Italians were still with them on the farm. The government said it was because it was impossible to obtain ships to repatriate them, but Father believed it was because the POWs continued to be useful to the economy. Whatever the reason, Maggie was beyond delighted. Giulio mentioned it seemed unfair that he couldn't get home, and that they were still under control of the army, not free men. But all Maggie wanted was for Rocco to stay with them forever. Even if she knew it was impossible.

While Rocco and Giulio waited for the bricks to dry, they would find other things around the farm to do. Sometimes Maggie would see them rolling forty-four gallon drums full of water from the dam to fill the small tank by the house. Father kept saying he'd get a windmill and hoses one day. Some of the water was used for the garden, which was Maggie's domain. Mother had asked her to grow things and rarely went near it herself, except to see what she could take for meals. Being from the city, and a clergyman's daughter, Phyllis didn't know anything about gardening and relied mostly on the order from town.

The men now also helped with the ploughing and seeding. Giulio was great with the horses and could work the fourteen-disc plough better than Father, or so

Charlie had said. Money would come in after harvest, which would be done with the old Sunshine harvester. Her father had also purchased some sheep, and Rocco, Charlie and Giulio watched them until fences could be built. Elders had helped them with finance for fencing materials and super, which they stored in a newly built bush shed.

'You need manure,' said Rocco, walking up alongside Maggie. He reached out and took the shovel from her hands. 'And you need a *zappa* too. I ask if I can make you one,' he said. Then he finished digging up the rest of the dirt bed.

Maggie knew she needed more manure but it was a long, slow process carting up horse poo from the stables. And she had no idea what a *zappa* was.

'Giulio and I finish with water. We help you with manure.' Rocco glanced behind them before smiling at her.

'It's okay, Mother has gone next door to visit Mrs Stewart.'

His smile grew as he gave the shovel back. His hands remained on it just long enough for them to touch. Giulio cleared his throat and Rocco let go. He started talking to Giulio in Italian and leading him towards the stables.

True to his word, Rocco came back with Giulio and a mountain of horse manure. They'd hooked up the old cart to Splinter and loaded it high. Now they set about unloading it over the area. Within the hour they had the manure turned into the dirt and had made more beds for her to plant things, although Maggie only had zucchinis and tomatoes.

'Come inside,' Rocco said while Giulio took the horse and cart back.

In the kitchen, Rocco pulled off the hessian sack covering the large sack of potatoes in the corner.

'What are you doing?' said Maggie.

He turned and reached for her hands. 'Here, put your hand out,' he said, but didn't let go or move away.

His eyes drank her in and Maggie experienced that headiness she always got around Rocco, made five times worse when he touched her. His gaze was so powerful, like he was reading her every thought.

Rocco glanced around the house, pulled her hands up to his lips and kissed them. Maggie's toes curled.

Eventually he let go of her hands and fished through the potato bag. He started putting the smallest ones in her hands.

'They have to be small,' he said while he sorted. 'Too big and they rot.'

When he was happy he had found enough they went back out to the garden. Then he showed her how to plant them.

'See, only this deep,' he said, indicating about the length of his thumb. 'You won't have to buy potatoes again.'

He smiled and Maggie didn't care about potatoes or the money they would save. She just saw Rocco and a happy life with him in it.

The lesson didn't end there. Next they walked through the bush, finding long sticks from dead trees, and he taught her how to hitch them together for the tomatoes to grow up.

'How do you know all this?' she asked him.

'My mother, very good garden. I help her.'

Maggie was just happy to be near him and watch the way he moved, how his hands worked or the way his brow creased when he was thinking. She loved his manly scent and the deep velvet of his voice. He was strong but so considerate of her needs.

'Margaret!' yelled Phyllis, startling them. She stepped from the back door of the cottage, marching closer to see what they were doing.

'Rocco and Giulio have helped me with the garden,' Maggie said, trying to keep her voice even and precise. 'They have just brought up some manure and Rocco is showing me how to grow potatoes. We won't have to buy any ever again.'

'Oh, well, that's good.' She paused for a moment, seeing what they had accomplished, and when she found nothing else to say turned back to the house. 'If you've finished up, can you help me in the house now, please?'

Maggie rolled her eyes and dusted off her hands. 'Thank you for your help, Rocco.' She gave him her best smile. He nodded but their eyes remained locked for what seemed like minutes. Knowing her mother would be watching, she turned on her heel and walked quickly back to the cottage, trying to hide her recent happiness.

* * *

The next morning Maggie was sad to find out that Rocco and Giulio had asked to borrow the bikes and go for a ride. She waited all day for them, finding excuses to go for walks to see Charlie or to check the horses, each time being disappointed that they weren't back.

She headed down to the stables again, this time with afternoon tea.

248

'Where have they gone, Charlie?' she whispered to her brother as they sat drinking

'I don't know. Would you like me to ask Father?'

Her eyes bulged and Charlie winked. He knew about her and Rocco, and remained silent about her meetings with him.

'Don't worry,' he said. 'He can't be far away.'

'Thanks, Charlie.' She threw her arms around him, giving him a quick hug. Thank God she still had one brother left.

'Hey, what are brothers for? Besides, if it wasn't for your help, Valerie may have never noticed me.'

'Oh, come on, Charlie. How could she resist you?' teased Maggie. Valerie was a cousin of one of her friends, and Charlie had taken a shine to her. Maggie had helped them become friends — well, more than friends now. Their father finished up with the truck he was working on and joined them, devouring the small slices of cake she'd brought. They discussed farm matters but no mention of Rocco and Giulio, much to Maggie's dismay.

Just as she was packing up the cups they heard a whistle. Around the corner of the stables came Rocco and Giulio on the bikes. They carried hessian sacks and Rocco had a metal contraption balanced on his bike.

'Ah, I was wondering how you were going. How is everyone?' John asked as he took a sack from Rocco so he could get off the bike. 'How are your backsides?' he added with a chuckle when he noticed how gingerly they dismounted.

'Long ride. But Mr Demasis good. He give you his wishes,' said Rocco, stretching a little.

Giulio had put the bike away and was rubbing his

249

backside when he thought no one was looking. But Maggie saw and she tried not to laugh.

'Is this it?' asked John as he reached for the metal tool.

'Yes,' said Rocco.

'What is it, Father?' said Charlie.

'Rocco went to the Demasises' to make this for Maggie to help in her garden. It's like a hoe.'

Her father smiled and Maggie felt all eyes on her. Rocco had ridden all that way for her. Not even Maggie would want to ride that far. The Demasises were an Italian family who had settled in the area long before the Second World War started, and they lived on the other side of town.

'What have you got in the sacks?' Charlie asked.

'Mrs Demasis, she give us seeds and clippings.' Rocco pulled out little paper bags. 'Tomatoes, beans, capsicums, oregano, basil. And we have more,' he said, gesturing to Giulio's bag. 'Mulberry and grapes.'

'Really?' said Maggie, looking into the bags. 'We can grow all that?'

'Si, I'll show you.' He quickly glanced at John. 'If it okay, Mistair Boss?'

John clapped Rocco on the shoulder. 'Of course it is. I'm just grateful for your help.' John turned to Maggie and rolled his eyes. 'I guess we'd better sort out a permanent water hose now. Actually, Maggie, maybe Rocco and Giulio could help you start a patch by the new house. We'll be moving there soon so it would be better to start the trees there, don't you think?'

'Yes, I agree. I'll ask mother where we can put it.' Maggie tried hard not to rub her hands together. This meant she could work on the garden by the house that

250

Rocco and Giulio were building. They would be working side by side and Maggie would have the perfect excuse to be near him far more often. She could just about jump into her father's arms and kiss him.

Phyllis took great pleasure in marking out the best spot for the garden. She sauntered back and forth, finger to her lip as if this were a critical decision, and Maggie was forced to keep quiet. Phyllis eventually decided on an area at the rear of the house — maybe because Rocco and Giulio had all their tools and bricks out the front. But Maggie wasn't going to complain.

Two days later, Rocco and Giulio were free to help her start the garden. They cleared the area, dug up dirt, carted in more manure and built a small fence to keep out the rabbits.

'Now I get to show you the *zappa*,' said Rocco when the garden bed was finally established.

He bent over, demonstrating the tool. The head was shaped like an axe but it was used sideways so it chipped at the earth. Perfect for making trough rows.

'Now, tomato go here,' he said, pointing to the well part of the row. 'It grows, we push dirt back against plant so then this area becomes water trough near roots.'

Over the coming weeks, he showed her how to cover the tomatoes and capsicums with twigs when the frosts came in, and then as the seedlings became established, they put in the stick tepees for the tomatoes.

'Do we need that many tomato plants?' she asked, brushing her dirty hands together.

'*Si*. Lots of tomatoes, make tomato sauce. I show you,' he said with a wink.

251

Maggie's pulse raced. She caught her lip in her teeth, trying to slow her breath. Rocco scanned the area, then ran into the house. The brick walls were now much taller than him. He turned back and gestured for her to follow. Maggie quickly checked for her mother before darting in after him.

The moment she stepped inside, Rocco grabbed her hand and pulled her towards him. Together they sank back against the corner, a hiding spot, protected by walls.

She was pressed against the cold hard wall but didn't notice it with Rocco's warm body touching hers, their hearts racing together. He raised his hand, brushing her hair back and then tracing the curve of her cheek. Next he bent down and brushed his lips against her neck.

'Sono innamorato di te,' he whispered against her ear.

Maggie felt her body pool with desire and longing. His words vibrated to her core, tingling her senses and driving her crazy.

'Kiss me, Rocco,' she said breathlessly.

His lips trailed up her neck to her cheek and then he claimed her lips. Her fingers threaded through his thick hair. She pressed her hips against him, wanting to feel every part of him. It took all her effort not to groan.

A banging noise broke them apart. Their breathing was heavy, their eyes locked. Her ears strained for her mother's voice but it was just Giulio, working on the front of the house. He'd often whistle a tune whenever he saw Phyllis, his way of warning them she was coming. But there was no whistle. She sighed with relief as Rocco kissed her forehead.

Maggie tugged on his shirt, pulling him closer, his

lips towards hers. She wanted just one more earth-shattering kiss before they parted, because she never knew just how long she'd have to wait for the next one.

26

It was a quiet drive home from Chiaravalle to begin with. After leaving Francesca's they felt so overwhelmed. They didn't want to leave but they knew Stefano had to get back to work, even though he kept telling them to take their time, that his work was nothing compared with what they were doing. How could a random stranger have so much understanding and emotion for them?

But it hadn't seemed right to chew up any more of Stefano's time; they'd worn him out translating, and besides, they could just fly home and ask Rocco to fill in the rest of the story.

They passed through tunnels and weaved around the big green mountains spotted with old castle-like buildings, but Flick was not really seeing any of it. Her mum was quiet in the back too, her head tilted to the window, staring out at the flashing landscape.

'Mum, Rocco married very late in life, didn't he? Was he still nursing a broken heart, do you think? Why didn't he go back to Maggie?' Flick spoke slowly, trying to pin down her thoughts as they raced around her head.

'I don't know, love. I'm asking myself the same things.' Toni leant forward. 'I guess we just have to wait until we get home and see him.'

'What do you think Nan will make of all this? Do you imagine she'll want to meet him?'

'I don't know,' Toni said again. 'It was a long time ago and they have separate lives now.'

They fell back to their own thoughts and Stefano remained politely quiet. Flick studied every detail of him, from his long fingers gripping the wheel to his lean forearms.

'Stefano, we really can't thank you enough for what you have done for us. How can we make it up to you?' she asked, shooting him a special smile.

'Your company has been plenty. I am very lucky. To see such a reunion is amazing.'

Flick couldn't see his eyes behind his sunglasses but his lips curled into a grin, and for a second she imagined what it would be like to kiss him. He moved one hand from the wheel, resting it on his leg, fingers splayed, taunting her. She clutched hers tightly in her lap. She had only just broken up with Chad, had her heart crushed yet again, and yet now here she was, thinking of another guy. A guy who lived in Italy? Flick, the girl who made bad choices and had bad timing.

Toni spoke up. 'You must let us repay you somehow. Maybe dinner on us?'

'No, no. Maybe I come to Australia one day and you can be tour guide.'

'You should come work for us over harvest. It's a great way to see Australia and get some cash at the same time. We have lots of overseas backpackers who do it,' said Flick.

'What is it you do for harvest?' he asked.

Toni went into great detail of the workings at harvest time. Long hot days in the header, right

255

down to how the machine worked to cut off the heads of wheat.

'But there is always a cold beer at the end of the day. You could be a great header driver for us,' she added. He was confident behind the wheel.

'It seems like a dream.'

'Well, this seemed like a dream to me too, and yet here we are in Italy!' said Toni.

When they arrived back in Montone, Stefano insisted that they have late lunch with him at the restaurant, as it was only two o'clock. They'd spent over four hours with Francesca, yet time had just flown.

Sofia was cleaning down the last table when they walked in. Flick could see the relief in her eyes that Stefano had returned, but didn't seem so pleased when he seated them at a table.

'Stay, relax. I'll go make us my favourite pasta,' he said and headed for the kitchen area. Sofia followed him, talking loudly as they both disappeared behind doors.

'She seems friendly,' said Toni.

Flick didn't miss the sarcasm. 'I know. Don't think she likes us.' By 'us' she meant herself, but it felt better to include her mum. 'I wonder what her story is.'

'Have you asked Stefano?'

Flick pretended to read the wine list. 'What's the point? We're not here for long.' She was unsettled by her own words. Why couldn't she just be normal and find normal men?

'Just because you live in different countries doesn't mean you can't have a new friend — or more, if it ever came to that. Don't be too dismissive,' whispered Toni.

'Maybe you should listen to your own advice,' Flick shot back, one eyebrow raised.

When Stefano reappeared ten minutes later, he was carrying three plates of pasta. It looked simple but the truffles made it taste amazing.

'Wow, truffles just for us?' said Toni.

Stefano shrugged. 'I find them myself with our dogs.'

'I guess it's no different to us catching fresh yabbies,' said Toni. 'People pay a lot for them in the city.'

They all tucked in, stomachs hungry, no one talking. It had been such a long morning. Flick had only a few strands of pasta left when Toni broke the silence.

'Is Sofia your sister?'

Flick nearly choked and reached for her water while trying to stop her eyes from smarting. She would throttle her mum later, but right now her ears were straining for his reply.

'Um, no. She is a good friend who has worked here with us for years. She's actually my older sister Martina's best friend.'

'Is your sister here?' Toni persisted.

'No. Martina lives in Roma with her boyfriend.'

Flick cleared her throat, finally able to breathe properly again.

'Lucky girl.'

'I don't think so. Roma is very busy. Are you planning to go?'

'Yes, we fly out from Rome. We take our car

back to Arezzo then catch the train to Rome,' explained Flick.

Stefano sighed, a sad smile on his face. 'I will be sad to see you go.'

'We thought about going to see Pietralunga this afternoon. I read there is an ancient castle there,' said Flick, not wanting to think of their departure yet.

Putting down his fork, he nodded. 'Yes, the fortress. It is from the Lombard period, around the eighth century.'

'Did you want to come with us?' she asked hopefully.

Already he was shaking his head. 'I am needed here now but come find me after. We could go for a walk at night, the lights are very pretty.'

'Sure, sounds great.' Flick was leaning closer, lost in his words, his smile and the deep, dark pools of his eyes. She'd totally forgotten her mum was sitting with them until Toni spoke.

'Well, that was delicious. Thank you once again, Stefano. You are a wonderful cook.' She excused herself for the bathroom.

Flick had hardly moved her gaze from Stefano's face. A strange gravity was holding her to him. Everything about him held her fascination. His long eyelashes, his lips and his smile.

He reached for Toni's plate and went to grab hers. 'It's okay, I'll bring it,' she said, helping him clean up. Inside the kitchen area she put the plate down and waved to Massimo. 'Grazie,' she called to him before turning to Stefano. 'Thanks again. I'll see you later.'

He nodded, his eyes intense. 'You come find me when you get back.'

★ ★ ★

On the way back from Pietralunga they stopped by the edge of the road to take a photo of Montone up on the hill in front of them. Such a majestic sight, straight from a story book.

Pietralunga had been lovely. They'd sat outside a shop enjoying another amazing coffee and pastry, checked out the local shops, seen the fortress. But when they got back to their car they found a parking ticket on their windscreen. That was universal at least.

'Can't say our trip has been boring,' said Toni with a chuckle as they headed back to Montone.

'No, not at all. I'm having the best time. I guess I do miss home, but I can see why you really wanted me to travel.'

Toni smiled but it wasn't an 'I told you so' one. Instead it was sincere and relieved. 'All I ever wanted was to show you was that there were more things in life than the farm. You can still go back, but I just wanted you to know you had options. I never had that.'

'I know, Mum. And I'm grateful. I really am. Are you having fun?'

'Yes, of course!' Toni stared out her window. 'I mean, finding Rocco is surreal, and meeting Francesca ... I don't really know if I'm processing it properly yet, but I'm certainly enjoying the travelling. I'm just starting to realise that this was once all I ever wanted but now, many years later, my dreams have changed. Now I see how much the farm means to me and how much I appreciate it. I miss the landscape, the work and even the bloody sheep. Somewhere over the years, I've changed. I used to think I was forced back onto the farm but now I think fate knew it was for me all along.'

For the first time in a long time, the smile Toni gave Flick seemed liberated. Her face lost its harshness, and instead radiated contentment and self-awareness.

'Well, I've always known that you belong on the land, Mum. I could have told you that!'

Flick parked the car outside the village wall while her mum nudged her playfully on the arm.

'Well, if you're so wise, then tell me what I should do about Jimmy?'

'You don't need me for that, Mum. You already know in your heart what you want; you just have to let yourself be happy. I know it's been hard finding out about Rocco, but Jimmy will always be there for you. So will I and so will Nan.'

Maggie's face appeared in her mind and Toni realised how much she was missing her mum. Her whole life they'd worked side by side, living together and helping each other. It's why the lie had been such a shock and why she'd felt so betrayed. But she still loved her dearly, and life wasn't the same without her nearby.

'Are you going to meet up with Stefano later?' Toni asked as they headed to their building.

'Do you think I should?

'Would you like to?'

Flick didn't hesitate. 'Yes.' She sighed. 'But . . . what if it's too soon after Chad?'

'Are you happy? Does it feel right? Have you *really* been missing Chad?' Toni asked seriously.

'Yes, yes and no.' Flick frowned. 'Does that make me an awful person?'

'Of course not! Don't be so hard on yourself. You're not marrying him. You're young — and you're in Italy! Go and live it up.'

'I will if you will,' Flick said with a chuckle. She never thought she'd see the day when they were giving each other dating advice.

For dinner, they tried another restaurant, called *Erba Luna*. It was set in the walls of Montone, which had once been ancient stables. It was gorgeous, with rock walls mixed with bricks, and high ceilings that arched up above them like in a chapel. The glow of the lighting off the rock wall was romantic and soft.

'I'm loving all this fancy eating out,' said Toni. They opted for a set menu, which started with a traditional sharing platter of fresh duck, porcini mushrooms and locally sourced truffles, all presented so beautifully. Next came three types of pasta, followed by steak sliced and spiced on a bed of rocket and paired with a red wine, which their chef, Claudio, chose to complement the meal. They finished with crepes filled with ice-cream alongside crushed-almond and marzipan pyramids.

'Just a little bit more exciting than the pub and club, hey? I'm not knocking pie and sauce or chips but it's nice to branch out,' said Flick as she scraped her dessert plate clean.

On their way home they walked back through the Piazza Fortebraccio, and Flick didn't have to wait long for Stefano to finish up. When he joined them, Toni said goodnight and pressed the door key into Flick's hand.

'Come this way,' said Stefano, reaching for her hand. 'It is a good place to see the lights of Umbertide.'

His hand entwined with hers, he led her to a lookout with a bench seat, the sounds of the night echoing around them.

'Do you bring all the Aussie tourists here?' she asked curiously.

Stefano looked at her seriously. 'No, but I have never met someone like you before.'

'Sure,' said Flick, a little embarrassed.

'It's true. I don't normally give up my work to help out tourists. But your smile and laugh is beautiful.' His eyes dropped to her lips and moved back to her eyes before he faced the lights of Umbertide.

Flick wasn't sure what was more enticing: the lights or Stefano's profile.

'Shall we sit?' He gestured to the bench seat.

Flick sat close to Stefano, wanting to feel his warmth as the night air cooled.

'It's so pretty. We don't get any lights at home, except at seeding time when I'm up on the hill and I can see all the other tractor lights all around me, like ground-level stars. It's long hours but I love it. Freshly turned earth is one of my favourite smells. In the morning, real early, it just makes all your senses come alive.'

'I love hearing you talk about your farm. It sounds amazing.'

'It is. It's nothing like here, but in its own raw natural way it's heaven.'

Stefano put his arm along the back of the chair and Flick found herself almost snuggling into his shoulder.

'I really miss my boys, though. I've never been gone from them so long before.'

'Boys?'

His worried tone made Flick laugh. 'Yes, Fella is my dog and Contractor is my horse. They're my boys.'

'Ah, I see.'

By the light of the nearby lamp she could see his relieved smile. He watched her carefully as she went into detail about her pets — how she had trained Fella, and how Contractor was clever and cheeky.

'I had a little dog, Goose. We went everywhere together,' he said. 'He was my best truffle-finding dog.'

'Goose?'

Stefano laughed. 'From that movie, *Top Gun*?'

'I loved that movie. What happened to Goose?'

'He died of old age.'

'Aw, but I'm sure he had a good life.' Flick reached for his hand. She didn't even think about it, didn't second-guess it. Touching Stefano just seemed right.

He moved his thumb across her hand in gentle strokes. She was so lost in the moment and was surprised when his other arm encircled her

263

properly. And that's how they stayed for the next three hours while they talked about their lives. It was only when she shivered that he suggested it was time go home.

Flick was stiff with the cold when she tried to stand. Being beside Stefano and lost in their conversation, she hadn't registered the weather or time. She decided it must be close to midnight.

A true gentleman, he walked her back to her door, their bodies close together, hands still tangled.

Montone was quiet. Even their breathing seemed loud, so they whispered as they walked. They stopped at her door, and Flick struggled to see his face in the darkness. Stefano bent down and whispered some Italian words in her ear.

His words sent electric pulses throughout her body. 'What did that mean? Actually, you still haven't told me what you said last time.' They were toe to toe, so close she could feel his heat.

'I said you had a beautiful smile.'

'Really? Thanks.'

'I just speak the truth.'

All Flick could think about was how close his lips were. 'And what did you just say then?'

'You want to know?'

She nodded as his hand rested on her shoulder. Slowly it moved upwards until he was caressing her face.

'I said, 'Can I kiss you?''

Thud, thud, thud, went her heart. 'Yes,' she squeaked. She had hardly finished getting her word out when his lips found hers. It was soft, sweet, and as thrilling as racing Contractor flat out across the paddock.

All too soon, Stefano pulled away. 'It is time for me to go. Thank you for a wonderful night, Felicity. I'll see you tomorrow, *si*?'

'*Si*,' she croaked.

'*Buonanotte*, Felicity.' Their hands broke apart and he sauntered away, leaving her alone, touching her lips in the narrow street by their door. A sweet, perfect kiss.

Fishing out the key from her pocket, she tried to open the door in the dark. With her body still buzzing and her mind still on the kiss it took several minutes for her to finally get inside.

'Have a good night?' came her mum's voice from her room.

Flick smiled. Toni was such a light sleeper, and she always made sure her daughter was home safe and sound.

'It was, Mum. Night.'

Flick climbed the stairs to her room and instead of going straight to bed she opened her window, sat on the sill and watched the twinkling lights of Umbertide, while her mind relived the best night of her life.

27

Maggie stood in her veggie garden as the sun rose, staring across the land between the swaying gum tree branches. She kept expecting to see Flick come riding along on Contractor, or Toni whizzing past in the ute. But it was unusually quiet and had been the five days since they left. Did she regret not going with them? She wasn't sure. Part of her longed to find Rocco and ask him the questions burning inside, some that had been lingering since he left.

But Italy was a long way from home, from everything she knew, and if she was being honest with herself, she was afraid. Afraid of finding him and afraid of not finding him. There were too many variables, and she wasn't sure if her old ticker was up to all that. Staying on Sunnyvale with Jimmy had seemed like the safest option, even if she missed her girls madly. With a bit of luck, Toni and Flick would be enjoying their time together, and hopefully they had found some information. Had they already found Rocco? Her pulse started to race and tingles shimmered across her body at just the thought of the possibilities.

With one international call she could ask them, but she'd decided she wouldn't want to hear bad news over the phone. It hadn't stopped her stalking past it every day or looking at Italy on the map Flick had left her with their itinerary.

'There you are, Maggie.' Jimmy stepped over the fence and came into the veggie garden, leaving Gypsy on the other side. 'Thinking of the girls?'

Maggie turned to the strapping man and smiled. 'Yes. It's only been five days but it feels like a month. It's not the same without them, is it?'

Jimmy scratched at the stubble on his chin. 'No.' He cleared his throat.

Maggie studied his profile. He was looking a little worse for wear — had done since Toni had left. She wasn't sure what had transpired between them but it had certainly upset him. He'd been working himself to the bone ever since. 'You look like a dog's breakfast, Jimmy. Why don't you come and have a cuppa with me? I have some caramel slice. You look like you could do with a break.' She put her hand on his shoulder and gave him a gentle squeeze. If she'd ever had a son, she would have liked him to be a lot like Jimmy.

The weariness she saw in his jade eyes cleared for the moment as he grinned. 'Sure, when can I ever say no to you?' He winked, tucked her hand into his arm and escorted her back to the house.

Because it was such a nice morning they brought their cuppas outside and sat on the verandah, while the magpies called out their morning song. Maggie picked up a small bit of slice from the plate between them. Jimmy leant forward, elbows on his knees while the steam rose from the cup between his hands.

'What's on your mind, Jimmy? I can see

267

something is bothering you.'

He shrugged and took a sip of his drink.

'Is it the farm?' she asked. 'Are you struggling to keep up with it all? Because I can help if you need it. I spent many years in the sheep yards myself.'

And she wouldn't hesitate to do it again. Jimmy and the girls had the farm covered, and Maggie was better off in the house keeping them fed than getting in their road. But on the odd occasion someone was sick or away she enjoyed masquerading as a farmer, feeding sheep or helping them draft. It made her feel youthful — although afterwards she felt anything but. Her hip tended to flare up and ache, along with her back.

'No, I'm managing all right.'

'So it's just Toni then?' she said bluntly.

Jimmy kept his head down, avoiding her eyes. He dragged his lip through his teeth but said nothing.

'I don't want to go sticking my nose where is doesn't belong but don't let it get you down. Whatever it is,' said Maggie. She sipped her tea while Jimmy leant back and reached for some slice. Eventually he met her gaze.

'Do you think this trip will change things?' he asked. 'Change them?'

'It depends. I'm not sure what they're going to find or how either of them will react. I'm not sure how I'll react. But one thing I am sure of is that both those girls think the world of you and that will never change.'

'You really think so?'

For a strong, reliable, happy-go-lucky man, Jimmy seemed very unsure. Matters of the heart could take down the strongest.

'Yes, I do. Just give her time.'

He ran a hand over his face. 'How is it that I tell you hardly anything, yet you know exactly what I'm thinking?' He sighed. 'Thanks, Maggie May.'

Gypsy shifted by his feet, looking rather glum.

'Do you think they've found him?' asked Jimmy.

'To tell you the truth, I'm trying not to think about it. But the more I try, the more I end up wondering. I guess we will know in a few more days.' Maggie felt that flutter begin in her chest again. Nervous excitement and dread. 'Is there anything I can help you with today? I can't cook any more, the freezer is full. But I need to do something.'

'I understand. You want to come with me while I feed the sheep and check the troughs?'

'I would love that.' Maggie felt relieved. She reached down and scratched Gypsy's head. The dog melted against her hand. 'So, where's Fella?'

Both Gypsy and Jimmy looked at her strangely. 'What do you mean? Isn't he with you?'

Maggie frowned. 'No. I haven't seen him since last night when I fed him and Contractor.'

'Oh, crap. Well, I haven't seen him since before then. Where could he be?' Jimmy clapped his hands. 'Gypsy, where is Fella?' She tilted her head, ears erect.

'I'll go check his pen and around the back of

the house. He likes the chooks, maybe he's watching the new chickens,' said Maggie. There was no point worrying yet, except she did. It wasn't like Fella to just disappear, especially when Gypsy was here.

'I'll go to the sheds and do a quick drive-around. I'll meet you back here in five.' Jimmy strode to the four-wheeler, whistling as he went. 'Fella!' he yelled.

Maggie checked everywhere, even inside Flick's bedroom. Nothing. She stood out on the verandah and called him again. There wasn't even a bark.

Jimmy came back, his brow creased. 'Buggered if I know where he'd be. It's so unlike him.'

'Do you think he's hurt? Snake bite? Maybe went off chasing rabbits and got lost.' *Or worse*, she almost said. Their last dog Bruce had been sprinting through the crop when he'd impaled himself on a mallee root he hadn't seen. She hoped to God Fella was fine. 'We need to find him, Jimmy.' Flick would be devastated.

'I know.' Jimmy swallowed hard. 'I'll go get the ute and we'll have a proper look around the farm.'

He walked back to the bike, his hands shoved deep into his pockets, shoulders hunched. Maggie felt the same. All thoughts of Rocco vanished as the need to find Fella became a priority. Maggie closed her eyes and prayed. *Please let us find him alive.*

28

As promised, Stefano drove them to Gubbio the following day. Had it been a straight road it would have taken them fifteen minutes. Add tight bends, hills, and being stuck on 60 kilometres an hour, and time doubled. Toni sat in the back again, but she didn't mind. She could still see plenty of the scenery. Flick and Stefano chatted away in the front. It was amazing they still found things to talk about after spending nearly all night at it.

Over breakfast Toni had quizzed Flick. All she said was that it was 'wonderful', but the rest Toni could read from her expression. She was walking on clouds, almost like a giggly schoolgirl as they waited to meet up with Stefano again. She didn't miss the heated smiles they shared as they greeted each other.

Toni was delighted for her daughter. After that messy business with Chad, a little holiday romance would do her the world of good. Sure, seeing the spark between Flick and Stefano made her heart long for Jimmy, but soon she would be home. Three more sleeps.

'So tomorrow you leave for Roma?' asked Stefano as he parked the car in an unmarked gravel car park, a catch in his voice.

Flick just nodded sadly.

'I wonder,' he started. 'I haven't seen my sister for a long time. Would you let me drive you to

Rome? We could return your car there and you would not have to drive back over the same roads to Arezzo.' Stefano sought out Toni's eyes in the rear-vision mirror. He knew it was her decision.

Flick was watching her too, lip caught between her teeth.

'Are you sure that wouldn't put you out?' Toni asked. 'It's fine by me if it's okay with you and your work.'

Both of the kids grinned with relief.

'My mum will be happy, I can take some things she has for Martina. They miss her.'

They parked the car and headed towards the outer wall of medieval Gubbio. Terracotta tiles on stone buildings started at the bottom of the hill and rose like a Lego structure up the slope. Flick and Stefano held hands beside her and Toni knew the release they must feel at having a few more days together. But really, was that a good thing or would it just make leaving harder?

Toni was thinking how unbearable the plane ride home might be with a daughter whose heart was aching. She could relate it all back to her and Jimmy. Should she take the chance of a broken heart too?

Inside the walls they walked around the medieval terraces and along narrow, steep streets lined with small cars. They found a ceramic shop with the most beautiful hand-painted plates and ornaments.

'Nan would love all this stuff,' said Flick, eyeing a massive jug.

Toni picked up a serving platter. 'Yes, she

would.' In that instant Toni wished her mother were here to experience this with them.

Walls, shelves and even the floor were covered with all sorts of ceramics. An elegant ornamental amphora with antique decoration and a beautiful hand-painted blue dragon took Toni's eye. Flick was drooling over some wall plates with yellow peacocks on a vibrant blue patterned background.

'I think she'd like this,' said Toni, picking up a two-piece handmade butter dish. 'She loves her butter soft.' Maggie had always used a butter dish, for as long as Toni could remember. She had a simple glass one but the top had a big crack in it. Toni stared at the dish in her hand but her mind was on Maggie. Was her mum doing all right at home? Was she keeping an eye on Jimmy? She'd left them both with issues unresolved and it plagued her mind. She wasn't sure how to fix either problem. Her mum wanted forgiveness, which maybe Toni could find eventually. But Jimmy? He wanted something special with her, or at least that's what she'd thought until he'd walked away. Toni just wished she knew what *she* wanted.

'Mum?' said Flick again. 'Are you okay?'

Toni glanced up and smiled. 'Mmm. I think we should get her this.'

They bubble-wrapped the gift to within an inch of its life and prayed it would survive the trip home. Stefano then led them to the Palazzo dei Consoli, a Gothic-style building around 60 metres high in an off-white limestone. It had a bell tower and big circular steps in a fan-shape

273

that you could walk under. In front of the building, a massive open area paved in redbrick herringbone contrasted with the limestone.

'This is completely full of people for *La Corsa dei Ceri*, the race of the Saints,' Stefano said. 'Lots of colour and fun.'

They followed Flick to the wall along the edge, which offered a view of Gubbio. Toni smiled at the sight and then turned to see Stefano with his arms around Flick. The two snuggling together made it all look so romantic, and Toni couldn't help imagining being there with someone special.

In one of the squares they stopped for morning tea, which was a slice of pizza. And not just any pizza. It was made with an amazingly light base and topped with only a few ingredients.

'We totally overload our pizzas,' said Flick through her mouthful. She rattled off all the things she'd put on the last pizza she'd made, causing Stefano's eyes to bulge. 'And we do the same with our pasta. We use mince but I've noticed here it's mainly just a light flavoursome sauce.'

While they were chatting Toni stopped by a tourist shop and bought a postcard. She intended on filling it out for Jimmy but then realised she'd beat it home. Plus, what would she say? 'I'm missing you'? How would he take that? In the end she wrote one it to Uncle Charlie, posted it off, and then bought a new magnet for the fridge. She'd started collecting a few; that way every time they went to the fridge she would have reminders of their travels.

Soon it was time to head back to Montone. Stefano had to work, and Toni and Flick had to clean up so they'd be ready to leave the next day.

'Mum, shall we do the 12-k walk this afternoon too?' asked Flick.

'Yeah, why not?'

When they walked Stefano to the restaurant, he went to tell his parents about the trip to Rome. Toni watched for a moment while Flick went to look at some felt hats and scarves at the shop opposite. Massimo seemed pleased that Stefano would be visiting his sister. But it was the look on Sofia's face as she overheard the exchange and went running to Stefano that gripped Toni's attention. A big three-way Italian conversation raged. Sofia's hand was on Stefano's arm and she was shaking her head. Stefano said something, and she pouted. His words had hurt. Toni wondered if Stefano even realised the depth of Sofia's feelings towards him. Lucky Flick had missed the commotion.

An hour later they started on their walk, taking the bit of paper with the directions with them. They strolled down a narrow bitumen road lined with grapes and figs, helped themselves to a few, and talked to some horses, which Toni knew would make Flick feel homesick. They reached overgrown dense green areas before heading over a few hills until they could see Montone in the distance. A farmer in his blue tractor was ploughing his paddock right beside them. The simple plough cut two deep gashes through the earth, curling dirt over on itself.

'Wow, see how deep they're going?' said Flick.

They stood over the ripped area, checking out the soil type, measuring the depth of the cut. Back home they only ever scratched the surface. It just showed how rich and fertile the soil was here.

Further on they passed some men moving sheep. Five white dogs walked along in front as the mob followed. 'You don't see that every day,' said Toni.

'You think if I paint Fella white and get him to lead the way, our sheep will follow?'

Toni laughed. 'I can't imagine that ever happening.' The little lambs that passed were so adorable. The sheep didn't even worry about them, just surged forward towards their next paddock.

They walked between crops of tall, leafy plants and had a big debate on what they could be, before agreeing they might be tobacco. One paddock definitely had sunflowers.

'It's so amazing, Mum,' said Flick, pausing on their steep climb and glancing across the green landscape. Flick gave her a silly smile. 'I can definitely see why you wanted me to travel. There's so much to learn, new things to see.'

Toni was silently pleased. 'Yes, there is. Farming here is different.'

'But then again, it's not. Did you see what that farmer was wearing? Boots and trackpants!' Flick laughed. 'That's me half the time.'

'Only because you slept in yours and couldn't be bothered changing. You were a lazy sod when you were home from high school.'

'Yeah, those were the days,' said Flick as if remembering twenty years before instead of three.

Toni put her arm around Flick's shoulders. 'You know, darling. I think we should make this a yearly thing — you and I having some time out together. What do you say?'

Flick opened her eyes wide. 'You mean a big trip overseas?'

'No, not necessarily. I would love to keep doing trips overseas — maybe we could travel to America and see how they farm there,' Toni said, getting excited. 'But, I mean just you and I go somewhere, whether it's to the coast or down south or even camping out in the bush someplace. I'm just really enjoying this personal time with you. I'd like to keep it going.' Toni smiled and Flick gave her one back.

'Yeah, I'd like that too, Mum.'

29

'This place is extreme,' said Flick as she watched the Rome traffic buzz around them like frantic flies. They had returned the car and were now waiting next to the train station at the taxi stand. People flooded out from the station. Queues of people with bags lined up waiting for a ride, others just stood around chatting. It smelt like a city: car fumes, cigarette smoke and damp cement, but you didn't notice it that much when you were busy gazing up at the buildings — long, square-bricked terraces with rows and rows of windows, some four levels, others six levels high, and dressed with shutters. Hotel Siracusa sat on the corner of one street. If only their hotel, the Priscilla, was that close. Along the busy one-way street sat scooters and bikes, parked so close they could topple like dominoes if pushed.

'I think we should walk, it would be quicker and cheaper,' said Stefano.

'Fine by us,' said Flick. She pulled out the map of Rome their hotel was marked on. It also had illustrations of all the sights, like the Colosseum and Pantheon, so they could plan something of a route for themselves.

Stefano studied it over her shoulder. His closeness made her contented. She wanted to take his hand, but walking the crazy streets of Rome with luggage would need to be done in single file.

'Okay, we go this way.'

And off they went. They crossed the main, cobblestoned road, the *click clack* of their bags along the uneven surface adding to the noise of the traffic. Flick saw a nun dressed in black with brown sandals running to cross the street, and most people around them seemed really well dressed. It looked like they were in a business area. Once safely on the other side, they dodged people on the narrow and uneven path, past parked bikes and around skip bins, and headed towards a massive building at the end of the street with a huge eagle on top of it. Near the end of Via Marsala was a tourist area, with little souvenir huts sprouting postcards or handbags and luggage.

They weaved left and right along different streets with names like Via Montebello and Via Cernaia, but in no time had found Via Calabria, the street their three-star hotel was on. There was a restaurant on the corner; the smell of coffee was alluring, and tables with white tablecloths and chairs sat outside along the pavement. All crammed together and looking like one whole structure, the buildings were six storeys high and it seemed like a seventh went down below the road.

'Did you see how many restaurants are around us? We won't have far to go,' said Flick as they powered past some tall trees and up the stairs to the Priscilla.

Franco, the enthusiastic manager with a lopsided smile and white jacket, checked them in, his keys jingling on his waist every time he moved. Their room nothing special but it was clean and the bathroom was surprisingly big. At least it only had a toilet and no bidet.

Stefano asked if he could leave his bag in their room. 'My sister can't pick me up until after her work. She will come to Priscilla at seven o'clock. Do you mind if I be your tour guide until then?' he asked Toni.

Flick found it so charming that he always checked with her mum first. He knew this was their holiday, their time together, and he didn't want to overstep.

'That would be great, Stefano. Then tomorrow we'll have more confidence to trek around Rome ourselves. Thank you.' Toni took his bag and sat it on the double bed in their room. 'We'd rather walk everywhere than take the subway. I've heard too many horror stories about bags getting stolen.'

Flick laughed at her mum, but truthfully she was a little afraid of it herself. Growing up in such wide-open spaces, the thought of cramped, overcrowded places filled her with dread.

They waited outside the room while Toni locked up. Flick had swapped her thongs for her walking shoes but kept her denim mini skirt on, along with a white strappy tank top. Stefano was wearing fitted jeans and a snug navy-blue shirt. She had to fight the urge to run her hand across his chest.

'Righto, let's go,' said Toni.

Outside, Stefano reached for her hand and Flick gladly let him. Everything felt so much more alive when she could touch him and she didn't want to waste a moment, as they would be flying home so soon. Instantly a wave of sadness hit, but she tried to bury it way down deep. She would not ruin the time they had left worrying about goodbyes.

'Bloody hell.' Toni had stopped, pointing to a compact car parked in the street. 'How in God's name did they get that in there?' The little white car was in a space between two trees with an inch either side.

Flick laughed. 'And look at that one.' She pointed to a black VW Beetle. All the cars around it were parked horizontally while it was vertical, making the most of a tiny space. 'You couldn't pay me to drive here. Look at them, they're nuts!'

People stopped next to parked cars and just left their cars, while others tried to drive around them. It was a free for all; you did what you had to. They noticed a car that had been parked in the middle of an intersection.

'He's probably gone for coffee, or picking something up. They all drive around it and he won't be long,' said Stefano.

'You lot crack me up,' Flick said teasingly, and squeezed his hand.

It was a feast for the senses: clothes shops, little delis, divine restaurants and many well-dressed locals speaking Italian. It was such a vibrant, modern city yet it held so much history, with ancient ruins scattered unexpectedly about. Flick felt like pinching herself. She was really in Rome.

'Do you know where we are?' Stefano asked eventually.

Flick walked to the edge of the nearby wall and looked down. She could see rows and rows of steps cascading down like a waterfall to a street at the bottom, where a fountain in the shape of an old boat seemed to sit in the middle of the road. People sat on the steps, not doing anything in particular, just enjoying the view or the feel of the place.

'The Spanish Steps,' said Toni. 'Amazing.' She headed off down the steps first; Flick followed and was glad she'd changed out of her thongs, as the steps would have been slippery.

Near the bottom she sat down with Stefano while Toni went to look at the fountain. He put his arm around her and Flick snuggled close.

'Sometimes I think this must all be a dream,' she said, smiling up at him.

Stefano played with a long strand of her hair. He let it fall before touching her lips with his finger. 'If it is, then don't wake me.'

She was drowning in his dark eyes and it felt as if they were the only two on the steps. Even the noise seemed to fade away, except for the faint thud of her heart. He was watching her, glancing at her lips. Her pulse quickened.

'What are you thinking about, *bella*?' he whispered.

'*Baciami*,' she said. *Kiss me.* It was the one word she'd looked up in the Italian dictionary after their night together in Montone.

Stefano smiled, delighted with her words. His eyes went to her lips again. 'You are so hard to resist,' he said, dropping his head so their lips met.

Flick closed her eyes, her fingers reaching up through his hair at the base of his neck. Her other hand rested against his chest as he pulled her closer. His tongue brushed across her lip and she welcomed his taste. Nothing was more powerful than this moment. It felt like she'd been waiting forever for this kiss, this overwhelming kiss in this perfect location, and with it she knew she'd just lost a little bit of her heart.

Stefano leant his forehead against hers and murmured something. Flick thought she could make out the words, '*É stato stupendo.*'

'Whatever you said, I agree,' Flick replied. With her lips still tingling, she tried to catch her breath. She'd never been kissed like that before. How was she going to be able to walk away from this guy?

'Smile, you two,' said Toni. She'd made her way back to them and stood poised with her camera.

Stefano kissed her cheek as Toni snapped a few photos. Flick knew she would be grateful to have this moment captured, especially when she was home and back to reality.

They walked on, past a man roasting chestnuts on a street corner, past shops overflowing with leather bags. Small streets crisscrossed and the buildings all towered many storeys above, giving the sensation they were in a maze. Flick found it somewhat unnerving that she couldn't see the horizon, that the only way to see the sky was to look straight up. But that only made things more spectacular when they opened into a square to find the Pantheon. It was as if they'd found the cherry in a pacman game.

'Stefano, can you take our picture, please?' Toni held out her camera to him, then grabbed Flick's hand and dragged her to a column, wrapping her girl tightly in her arms.

'You don't mind Stefano being with us?' Flick whispered.

'Of course not. Think of all the photos we'll have together now,' Toni teased.

The last stop was the magical Trevi Fountain.

'Is that Neptune?' Flick asked, pointing to the beautifully carved man in a shell-like chariot.

'No, Ocean, son of Sky and Vesta,' replied Stefano.

Like that clears it up, thought Flick, who didn't know much about the gods.

She turned back to the statues of two men with fish-like tails, holding a horse each. She was transfixed. How did they make the horses so lifelike? She could see Contractor's strength and spirit in both of them, inexplicably carved into the marble.

'Here,' said Stefano, handing Flick and Toni some money. 'Throw a coin in.'

Standing at the edge of the huge fountain, Flick gripped her coin. Others around them were doing the same thing; coins glittered at the bottom of the fountain like scales on a fish. She glanced at Stefano. He winked at her, kissed his coin and threw it in. She wondered if he'd wished the same thing as her: to be together again someday. Kissing her own coin for extra luck she threw it in, watching it glide through the clear water to the bottom.

Toni held out her hand, coin still sitting on it. 'I don't know what to wish for,' she told Flick. 'I just realised I have everything I could possibly want.'

'Aw, Mum.' Flick touched her arm. 'Well, then wish for a fantastic harvest.'

'Yes, yes, you're right.' Toni scrunched her eyes and threw in the coin, but it didn't look like she was thinking of the harvest.

Stefano tucked Flick back against his chest. His chin rested against her neck as he whispered, 'A coin in the Trevi means you will return to Rome. I hope you and I can be here again sometime.'

Flick tilted her head towards him. 'So you don't actually get a wish?' She felt a little disappointed.

Stefano shrugged. 'But that is my wish. That we would both return here.' He kissed her cheek.

Flick nuzzled in close. Yes, that was her wish too.

★ ★ ★

Before Flick knew it they were sitting on the steps of the hotel, waiting for Stefano's sister. Toni had stayed in the room, giving them some time together.

Time together. Time had gone too fast. Flick just wanted to hold him close and kiss him forever. His lips were never far from her skin, and they made as much contact as possible, right down to their feet.

'I do not regret meeting you, Felicity. You are

not like any girl I have met,' he said softly.

'That's because I'm an Aussie country gal,' Flick said flamboyantly.

'Maybe. You are funny, beautiful, you have life and you are *gioia mia*. My joy.'

Flick wrapped herself around him, wanting to tell him what he meant to her, but she knew the words would catch in her throat and she didn't want tears. Not now.

'We will stay in touch, Stefano, won't we? Email me when you can.'

'*Si*.'

Flick nestled into his neck. Stefano smelt like rosemary and maybe cardamom, fresh and outdoorsy. Was she in love with him? Was that possible after just a few days? Or was it just the excitement of Italy and Stefano's good looks mixed in with his Italian accent? But they had talked like she had never talked with a guy before. And he hadn't pressured her for anything more, seeming content just to be in her company.

The violent sound of a horn tooting made them jump. A car had pulled up behind the row of parked cars and was waiting.

'That's Martina.' Stefano threw his arms around Flick. 'I will miss you.'

'Me too.' Someone had reached into her belly and was twisting her insides. The lump in her throat was so big she couldn't speak. But she didn't have to. Stefano found her lips and kissed her. Flick clung to him desperately. They must have been a sight, standing in the street, cars passing by, but all she could think about was the taste of his lips and the strength of his embrace. Pressed so close she could feel him and his hunger for her.

'*Bella*, I must go,' he said between kisses. 'Have a good time tomorrow, stay in touch, *si*? *Arrivederci*. I will miss you.' After one last kiss he turned and was in the passenger seat before Flick had time to register his absence. Stefano stuck his arm out the window and waved goodbye, and the little black car shot off down the street, mingling with the chaos of Rome.

30

'Have you finished darning those socks yet?' asked Phyllis as she picked up another box of plates and things from the cottage. Today was moving day.

'Nearly done.'

'Good. Then you can help me carry the treadle Singer to the house after you've brought this over.' She gestured to the last box on the table.

Phyllis strutted out of the cottage like the Queen. The day before, Charlie had come to get them, and they'd watched as Giulio had handed Father the doorknob, the item they'd especially left until last. They'd all applauded as Father has screwed it in. Then there was a frenzy of handshaking and back-patting. All Mother had mustered was a mumbled 'thank you' to Giulio and Rocco. She'd thanked Father and Charlie, of course, but they'd only helped with the roof and inside. It was Rocco and Giulio who had made every brick, built every fireplace and given two years of their life for it.

'Ouch.' Maggie accidently pricked herself. Blood spotted her fingertip, her anger making her careless. She shouldn't dwell on it, but her mother's treatment of Rocco and Giulio always made her temperature rise.

Maggie finished off the socks then packed up the sewing gear. She'd have to come back for the machine. Snapping the lid on the tin of buttons, cotton and needles, she placed it in the box her mother had left. Maggie fixed her skirt straight, pinched her cheeks and checked her soft curls were in place before picking up the box and heading to the new house. The only things left were the beds and tables, the sewing machine and the meat safe. Charlie and Father were bringing the ute around to load up shortly, after they'd finished erecting the new fence by the house.

Outside, she squinted until she'd adjusted to the bright light of the sun. She paused to look back at the cottage. Weatherboard and tin, hessian and wood, dusty floorboards and cold dirt. She would miss it; it had been home since she could remember, but at least the new house had no holes for snakes and mice to come through. That was something she wouldn't miss.

Now that the house was finished, Rocco and Giulio were back doing farm work, probably out in the paddock building fences or tending to the horses. But just in case she bumped into Rocco, she always checked she was presentable. Although they never had much time alone together, just being around each other was enough. Charlie and Giulio knew of their affections and would turn their backs while they stole some moments to talk. Both men had promised to keep the secret, and Maggie worked hard on not being caught by her parents, although Charlie believed that Father had an inkling. If he did, he never said anything.

It was a fair walk to the house, and Maggie kept her pace steady and slow so not to raise a sweat.

'Maggie!' yelled Charlie as he jogged towards her. 'Something's happening. I have to get Rocco and Giulio.' He brushed past her, like a brewing storm.

She spun as he continued towards the paddock, watching his retreating body. Hugging the box to her chest, she quickly picked up her pace. Father would tell her what was going on.

She walked through the gimlet trees and around the corner of the new house, where she saw her father leaning against his shovel as he spoke to a man beside the all too familiar truck covered with canvas. Mr Tweedie. Was it canteen day already? Maggie placed the box by the front door and walked over to where her father stood. He'd been working hard this morning on setting out a garden area for Mother. They were halfway through erecting a small fence.

'Hello, Miss Margaret.' Mr Tweedie nodded his head towards her; he was still in his green uniform, which always reminded her of her brothers. She'd be happy if she never saw it ever again.

'Mr Tweedie. Father,' she said, 'is something happening?' Her heart was beating faster.

'He's here for the lads,' said Father with a glum expression.

Her stomach cramped and her panic rose. *Now?* No, they couldn't be. She wasn't ready. She hadn't said goodbye. They couldn't leave like this. She needed more time with Rocco.

John frowned and Maggie instantly tried to retract all her fearful thoughts from her face. Had he sensed her panic and seen her devastation?

She swallowed and tried to smile. Turning to Mr Tweedie she asked, 'Are you taking them now?' Hopefully no one had noticed the small tremor in her voice.

'No, lass. Not yet. I'm just here to tell them the good news. Ah, here they are.'

Charlie returned with the Italians, all jogging to join them by the truck, dust lifted from their heavy steps.

'Sir,' said Rocco and Giùlio, greeting Captain Tweedie. Maggie was watching Rocco, waiting for the quick glance her way. When his brown eyes found hers, so much passed between them in that tiny moment: how much he longed to reach for her, his desire, his happiness, to be near her. She saw his face change instantly when he noticed her terror. He was no doubt wondering what could be so bad.

'You're going home, boys,' said Mr Tweedie, drawing Rocco's attention back to him.

'Truly?' said Giulio. He rubbed his hands together, his grin huge.

'When?' asked Rocco, who didn't exude the same excitement as Giulio.

'There's a ship that's coming in next week, The HT *Chitral*. I will come to collect you on Monday. We will go back to Northam, where we'll process your papers before loading you up on the ship. Then it sets sail on Friday to Naples.'

Giulio thumped Rocco on the back and spoke to him in Italian.

Rocco smiled. 'Yes, it will be great to be home.'

No one but Maggie noticed the lack of excitement in Rocco's eyes, and part of her was relieved to know he wasn't so eager to leave.

'Good. Have your stuff packed and ready. I'll be here Monday morning,' said Mr Tweedie.

That gave Maggie almost three days. Her stomach flipped and a wave of dizziness flushed through body. Scrunching her toes, she willed herself to stay upright and fight the faintness. She could not go to pieces here in front of them all. Tilting her head up, she forced herself to focus on the cockies screeching in the trees above her head. She let the noise drown her thoughts. Later she would cry; now she must stand strong.

The leaves flittered on the small hint of a breeze, sun danced on the eucalyptus leaves like diamonds while the conversation continued. She felt like she was slowly dying while life went on around her. She couldn't even risk glancing at Rocco. Seeing his face would be too much. Those lips, his eyes — *oh*, she would never feel his fingers caress her skin again.

Backing away from the group, Maggie picked up the box then headed inside to hide. Phyllis was walking down the wide corridor, her shoes clicking against the wooden floors. Maggie was growing weary of that sound already, her mother strutting the rooms as if on a routine inspection. It was a house of beauty, its high ceilings giving a feeling of space, and the brick walls felt safe and solid.

Maggie hoped the click of Mother's shoes would hide the awfully loud sound of her heart pounding — and possibly breaking. Maggie forced herself to hold it together until she was alone.

'They leave back to their families yet where are my boys? When do they get to come home? It will be a relief to have the prisoners gone.' Phyllis smiled and Maggie resisted the urge to slap her across the face.

For two years, Rocco and Giulio had been like family. Even Charlie regarded them as brothers. He'd once told her it was like having Thomas and George with them. Even Father treated them with such kindness, joking and laughing with them. Maggie knew he would miss them. It was only Mother who had never let them into her heart.

In her head, Maggie was screaming at her, telling her exactly how mean and horrible she was. For the moment she relished the anger, helping to control her heartbreak and tears.

'Just put that in the spare room, please,' said Phyllis as she continued out the front door.

Maggie dropped the box in the room as a sob broke free. She ran out the back door, tears already falling. She weaved her way through the gimlets and gum trees. Branches slapped at her face and shrubs scratched at her legs but she ran with blind fury. Nothing was more painful than how she felt now.

Contractor neighed as she ran into the thatched stables and headed straight for the first stall, where they stored some of the hay. The smell of horse manure and the leather from the harnesses had a calming effect. She climbed up the pile of straw, then lay down so her hand fell through the gap into Contractor's stall. As if being called, he wandered over and nuzzled her hand. Just the feel of him helped as the tears came in big howls.

When Charlie found her half an hour later, her face was still damp but her body had stopped shaking. Contractor had not left her side the whole time. She'd stared at the white blaze on his nose as if it were a hypnotic fire that held all the answers.

'Maggie?' Charlie sat down in the straw next to her. 'I'm sorry,' he said. 'I'm going to miss him too.'

Fresh tears welled in her eyes. 'What am I going to do, Charlie? I love him.' She'd never spoken those words out loud before, had never told Rocco, but now it all seemed pointless.

'Oh, sis,' he said and reached out for her.

She cried some more in his arms, glad that someone was on her side and understood. 'I don't want to say goodbye, Charlie. I wish I could go with him or that he could stay.'

'You know that's not possible. In a while, he might

be able to come back. If you truly love him, then it will work.'

Maggie smiled through her tears. No one had a softer heart than her Charlie. She wiped her eyes and gripped his arms. 'Could you help me, Charlie? I want some time alone to say goodbye.'

He nodded. 'Clean yourself up. Mother is already asking where you went.' Maggie sat up, brushed the straw from her clothes, and wiped her face on the bottom of her skirts. 'Now, we have five minutes to think up a plan before you need to show yourself.'

Together they sat in silence for the few minutes they had left to compose themselves, Contractor straining his head over the rail to join them. Maggie gave him a pat and almost laughed at his intuition.

'I've got it!' said Charlie eventually. 'We have church on Sunday. Just fake being sick and you can stay home. I'm meeting up with Valerie, so I'll get Mother and Father to visit with her family after church,' he said with a smile.

Charlie had been smitten with Val for the last year. Each holiday she came to stay at her uncle's farm and Charlie always found a reason to visit. Maggie liked Val; she was a pretty city girl but was sweet and a perfect match for Charlie.

'Are you going to propose?' she asked hopefully. 'I know she cares for you.'

He gave her a sly smile. 'I have been planning on it. Do you think she'd have me?'

'Yes, of course, Charlie.'

He let out his breath. He was nervous. Maybe he really was going to propose.

'Great. Well, that's settled, then. Sunday you can say your goodbye.'

Hearing him say it lifted a weight off her chest — at least now she knew she would have some special time alone with Rocco — but this relief was soon replaced with an anxious energy. She stood up. 'I'd better go find Mother.'

'And I need to help Father put up the fence.'

They crawled out of the hay and brushed each other off, then embraced.

'It will be okay, Maggie. I'm still here.'

'Thanks, Charlie.' She went over and kissed Contractor's nose. 'You too, boy.'

'Hey, he did nothing,' said Charlie as he followed her out.

'He didn't need to,' said Maggie with a laugh and darted off towards the cottage, leaving Charlie to wander back to the house alone.

*   *   *

That night Maggie saw Rocco again. He was sitting across from her at the table, seemingly paying attention to what her father was talking about but beneath the surface his legs were entwined with Maggie's. They hadn't been able to discuss his impending departure, just a quick 'hello' before dinner. She was bursting at the seams wanting to tell him about Sunday but it would have to wait. Hopefully tomorrow she'd be able to find some unsupervised time. But for now, being able to see and touch him was enough. When Mother got up to fetch the sauce Rocco's eyes stayed watching her, sending her unspoken messages from his heart. His dark eyes were heavy with longing and she knew exactly how he felt.

31

Finally landing back on home soil and walking into the familiar airport Toni and Flick both sighed with relief. Nothing beat coming home.

'Now this is a good feeling,' said Toni.

'Even better when we get back to Sunnyvale,' said Flick.

They navigated their way out of the airport to their car. Outside, the West Australian air smelt good. She sucked in breaths; everything felt familiar. The sun on her skin had that typical bite and the sky felt like home.

'Well, we know how to get to Quairading,' said Flick as she drove them out of the city.

They'd eaten on the plane and didn't feel like stopping again. Rocco was calling to them, and neither wanted to wait.

'We've been through it before. Wouldn't it be funny if we've actually driven past his farm, Mum?'

'Yes, that would be quite strange.' Toni turned to Flick. 'It's all been rather strange, hasn't it? Florence views, Umbria walks, coins in the Trevi, kisses at the Spanish Steps.' Toni sighed. Already it was starting to feel like a dream.

Flick giggled. 'I know. It all seems so surreal. But we did all that. It was so amazing. I'm glad we're nearly home but I wish we could have explored more.' She pursed her lips. 'I think I've been bitten by the travel bug.'

It was Toni's turn to laugh.

'Now we have the next step in our journey. Rocco is a mere two hours away. How do you feel, Mum?'

Toni sank back into her seat and watched the trees flash past as they headed through the hills of Perth and into the country. Flick's question hung in the air while Toni tried to formulate a reply. Did she tell her daughter the truth — that she was a crazy mixture of nerves and dread, fear and excitement, longing and panic? One minute she wanted Flick to drive faster to reach Rocco sooner, and the next moment she was eyeing the door handle as if it were an eject button that would fling her from this situation.

'Mum?'

Toni drew a deep breath and let it slide out between her teeth. 'I honestly don't know, Felicity. I'm feeling every emotion at the moment. It's easier not to think about it.'

'Okay. Maybe a distraction will help.' Flick turned up the radio.

The music didn't help but when the talkback came on, Toni found it easier to focus on their conversations and give her mind a rest.

Soon the trees gave way to the dry hills of York, and they drove further on until wide paddocks full of ripening crops made them feel closer to home. Nearly two hours after leaving Perth they arrived in Quairading and stopped at the BP roadhouse, where they hoped to find someone who'd know pretty much everyone in town.

'Um, excuse me,' said Toni to the young girl

297

behind the counter. 'I'm trying to find Rocco Valducci's farm?'

The girl, who looked not much older than Flick, smiled. 'Sure. You head out the road past the bins, heading to Corrigin, then take the Melba Road on your left and you can't miss it. It'll have a sign.'

'Thanks, that's great.' Toni clenched her fists and bought four chocolate bars. She needed comfort food.

'What's this for?' said Flick as Toni got back in the car and held out the chocolates.

'Just hungry,' she said. But looking at them now she realised she wasn't. Still, she opened one and started eating. Not even the sweet chocolate could take her mind off where they were going.

Toni gave Flick the directions, and five minutes after turning down Melba Road they spotted the sign as they drove up a small rise.

Flick stopped beside it. 'Oh my God, Mum.'

The large sign, quite faded, read 'R&C Valducci & Son', and underneath that in bold blue was the name 'Maggie Downs'.

'Take a photo with your camera, Mum, so we can show Nan.'

Down the driveway they went, river gums along either side, and new straight fences and wide paddocks beyond. 'His crops are nice,' Toni commented. 'Some look close to harvesting.'

Two homesteads came into view. The first one was newer, like a transportable, and the one in among some bush on the opposite side of the road was older, but still clearly lived in. 'Try that old one. My guess is the newer one is the son's.'

'You mean your half-brother's,' said Flick.

Toni's hand shot to her mouth as those words sank in. Flick was right. She had a brother. 'A younger brother,' she said, dropping her hand and letting her smile grow. 'It's surreal.'

'That means I have uncles and aunties. Finally. And cousins!' Flick let out a nervous giggle.

Both of them were jittery and overtired. But this was something that couldn't be put off for another day. They were so close. Maybe the chocolates had been a bad idea.

'Let's do this before I chicken out,' said Toni. She got out of the car and stood beside Flick. It took two seconds before she gripped Flick's arm in a fit of panic. 'Oh my God. Maybe we should have called first? What if we give him a heart attack? What if he doesn't believe us?' Toni felt the world start to spin around her.

'Mum! Calm down.' Flick was now holding her arms and shaking her slightly. 'Deep breaths, okay?'

Toni tried but her heart and head were racing.

'There is no other way. This isn't something you want to discuss over the phone. And I'm sure we won't kill him with shock.' Flick paused. 'Well, I'm pretty sure.' She pulled a face but it didn't reassure Toni one bit. Her skin was feeling damp, her head light. 'Uh, Mum, are you okay? You look like you're about to pass out.'

'I might,' said Toni as she tried to get a grip.

'Do you want me to tell him?'

Toni shook her head. She was so frozen in

doubt and panic that she wasn't even sure if she could walk.

A tanned, lean boy came running out of the house but paused when he saw them. He had to be around twelve and was a typical farm kid in worn jeans and boots.

Toni straightened her back and tried to take some control. 'Hello,' she said softly.

'Hello,' he replied. He cocked his head to the side, his eyes squinting. 'Who are you?'

'I'm Toni and this is my daughter, Flick. And you are?'

'Noah,' he said. 'Are you here to see my granddad?'

Toni stumbled over her own tongue, which upon hearing the word 'grandad' had seemed to swell in her mouth.

'Yes, is he here?' asked Flick.

Noah nodded. 'Grandad!' he shouted. 'You have visitors.' Then he gave them a wave, walked past them to the nearby motorbike and took off towards some sheds in the distance.

'Cool kid. A nephew.' Flick paused, her eyes growing wide. 'My cousin.'

Toni loved seeing Flick's excitement and wished she felt the same. So many new faces. Would Rocco allow her into his family? Would she even get to know Noah and his family? How would this meeting end?

They headed towards the front door. The flywire door opened before they got there.

'Hello?' said the man who walked out.

Toni stopped under the verandah, her body stationary as she recognised the man from all the

300

photos. But the familiarity didn't come only from those photos — she also saw herself in his eyes. The same deep browns that were neither like her mum's nor like Arthur's. Seeing that connection, feeling an even deeper sensation of belonging and recognition, made her speechless.

Flick stepped forward, holding out her hand. 'Rocco? Rocco Valducci?'

'Yes,' he said, shaking her hand, but his eyes kept coming back to Toni's as if trying to figure out something.

Could he see Maggie in her, or could he see himself, she wondered. Did he even know what it was that drew him to her face?

'My name is Flick and this is my mother, Toni. We are from Pingaring and I think you know our farm, Sunnyvale?'

Rocco blinked rapidly and let out a breath. 'Sunnyvale. Oh, I haven't heard that name in a long time.'

Toni couldn't stop studying him. He was tall, tanned, and dressed in blue cotton work pants and a shirt. Boots sat near the door, and Toni could tell he was active on the farm. She could see it in the strength of his arms and the straightness of his back. Age had threaded itself into his skin and lightened his hair but underneath, strong bones and muscle held him sturdy. His face was aged but his eyes held fight and determination, and he by no means seemed his seventy-six years.

'Is there somewhere we can sit down and talk?' asked Flick.

Rocco went pale and gestured them into his

301

house. 'Please, come in.'

Slipping off their boots, they followed him down the passageway to the dining room and sat at the square pine table. It was an old house but it was clean and tidy, and they had made the best of its aging features, with jarrah doors, frames and floors. Toni saw photos of kids on the wall, piles of farming magazines. It had a woman's touch, warm and homely.

'Is this about Maggie?' he asked, clenching his hands together. 'Has she passed away?' His mouth was set in a firm line, his brow creased.

Toni felt like crying right there and then. For Rocco to mention her mother's name was dreamlike, and to feel the emotion in his words was more than she could bear. Sliding her hand across the table she held his hand and shook her head.

'No. She's fine. Maggie is my mother. My full name is Antonia.' She watched relief flush his face, followed by familiarity as she said her name. 'Mum just recently told me that you are my father.' A tear escaped and trailed down her cheek. Toni's breathing stopped as the milliseconds ticked by like minutes while she waited for Rocco to reply. She didn't know what she was expecting but the way he drew his hand back and away from her stung more than any wasp bite.

Rocco leant back in his chair, his eyes set in his lap. Abruptly he stood and fell against the sink. Toni glanced at Flick, who shrugged slightly. Did they wait for him to respond?

His hand banged against the bench, causing

302

them to jump. 'No,' he said shaking his head. 'It's not true.' Rocco slowly turned his head, his eyes piercing.

'I'm sorry to tell you like this, if there was a better way . . . ' Toni's voice faded away. What could she say to make it all better? 'It was a shock to me too. I only just found out after fifty-three years.' Rocco just stood there, his expression hard and unreadable. 'But it makes sense now, why I didn't look like my father. I have your eyes,' she whispered.

As the words left her lips, his gaze found her eyes as if to see for himself. Toni saw the familiarity, the realisation. His wide shoulders begun to shake. Toni and Flick stood up uncertainly and shared a glance.

Rocco clung to the bench top as tears begun to slide down his weathered face. It was as if the world had come crashing down on him; his mouth contorted in pain and Toni covered her own mouth to stop her cries. She didn't know what to do or how to stop him from hurting.

A girl, about ten, came running in calling for her grandad. The girl's mother followed, then stopped abruptly when she saw Toni and Flick. The woman took one look at Rocco and rushed to his side.

'Dad? Dad, what's wrong? Are you okay?' She held his arms but the man seemed inconsolable. The woman with shoulder-length auburn hair turned to face them, her face flushed. 'Who are you? What is happening here?' She shot them accusing looks. 'Dad?' she said, turning back to him. Rocco let her hold him tightly but it was like he'd disappeared from the room, lost in his own grief. 'Someone tell me what's going on!' she demanded angrily.

'Mum, what's wrong with Grandad?' said the little girl, beginning to cry.

'It's okay, Holly. Come here,' said the woman as she reached out for her. 'Grandad's just upset. He'll be fine,' she said, although her face didn't show it.

Toni didn't know if it was her place to tell the secret, but she was hardly holding herself together. Rocco was in tears, she was in tears, and so was little Holly, and her half-sister looked ready to kill her. What had she done?

'Maybe we'd better go,' said Flick, who looked just as pale and confused. 'I'm sorry, we didn't mean to cause any problems. Come on, Mum, let's give him some space.'

'I think that would be best,' spat the mother, who seemed torn between wanting to interrogate them and consoling her father. 'Dad, talk to me,' she whispered, deciding he was more important than the strangers in his house.

Toni felt rejected but tried hard to remember how she'd reacted to the news. 'I'm so sorry,' she managed between her own sobs. Flick put her arm around her and guided her away from Holly's frightened eyes and her mother's outrage.

32

Flick glanced across at her mum again, then back to the road. She'd said nothing since they'd left Rocco. To start with, Flick was just giving her time to process, but now — well, they were nearly home and it was time to talk.

'You okay, Mum?' she asked again.

Toni was staring at the passing paddocks.

'Mum!' she said a bit louder, and waited till Toni turned.

'Hmm?'

'It was a shock for him. Remember how you reacted to the news?' Poor Rocco had looked like he'd been slapped with a wet fish. At least her mum had had time to get used to the idea before facing her dad. Rocco, on the other hand, had to deal with it face-on. The guy had gone deathly pale, and Flick had been worried they'd brought on a heart attack after all. Flick's stomach rolled as she remembered the look on her mum's face when Rocco had withdrawn his hand. That one movement had been her undoing. She'd been gutted, and Flick had felt its effects ripple through her own body.

Flick sighed. She was utterly exhausted. It had been such an incredibly long, emotional day of flying halfway around the planet, driving across the state, and then finally pulling into Maggie Downs to meet Rocco. She couldn't wait to get home and sleep for a week.

Except she couldn't even think about resting just yet — they had Maggie to face first.

'Please tell me how you're doing?'

Toni eventually turned and acknowledged her question. 'I'll be all right.' Toni shrugged. 'I didn't know what to expect, but it wasn't that.' A rush of breath left her lips. 'Maybe I had built up a perfect joyful reunion in my mind. I knew I was getting my hopes up.'

'Mum, you wouldn't be normal if you didn't hope for that. You have to let him get over the shock. When Nan told you, she was someone you love. We were complete strangers to him. Imagine how hard that would have been to take. Think of how you reacted with Nan?'

Toni turned back to the yellow crops flashing past the window. 'I know you're right . . . but it still feels awful.'

'And I'm sure Nan still feels awful too.'

Flick saw her mum nod. Maybe now she might understand it from Nan's perspective. Maybe now they could repair their rift.

'What shall we tell Nan?' Flick asked as she neared their driveway. Both of them stopped talking as they turned into it and started driving towards the house. Flick had never been so relieved to come home. She could almost cry from the joy. Glancing across she noticed her mum sit up and take note too. Her shoulders relaxed. She even smiled.

'God, I missed this place,' said Toni. And as they pulled up outside the house, she finally replied to Flick's question. 'We tell her the truth, I guess.'

Flick honked the horn, but she needn't have bothered as Nan was already running onto the verandah, apron on and tea towel hanging from her hands. She threw it onto the nearby chair and headed towards the car. Jimmy came running from the direction of the shed with Gypsy and Fella in tow. Flick bit her lip as she felt the relief of coming home, the exhaustion making her emotional.

She flung open her door and was mobbed as two dogs launched at them. 'Fella, Gypsy! Missed you guys.' Gypsy wandered off after saying hi, but Fella stayed glued to her side, racing around her feet and barking. He was so thrilled, his bark was becoming a squeak.

'He totally was lost without you,' said Jimmy. He pushed past Fella to grab her into a tight hug. 'We actually thought we'd lost the bugger. Gave us a fright. The little mutt was curled up beside Contractor. Wouldn't even come when we called.' Jimmy stepped back and smiled. 'Wow, you're a sight for sore eyes. Tired?' he asked.

'Yes, very. Nothing a cuppa wouldn't fix.' Flick stepped into Maggie's waiting embrace. '*Ciao*, Nan,' she said.

'Oh, lah-dee-dah,' teased Jimmy, and Maggie laughed.

'I'm so glad you're both home.' Maggie grasped Flick's head in her hands and kissed her forehead.

Toni stepped towards Maggie. 'Hey, Mum.'

'Hello, my baby,' Maggie said with a grin as she let Flick go. 'How are you?'

Toni didn't reply but stepped into Maggie's

arms and held her tight. Flick smiled stupidly as she watched them finally reunite. She glanced at Jimmy, who was also grinning. He gave her a wink as if to say, 'Job well done.'

'I missed you, Mum,' Toni said at last. She clung to Maggie as if she held all the answers to her problems.

'I missed you too, love.'

They pulled apart and both wiped the corners of their eyes.

'We have so much to tell you,' said Flick. 'Is the kettle on? Let's unpack later.'

'Yes, great idea,' said Toni with a sigh. 'It's been a bloody long day — and night! But I'm having a beer,' she said. Toni glanced at Jimmy. 'You want one?' she asked as she headed to the fridge on the verandah.

Jimmy's smile slid away. 'Please, thanks.'

Flick tucked Maggie's arm in hers and they all headed inside to sit around the table. She made herself and Maggie a coffee, of the instant kind.

'This coffee is nothing like Italian coffee,' said Flick. 'I wish we'd brought some back. It was divine.' If she closed her eyes and thought really hard she could almost smell the perfectly brewed coffee.

'Are we going to get this every morning at breakfast from now on?' Jimmy raised an eyebrow.

'Maybe,' she teased.

Maggie's eyes swam with emotion and unanswered questions. She pursed her lips but never asked. Flick knew she was fighting between wanting to know and not wanting to know. Toni had worn the same expression not that long ago.

The table fell silent. Jimmy sipped his beer and Flick looked to Toni, waiting for her to explain about Rocco.

Toni wriggled in her chair and cleared her throat. 'I guess we should get this over with. Mum, we found out Rocco is alive.'

Maggie swallowed hard and blinked rapidly.

'He actually lives here in Australia,' added Flick. She figured she'd better just blurt it all out, like ripping off a band-aid. Besides, her mum could probably use the help.

'What?' Maggie whispered. 'Here? How can that be? You have just been all the way to Italy.'

'That's right, where we found his family, who told us that Rocco lives here in Western Australia,' Flick explained.

'He came back to Australia for you, so his sister said,' Toni continued. 'Ended up buying land in Quairading, where he still lives to this day with his family.'

'He came back,' Maggie said softly. Her shoulders had drooped forward and for the first time in years, she seemed old and frail.

Toni nodded.

'Nan, he got married late in life and had two kids. I don't know why he didn't come and find you,' said Flick. 'I'm so sorry.'

'Maybe he did,' said Jimmy, startling them all.

The women turned to him like guns trained on a target. 'What if he did come by and ran into your parents first or something? Would they really want to tell you Rocco was there when by this time you were married with a kid? I know I wouldn't want to upset my daughter's new life, especially if she was happy.'

The table fell silent. They all knew he was right.

'Yeah, a respectable local man or an ex-prisoner of war with nothing? I know what I would have done,' said Flick, watching Maggie carefully.

'So he lives here?' Maggie asked.

'Yes. In Quairading, of all places!' Flick thought she had better deliver the next bit of news. Her mum was still struggling with it herself. 'We stopped by his farm on the way home. It's called Maggie Downs.'

Maggie went pasty and started shaking her head. 'No. Really? You've been there? Already? What did he say?'

Flick nervously watched her mum and nan, hoping neither of them would break and shatter. It had been one of those days and she wasn't sure how much more her mum could take.

'Well, we told him the truth and he kind of went into shock. Then his daughter came in and she was confused and angry with us so we thought it best to leave. He'll need time. He was really upset, Nan.' The image of Rocco, a strong able man, falling to pieces, flashed in her mind, and she felt the prickle of tears. Flick nodded, trying to convince them all she was right. 'It was a little emotional for all of us.' She glanced at her mum who sat quietly, beer untouched in her hand.

Maggie reached over to Toni. 'I'm sorry. I didn't want to put you through any of this.'

'It's okay, Mum. I understand.' Toni leant forward. 'We did meet Francesca, though, and she was lovely.'

'Rocco's little sister? Really?'

'Yes, with the help of a very handsome young local man named Stefano, but that is another story entirely . . . '

Maggie cleared her throat, straightened her shoulders, and plastered on a smile. 'Right, I want to hear all about it.'

But as Flick started recounting their trip from the beginning, she could see Toni's mind was far away — no doubt thinking of Rocco and how he was coping. At least she had an idea of what he would be going through. Flick just hoped that in time Rocco would be interested in meeting them all. Sure, she was an optimist but she really did hope a family reunion was possible.

Jimmy stood up, only five minutes into her story — they hadn't even arrived at Montone yet — and excused himself.

'Sorry, I've got to go feed the sheep before I forget. I'll leave you to catch up.' He gave Flick a wink. 'You can fill me in later.'

'You don't have to go, Jimmy,' said Toni. 'The sheep will be all right, won't they?'

It was late in the afternoon, after all. Flick watched Jimmy shrug, and tried to figure out the expression on his face.

'I've got them in the white dam paddock and I haven't got around to checking if the back fence is still up after that last rain. Don't want them getting out. Will just be a quick trip.' His smile was short and sharp before he turned and left.

They all watched him leave, the door shutting behind him. Toni tilted her head. 'How was he while we were away?'

Maggie shook her head. 'He was rather miserable without you both.'

'Really?'

'Antonia, I think you know,' was all Maggie said.

Flick shivered from the intensity of their gaze, Nan with her all-knowing eyes and Toni who seemed to understand them fully.

Toni reached for Maggie's weathered, slightly spotted hand with its paper-thin skin. It was still a source of strength. 'Yes, Mum. I do know.' Toni stood up, surprising them both. A smile crept across her face. 'Well, if you'll excuse me, I have something I must do.'

Then she turned and headed for the door.

33

Toni ran out the house after Jimmy, who was striding towards the shed.

'Jimmy,' she called, but he didn't slow. When she was close enough she reached out and pulled on his arm. 'Wait up, I want to talk to you,' she said rather gruffly.

'It's okay, I don't need any help,' he said, facing her.

God, he was handsome. His blond hair was clipped, his stubble at that perfect length that she found sexy. 'Good, 'cos I wasn't going to offer you any.'

He blinked. Confused.

Toni reached out and caressed his face. It was now or never. She was throwing all her chips on the table. 'I just wanted to tell you something that I probably should have told you a long time ago — I care for you, Jimmy. Actually, I'm in love with you.' Tears threatened but she blinked them away.

Jimmy's eyes shimmered in the dying light, realisation turning them a darker shade of jade. 'What was that? I think I missed it.'

Toni smiled. It was rare that she ever caught Jimmy off guard. 'I think you heard me. So what do you think? Have I missed the boat?' Her heart stopped. Everything was hanging on his reply.

Jimmy closed his eyes, then he reached for her,

pulling her into his arms with a strong wildness. 'No, you haven't missed the boat.'

Jimmy smelt like home: the sunshine, dirt and eucalyptus all rolled into one. God, it was so good to be back in his arms. Toni sucked in deep breaths of him. She'd needed this hug. She'd needed it at Rocco's just as much as she'd needed it back when Maggie had told her the news about Rocco. The difference was that only now did she realise it, and only now did she let herself surrender to it.

'I missed you like crazy,' he murmured next to her ear.

She wanted to stay in his embrace forever, savouring the feel of his stubble against her cheek, the beat of his heart against her chest. It was heaven.

He pulled back so he could see her face. 'So, you didn't find any nice Italians over there, then?' The cheeky grin she'd missed so much finally reappeared.

'Yes, I did actually. A gorgeous bloke called Stefano. Such a gentleman.' Toni almost laughed when Jimmy's face darkened. She'd never seen him jealous before. She rather liked it on him. 'And he and Flick got on like a house on fire.' She felt giddy and excited, high on life — or was it love? Whatever it was she felt free, like she didn't have to keep part of herself locked away any more.

'Really? You sure she was all right with him? Is he worthy?'

And that right there was the main reason she loved Jimmy with all her heart. He loved her daughter as if she were his own, and that was just fine by her.

'Yes. Let's get going and feed the sheep, shall we? And I'll tell you all about our trip.'

'No.'

'No?' Toni was puzzled.

Jimmy smiled. 'I've waited all this time; I'm not going anywhere yet with unfinished business.' He caressed her face, then, holding her chin, he tilted it up and found her lips.

Toni let out a whimper and melted against him. He held her with those strong arms. Heat was burning through her.

Jimmy groaned and pulled back. 'We'd better go or I'm not going to stop.' There was no cheeky smile or teasing spark in his eyes. He was deadly serious.

The sun was starting to set in the west. Toni realised just how long her day had been, yet being in Jimmy's arms filled her with energy she didn't realise she had.

'Who said I want you to stop?' She loved the way his body reacted to her words.

Jimmy was watching her carefully. 'Are you sure about this? About us?'

'Even with everything that's happened, I've never been more sure. I don't want to waste any more time. I want to live in the moment.' Toni cocked an eyebrow. 'Are *you* sure about us?'

'I've always been sure,' he said seriously. 'I think I loved you from the moment I set eyes on you.' An evil glint flicked across his eyes. 'Or maybe it was when I caught you skinny-dipping in the dam a few years ago.'

Toni threw her head back and laughed.

'God, I've missed that sound,' he said.

Passion swept into his gaze and Toni's body tingled enough to curl her toes as Jimmy found her lips once again.

34

Flick sat on Contractor as the sun rose on another beautiful day. Bright orange blazed across the tops of the crop, lighting them on fire.

'I really did miss being with you guys,' she said. It had nearly been two weeks since they'd arrived back from Italy. Leaning forward, she wrapped her arms around Contractor's neck. 'Did you miss me while I was away? I see you have a soft spot for Jimmy now too.'

Fella barked at the mention of Jimmy's name and stood up, glancing around. Flick laughed. 'He's not here, Fella.' She breathed in deeply. There really was nothing like home. Flick slid down from Contractor and walked towards the crop. Tall stalks held heads of wheat; Flick snapped one off and ground it between her hands, releasing the grain. So different from the big leafy tobacco plants in Italy.

The crops looked good this year: no frost, just plump grains. She flicked off the chaff and tipped the wheat into her mouth, chewing and crunching on the seeds. Grandad always chewed the grain as if it was gum. They would go crop inspecting together and Flick would retrieve some heads for him to study. He always called her his long legs. Sometimes he'd ask her to run through the crop, do cartwheels and jump around. The smile on his face was always worth it.

Flick pulled herself up onto Contractor. 'Come on, time to head home.' They were getting the header and field bins set up today. Jimmy wanted to take off a sample of barley for testing. And Flick wanted to check her email again. She and Stefano had been sending emails every day since she'd got home. She still had his first one pinned up in her room.

Buongiorno bella Felicity,
I hope you arrived home well. I miss you
so much. I came home with my family in
Montone. Coming home was hard without
you. I see you everywhere. Everything is
back to the way it was but it feels empty
without you.
A più tardi,
Stefano.

They talked about everything. She'd told him about their flight home, meeting Rocco, and Nan's reaction to the news. She'd told him how happy Fella and Contractor were now that she was back, and spoke of how much she missed him. And really, she did. While part of her had always hoped that it was little more than a holiday fling, Flick couldn't deny that Stefano was on her mind all the time. She missed him with an ache that cut deep to her core — a pain that hurt far more than her break-up with Chad.

It made her realise how hard it must have been for Nan to say goodbye to the man she loved. Flick wasn't sure if she was in love with Stefano but it felt darn close.

Once she'd put Contractor back in the stables and fed him, she made her way over to the old house. Jimmy had moved in, and his stuff filled up the house — stray clothes, boots and CDs, making it feel warm and lived-in. Flick was also adding her own personal flair to the mix — her shoes, hats and collection of snow domes. While she'd been overseas Jimmy had finished setting up the spare rooms, no doubt ready for his family to visit, and in doing so had made the house feel complete.

The floorboards creaked under her steps. The wide passageway felt bright with the cream-coloured walls against the wooden floor. Jimmy had even hung up some of the black and white photos Flick had found of the house after it was built. He'd framed them with jarrah panels from the old shearing shed. They were rustic, even with nail holes, but Jimmy had brought them to life and it just suited the warmth of their house.

Flick headed straight into the lounge room by the kitchen, where she had set up the new computer. It had arrived while she was away, and Jimmy and the local computer guy, Russ, had set it up for her. At least this way she had privacy when reading her emails. Jimmy wasn't likely to look over her shoulder — not like Nan and Mum.

She flicked on the computer, happy that it started up more quickly than the old one. Clicking on her mailbox she watched as a message downloaded. It was from Stefano.

With a whoop of delight she started reading, at first zooming through it quickly but then going back to read it again and again.

Buongiorno bella Felicity,
Si, I still miss you. I go to the lights of
Umbertide most nights to feel close to you.
Sofia thinks I am silly but I know it is
more. I feel it in my heart. We had new
Aussie tourists in Montone, an older
couple but their accent reminded me of
you. Because I miss you I have talked to
my parents about coming to Australia as I
have the money put aside. They are happy
for me to go and experience your country.
They gave me two months. Can I still
visit? You use me for harvest, si? I wait
your reply.
A più tardi,
Stefano.

'Flick, are you in here?' yelled Jimmy.

'Yeah,' she yelled back, then heard the creaks as he came down the passageway.

'I need your help, can you drive the tractor with the field bin to the paddock while I take the header? Your mum had to go into town to get oil and grease for the truck.' He frowned when he saw her face. 'What's up?'

Flick felt like she was going to burst. 'I just had an email from Stefano. He wants to come help us with harvest, if it's still okay.' She knew she was probably grinning like the Cheshire cat. 'Is that all right?'

Jimmy laughed. 'Don't know why you're asking me, I just work here. You need to check with the boss.'

'Well, she's the one who offered it to him

when we were over there, so she should be cool with it.' Flick swivelled her chair around and tilted her head. 'Hey, I consider you a boss here.' She gave him a wink. 'Especially seeing as you're dating the big boss,' she teased.

Red flushed across Jimmy's face and even reached his ears. He dug his hands into his jean pockets.

'Come on, Jimmy, I'm absolutely delighted. Surely I deserve a hug for all the ground work I did in Italy.'

He smiled and opened his arms. 'What ground work?' he asked as she stepped into his embrace.

Flick felt safe in his arms, protected. Was this what it felt like to have a real dad? She squeezed him tight before letting him go. 'Yeah, you know, a nudge nudge here and a hint hint there. She just needed to know that it was fine to have what she wanted. Life's short, you know?' Flick picked up her sunglasses and put on her green John Deere cap. 'I think seeing me with Stefano may have helped with that too.'

'Well, I'm glad he's coming here. Now I can give him the third degree and see what he's really like. Not all this sweet and nice stuff you and Toni keep spruiking.'

Flick gave the computer one last glance; she'd get back to Stefano this afternoon once she'd talked to Mum. She slapped Jimmy's arm as she headed to the front door. 'We didn't exaggerate, Jimmy.'

'What? He couldn't possibly be as cool as me.'

He flicked her hat off her head but she caught it on the way down. They shoved each other while trying to get their boots on; Jimmy fell back onto the wall and Flick ended up on her knees, laughing.

'Race you to the shed,' he called, sprinting off, his boots thudding across the verandah.

While Jimmy was young at heart, his body wasn't. He didn't stand a chance as Flick rounded him up. Even in her work boots she glided past, chuckles erupting from her throat while the dogs barked and joined in the fun.

She ran around the edge of the shed and leant against the tyre of the tractor, quickly trying to catch her breath. 'What took you so long?'

Jimmy stopped and bent over, breathing like a smoker. 'I'm going to regret that tomorrow. Probably pulled a few muscles.'

'Come on, old man, don't we have work to do?' She climbed in after lifting Fella up.

'You cheeky — '

The rest of Jimmy's words were lost in the slamming of the door. She pulled a face as he gingerly walked to the header. He slapped his backside and she snorted. Their code for 'kiss my arse'.

Flick warmed up the tractor, reached for the two-way, and waited until Jimmy was inside the header. He would have Gypsy in there too. 'So, boss, where to?'

'Meet you at the new land. Can you open the gate and have the fence down for me?' came his reply.

'Roger, ten four, old yella out,' she teased.

Old yella was what they called the tractor she was driving. It had been yellow once, but now it was faded and rusty. Still reliable, though — they didn't make them like this any more.

Jimmy's voice crackled out over the old speaker in the tractor. 'Maggie, you there?'

'Yes, Jimmy,' came her reply from the house. 'We're ready for that ride.'

'Roger, big boss, old duck out,' she said.

Flick burst out laughing. 'Good one, Nan.'

Life was finally back on track. Mum was back eating meals with Nan and they talked like they'd used to. And best of all, Flick wasn't stuck in the middle any more.

She took off down the back track, Jimmy following, until they hit the gravel road that went through their farm. Here Flick stopped and opened the double gate into their neighbours' paddock — it was a tight fit and she'd have to direct Jimmy through. Every harvest they went through McKenna's paddocks. It was handy having great neighbours.

Nan came charging through with the ute, drove through the bush to overtake Jimmy so she could get in front and open the rest of the gates for him on their neighbours' farm. Flick waved as she drove past, following the rough track along the fence line.

She wiped the sweat from under her hat and indicated for Jimmy to lift the comb and come slightly left. With an inch or so either side, he crept through and followed Maggie while Flick finished shutting the old gate.

Flick took the nature reserve track to get to their barley paddock and made her way to the fence that they shared with their neighbours. She could see Nan driving through McKenna's paddock, scaring his sheep towards the far corner.

'Fancy meeting you here,' said Flick to Maggie as she began unhitching the wire from the posts that held the boundary fence. Two massive rocks sat by each post. Farmers' tool number thirty-two.

'Ready to go?' asked Nan.

'Yep.'

Nan helped pull the wire down so it was flat on the ground. Quickly Flick put the rock on it. They did the same at the other post just as Jimmy approached. Nan took out a hankie from her pocket and started waving it at Jimmy, as if his red header was an angry bull. 'Olé!' she cried.

Flick giggled while Jimmy drove the header straight through and continued into the paddock, harvesting the barley while Flick righted the fence after Nan had brought the ute through.

Fella jumped on the back of the ute and Flick got in while they waited for Jimmy to collect enough for a sample.

'It's so good to see you and Toni so happy. It makes this old duck's heart swell,' said Maggie, reaching for Flick's hand and giving it a squeeze. Her eyes sparkled with joy and her face rippled with lines as she smiled.

'And I'm glad you and Mum are back to normal again.'

'Yes, so am I. She asked me last night after dinner to tell her about him, when he arrived on Sunnyvale. It was so good to share that with her and for Toni to be interested. I just wish Rocco had taken the news better.'

'I agree. Do you think Mum is handling it okay?'

'She seems to be. Maybe being with Jimmy, she's happy and isn't giving it much thought,' said Maggie.

'How about you, Nan? Are you still thinking about Rocco?' asked Flick.

Maggie pulled a loose thread on the hankie in her lap, her head bent down. 'Oh, I will always think of him, love. I have done my whole life, so why stop now?' She gave Flick a weak smile. 'But I do wonder what he's thinking of all this. Is he curious about Toni and me? Will he ever want to see us?'

'Do you think he'll ever make contact? He knows where we live. Or should we try again?'

Maggie shook her head. 'No, I don't think we should. He knows now, he knows where we are, so the ball is in his court. But I don't think we should wait. We need to move on with our lives.'

Flick agreed but she couldn't help wondering how Nan had tried to move on with her life fifty-three years ago.

35

Maggie buried down into her bed, hiding under the sheet. Last night she'd gone to bed before dinner, complaining she didn't feel well. It killed her not to sit across from Rocco but she had to do it to keep her mother from getting suspicious. During the night she'd also taken some pepper, which she started smelling in the morning to cause sneezing and red eyes. As an added precaution, she kept her hands on her forehead, hoping to keep it feeling hot. Her stomach gurgled. She wished her parents and Charlie would leave for church so she could have breakfast.

Maggie smelt her mother's suffocating perfume before she heard her. She tugged down her sheet, keeping her eyes droopy.

'Margaret, are you awake?' Phyllis felt for Maggie's temperature. 'You do feel hot. Do you want me to stay home?'

Maggie slowly shook her head and tried to croak out some words. 'No. It's just a flu. I'll be fine. I just want to sleep.' She let her eyes close and tucked herself into her pillow.

'All right, then. I've left some chicken broth on the stovetop. Try and have some.'

'Yes, Mother. Thank you.'

'We are heading off now. Charlie is rather excited to see Valerie again. She's a lovely girl.'

Maggie knew her mother approved of Valerie and her background. She was from a wealthy family and her father worked in government. It was the cherry on the cake.

'Say hello to Arthur for me,' said Maggie and watched her mother smile and then leave.

Charlie stuck his head in a moment later. 'All good, sis. We're leaving now.' Maggie propped herself up on her elbows and Charlie laughed. 'You do look sick.'

She pulled a face but then smiled. 'Thanks, Charlie.' He was giving her the best gift ever.

'I'll try hard to keep them away for as long as I can and when we get back I'll drive around so you know we're home.' He winked and ducked off before she could thank him again.

Straining her ears, she heard the ute leave, and gave it two minutes before jumping out of bed to get cleaned up.

They had completely moved into the new house and Maggie did love the space. She had a big room to herself and it didn't creak like her old one, nor did it let the wind in. The high ceilings helped give it that spacious feeling, and the dining room was big enough for a large table. No more sitting crammed together around their old small one, knees practically bumping the person opposite, with no room to put a serving dish between their plates. And most importantly, Rocco had helped build it. His hands had been on every brick.

She slipped on her pale-blue button-up blouse and long A-line skirt and then had breakfast. Once she'd washed her face, put on some make-up and brushed her hair, she skipped out the house and towards the cottage. Father had told the men not to work, just to enjoy their last few days on the farm. 'Go shooting or go for a ride on Contractor. Relax,' he'd said.

When she got to the cottage, Rocco was sitting on the step outside his little tin room. Maggie stopped running and slowed to an elegant walk. Rocco's arms were resting on his knees and he wore a singlet with braces for his pants. The sight of him made her breathless. His body glistened in the morning sunlight and only made her nervousness rise. He saw her and stood quickly, walking towards her.

'Maggie.'

'Morning, Rocco,' she said shyly and glanced around.

'Giulio has gone for a ride on Contractor. He said he will be gone till lunch.'

Maggie nodded as they stood watching each other. 'I can't believe you leave tomorrow. I can't bear to think about it,' she said. Too late — the emotions swamped her and tears threatened.

'No, *amore mio.*' *My love.* Rocco moved to take her hands into his. 'Don't cry.'

A tear fell before she could stop it. 'I wish I could go with you to Italy. Maybe we could run away?' She looked up into his beautiful brown eyes. Hoping. Dreaming.

Rocco shook his head as he thumbed away the tear. 'No, I must return home.'

'But we'd be together and that's all we need,' she said. She couldn't imagine a life without Rocco. For so long she'd had to hide her feelings for him.

'What about Charlie and your parents? You would miss them. I cannot let you give all this up for me. What would they do if they caught us? What would we do? Where would we go?'

Maggie turned away, ripping herself from his arms so he couldn't see the sobs starting to take over her body.

328

'Don't you care about me?' She felt as if the Clydesdales were tearing out her heart with a rough rope, surging forward like they did when digging up the paddock. Any moment now she'd hear it pop from her chest. Maybe then it wouldn't ache so much.

'Maggie, Maggie.' He wrapped his arms around her from behind, holding her against his chest, his lips by her ear. 'How could you ever think that? I love you.' As if to show how much he really meant it, he said it in Italian too. 'Ti amo.'

She went limp in his arms. Oh, how she'd missed his touch. Stolen hugs here, sneaking kisses there; it's all they'd ever had. Now she could truly be his. Spinning in his arms, she looked up into his eyes.

'I love you too, Rocco. I don't know how I'm going to go on without you.'

Rocco smiled sadly. 'You will, because you are strong, amore mio. I will write to you and you know I am coming back. We will get our own land and we can start a life together. Think to the future. Our future.' Rocco kissed her tear-stained cheeks, her nose, her eyes. 'I love the blue of your eyes, just like the skies here.'

Maggie grinned. His kisses and words were making the pain ease. She reached up for his face, holding it still. They gazed at each other as if trying to memorise every line and contour.

'Let's not talk of sad things now.'

She stood up onto her toes, her lips meeting his. She sighed softly as he squeezed her against him, their kisses growing deeper. An electric thrill ran through her body when their tongues touched. Her body was alive, burning with a need for more. Maggie pulled away.

'Come with me.' She took his hand and led him into the empty cottage. Father had bought Mother a new bed for the house so the old one remained in the cottage. Maggie had plans for it, and had smuggled an old sheet out of the new house from under her mother's nose.

'In here,' she said, guiding him into her parents' old room. The door squeaked shut.

Maggie let go of his hand and started to undo the buttons on her blouse. Rocco stood beside her, watching her fumbling fingers. When she'd undone the last one he took her fingers and kissed them. Not rushing, he bent to kiss her again. Maggie felt like she was floating on air. Rocco made her forget her surroundings and he made her feel alive. With her hands pressed flat against his chest she moved them up and flicked off his braces. Rocco arched back and whipped his singlet off over his head in a smooth motion. Maggie didn't know where it landed, as her eyes were glued to the half-naked man in front of her. This would be her first time but she was ready. She loved Rocco with every fibre and cell of her body. She wanted to be with him, to reinforce their love.

Tenderly she touched him. His skin was warm and his chest strong and tight. Low in her belly the fire burned; it wanted more. Maggie shrugged off her blouse and laid it over the metal end of the bed. Mother wouldn't be impressed if she got it dirty. She did the same with her skirt, then stood before him in her undergarments. Rocco dropped his pants, standing only in his worn cotton briefs.

Maggie felt shy in just her cotton bloomers and pointed bra, especially when Rocco stared at her with such desire. No one had ever looked at her this way,

330

but it mirrored how she felt.

She unclasped her bra, letting the straps slide down her arms.

'Oh, *dio mio!*' he muttered.

Next went her cotton bloomers, and Rocco followed her lead until they stood naked in front of each other. Having three brothers, Maggie had seen the male anatomy, knew what it looked like and had giggled with her friends about it, but this was completely different. He was hard and she was fascinated. She felt wet with wanting. He'd brought this feeling on many times before with their stolen kisses and groping moments but now, now the hunger was more like an ache. She wanted to be with him.

Rocco stepped in and reached for her waist. As his mouth found hers, Maggie had no second thoughts. None at all.

*   *   *

Afterwards, Rocco stroked her hair as they lay curled up together. 'What are you thinking, *amore mio*? Not too painful?'

Maggie shook her head against his chest. 'No,' she said with a smile. 'It was beautiful.' She'd been so consumed by Rocco she didn't remember feeling much pain at all. Her fingers played along his chest, through his dark scattering of hair.

'How long have we got?' he asked.

'Charlie was hoping to keep them away for lunch.'

He nodded and kissed her forehead. Instead of discussing the elephant in the room, they took a different path and dreamt out loud. They talked of having their own farm and how their life would be.

Maggie dreamt of being on Sunnyvale, but she knew her mother would never allow it. But wherever Rocco was, that would be her new home.

The cottage was quiet except for their voices. The morning passed while they discussed their possible future. A name for their farm caused much debate.

'I still like Maggie's Hill the best,' said Rocco.

'What if we have flat land?' she teased. 'We could call it Sunnyvale two? When you build our beautiful home, I will help you,' said Maggie. She'd be right beside him for everything.

'With many rooms we can fill with children,' he said eagerly. 'If we have a girl, we can call her Phyllis.'

'No,' scoffed Maggie, propping herself up so she could gaze into his eyes. 'I'd rather call our girl Charlie, or even name her after your mother.'

'Antonia? You'd do that?'

'Of course, Rocco. You've told me so much about your family, I feel as if I know them. I'd even call her Francesca after your little sister.'

His eyes saddened. 'I miss her so. I have been gone for so long.' Maggie snuggled closer. 'I hope Mama still has her garden. I can see her watering with the old bucket and Francesca eating peas while Mama's not looking.'

In four years his little sister would have become a young woman. She could even be married.

'What do you miss the most?' she asked.

'That easy. Mama's polenta and the *cappelletti* in broth. Lots of pasta and ... *legumi*?' After much discussion, Maggie eventually worked out he meant chickpeas and lentils. 'In Italy they are called *la carne dei poveri*, 'poor man's meat'. My *padre* hunts wild pig, gets ham sometimes, rabbit too.'

Maggie tried to imagine his father walking a land unfamiliar to her and hunting much like they did. Rocco sighed contentedly.

She smiled. 'You sound so close to your mama.'

'*Una buona mamma vale cento maestre.*'

'What's that mean?'

'Old Italian words. 'A good mama is worth a hundred teachers.''

Maggie wondered if her mother fitted into that saying. She had taught Maggie how to sew, cook and behave like a lady, after all.

'May I ask you again what it was like at war?' she said softly. She often wondered what her brothers had been through. Would Rocco be up to telling her now?

He stiffened slightly, his chin brushing past her hair as he nodded. 'It was awful. Watching friends die by me.' He closed his eyes as if trying to shut out the vivid memories. Maggie tilted her head back and kissed his cheek before nuzzling against his chest. She wanted to know everything about Rocco, even the darkest, hardest parts.

'I was captured in Sidi Barrani, in Egypt. I was in the Italian 10th Army, we were waiting for supplies and more help. The British got us by surprise. They had big guns, aircraft and armour. Most of us went willingly when captured. Twenty thousand prisoners. It was dry, dusty desert land. So dead from what we were used to. Sandstorms would blast us.' He put his hand on his face as if protecting it. 'I thought it hell but then we were shipped off to India and put in camps. We hardly lived, sometimes only an onion to get us through the day.' He exhaled heavily. 'So coming to Australia and then to Sunnyvale . . . ' He paused, dragging his hand away and caressing her face. 'It felt like heaven.'

'India sounds awful.'

Rocco turned away. 'It was.'

Maggie kissed him along his torso until he squirmed and laughed. 'I'm glad you came here,' she said, stopping to be serious. Maggie shifted so she lay on top of him. A heated spark flitted through his eyes and she almost giggled with delight.

'Me too. Living through the war was worth it just to meet you.'

Tears welled in Maggie's eyes. Rocco smiled and wiped them away. 'I will love you forever.'

'Me too.' Maggie felt the heat building again. If she was a little tender she had forgotten about it.

'*Voglio fare l'amore con te.*'

She didn't know what he'd said — something about love. But she didn't need to know, because she could see it in his eyes. He wanted her again and she was ready to love him even more.

* * *

The time for Giulio and Rocco's departure came on Monday at nine-thirty. Rocco had told her she couldn't cry, that she had to be brave. 'Don't think of this as goodbye,' he'd said. '*A più tardi,* for now.'

Maggie was trying hard to remember that as she watched Mr Tweedie's truck pull up in front of their house. She felt physically ill and couldn't even find a smile for the captain.

Giulio and Rocco had their small bags packed and were sitting out the front of the house, waiting. In the meantime they had helped Charlie and Father with the garden.

After Father said hello to Mr Tweedie, he held his hand out to Giulio and then Rocco. 'I wish you blokes all the best. Thank you for being a part of our farm and family. I will miss you. It was like having my sons back.'

Maggie fought the tears as she watched her father struggling to say goodbye. Charlie shook their hands and grabbed them like he used to with Thomas and George. Surprising everyone, Mother actually hugged them — probably because she was overjoyed at their departure. Maggie, on the other hand, felt two seconds away from a shattering breakdown, like the glass bottles they'd shot at as kids. Millions of shimmering pieces on the ground.

'*Arrivederci*, Giulio. I will miss you.' And she would. He was a lot like Thomas in that calm, gentlemanly way. He always had time for Maggie and Charlie, and worked hard to please their father.

'Goodbye, Miss Maggie,' he said, kissing her cheek.

Maggie swallowed hard. Rocco was next. She gave him a hug, trying to keep it just like Giulio's. '*Arrivederci*, Rocco.'

'*A più tardi.*'

Maggie smiled. Rocco had been refusing to say goodbye, instead insisting on 'see you later'. She kissed his cheek and it was probably obvious to everyone that it was longer and more heartfelt than her farewell to Giulio, but she didn't care. The man she loved was leaving and it could be years before she saw him again. How would she make it through each day?

'Here, take these photos with you,' said John.

Maggie stepped back while scrunching her hands so tightly her nails would leave a mark, or even blood, in her palms.

'Thank you.'

Rocco pulled out a bit of paper from his pocket. 'My old address. I hope you will stay in touch.' John nodded and put it in his pocket.

One day soon she'd casually ask to write him a letter and hope her mother didn't make a fuss.

'Let's away, I have another farm to visit,' said Mr Tweedie, and he shook John's hand before walking to his truck.

Rocco and Giulio followed. Throwing their tiny bags into the back they climbed up under the canvas, taking not much more than they'd arrived with.

Mr Tweedie waved before turning the truck. Mother had already gone back into the house, but Charlie and Father stayed by her side as they watched the truck leave. Maggie couldn't stop the tears as she saw Rocco waving from the back. Charlie tucked her under his arm and stood with her long after the truck had rumbled away in the dust and disappeared from view.

36

Nothing was more rewarding than sitting in the header as it chomped through your hard-earnt crop. Toni smiled and glanced at Fella curled up by her feet. The radio played some Cold Chisel while she bounced along the paddock as the header reel turned. In front was Jimmy in the other, much older, red header. She liked knowing he was close by. The barley was making malt grade so there was plenty to be happy about.

Flick was on her way to the airport to collect Stefano, who was due to arrive tomorrow at 7 a.m. She'd gone down to stay the night in Perth so she could be there early to meet his flight. The grin on her face had been a permanent fixture of late, her excitement uncontainable. For once her farm chores had been completed with gusto. Toni hoped Stefano would be ready for work when he got here, because he'd be thrown right in.

'I think I've got a flat, Toni,' came Jimmy's voice over the two-way.

'Ah, shit,' she mumbled to herself. Bloody bad timing.

She reached for the handpiece and replied. 'Front or back?'

'Front.'

Toni cursed again. Bigger tyre meant bigger bill. 'Okay. I'm on my way.'

'A root?' she asked when she arrived on the scene. His body was tucked under the header so he could see the inside of the tyre.

'Yeah, something like that,' came his muffled reply. 'Through the side too.'

Jimmy backed out and rubbed his face as he cursed. She could see he felt bad; they didn't like outlaying extra money. Toni wanted to caress his face and ease the worry away. He was as invested in this farm as she was and it cemented her feelings for him.

Jimmy lifted off his akubra and swiped at his brow. 'The field bins are full so I'll go get the truck and deliver a load.'

That was a good plan, not much else they could do. 'And I'll go call Tyrepower to see if they can send someone out. Bit of luck, they have one to go straight on.' Toni was about to head to the ute parked by the field bin but Jimmy reached out, his hand sliding around her hip and dragging her towards him.

'And where do you think you're going?' he said with a sexy growl.

Toni relaxed into his arms. There was always time for Jimmy, a kiss or a touch didn't chew up much time and she enjoyed the reminders that they were together. Things were different now. She could reach out and touch him if she wanted.

Jimmy lifted her hat, watching her eyes before dropping his gaze to her lips. His other hand reached behind her neck and slowly he brought her closer. In an instant, Toni had gone from worrying about the header tyre to completely forgetting they were in a paddock as his kisses consumed her. She loved everything about this man.

With a groan Jimmy pulled away. As the passion faded, his green eyes turned to mischief. 'So what are you up to tonight?'

'Nothing, why?' she asked.

Jimmy played with the top of her shirt buttons. 'Well, with Flick away I have the house to myself, so I was wondering if you'd like to come to dinner.'

Her eyebrows rose. 'Dinner? Really?'

'I can cook more than just a barbecue, you know,' he said, half offended. 'How does chow mein sound?'

'It sounds good. What time do you want me and what should I wear? Is this a formal date?'

Jimmy's smile was dangerously heated. 'Whenever you're ready and you can wear nothing if you like. But if you want to actually eat I suggest you wear some form of clothing, otherwise I'll be too busy devouring you.' He leant forward and nuzzled her neck.

An outbreak of goosebumps spread over Toni's body in the heat of the afternoon. She grinned wickedly. 'Okay. I'd like to actually eat something you've cooked.'

He nibbled on her earlobe in between words. 'Believe me, it will be so delicious I promise you'll be coming back for more.'

Toni wasn't sure if they were talking about food any more; she was struggling to hold a thought. With a last peck on her lips, he righted her hat and stood back out of arm's reach.

'I'd better get back to work before my boss takes it outta my hide,' he said with a grimace.

Toni laughed. 'Yeah, she's a piece of work so I'd toe the line if I was you.' She whistled to Fella and turned towards the ute. 'You want a lift to the truck?' It sat over by the fence line.

'Nah, the walk will do me good.'

Toni jumped into the ute and watched him walking with Gypsy. How had she got so lucky? Then she thought about dinner tonight and her body tensed. Hell, she knew what was implied. They hadn't taken the next step yet. She wanted it but it had been a long, long time between drinks. So long, in fact, that the spiders had done away with their cobwebs and had built their own two-storey mansions. Toni forced the thought from her mind. It was time to get back on the bike.

At the house, she headed straight to the office.

'What's wrong, dear?' asked Maggie poking her head around the doorway.

'Got a flat on Jimmy's header. What are you cooking? It smells divine.'

'I'm trying a new orange cake recipe; it will be ready in ten minutes if you want to try some. Maybe you could take some back to Jimmy?' Maggie came and sat beside her on the spare seat against the wall. 'So, how are you really going? I know you're busy with harvest but I do worry.'

Toni leant back in her chair. 'I'm fine, Mum,' she said with a sigh.

'It's just, Rocco hasn't made contact and I didn't want you to get your hopes up like I did

340

all those years ago.'

Pain shot through her chest at her mum's words. Being with Jimmy and having harvest had kept her mind busy, but lurking deep down was hope that Rocco would seek her out. Is this how her mum had felt after he'd left? Constantly living with anticipation, only to have it fade into nothing? Or did her mum still have some of that optimism, even today?

'Do you wish he'd visit?'

Now it was Maggie's turn to sigh. 'I sometimes think that I'm happy with life, I have my family . . . yet I still wonder. I still want to know why.'

'Well, at least it's all out in the open now. Everyone is aware. There's no going back and I'm glad that there are no more secrets between us,' said Toni. 'There *are* no more secrets, right?'

Maggie smiled reassuringly. 'Yes, Antonia. That was the only thing I ever kept from you and I believed I was doing it for the right reasons.'

'I know that now, Mum.' They sat quietly, watching each other.

'Don't forget to stop by the kitchen before you head out.' Maggie got up and Toni did too, reaching out to hug her mum tightly.

Maggie disappeared back into the kitchen while Toni began searching for her dad's teledex. She lifted up papers and opened drawers. Since Flick had rattled through the office to take what she wanted to the other house, Toni was having trouble finding anything.

With a sigh, she picked up the phone directory and thumped it on the table to search for the

Tyrepower number.

Luck was in: they had a spare tyre and a bloke who could fit it. He'd be out in two hours. Toni grinned with relief as she put the phone down. If it had been the middle of harvest, they wouldn't have been so lucky.

Leaning back on her chair, Toni stared at the phonebook. Finding Rocco had made her think about Simon and all that Felicity could be missing out on. With everything going on and with all the things Flick had said, she realised just how important it was for Flick to know her dad, to see the other half of her DNA. After all, Toni had felt the connection just seeing Rocco, seeing the resemblance. What if she could give that to Flick? It could be fraught with danger; she could be putting Flick at risk of being disappointed or going through something similar to Toni. But she knew Flick was strong and would survive anything thrown her way.

Her hand hovered over the numbers on the phone. It was time to grow a pair and do what she should have done a long time ago.

She dialled Stan's number and listened as it rang.

'Hi Stan, it's Toni here. I'm chasing your help.' If anyone could remember the names of the guys who worked on that crew, it would be Stan. He ran the shop back then and practically fed and housed that crew. Plus, he knew everything about everyone.

'Yeah, I remember those guys. Simon's last name you want, hey?' He paused thinking. 'I can't remember it off the top of me head. But I'll tell you what. I set up an account for them all back in the day and I've got the old accounts out in the shed. If you give me a few hours, I bet you I can find his last name.'

'Really, Stan? That would be awesome.'

'Did he not pay a debt or something?' enquired Stan.

'No. I'm just trying to track him down because he's Felicity's father.'

The phone fell silent for a long second. 'Oh, right. Well, I'll call you back soon. I'm sure it's here, Toni. We'll find him.'

'I hope so, Stan. I'm not sure how else to find him without a last name.' Toni hung up the phone and leant back in the chair. She felt a rolling sickness but she pushed it aside, because she knew she was doing the right thing by Flick. Regardless of how it made her feel.

★ ★ ★

Toni touched up her lipstick, checked the soft, smoky eye shadow against her dark eyes and adjusted her black dress. It was actually one of Flick's. Toni had nothing sexy and fun of her own so she'd gone searching through Flick's clothes while she was waiting for the tyre to be fixed. She'd found the little black dress, which frankly looked little more than a nightie, and had instantly put it back. But she did want something that would surprise Jimmy, and the dress would certainly do that. So she'd taken it along with two others to try. Toni wasn't worrying too much about the shoes — she wasn't planning to wear them for long.

The soft black fabric clung to her curves and strained at her bust, making Toni feel very exposed. It was a far cry from her usual jeans and singlets. If she bent over, the dress rose up over her bum. How could anyone actually wear this out in public without making a spectacle of themselves?

She turned away from the mirror and dabbed on a little perfume that she kept for special occasions. Then she reached for her long jacket, covering herself up. She'd feel silly walking around the farm in this dress.

Slipping on her thongs, she stuck her head around the lounge room doorframe. 'I'm heading over now, Mum. If you need anything, call us on the two-way.'

Maggie looked up from her knitting. 'I won't need you,' she said with a smile. 'I've got some whipped cream in the fridge if you want it,' she added with a chuckle.

'Oh my God, Mum. No.' Toni blushed and headed for the door, feeling young and in love. It was like she was living her youth all over again.

Outside, Fella followed her closely and Contractor whined from his stall. They'd both missed Flick today. At the door of the old house, she slipped off her thongs and jacket. The smell of spices floated through the open flywire door. Fella curled up on the verandah as Toni entered.

U2's song, 'With or Without You', played from the lounge room and she could hear Jimmy singing along with it. She crept down the passage, hoping the song hid the creaks of the floorboards. In the dining area by the kitchen he'd set up the table with glasses, wine and candles. Toni's heart skipped a beat. She'd never had a proper romantic candlelit dinner before.

Jimmy was leaning over the stove, a tea towel over his shoulder while he stirred. His was moving to the music, and his bum looking perfect in his stonewash jeans. He was also barefoot. She crept closer until she could smell his alluring aftershave over the cooking meal.

Toni leant against the bench and tried to strike an alluring pose. 'Something smells good.'

Jimmy turned with a start, the wooden spoon held in his hand. The black dress was worth the look on his face. He drank her in, every curve and every dip, and for once Toni felt powerful and seductive.

'Wow.' He swallowed, his eyes still roaming.

Toni felt shivers of anticipation. 'How's dinner going?' she asked and tried not to smile as his eyes widened. He'd forgotten all about it bubbling away on the stove.

Quickly he turned to stir it. 'It's nearly ready. Ah, shit, it'll do.' He flicked off the burner, threw down his tea towel and swept her up in his arms. 'My God, what are you wearing?' he mumbled. He buried his head against her neck and dragged his lips across her skin.

'You told me to wear something, I thought this was appropriate. A little black dress is good for any occasion,' she teased while her hands gripped his back.

'You got the 'little' bit right.' He pulled away so he could see her again. 'Damn.' He took her face in his hands and kissed her. 'You look amazing. Please tell me you're not hungry?'

'Oh, I'm hungry,' she purred. Jimmy groaned and Toni chuckled. 'Come on, I'll help you. What needs doing?'

He sprang back and guarded the stove. 'No, you go and sit down and pour us some wine. I've got this.' He shot her a look warning her to behave.

Toni went back to the table and opened the wine. It probably wasn't the time, but she wanted to be upfront and honest with Jimmy. 'I went searching for Flick's father, Simon, today.' She wasn't sure how Jimmy would take it, as he was pretty protective of Flick in his own way.

'Oh, right.' Then he was quiet.

'Well? What do you think? Bad idea?'

'What made you do it?' he asked.

Toni crossed her legs and began to bounce her leg. 'I guess everything with Rocco. I'm glad I know about him I've seen him and I know he's out there. And it got me thinking about Flick and all the times she's asked me about Simon. I just tried to put myself in her shoes, regardless of how much I want to protect her.'

Jimmy turned. 'And it's what she wants, isn't it.' Toni nodded and her shoulders dropped as if in surrender. 'You have to do what's best for Flick.' He gave her a reassuring smile. 'Did you have any luck?'

'Yes, actually. Stan found his name in some old records. Simon Templeton is his name.' They stared at each other, both understanding the massive can of worms this had opened up.

'You did a good thing. That would have been hard, but I'm proud of you.'

His confirmation eased her mind. She hoped Simon was half the man Jimmy was. 'I'm thinking I might try to contact Simon first, try to spare Flick any shock or rejection before I tell her any of this.'

'That's a good plan. I'll be with you through it all,' said Jimmy softly as he put their plates on the table and joined her.

Toni unclenched her hand and her leg stopped moving. 'Thanks, Jimmy.' Now that she'd cleared the air she felt so much more relaxed.

'Grub's up, babe.'

She loved it when he called her by his pet names. It still surprised her, and gave her a thrill.

'This smells great.' Picking up a fork, she scooped up some of the rice and mince. 'Mmm, delicious.' Jimmy hadn't touched his yet, he was too busy watching her. 'You going to eat?' He didn't move. 'You might need it for stamina.'

He picked up his fork and started shovelling food in.

She laughed, but the anticipation was affecting both of them and comments like that weren't helping. So Toni steered the conversation back to farming. They talked harvest until the bottle of wine was nearly empty and their plates had been scraped clean. Toni stood to clear the table.

'No,' said Jimmy, reaching for her hand. 'Leave them. I'll clean up in the morning.' He pulled her towards him, his arms circling her waist. 'Dance with me.'

'You've Lost That Lovin' Feelin'' by The

347

Righteous Brothers echoed down the hallway from the stereo as they started to sway.

Jimmy's hands moved down over her backside. He raised a brow. 'Did you rip off the bottom of this dress?' He didn't wait for her reply. 'I like it, but as long as you only wear it for me.'

Toni pushed against his chest, his heart pounding strongly. She moved her hands to the buttons on his blue dress shirt and one by one slipped them undone until she could part the material and touch his skin. Light-coloured hairs brushed her fingers as she explored the firm muscles. Jimmy pulled her closer so she couldn't miss his arousal. She kissed his chest, moving up towards his neck, her hands following until they entwined behind his neck. He moaned when she nibbled on his earlobe and whispered, 'I love you, James.'

He claimed her lips and she no longer heard the music, just the rhythm of their hearts. With strong arms he lifted her up. Toni wrapped her legs around his waist and he carried her towards his room. He set her down beside the bed and Toni unzipped the dress and slipped the straps down. The sheer fabric fell to the floor, leaving her standing in the sexiest briefs she owned.

But her lack of fancy underwear didn't kill the heat glowing in Jimmy's eyes. He shrugged off his shirt and reached for Toni. With gentle hands and warm lips he tasted and teased each breast until Toni was burning with desire. She started undoing the buttons on his jeans, all her previous anxiety falling away as they stood naked, facing each other. She felt nothing but love and

348

passion, and it pulsed through her. Jimmy reached for her, caressing her face.

'You have made me the happiest man in the world, Antonia Stewart. I love you so much.'

Toni grinned while trying to take in the masculine beauty that was James. So magnificent and strong, but it was his chest that consumed most of her attention, for that was where his heart lay, filled with a gentleness that made him who he was. She traced a finger over his lips, gazed into those jade depths and was ready to give herself to the man she loved.

37

Flick's bum was starting to go numb. She'd been so excited she'd got to the airport an hour before Stefano's flight was due, which didn't stop her checking every face from every flight that landed.

She chewed her nail as his plane finally started to disembark. But the moment Stefano cruised out the gate, her anxiety disappeared. Any worry that her feelings might have just been a holiday romance fled upon seeing his face. He looked full of relaxed confidence, wearing jeans and a snug white T-shirt. He had a small carry bag over one shoulder and sunglasses on top of his head. It was like all her birthdays had come at once.

'Stefano!' she called, waving madly. One look at each other and they were running, colliding into an embrace and kissing. Some old guy nearby clapped, bringing them back into the real world. Flick pulled back to study him. 'Oh my God. You're here. I can't believe it.'

'Me too. You are just as beautiful as I remember.' He cupped her face and kissed her cheeks softly.

'*Come stai?*' she said with a grin.

'I am well, thank you. Have you been practising?'

'*Forse.*' Maybe.

Stefano chuckled. 'I can help you learn more.'

Flick was floating on air. She gripped Stefano, hugging him tightly, afraid this was all a dream.

He threaded his hand through her hair and whispered her name, causing ripples of delight. She'd missed his scent, crisp and fresh like the lush outdoors of his Montone home.

'Come on, let me take you home,' she said moments later. The area by the gate had cleared, leaving them partially alone.

'I like that.' He kept his arm around her and together they walked towards the baggage area.

Soon she whisked him away from the airport and drove him three hours inland, to where the paddocks were long and wide and the earth dry. It was strange to see him in awe of the landscape. It was a total role reversal.

'I like being the tour guide,' she said.

He gazed back out the window again. 'I just can't believe the space. I can see so far. And the road. It is so straight, and where are all the cars? Are we the only ones here?'

Flick laughed. 'It feels like it sometimes.' She'd stopped at the Corrigin roadhouse for lunch and bought him a pie with sauce to try. Watching him eat it had been highly entertaining.

She slowed down along the Tin Horse Highway out of Kulin to show him all the tin horses along the side of the road. She loved watching him experience something new, and answering all his questions about the different things he saw. The big dams were something he found fascinating, and Flick promised him they'd go swimming in them soon. 'Especially coming into harvest. We'll have hot days that will be over forty degrees.' She knew he'd never experienced that kind of heat before; in Montone they even had snow. Flick felt a desire to go back just to see the village coated in white.

'Well, this is our home. This is Sunnyvale,' she said as they drove through the open farm gates. Flick pointed out Contractor, the homestead, the sheds and then the old house, where she stopped. They carried his cases inside into her room and she gave him a quick tour.

'So this is the house Rocco helped to build,' he said, glancing up at the high ceilings.

'Sure is.' She reached for his hand. 'Come, I want you to meet my nan before we go to work. Unless you would like to catch up on some sleep?'

'I cannot sleep. I just arrived,' he said, raising his brow.

'Are you sure?'

'Of course. I will sleep tonight. I want to see this harvesting.'

'All right. This way, quick tour first,' she said as they walked to the homestead. 'This is Nan and Mum's veggie garden. What do you think? In Italy everyone seemed to grow tomatoes and edible things instead of roses but in Oz we are the other way around.'

'I am impressed. A lot like Francesca's garden.'

Flick agreed. Inside they found Maggie in the lounge, knitting. 'Nan, I'd like you to meet someone special.'

Maggie glanced up over her knitting glasses. 'Oh my,' she said with a smile. 'You must be Stefano.'

'*Si, Signora*, hello.'

Flick held back her laugh as she watched her nan fumble to put away her knitting before getting up. Stefano embraced her and kissed her cheeks, causing them to flush.

'Oh, he is a bit dishy,' said Maggie. 'Do you want something to eat? Drink?'

'Yes, let's have a quick cuppa before we head out into the paddock,' said Flick.

As Maggie headed to the kitchen to put the kettle on, Flick gave Stefano a look around the house. He stopped at the side table and picked up a photo of Flick when she was eight, riding on a sheep's back during shearing. Her booted feet were kicked out, her head thrown back, laughing as her akubra hat fell to the ground. She did look a bit wild and free, but that was what life was like growing up as a farm kid.

'I love this.' He touched the frame and shot her a wink.

It was one of her favourites too.

'Come on, kettle's boiled,' shouted Nan from the kitchen.

Nan asked Stefano about his flight and what he thought of Australia so far.

'Different but beautiful.' He glanced at Flick as he spoke the last word.

'Say something to Nan in Italian,' asked Flick.

'È stato veramente un piacere conoscerti.' His words were like velvet.

'Oh my,' said Nan. 'I always loved hearing Rocco speak Italian. He taught me a bit but it's all lost to me now,' she said sadly. Maggie took a breath and smiled. 'But I'm so glad you're here, Stefano. It will be lovely having you around.' She caught Flick's eye and smiled.

Flick reached for his hand.

'Stefano?' Toni shot in through the door. 'I just saw the car outside. I can't believe you're here.' Stefano stood up and Toni greeted him with a warm hug like they were long lost friends. 'Welcome to Sunnyvale.'

'Thank you. It is amazing.'

Flick was grinning like a fool but she couldn't help it.

'You haven't seen anything yet,' said Toni letting him go. 'How are you feeling after your flight?'

'I am good. I did sleep in the car a little,' he admitted. 'I'm ready to see more.'

Toni reached out and squeezed Flick's shoulder before turning back to Stefano. 'It is just so fantastic to have you here.'

Flick couldn't agree more.

★　★　★

There had always been plenty of room in the header when she was a little girl. Now sitting on the esky wasn't as fun. Luckily Stefano was picking up header-driving like a duck to water and she could give her backside a break.

'Yep, you've got it,' she said as he lined up the field bin and started emptying out the header box.

His dark eyes danced. 'This is *incredibile*! This header is *enorme*. I can't wait to email my family some photos.'

Flick laughed. 'A week here will feel like a month.'

'I'm counting on it,' he said and leant towards her, kissing her cheek softly.

He smelt amazing, considering he'd slept on the plane and was probably dying for a shower. Flick had missed everything about him. She turned her head and found his lips. The kiss deepened and the temperature in the header rose.

'You're empty there, kiddo,' said Jimmy.

Stefano jumped in surprise. 'What was that?'

'Oh, that was just Jimmy on the two-way. You'll meet him soon.' She motioned for Stefano to turn off the auger while she reached for the two-way. 'Just showing Stefano the ropes,' she replied.

Jimmy's chuckle crackled back down the two-way. 'I don't think they're the ropes we had in mind,' he teased.

Flick looked out the window and saw Jimmy hanging out his header door with the handpiece in his hand. They'd been sprung.

'G'day Stefano, nice to see you,' said Jimmy, giving them a wave.

Flick held out the handpiece to Stefano. 'Just hold that button down when you talk and let it go when you're done.'

Stefano gave her a worried glance and spoke into the two-way. 'Hello, Jimmy. Nice to see you too.'

'We'll have beers later and catch up properly,' said Jimmy. 'Big boss out.'

Flick took the microphone. 'Yeah, you wish,' she teased, before sliding it into its holder. She watched his header drive into the barley. 'Jimmy lives with me in the old house so we'll catch up with him tonight, and Nan has organised a big feast to welcome you.'

'I could get used to this.' Stefano reached for her hand, holding it tight.

Flick grinned. 'Me too.'

At around seven-thirty, not long before sunset, Toni came and gave them a break on the header. 'Why don't you take Stefano on a tour?' she'd said. 'I think his day has been long enough.'

Flick could have hugged her mum to death. Since Toni and Jimmy had become an item, Toni had been so much easier to live with. Happier and more easygoing. Maybe the trip away together had helped too.

They took the quad bike back to Contractor's stall. 'This is my boy. Contractor, come and meet Stefano.' Flick held out her hand and Contractor shook his head and kicked at the ground. 'Come on, don't be silly.'

Eventually the horse stepped towards them and let Flick rub his nose. Stefano reached out and did the same. 'He's big.'

'I'll teach you to ride him if you like. Good fun.' After checking the water she gestured back to the bike. 'Hop on, I want to show you something.' Fella jumped up and Flick had to shoo him off. 'Not this time, Fella, you have to run.'

'Motorbikes, horses, headers, trucks, tractors. This place is *meraviglioso*, um, wonderful,' he said. 'Full of fun toys.' He climbed on behind Flick and wrapped his arms tight around her waist.

'Expensive toys,' she clarified.

Flick took him up to the paddock, which had the best vantage point for the sunsets. Fella followed them at a cracking pace, slobbery tongue hanging out, total exhilaration in his eyes. She stopped the bike by a massive gum tree on the edge of the paddock. The sun was already starting to set, and orange and pink streaks filled the sky where the rays caught on the wispy clouds. She got off the bike, reaching for Stefano's hand, and led him to a smooth spot on the ground for them to sit.

He wrapped his arm over her shoulder and they sat in silence as the sun dipped below the horizon.

'It's no sunset over the hills in Montone but it's still pretty special,' she said.

'It's magical. It's so different here.' He turned to her. 'But everything is magical with you by my side. I'm so glad I came.' He kissed the top of her nose. 'I have never felt this connection before.'

'I know. I really feel the same way.' Flick tugged at some straw. 'So . . . what did Sofia think about your trip?'

He frowned. 'She not happy at all. I did not realise.' He shrugged.

'So you finally saw how much she likes you? Mum and I could both see within a few days that she had a little something going for you.'

With his foot he dug at the dirt. 'Maybe I didn't want to see it. She has been a friend of our family for years.'

'I'm sure she'll always remain a close friend.'

'I hope so.' They glanced at each other and smiled. Then Stefano pounced on her like a tiger, rolling her over until she was on top of him and they were both laughing. 'Now this is much better.' He let her slide to his side and they lay there on the dirt, watching the sun fall from the sky.

And he was so right. Flick never would have guessed that she'd find love on her trip to Italy, nor did she think it would follow her home to Sunnyvale. Life was full of surprises.

38

Maggie had just finished putting away the dishes from breakfast. She'd treated them all with hearty bacon and egg toasties full of caramelised onions. She took great delight in feeding them well. That's how she showed her love for them, through their bellies. And if she didn't keep busy doing things like cooking, or keeping the garden going or running around in the ute, then she knew she'd probably shrivel up and die. Her body was built for work, and if she kept it busy, then there was less chance it would deteriorate. Well, that was her plan and she was sticking to it. Hopefully the girls would look after her if she got too bad later on in life. Sunnyvale was her home and she'd be more than happy to die here. She wanted to be interned in its earth, just like the many loved pets she'd had over her lifetime.

'Are you there, Flick?' came Stefano's voice over the two-way.

'Yep. What's up?'

'Needing fuel soon. You free?'

'Sure am, see you in five.'

Maggie smiled. Flick was absolutely smitten with Stefano and she could see why. The young man was lovely. He'd complimented her on her papadelle ragu last night, high praise considering his family was in the restaurant business. Maggie had been trying new recipes after Flick showed her how to find them on the internet. Most were Italy-inspired.

Maggie had told Jimmy he could learn a thing or two from Stefano's manners, and he'd replied by sweeping her up into a hug and kissing her on the cheek. 'How will that do?' he'd said. Such a cheeky lout, but she loved him. And so did Toni. Maggie had never seen her daughter so deliriously happy before, except when Felicity was born.

Maggie started humming an old tune and realised it was one she'd heard Rocco and Giulio sing many times. Strange that she would remember it now. Stefano had certainly triggered certain memories. Just hearing his Italian accent made her feel happy and sad all at once. Good memories, heartbreaking memories. It seemed so long ago, those two years with Rocco. Yet they still haunted her dreams and crept into her thoughts; they had all her life. For years she'd looked at the photos of him, sneaking glances while Arthur was out working. She'd hold the snake he made her close to her heart and remember their shared dreams.

'Time you cooked something new,' she muttered to herself, trying to steer her mind to more practical thoughts. Opening the drawer, she pulled out her favourite CWA cookbook and thought about dinner.

But something caught her eye out the window.

Who would be stopping by to visit during harvest? Did they have sheep out? she wondered.

Taking off her apron, she placed it over the back of a chair and headed outside. The sun was bright, the day warm already, and her blue cotton dress was perfect for the rising heat. She looked at the strange ute by the house. Not one she recognised. *Please don't let it be a salesman.*

Maggie stepped to the edge of the verandah as an older man in a hat walked closer. He looked like your average farmer in work clothes.

'Hello,' she said politely. She saw the man's face and something about his eyes took her breath away. Her hand went to her chest, her heart started pounding.

'*Ciao*, Maggie. You look as beautiful as ever.'

He stepped up, joining her on the verandah, giving her a full view of his face. *It couldn't be?*

'Rocco?' she whispered.

He dropped his wide shoulders, relaxing. 'I wasn't sure if you'd recognise me. I'd know you in a crowd though, same blue eyes. Like the sky.'

'Oh my.' A quivering hand went to her mouth. It was her Rocco. She could see the young man he used to be. The same face, only more lines. The same full hair, only now grey. But his eyes had never changed. In them she saw the handsome man she'd loved. Without realising it, her arms went around him and she sank against his chest. It still felt like she belonged here. Her body was alive as it remembered his embrace. A flood of feelings rushed forward, she felt dizzy and her legs threatened to give way.

'Rocco.'

Rocco kissed the top of her head before pulling away slightly. 'Here, let's sit down.' He helped her to the chair.

Maggie couldn't take her eyes off him; she

361

couldn't believe it was him, even though his touch was real. He'd lived in her memories for so long. Some days she'd tried to picture how he would have aged, but the 1946 version always won.

'Is it really you?'

He took both her hands, holding them while his thumbs rubbed gentle circles. 'It's me. You look good, Maggie. Life has treated you well.' She smiled and reached out. He closed his eyes as she caressed his face. 'I'm sorry to hear about the passing of Arthur,' he murmured.

Maggie dropped her hand. 'How did you know about Arthur?'

'I saw it in the paper a few years back.'

She nodded, but her mind was racing. What did he think about her being married to Arthur? Why didn't he ever try to make contact, even just to say hello, or would his wife disapprove?

'I hope you don't mind, but I had to come and see you. All my life I've carried you in my heart.'

It had never for one moment occurred to Maggie that Rocco might come after all these years. 'Does your wife know you're here?' she asked. 'Francesca told the girls you were married.' Maggie held her breath.

'I was married. She left me fifteen years ago. Carol lives in Perth, not far from our daughter, Susan. I'm on the farm with my son, Mark, and his family.'

Listening to Rocco mention his kids caused her chest to ache. They were supposed to have been together, making their own family. Tears started welling in Maggie's eyes. It should have been her alongside Rocco all those years.

'Why didn't you come back for me?' she said as tears fell to her lips.

'Oh, Maggie.' Rocco's face twisted in pain as he scooted her into his arms, his lids blinking away his own tears. 'I did come for you. Didn't you get my letters? I sent you many while I was in Italy, asking you to wait for me and telling you how much I still loved you.'

Maggie laughed and cried at the same time. 'Oh, I got them eventually, fifty-three years later.' Confusion etched across his face. 'My grand-daughter found them when she was renovating the house you built. I think my mother hid them from me. None of them were opened.'

'Oh my lord.' He shook his head. 'I told myself many reasons why you never replied over those years, but I never gave up hope.'

'I went to write you but no one could find your address. I'm starting to wonder if that was my mother's doing also.'

Rocco shook his head. 'I'm starting to think you were right not to name our child Phyllis.'

Maggie chuckled through her tears. 'I did warn you.' She pulled out a hankie and dabbed at her eyes. 'You said you came for me? I never saw you. Did my mother stop you?'

He took a deep breath. 'I'll start at the beginning, shall I?'

Maggie nodded. 'That sounds good. Do you want to walk while we talk?'

'Can we see the cottage?'

'What's left of it, sure.' Together they stood but Rocco held her hand in his tightly.

'I'm not letting you go again, Maggie, so you'd better get used to it.'

A fresh wave of tears spilled out and she threw herself into his arms. Years of frustration, regret, hopes and dreams melded together as she clung to Rocco. How could life have been so cruel to them? How could Phyllis?

'I've missed you so much, Rocco. I feel like I've been waiting my whole life for this moment.'

'I too have been waiting. Life has not felt complete until now.'

They began their journey to where the old cottage used to stand, and Rocco commenced his story.

'The boat took me to Naples, I went back to my family. I tried to find work until I could get back to Australia and to you. Even though I didn't hear from you it never stopped me. As soon as immigration for Australia reopened I did not hesitate to find a farmer willing to nominate me. The Williamsons took me on and I worked with them and many others, saving money to buy my own farm.'

'Which you did,' said Maggie with a proud smile. 'Maggie Downs.'

'Yes, after you, *bella*. I came to see you the moment I could get a break and the Williamsons let me take their ute. I arrived back on Sunnyvale nearly four years after I had left. It was too long, but it was the best that I could do.'

Maggie nodded, listening intently. 'Of course. It was a miracle you made it back here at all.'

'I thought Phyllis wouldn't be so happy to see me. For all I knew you might have moved. I had no idea what I was walking into. And I hadn't sent you a letter since arriving in Australia, I was trying to keep it a surprise.' He shrugged. 'But upon seeing Sunnyvale and the house, it was as if I'd never left. A great wave of happiness ran through me. Finally I would have you back in my arms.'

'Until my mother did something, right?'

Maggie stopped. They were just by the old cottage. All that remained was some dry wood and the old stove in a mound of dirt. It was hard to believe they had been together in that cottage, which was now collapsing back down into the earth. Even the stables were gone, but in her mind Maggie saw them clearly. The Clydesdales as they had been, and Contractor.

'No,' said Rocco.

'No? What do you mean?' She turned to face him. Was it her father? Surely not.

'Arthur came to the ute. He recognised me straightaway.'

'Arthur?' Maggie's mouth dropped open. What had Arthur done?

'I said I wanted to see you and he said that his wife was unavailable. God, Maggie, his words shocked me. I couldn't believe it. You never had feelings for Arthur, even though it's what everyone else seemed to want. I couldn't believe it but then you came running outside, chasing a little girl. You took my breath away as you laughed. Finally here you were, like a dream come true. So beautiful. But you belonged to another man and you seemed happy. You scooped up your child and went back inside.

That was the last time I ever saw you.'

He ran his hand over his face and sighed. 'Arthur said he didn't want me around. That you had moved on and had started a family and you were happy. As I drove away all I could think about was how that was supposed to have been our family growing up in this home together.'

Maggie gripped Rocco's arms, her heart breaking as she swallowed back the sobs of despair. 'No, Rocco. Oh no.' She put her hands on his face, looked deep into his hurting brown eyes. 'That little girl was Antonia and she was your baby.'

His face went blurry and she tried frantically to blink away the tears.

Rocco's face twisted in pain. 'I know that now. When Antonia and her daughter came by and told me, it was such a shock. At first I wouldn't let myself believe it but when I finally let myself see her . . . my God, she was me . . . and so much of my sister, Francesca. Nothing about her looked like Arthur and I knew it was the truth.' Rocco sniffed back his tears. 'I lost it, Maggie. All the years, our dreams, our hopes, all wasted. We had a daughter and I hadn't been there.' Tears dropped from his cheeks like rain. 'I fell to pieces. I'm not proud of how selfish I was and I regret not stopping them from leaving. I needed some time. It was just so much to take in. I had my own family to consider.'

'I know. I felt the same when I finally got your letters. It was so overwhelming knowing that you'd intended to come for me. I'd held onto hope for so long, I was so sure our future was together.' Maggie wished she could take away the pain, take back time and change things. If only she'd seen that ute that day. If only her mother hadn't hid her letters. If only Arthur had told Rocco the truth.

She gestured for him to sit on the ground. 'Let me tell you my story now.' Maggie sat in the dirt beside him. Nothing else seemed to register, not the uncomfortable stones or the little ants crawling about. She only had concern for Rocco. 'After you left I struggled to get by. Each day was as painful as the last but Charlie tried hard to help. Although with him marrying Valerie he was preoccupied. He knew how much I loved you. But a few weeks later I realised I was pregnant. I was so happy, I was carrying your baby, our baby. It gave me the courage to continue. But I realised that if mother found out she'd send me away or give our baby away. Arthur found me sobbing one day when I was getting the cows in. He held me tight and listened to my story. He said he'd marry me and pretend the baby was his.'

Maggie paused, remembering it like yesterday. The smell of the cows and Arthur's musty scent. 'It seemed like the only option, one where I could stay and keep our baby. I kept waiting for your letters, hoping you'd come back for me, but the days went on. I married Arthur and Antonia came along. Even though life went on, you were still in my heart. And Toni had your eyes. How could I forget you when every time I looked at her I saw you?'

Rocco smiled. 'You called her Antonia, after my mother?'

'That's what we'd decided, right? It wasn't going to be Phyllis.' They both chuckled and wiped away tears. 'It just seems like a waste,' she said eventually.

'No, don't think of it like that, Maggie. I have two children I love, Mark and Susan, and grandchildren who are wonderful. We can't go back in time and make life how we wanted it, but we can start now. I'd like to get to know you again, and my daughter. If she'd have me?'

Maggie smiled. 'I'm sure she would. She had a difficult time with Arthur, mostly after his accident. Don't get me wrong, Arthur was a wonderful father and he loved us dearly. I eventually grew to love and respect him, Rocco. I can't say my life was horrible either, but you were never far from my thoughts. Arthur gave us a great life, and I guess I can see why he did what he did. He loved me and in those years he loved Toni like his own. As it transpired, Arthur couldn't have any children, so she was the light of his life.'

'And I remember how you used to laugh about him and how your families wanted to set you up. Well, it must have pleased them all when you married.'

'Yes, it did. I think that's why it was so easy to fool everyone about Toni. Except for Charlie. He was my confidant.'

'Oh, dear Charlie, how is he?'

'Still alive and kicking. He moved to the city to be with Val after Arthur and I married. They have two girls. He would love to meet you again. You were like a brother to him.'

'As he was for me.' Rocco wrapped his arm around Maggie. 'Can we start our life again now? I know we are in the middle of harvest, but will you visit my farm and meet my family? They know all about you, the one who got away.'

Maggie laughed and squeezed his hand as if to prove she wasn't going anywhere. 'That sounds perfect. Will you write to me?'

'I'd love to. After all, you were the one to teach me how to read and write English, *amore mio*.'

Her heart melted at the Italian words for 'my love'.

They gazed at each other while a magpie sang in a nearby tree. If she closed her eyes, it was just like fifty-five years ago when Rocco had first kissed her. Her heart raced and the feel of his soft kiss was heaven. His arms were still strong, a man who worked hard even in his seventies, and he still smelt like Rocco.

'I've never stopped loving you,' Rocco whispered against her lips.

And in that moment Maggie was eighteen again.

39

Maggie looked through the kitchen window, watching the man she loved with his daughter. Sniffling, she wiped away a tear. It still moved her, seeing them together. They often spent hours walking around, talking farms. On one of the many nights he stayed, he'd mentioned how amazed he was with Toni, how she could give Mark a few lessons on farming. 'She's so bright and runs this farm so well, she was born for it,' he'd said with a smile.

Maggie loved it when Rocco cooked meals for them that his mother had taught him. Often Stefano would join him, and they would create Italian feasts. It was like having their own Italian restaurant on the farm. So much had happened over the two months since Rocco had come home.

Maggie wanted to be by Rocco's side always but she gave him up gladly for Toni. Even so, she kept her eyes on them. Like today: Rocco was asking Toni something very important, and Maggie was dying to know the answer.

'Mum, you can come out now!' yelled Toni.

Grabbing a tea towel she walked out, pretending to dry her hands as if she'd been doing the dishes and not trying to eavesdrop.

The sun was setting on another day outside. It was still very hot but their harvest was done, and finally they could all rest easy. Flick rode up on

Contractor, with Stefano alongside on the motorbike and Fella trying to keep up.

'Looks like everyone is just in time,' said Toni.

'Hey, Nonno,' said Flick, testing out the new affectionate name. She dismounted and, keeping the reins in one hand, walked over to give him a hug. 'You just get here?'

'About an hour ago.'

Rocco's eyes sparkled any time he hugged Flick or Toni. It melted Maggie's heart, knowing the girls still had someone to count on. She knew they missed Arthur; even Maggie still missed him. He would always be remembered and never left out of their family. Their feelings for Rocco would never detract from that.

'*Ciao*, Rocco,' said Stefano as they shook hands.

Flick shot him a dirty look. Rocco and Stefano had been banned from speaking Italian in Flick's company unless they were teaching her. But when they were alone they would go back to their native language and Maggie would sit and listen, not understanding a word of it but loving how it sounded.

'Rocco is coming to live with Mum,' said Toni.

'Really?' said Flick.

'If that's all right with all of you,' said Rocco. 'Mark's been trying to get me off the farm for years, for some reason he thinks I interfere too much. But I promise only to help out when you need me here. You're the boss,' he said directly to Toni.

'As long as you remember that, then we are good,' Toni teased.

'Then I say, yay,' said Flick. 'Does this mean you're going to move in with Jimmy, Mum?'

'She bloody well better be,' said Jimmy as he joined them, walking from the sheds with Gypsy by his side.

Toni nodded but her face looked grave. Maggie knew she wasn't finished. She may have happened to overhear that Toni had some important news for Flick.

'Flick, I know you and Stefano are heading off tomorrow on your sightseeing adventure down south. I'm sure Stefano will love the Margaret River beaches and hopefully won't come back with a surfboard.' They laughed. 'Stefano, it's been truly wonderful having you on Sunnyvale, you will be missed around here.'

'Here, here!' shouted Jimmy.

'I'm so glad you're staying another month.'

'Or more,' said Flick with a grin.

'But just make sure to come back and spend some time with us again.'

'*Grazie*, Toni. Of course.' Stefano blew her a kiss.

Toni cleared her throat and faced her daughter. 'Before you leave I need to give you this.'

Flick screwed up her face. 'What is it? Travel money?' she said hopefully.

Toni pulled out a piece of paper from her pocket and handed it to her.

Flick read the scrap. 'Simon Templeton.' Her eyes flew back to Toni. 'As in, my father Simon?'

'Yes, I discovered his last name. And after some more searching I found him. He works at his family's winery — that's the address and his number.'

Maggie put a hand on Toni's shoulder. She was so proud of Toni for doing what was right. Rocco glanced up at Maggie and smiled. Finally they had their big family.

'What . . . ?' Flick's face was frozen in shock.

Everyone went silent, watching and waiting for an explosion or tears. Instead she threw Contractor's reins at Stefano and flung her arms around Toni. 'Oh, thank you, thank you, Mum. I can't believe you found him.'

'So this is okay?'

'It's perfect. I can't believe it.'

Toni held up her hands. 'Just don't get your hopes up. He's still getting used to the idea but he does want to meet you.'

Flick gave her a smile that said she understood all too well.

Maggie clasped her hands together. 'I think this is cause for celebration.' She opened the beer fridge on the verandah and passed beers out.

Stefano tied Contractor and eagerly reached for a bottle. He'd embraced beer while working up a thirst over harvest. He cracked the top and joined everyone as they sat along the edge of the verandah, facing the setting sun with cold beers in their hands.

Maggie propped her beer between her legs and wrapped an arm around Antonia and Felicity, and pulled them both close.

'Now, that's a perfect shot,' said Jimmy, pretending his hands were a camera. 'The

Sunnyvale girls. Stubborn, gorgeous, and the loves of my life.'

They all laughed as the sun dipped into the earth like a gold coin. Contractor neighed, galahs squawked and Fella chased Gypsy around the motorbike. Maggie smiled, her eyes misting. It was remarkable how long she'd held onto her hope, even when she thought she'd lost it all. Rocco squeezed her hand and she felt alive. Some dreams never die, no matter where your life takes you.

Acknowledgements

Our area has a history with the Italian POWs, one that I wanted to dive into and write about. I couldn't have done this without the help of others. Many thanks go to Ross and Lorna Murray for the stories and memories of Giulio and life in the 1940s. It was so amazing to learn about Giulio, to follow his story to the end and to be able to weave some of it into my own story. Thanks to my friends Lea and Yogi Murray for allowing me use your farm, Sunnyvale, and your stories as inspiration. It was great to see what was left of the old cottage. The tours around the farm were fun and an excuse to come out for a cuppa.

Searching for Giulio led me on a trip to Italy, where I met his daughters, Carla and Isalda, along with their immediate family, who were all just lovely. It wouldn't have happened without the help of Mimmo Maurelli and Giulio's granddaughter, Silvia Borioni, whose translating made our meetings possible. I will be forever grateful to you both. My time in Italy was very surreal and beautiful.

To my aunty Lorna Madson, Gaye Bario and my mum, Sue. Thanks for the most amazing trip ever. Memories I'll treasure. Well, most of them anyway — maybe not the time we were locked in the Florence train station toilets!

Thanks also to Kath Garard, Lina Varone and

Bice Di Franco for the information and titbits. They all help give this story depth and truth.

Thank you to the amazing Ali Watts, as always. To the Penguin team who I've worked with, or have helped me out, thank you Jo Rosenberg, Chantelle Sturt, Laura Thomas, Kym Steinke, Louise McCall and Julia Rauch.

I have special writing friends who I can call upon when in need. Rachael Johns, Margareta Osborn, Cathryn Hein and Fleur McDonald to name a few, thank you for all your support! Especially Rach, I can't thank you enough for the wonderful cover quote.

I have an amazing husband who kept the home fires burning while I was away on my trip, and if it weren't for him, the trip wouldn't have happened and this book would have been ten times harder to write. Thank you, Darryl, for being so supportive and being a fantastic dad to Mac and Blake. We are so lucky to have you.

Lastly, thank you to all my family, fans and supporters who help me get through. I can because of you.